He crushed her against him...

Jacob's mouth was hard, bruising, as if he could not get enough of her, and her own lips, too numb to react, yielded. Laurel felt his tongue push past her teeth, boldly, deeply into her mouth, and she was horrified by the traitorous sensations raging rampant in her body at his assault. When his hand reached her breast, she momentarily recovered, flailing at his back with her fists. But he took no note as his fingertips teased her flesh through the cloth of her dress. The sensations aroused by his touch were potent, titillating; she shuddered with desire and surprise. Raining her face with kisses, he whispered, "Easy, love, easy."

She was touched by his words and by his soft, sensuous kisses, and all at once she found herself wanting to drown in him. Her hands moved to encircle his body tentatively, then caressed the corded muscles of his back as she half-sobbed his name...

*   *   *   *

Eugenia Riley's First Fabulous Romance,

Ecstasy's Triumph

...got five stars from *Barbra Critiques*. *Romantic Times* called it "Splendid reading with lots of plantation passion." And the editor of *Heart Line* wrote "It's terrific!! I loved it!! The plot and characters are great!"

**Now Eugenia Riley has done it again
—and more—in**

Laurel's Love

Eugenia Riley

WARNER BOOKS

A Warner Communications Company

WARNER BOOKS EDITION

Copyright © 1986 by Eugenia Riley

Warner Books, Inc.
666 Fifth Avenue
New York, N.Y. 10103

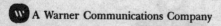 A Warner Communications Company

Printed in the United States of America

First Printing: October, 1986

10 9 8 7 6 5 4 3 2 1

To my precious Aunt Sister, with great love—
thank you for always believing I was wonderful,
even when I didn't.

The author acknowledges, with gratitude, the following sources consulted in the writing of this book:

Bob's Galveston Reader, written and published by Bob Nesbitt, Galveston, 1983.

Campfires and Battlegrounds: A Pictorial Narrative of the Civil War, by Rossiter Johnson, New York, The Civil War Press, 1977.

Fabulous New Orleans, by Lyle Saxon, New Orleans, Robert L. Crager and Company, 1950.

Galveston: History of the Island and the City, by Charles W. Hayes, Austin, Jenkins Garrett Press, 1974.

Indianola, The Mother of Western Texas, by Brownson Malsch, Austin, Shoal Creek Publishers, 1978.

Ray Miller's Galveston, by Ray Miller, Houston, Cordovan Press, 1983.

The Galveston That Was, by Howard Barnstone, New York, MacMillan, 1967.

The Treasures of Galveston Bay, by Carroll Lewis, Waco, Texian Press, 1977.

Visions of Glory: Texans on the Southwestern Frontier, by Stephen B. Oates, Norman, University of Oklahoma Press, 1970.

Author's Note

This novel is a work of fiction in which are depicted many actual figures from the history of the times. While some situations and certain details of characterization involving these figures are fictitious, every effort has been made to be as faithful as possible to historical fact in the portrayal of these persons. Exact dates are used whenever possible and available, though a few obscure events have been assigned a date consistent with the story line and with the overall historical framework.

All nonhistorical characters in the novel are imaginary. Jacob Lafflin is a fictional character. The name Lafflin is used in support of the theory that a well-known nineteenth-century historical figure, in his later years, took the assumed name of John Lafflin and later settled with his wife in Missouri. Jacob Lafflin is the imaginary son of John Lafflin.

Chapter One

"Damned Yankees!" said Laurel Ashland, as she sat upon her bed at Ursuline Academy, dangling slim legs over the side of the mattress as she again read the letter that had just arrived from Brazos Bend.

"Just look at the date on this letter, Fancy," the raven-haired girl told her black maid. "August twelfth—two months ago." Laurel's beautifully shaped mouth formed a pout. "Mail service since the war began has been abominable, Fancy, abominable. Mother makes no mention of my birthday—I'm seventeen this very day, and my sole consolation will be rolling bandages for Witch St. Pierre!"

Across the room, fourteen-year-old Fancy clapped a black hand over her gaping mouth. "Miss Laurel, if Mother St. Pierre hear you saying that, she take the knuckle-rapper to you!"

Squaring her shoulders, Laurel replied stoutly, "Fiddlesticks, Fancy. My daddy would boil her highness in her own juices if she touched a hair on my head."

1

Young Fancy's back grew straight as the chair in which she sat as she retorted, "You best think again, Miss Laurel. Your daddy off fighting the Yankees—he ain't going to save you from Mother!"

Laurel scowled indignantly at her servant. "Fancy, of all the things to say! My mother makes no mention of Daddy in her letter. He may be in the direst predicament at this very moment. It's all I can do not to take to my bed with the grief and the fear of it, and you have to remind me!"

"Miss Laurel, you ain't feared of nothing, 'cept you won't git your own way," Fancy replied.

Laurel stood up, her yellow muslin skirts flouncing. "Tell me, Fancy, how would you like to sleep in the kitchen for a week or two?" she asked with a saucy tilt of her head.

Now the cottonade-clothed slave was also standing, her fearful eyes whitening as she backed away. "Oh no, Miss Laurel, please don't send me to the kitchen! They is rats in the kitchen and I is scared of them!"

"Oh very well," Laurel conceded grumpily, taking her seat again. "You don't have to fly into a swivet about it."

"Yes 'um."

Laurel smoothed her skirts about her and again took up the letter. For long moments, she scrutinized her mother's handwriting, her brow furrowing into a deep frown. Fancy, noting her mistress's preoccupation, returned to her chair and silently watched the older girl.

Soon, Laurel sighed heavily and looked up, distractedly brushing a thick black curl from her forehead. "Listen to this, Fancy. 'My darling, I realize that you miss us and are aching to be home. Believe me, Cammie and I think only of the day we shall all be reunited. But, sweetheart, all the men are gone. There is simply no one we can send to fetch you safely home. Please, love, do not attempt to travel to Houston by steamboat. We were touched by your willingness to do this, but you must remember that even if you reached Houston, there would be no one to accompany you overland to the Brazos. Don't forget that lawlessness has been rampant since the men left the state. I should be heartsick with worry about you out upon the trail. Your other idea—that of journeying to the mouth of the Brazos at Valasco—must also be abandoned, dear. You must stay at the academy with the good sisters, where you will be safe, for we have heard rumors of Yankees in the Gulf.''

Laurel tossed the letter aside, looking at her maid, her blue eyes incredulous. "Where we will be safe, indeed! Can you believe it, Fancy? Rumors of Yankees in the Gulf! What would my mother say if she knew that just yesterday the Yankees raised their deplorable flag on our customs house?'' Sighing breathlessly, she continued, "Ah, the shame of it all, Fancy. To be abandoned by one's own family."

Laurel stood up, walked to the window, and drew up the sash. As the mild, salty Gulf breeze caressed her face, she looked past rows of prairie grass to the sandy beach beyond. Her second-story vantage point afforded her a good view of the Gulf of Mexico and, in the distance, two small black shapes bobbing on the waves—the Yankee steamers *Harriet Lane* and *Clifton.*

"Ah, the shame of it all," she repeated sadly. "To be the only student left in this godforsaken establishment—all my friends, all the soldiers, gone. Only Yankees now. Fancy, we're at the mercy of the damned Yankees!"

"Miss Laurel!" Fancy squealed.

Laurel turned dramatically to the slave. "It's true, Fancy. It's only a matter of time before the whole lot of them descend upon us." Moving closer, she added, "We'll all be summarily executed, I'm sure. I've heard it a thousand times—the Yankees are cutthroats who hold no quarter."

"Oh no, Miss Laurel!" Fancy cried, bolting to her feet and clutching the back of her chair with trembling fingers that made the chair legs dance. "You is telling tales again."

"We'll all no doubt be ravished prior to the executions," Laurel declared, sweeping to the dresser and picking up her hairbrush. "I do wonder how old Mother St. Pierre will like having a taste of the carnal before she meets her maker. Though I've heard the Yankees are ugly beasts, with vile breath and whiskey paunches, the lot of them. If the truth were known, however, I should swear Mother St. Pierre dreams each night of just such an outrage." Laurel pulled a mass of hair from her hairbrush and pushed it through the hole in the porcelain hair jar on the dresser.

Fancy came up behind Laurel, her fingers trembling as she unfastened the buttons on Laurel's frock. "Miss Laurel, hush this wicked talk of yourn. You is late for your nap, and Mother say if she catch you about, you is ironing sheets the whole afternoon."

"The old biddy," Laurel complained, turning to the slave. "On my birthday, no less! Doesn't the Constitution forbid cruel and unusual punishment?" She bit her lip. "Oh, but that's their Constitution now, isn't it, Fancy? I suppose I've no choice but to take to my bed."

Fancy pulled the yellow muslin over her mistress's head and hung the frock in the mahogany armoire as the chemise-clad Laurel removed her slippers, drew back the quilt, and settled herself upon the knitted counterpane.

As Fancy pulled the mosquito bar to the end of the Mallard tester bed, Laurel commented sadly, "Mother St. Pierre is insane, Fancy, I'm sure of it. What do we do each day but scrub floors, roll bandages, iron sheets? Yet to this day we've not had a single wounded soldier arrive! Even when the Yankee commander suggested rather vehemently that we all take our leave, what does Mother say but that we're staying to ensure the care of the glorious wounded?" Gesturing impatiently, she beseeched the slave, "*What* wounded, Fancy? I tell you, Mother's taken leave of her senses. A phantom mother superior ruling a phantom hospital. Sheer lunacy, Fancy.''

''You hush, Miss Laurel,'' Fancy scolded, hands on hips as she glowered down at her mistress. ''Mother be by anytime to see if you resting.''

''I suppose you're right,'' Laurel conceded. Lowering her black eyelashes, she muttered, ''It's just that everything is such a bore, Fancy. Such a damned bore.''

''Hush up and count your blessings, Miss Laurel. You could have it a mess worse than being bort. You is fed and you is safe—for now. You is going to pray to be bort when that Yankee shell start flappin' your skirts.''

Scowling, Laurel opened one blue eye and thrust the pink tip of her tongue at the slave before she again feigned a dignified repose.

Fancy shook her head as she went off to the dresser. She straightened the eyelet dresser scarf and placed the toiletry items in a neat row. Catching her mistress's reflection in the beveled mirror above the dresser, she shook her head and mumbled under her breath, ''Too purty for her own good.''

Fancy turned, studying her mistress. Silky, luxuriant black curls cascaded upon the pillow, a startling contrast to Laurel's pink and white face. The girls's nose was beautifully boned, her mouth wide and slightly full, her high cheekbones covered with a delicate pink flush.

''Black-haired angel,'' Fancy murmured. ''With eyes so blue to charm the devil hisself from the ground, and a heart full of 'nuff sin to run him back to hell.''

''Did you say something, Fancy?'' Laurel breathed from the bed as she stretched luxuriously, her eyes still closed.

''No 'um,'' Fancy whispered back.

As Laurel turned and began to breathe deeply and regularly, Fancy heaved a sigh of relief. When she was sure her mistress was fast asleep, she tiptoed toward the armoire.

She was reaching for the handle on the wardrobe when suddenly, the door to Laurel's room opened.

Fancy could feel beads of perspiration pop out on her forehead as she turned to face Mother Celeste St. Pierre. The Frenchwoman was clothed in a black habit; steel-gray eyes stared past sharp features to gaze at Fancy dispassionately.

Fancy hastily curtsied, then slithered to her pallet beyond Laurel's bed, out of Mother St. Pierre's sight.

Tiptoeing toward the bed, Mother St. Pierre briefly scrutinized the young belle from Washington-on-the-Brazos who was, at present, her sole charge. Then, sniffing disdainfully, she turned and left the room.

Fancy sprang up from her pallet. "That a close call. I best go before she come again."

Fancy opened the wardrobe doors. Nervously glancing over her shoulder at the sleeping Laurel, she gingerly pulled out a small cedar chest.

"You is not going wid me this time, Miss Laurel," Fancy muttered to herself as she took the chest to her pallet. "Mother say she dose me wid calomel if'n you loose again." Fancy removed a white silk dress and a large handful of trinkets from the chest. "Though you need to go, Miss Laurel. Sweet Jesus, you is bad. Miss Emilie, she try wid them other two, Miss Cammie and Mister Charles. But when you come along, she just give up and let your daddy have his way. Be a sin the way that man spoilt you rotten. And lettin' you run wild wid boys and wear britches from a baby. I is thankful Miss Emilie stand up to your daddy and send you here to school, but Mother St. Pierre don't know what to do wid you, neither." Shaking her head as she glanced up at Laurel's bed, Fancy expostulated, "You is might purty, Miss Laurel, but you is never going to be a lady."

Fancy doffed her blue cottonade dress and quickly donned the white silk garment. Hurrying to the dresser, she put on the beads, pearls, and gold and silver bracelets she had taken from the chest. The trinkets were the collections of a lifetime—gifts from Laurel, all, beginning with the time twelve years earlier, when five-year-old Laurel had dressed up her black "baby" in the finest eyelet and pearls and nicknamed her Fancy.

Fancy pinned a turquoise brooch to the white turban that held her fuzzy black hair. Satisfied with her appearance, she was heading for the door when she heard her mistress sneeze.

Fancy froze in her tracks. After a moment, she turned timidly and saw Laurel frowning in her sleep as the Gulf breeze billowed the lace-trimmed curtains. Moving closer, Fancy saw the gooseflesh on Laurel's arms and legs.

Cautiously, Fancy parted the mosquito netting and reached for the quilt. But she gasped sharply as she heard her own bracelets jangling.

Laurel Ashland's eyes flew open. "Fancy, where the devil do you think you're going?" she demanded, sitting up.

Fancy's lower lip quivered as she backed away from her irate mistress.

Laurel sprang to her feet. "You're going to the ring shout, aren't you? Oh, how could you forget me on my birthday!"

"Miss Laurel, Mother say she dose me good if'n you loose again!"

"Well, the old battle-ax can't hang us until she catches us." Laurel began to pace, scowling, while Fancy bit her lip miserably. "Was that Mother St. Pierre who checked on me just now?" the older girl demanded.

"Yes 'um."

"Good. Then she probably won't be back for a while." Laurel paused at her bed; then, nodding to herself resolutely, she grabbed a pillow and tossed it at Fancy. "Help me stuff this bed. I'm going with you, Fancy."

"Oh, no 'um, no 'um!" Fancy pleaded.

"Oh yes. You're not leaving me here to go mad staring at these prison walls. You'll help me, Fancy, or I'll tell Mother we were at the ring shout last time also—not walking the beach, as you lied to her."

"Miss Laurel, have mercy!" Fancy wailed.

"Mercy, indeed! How much mercy have you shown me? Either we both go or we both stay. Which is it, Fancy?"

Her lower lip trembling, Fancy came over to help her mistress stuff the bed.

The servant then dressed the older girl in a simple white dimity frock. As a finishing touch, Laurel took her grandmother Barrett's gold and sapphire brooch from her jewelry box, pinned it to a blue velvet ribbon, and hung it about her neck. "There," she pronounced, eyeing her handiwork with approval. "Now, Fancy, fetch me a turban. Two servants out on the streets will catch little interest."

"Yes 'um," Fancy croaked.

As the slave searched for a clean turban, Laurel began pinning her silky black tresses atop her head, frowning at her reflection as she worked.

Fancy waited patiently as her mistress completed the task, then the slave tied the turban about Laurel's head. "We is going to git caught," the black girl said morosely. "Caught by Mother, or caught by them Yankees."

"Nonsense," Laurel assured the slave. "Mother will assume I'm still napping. As for the Yankees—are you silly enough to believe everything I say? Actually, the Yankees have yet to fire a shot at anyone. They're cowards, of course. Sister Mary Joseph told me the cravens had their flag up at the customs house yesterday for only a quarter hour—then they removed it and retreated to their vessels. You see, Fancy, this entire occupation business is merely a token affair. The Yankees just want to spoil everyone's fun with their silly blockade. So they sit in the Gulf in their boats—looking quite foolish, I might add—as they have for months." She stood, turning to face Fancy. "Now, let's go. It's my birthday and, by damn, I'm going to have a good time!"

"Miss Laurel, your language a sin. It ain't proper a young lady cuss like a street wench. You is never going to marry talkin' like that."

Laurel shrugged. "Small chance of me marrying anyway, with all the boys gone." She half-smiled. "I wonder if the Yankees truly are as ugly as I've heard."

Fancy shrieked her horror, throwing a hand over her mouth.

"For heaven's sake, quit fretting, Fancy! I'm sure we won't even see any Yankees. Not a soul was stirring last time, remember?" She laughed ruefully. "Though I'd almost rather risk a few stray bullets than rot of boredom here."

"Miss Laurel, you is going to git us kilt!" Fancy squealed.

"Don't be absurd—we'll be fine," Laurel scolded. "I'll take care of you, Fancy. Aren't I always perfectly cautious?"

Fancy was too amazed to even attempt a reply.

"Now quit gaping and check the hallway. We must hurry before Mother decides to make another round."

Rolling her eyes heavenward, Fancy went to the door and gently creaked it open. She motioned for Laurel to join her, and the two eased themselves into the hallway. Closing the door, they tiptoed down the long oriental runner that led to the stairs. But they had gone only a few feet when they heard the sound of rapid French coming from the stairwell. The two girls dived into a tiny alcove just as Mother St. Pierre and Sister Agnes stepped into the hallway.

Pressed on either side of a dormer window, the girls held their breath as the two sisters passed them without even glancing in their direction. Then Laurel pulled the wild-eyed

Fancy back into the hallway, and the two dashed on tiptoe for the stairs.

Down the hall, Mother St. Pierre turned to Sister Agnes. "*Attendez*, Sister. I heard a sound—a titter, a giggle, almost. Did you hear it, Sister?"

The older nun shook her head. "I hear nothing, Mother."

Mother St. Pierre waved off her companion. "Your hearing is poor, Sister, since your bout with the ague last winter." She turned, staring hard at a door a few feet away. "Ah, *excusez-moi*, Sister."

Mother St. Pierre crept to the door of Laurel Ashland's room. Turning the knob, she peered inside. Then, shrugging, she closed the door and rejoined her companion. "*C'est un mystère, n'est-ce pas*, Sister?"

Sister Agnes nodded solemnly. "*Oui*, Mother. Perhaps a rat is loose."

Chapter
Two

OCTOBER 10, 1862

All was quiet on Twenty-fifth Street save for the sound of seagulls flying overhead. Pushed along by the Gulf breeze, Laurel and Fancy hurried past deserted homes and shops. They lifted their skirts as they swept along, shielding the hems of their gowns from the inevitable sand grinding beneath their slippers on the walkway.

"We is in trouble. Oh Lord, we is in trouble!" Fancy panted as she scampered along, trying to keep pace with her taller, long-legged mistress.

"Don't be a rabbit, Fancy," Laurel retorted. "You were all set to indulge in these shenanigans alone, leaving me without a whit of remorse. Your worries come a bit late."

Fancy was about to gasp out a retort when, suddenly, her eyes rolled wildly in her head and she jerked to a halt. "Oh, God! The sister!"

Laurel also stopped, glancing from her fear-frozen servant to the black-clothed figure approaching them from the

next block. Quickly assessing the situation, Laurel grabbed
Fancy, dragging the younger girl around the corner of St.
John's Church. Pushing the servant against the side entrance
of the edifice, Laurel clapped a hand over the mouth of her
half-hysterical maid. Then, peering out from the recessed
doorway, Laurel watched, scowling, as the basket-toting
sister crept into view.

Before continuing, Sister St. Augustin paused on the
walkway, a frown of curiosity tugging at her tight mouth.
Her eyes slowly sweeping the oleander-edged churchyard,
she shrugged, then went on her way.

"She seen us, I just know it!" Fancy exclaimed when
Laurel finally released her. "Sister St. Pierre sent her to
hunt us up!"

"Of course, Fancy," Laurel replied sarcastically. "That's
why she's carrying a basket of fruit!" Tugging Fancy toward
the street, she added archly, "Silly chit! St. Augustin is
merely fetching the produce from the central market, as she
does every afternoon!"

"But she seen us!" Fancy insisted, tripping along behind
Laurel as the two turned onto Broadway.

"She saw two slaves going to the market for their
mistress—that and nothing more!" Laurel insisted.

"But Miss Laurel, you is white!"

Her eyes beseeching the heavens, Laurel gritted, "Of
course I'm white, Fancy! She'll assume I'm a quadroon or
an octoroon. Anyway, the old crab is blind as a bat. She
couldn't possibly recognize me with my hair under this
turban."

"Well, I s'pose you is right," Fancy conceded, her black
brow puckered as they hurried along. "We could be toting
fruit today. But, oh, Miss Laurel—we ain't got no baskets!"

Fancy's mistress groaned her frustration.

Laurel dragged Fancy past the stately brick J. M. Brown
residence and the other frame houses on Broadway. Then

the two turned down Twenty-second Street, continuing four blocks to the Virginia House Hotel, a one-and-a-half story frame building on the corner of Twenty-second Street and Post Office.

Normally, slaves would not enter the front door of a business establishment or home. But since most of the residents of Galveston had fled with the news of imminent Yankee occupation, decorum could be abandoned. Thus, the girls hurried up the board steps, past the sign near the portal, which read: "Not a rat or a mouse, Dare enter the Virginia House."

Entering the building, the girls proceeded down a central corridor to the first door on the left. Inside the large block-paneled room, about a dozen blacks had gathered. All were now busy moving the contents of the dining hall—assorted chairs and tables—to the sides of the room.

"Why, Mam'zelle Laurel—Fancy!" a tall black woman called out.

Laurel turned, recognizing Reba, a magnificently proportioned bronze Negro. The gold-eyed Trinidad beauty moved toward them like a sleek, graceful cat. She wore a purple velvet dress, gold earrings and bracelets, and a vividly patterned turban secured with a ruby brooch. By sinister contrast, Reba wore about her neck a mahogany amulet of a snake. Viewing the charm, Laurel felt strangely chilled as she stared at the serpent's gaping mouth and bared fangs.

Reba smiled enigmatically, stroking the wooden snake with honey-gold fingers. "You like L'Loa, Mam'zelle Laurel? Perhaps I trade it for the blue stones you wear."

Laurel's hand protectively clutched the sapphire and gold brooch that hung about her neck on a blue velvet ribbon. "Reba, you'd best keep your yellow eyes off my great-grandmother's jewelry!"

Reba shrugged, undaunted. Watching her, Laurel felt uneasy. Reba was a free woman of color who had come to

Galveston from New Orleans three years earlier. Before the war forced the evacuation of most of Galveston's residents, Reba had supported herself by performing voodoo-style chants and dances at Taylor's House of Public Entertainment, a feat that caused her to be revered—and feared—by Galveston's population of blacks. Although Reba had been unsuccessful in converting any of the island Negroes to the worship of vodun, she was a frequent visitor at the shouts, seeming to view the proceedings with perverse fascination, much as Laurel did.

Now, Laurel looked around the room expectantly, noting that a large area of the rough cedar floor had been cleared. "Shall we soon begin?" she inquired of Reba.

"Mam'zelle Laurel, have you permission to be about today?" Reba taunted in return.

"Of course, Reba. Attending shouts is required curriculum at St. Ursuline's," Laurel replied flippantly. Nodding toward a banjo leaning against the wall, she questioned, "Where are Henry and Ben?"

"They are checking on M'sieur Verdene at the grog shop near the Strand."

"Ah." Laurel nodded. "You'd be in big trouble if the owner of this establishment caught you staying here, wouldn't you, Reba?"

The woman shrugged. "The man is too *ivre* to know the *différence.*" A provocative smile twisting her lips, she asked Laurel, "What would your *papa* say if he knew you were here, Mam'zelle?"

"My daddy let me attend the shouts at Brazos Bend when I was little," Laurel defended haughtily. Noting Reba's doubtful look, she continued, "Being one of the more enlightened of the landowners, Daddy thought the shouts a harmless enough pastime and did not forbid them, as many of our neighbors did."

In the corner, a baby squealed raucously upon his pallet

and an older girl handed him a bit of bacon fat just as the front door flew open noisily. Within seconds, two blacks Laurel recognized as Ben and Henry came into the room.

"Mister Verdene winning at cards against Mister Bailey and Mister Finch," Henry announced.

"And he just finish wid one bottle and buy more whiskey," Ben added, grinning, as he threw off a tattered overcoat and took up his banjo.

Henry also cast aside his overcoat, moving with the others toward the center of the room. Despite the balmy weather, Henry and Ben had worn the coats to hide their flashy clothing—white pantaloons and bright yellow linen jackets. As the dozen men and women formed a circle, Laurel considered the bright apparel the Negroes wore. The men were dressed similarly to Henry and Ben, while the women wore their finest frocks of silk or velvet, embellished by scarves, trinkets, and bright turbans. When attending the tribalistic rituals, the island blacks wore only their best garments and jewelry—often, the painstaking accumulations of a lifetime, as in Fancy's case.

Laurel watched Sister Suki, the middle-aged unofficial leader of the gathering, move toward the center of the circle. Realizing the ceremony was about to begin, Laurel knew a fleeting moment of guilt. True, her father had let her attend the ring shouts as a child—unlike other planters in the vicinity, he did not fear that such affairs were used to plot insurrections. But he had taken her aside on her eleventh birthday, quietly informing her that she would not be allowed to participate in the future—for reasons she would understand when she was older.

Now, watching the black bodies sway sensuously in anticipation of the rite, Laurel understood the reasons. But she pushed aside her anxieties, awaiting the event with unabashed eagerness.

Behind them, Ben strummed a chord on his banjo. Sister

Suki, looking more corpulent than ever in her crimson silk dress, raised her heavy arms and began to chant: "When I git to Heaven, going to sing and shout, Nobody there for to turn me out."

With that, the blacks began to move in a circle, shuffling along, and yet, as if by magic, tapping their heels in time and clapping their hands as they repeated Sister Suki's words. Laurel was familiar with the chant and the meaning of its words—the entire ring-shout movement was a result of the blacks being banned from the churches of their white masters.

Round and round the circle went, more rapidly each time, the movements of the blacks taking on a primal, ritualistic abandon, augmented with wild shouts of "Amen!" and "Sweet Jesus!" The two youngsters on the pallet watched with awestruck fascination while Laurel struggled to keep time with the untamed, increasing tempo of the dance.

Sister Suki was the focal point—moving her fleshy breasts and hips provocatively, her hands and face stretched heavenward as she led the ritual. Soon Suki's face twisted in an orgasmic grimace, tears streaming from her closed eyes as she hoarsely screamed the chant—"Ain't no one there for to turn me out!"—until it became a primitive, incoherent cry.

Faster and faster the circle went, the banjo strumming a reckless cadence, until the blacks began to attain a state of frenzied ecstasy—the spirit moving within them. Presently, the shout knew its first casualty—a young woman, faint and trembling, fell to the floor, moaning and crying. Two others soon joined her, but the ring closed up, became tighter, moving at a frantic pace.

To watch the blacks—sobbing, writhing, their eyes rolling wildly—was one of the most captivating sights Laurel Ashland had ever witnessed. Laurel clapped and raced about with the others, her blue eyes huge as she viewed the voluptuous movements of the Negroes, while the music, the pace, ignited her senses to a soaring exultation.

As one of the older men fell, panting hoarsely, to his knees, a deep masculine voice demanded, "What the devil is going on here?"

At the sound of this alien voice, the blacks froze in their tracks, the ring jerking to a halt. A dozen sets of eyes cautiously rolled toward the archway leading to the hall. There stood a tall, black-haired naval officer and about ten seamen dressed in blue uniforms and round white caps.

Fancy and another young woman simultaneously screamed and swooned. Sister Suki's hand flew to her heart, while Reba stared at the sailors implacably.

Laurel Ashland's eyes grew wild and vivid as the Gulf before a storm. "Yankees!" she gasped.

Chapter
Three

For a moment, time hung suspended. The characters assembled in the middle of the dining hall might have been statues in the park, their feet mortared to the spot.

Then, as if on cue, pandemonium broke loose. Most of the blacks fled the room, grabbing the children as they went, amid cries of, "Oh God—Yankees!" and "Sweet Jesus, save us!" Evidently, the blacks believed the warnings their masters had issued about the wickedness of the Yankees, for within seconds only three women remained— Fancy, who was still unconscious, Reba, who continued to stare at the sailors impassively, and Laurel, who continued to look quite statuesque, despite her efforts not to show fear.

The sailors assembled in the doorway found the mass hysteria of the blacks amusing, and chuckled to one another. However, their leader seemed to see no need for levity; uttering a harsh command, he walked purposefully toward Laurel and Reba.

All was silence as the tall officer studied Laurel's figure with a probing detachment. As Laurel bravely met his piercing gaze, it occurred to her that he was one of the most handsome men she had ever seen. Though she liked to think of her beloved father as the most handsome man in the world, this man came close. Dressed in an immaculate navy-blue brass-buttoned uniform, his broad shoulders were accented by gold officer's bars. His face was classically proportioned—straight nose, firm chin, wide mouth, deeply recessed dark brown eyes. His hair was black, wavy, and thick, and Laurel found herself inanely wondering what it would feel like to run her fingers through it. He looked to be in his late twenties, his physique hard-muscled yet youthfully trim.

The Yankee took a step closer to Laurel, one sun-browned hand resting on the ivory hilt of his sword, while his other hand held a blue cap. He glanced, frowning, from Laurel to Reba, then back to Laurel. "Where is the owner of this establishment?" he questioned Laurel in the same deep voice.

Looking up at him, Laurel noted the faintest shadow of whiskers on his bronzed face. Her eyes swept the hard line of his jaw, moved down his neck, stopping at the black of his cravat. Though Laurel knew this man was the enemy, he possessed the tantalizing allure of forbidden fruit, and she found herself wondering if his chest was as brown as his face, neck, and hands.

The officer shifted uncomfortably from foot to foot. "Well, girl? Are you deaf and dumb? Or have you never seen a grown man before?"

There was an undercurrent of insolence in the man's tone that sent ire racing through Laurel's veins. Arching a delicate black brow, she countered, "Frankly, sir, you're simply the ugliest man I've ever seen."

Behind the officer, the dozen sailors laughed uproariously

at Laurel's outrageous remark. But the officer's harsh command of "Silence!" was met with instant obedience; the men quieted and drew themselves to an attitude of attention. Laurel began to wonder uneasily if this young officer was not a man to be trifled with.

With an air of strained patience, the Yankee again turned to Laurel. "If you're through flattering my ego, miss, kindly answer my question."

His tone brooked no challenge, and Laurel hastily informed him, "The owner of this establishment is unavailable, sir."

"And just where, pray tell, is he hiding?" the officer pursued.

Laurel found a smile tugging at her lips. "He's at a nearby grog shop."

Dismissing Laurel, the soldier turned to Reba. For a moment, his dark brown eyes scrutinized the snake charm hanging about her neck, then he softly ordered, "Fetch the man."

Reba, who had watched the entire exchange with an unflinching lack of emotion, murmured, "*Oui*, m'sieur." But she slanted the Yankee an ambiguous smile before she left the room.

The officer turned to a stocky seaman. "Carter, inspect the surroundings."

"Aye, sir," the sandy-haired, broad-faced sailor replied. Issuing crisp orders to the other sailors, the seaman led the men from the room.

The Yankee's eyes again fixed upon Laurel. Without shifting his gaze, he pointed toward the prone Fancy on the floor and commented, "Now, girl, tell me what manner of mischief you people have been indulging in today."

As if on cue, Fancy, at Laurel's feet, began to moan and flail about, and Laurel realized with some guilt that her preoccupation with the Yankee had caused her to forget her servant utterly. Now she leaned over, pulling the younger girl to her knees.

"Miss Laurel, what happening?" the befuddled girl asked hoarsely.

Laurel shrugged. "Nothing, Fancy. It's just the Yankees have landed."

"God—Yankees!" the girl shrieked. Then she spotted the tall officer and again fainted dead away.

"Most hysterical bunch of women I've ever seen," the Yankee muttered grimly, striding quickly to the listless servant. Kneeling, he shook Fancy vigorously until the slave opened her eyes. "There, girl, don't fret. I've been fed today. If you mind your manners, you'll doubtless escape being eaten."

Shrieking and quivering at the officer's comment, Fancy threw her arms about her mistress's skirts and clung to the older girl.

Laurel's jaw dropped as she watched the Yankee stride off. "Why you insolent beast!" she stormed. "Just look what you've done to my Fancy!"

The tall Yankee shrugged. "I awakened her, didn't I? You'd both best remember that my patience is not limitless." Moving to the side of the room, he lifted a small table and a chair from a pile of furniture, then carried both items to the center of the room. Casually tossing his blue cap toward the wall—where it landed, squarely, on a wooden peg—he then wearily sat down upon the ladder-back chair and again stared curiously at Laurel. "Now, girl, I repeat—what ritual were you folks staging?"

Setting her jaw defiantly, Laurel leaned over and patted her wailing servant on the head. "There, Fancy, hush before this monster has you cast into the oven." She felt the servant stiffening, clenching black arms about Laurel's skirts so hard that for a moment, the older girl tottered to keep her balance.

Looking up, Laurel met the Yankee's gaze evenly as the man regarded the scene between the two girls with amused cynicism. Squaring her shoulders with great dignity, Laurel announced, "We were praying, sir."

"Praying?" the officer reiterated incredulously, laughing so hard his chair nearly tilted over backward. Leveling the chair, he again exclaimed, more sternly, "Praying? Don't tell me that pagan writhing and swooning constituted a prayer?"

"The swooning was mostly due to you, sir!" Laurel retorted tartly.

Across the room, the handsome Yankee struggled not to grin; then, losing the battle, he smiled broadly, revealing even white teeth. "Well, girl, considering the result of your supplications, you certainly can't claim your prayers were answered. But then—I suppose that depends on to whom you were praying."

Laurel scowled, remembering Reba's snake amulet. "Are you implying, sir, that we were practicing voodoo?"

"Were you?"

"If we were, sir, I can assure you we would have dispatched you to the bowels of the earth by now!"

The Yankee sighed, sitting up straight and resting bronze hands on the table top. "This repartee is getting tiresome, young lady." His dark eyes swept Laurel's figure appraisingly, moving upward to lock with her cold sapphire gaze. "Now tell me, blue eyes, who are you and what are you doing here?"

Hearing the officer's words, Fancy stiffened, looking up at her mistress in fright. Pulling the servant to her feet, Laurel said casually, "That's none of your damned business, sir."

It happened simultaneously—Fancy gasped, the Yankee whistled, and from the archway, a nasal voice inquired, "Real little hellcat, ain't she, sir?"

The Yankee officer turned, frowning grimly, to the sandy-haired sailor who had just reentered the room. "If I desire your opinion, Chief Carter, I'll ask for it!"

The burly seaman instantly replied, "Aye, sir," his lashless eyelids blinking rapidly over watery blue eyes.

Noting the humility of the husky seaman, Laurel began to regret her hasty invective. She struggled not to flinch as the tall Yankee got to his feet and approached her, his boots pounding ominously on the cedar floor.

"What a foul-mouthed wench you are," he remarked, his voice dangerously soft. Stopping just inches away from Laurel, he continued, "You'd best guard your tongue, miss, for your uncooperative remarks could easily be regarded as hostile behavior. And any Confederate acting in a hostile manner is to be taken to the commodore's flagship immediately. Would you prefer to be questioned by Commander Renshaw himself?"

Laurel gulped, realizing at last that she was not playing a game with this man. He was deadly serious. She *could* be taken to a Yankee ship—perhaps cast in irons, even shipped north. "No, sir," she said, lowering her gaze to the floor.

But a brown finger tilted her chin, forcing her to look up into the Yankee's penetrating eyes. "Your name?" he asked.

"Laurel Ashland, sir."

The Yankee released her chin. "And your business in this establishment?"

Laurel hesitated, a thousand thoughts swirling in her mind. If she told the Yankee the truth, she and Fancy would no doubt be bundled back to the academy, there to await death by boredom—if old Mother St. Pierre didn't murder them both first. But if she stayed here, she would be in the thick of the action—not to mention the danger—and she might even be able to help the South. She had heard of lady spies from the Confederacy who recklessly crossed into

Union territory, and she suddenly found the idea of betraying this arrogant stranger tantalizing.

"Well, girl?" the Yankee impatiently pursued.

Laurel quickly made her decision. "I work here, sir."

Fancy, who had spent the past few moments cowering behind Laurel, now screeched, "Miss Laurel!" then clapped a black hand over her quivering mouth, gaping at her mistress with eyes that threatened to pop out of her head.

The soldier glowered at Fancy, then turned to Laurel. "What the devil ails the girl? Is she simple-minded?"

"No sir," Laurel retorted. Turning to the servant, she ordered hoarsely, "Fancy, you hush up, now. Go fetch a chair and be seated."

Muttering "Yes 'um," the shorter girl lumbered off to seat herself in the corner of the room.

Laurel turned back to the Yankee, her smooth features belying the turmoil within as she planned what she would next say to the handsome but dangerous officer. "It's just that poor Fancy is half out of her mind with the grief of it," she informed him in a dramatic whisper.

"The grief of what, pray tell?"

"Of seeing her mistress toiling for her keep."

"And should that be such a tragedy?"

"Certainly, sir, since I hail from one of the finest families in the South," Laurel retorted airily.

"Indeed?" the Yankee laughed, staring at the blue turban binding Laurel's hair.

Laurel scowled and strolled away as she continued proudly, "My father recently sold our estate in Tennessee, and we began our journey to Texas, seeking more fertile lands. Then, due to the cruelties of fate, our ship ran aground off San Luis Pass. All our darkies drowned, save Fancy here."

The officer nodded toward Fancy, who sat, face aghast, in the corner of the room. "The wench swims?"

"Oh yes, sir," Laurel replied, moving closer to the

Yankee. "As a baby, she fell into a well and learned to swim in a hurry."

The Yankee again glanced at the servant, who now looked totally horror-stricken. "Remarkable," he uttered. Turning to Laurel, he urged, "Pray continue with your fascinating tale, Miss Ashland."

"Well, as I said, our slaves—quite a large investment—perished off the Pass. My father helped Mother swim to shore, while I pulled along my baby brother—er, Casper Ashland the Third."

The Yankee raised a black brow. "You also swim, Miss Ashland?"

"Of course. This *is* Galveston, sir."

"But I thought you had just gotten off the boat from Tennessee."

Laurel shrugged.

The Yankee's dark eyes narrowed. "Where is your... erstwhile family now, Miss Ashland?"

Laurel sighed. "Ah, sir, how pitiless is chance! The water gave the lot of them a deathly chill and one by one, they perished from malaria."

"Tragic," he murmured.

"At any rate, with our fortune—not to mention our slaves—at the bottom of the Gulf, and the subsequent death of all my relations, Fancy and I had no choice but to seek employment in these humble surroundings."

Laurel finished her story and eyed the Yankee warily. His face was a curious mixture of emotions—half vexation, half amused contempt. She gulped, not sure whether he was going to laugh in her face or place her under arrest.

Before the officer could gather his thoughts, the man called Carter stepped forward. "Begging your pardon, sir, but the wench is lying through her teeth. She's just putting on airs cause she won't own up to her black blood. Just look at the way she's dressed, sir. Ain't no doubt she's a quadroon—I see such in New Orleans."

"How dare you say such things!" Laurel hissed at the burly seaman.

The officer stroked his chin thoughtfully. "You have a point, Carter. I do believe the girl is lying."

Laurel glared at the Yankee, her bright blue eyes incredulous. "You don't believe me?"

The tall officer laughed shortly. "You're undoubtedly a remarkable swimmer, Miss Ashland. Do you have any idea how dangerous the currents are off San Luis Pass?"

Laurel bit her lip, for once at a loss for words.

"Sir, I got an idea," Carter interjected. "I seen a cistern out back. Why not throw in the girl—or her maid—and test out the story?"

In the corner of the room, Fancy squealed with fear, while the officer chuckled. "Not a bad idea. Or perhaps Miss Ashland would prefer a dip in the Gulf."

Despite her racing heart, Laurel drew herself up with dignity. "If you choose not to believe me, sir, that is your misfortune. But be assured that the truth is on my side." Before the Yankee could comment, she hastily changed the subject. "Now that I've given you my family history, as well as my reasons for being in this establishment, might I request the same courtesy of *you*?" Tilting her chin arrogantly, she inquired, "Who are you, sir, and what are you doing here?"

The Yankee grinned lazily and took a step closer to Laurel. Evidently much amused by her bravado, he bowed deeply, then announced, "I'm Lieutenant Jacob Lafflin, miss, captain of the *Owasco*. As to what I'm doing here—" his brown eyes sparkled with triumph as his hand lifted her chin—"I'm here to demand your unconditional surrender."

Chapter Four

OCTOBER 10, 1862

Infuriated, Laurel threw off Lieutenant Lafflin's grasp and drew back her hand to strike him. But the sound of loud voices in the hallway distracted her; she turned, with the others, toward the archway.

Portly and balding, Hans Verdene walked unsteadily into the dining hall, calling over his shoulder to Reba, "You'd best have a damn good reason for fetching me, wench! First time I've had a winning streak since this wretched war began!"

Suddenly, Verdene halted in his tracks as he spotted the Yankees assembled in the dining hall. His florid face whitening, he inquired unsteadily of Jacob Lafflin, "Explain this—this intrusion, sir!"

"You are the owner of this establishment?" Lafflin countered coldly.

Awkwardly shifting his beaver hat from hand to hand, the shorter man nodded and replied, "Yes, sir. I'm Hans Verdene."

Dispassionately appraising Verdene, Lafflin announced, "I'm Lieutenant Jacob Lafflin, captain of the *Owasco*. I've been assigned command of the ground forces occupying this island and hereby inform you that we shall be quartering in your establishment, sir."

The barrel-chested Verdene drew himself up haughtily. "You would steal a man's business, sir, without so much as a by your leave?"

His face tense, Lafflin strode to the front window of the dining hall, parting the chintz curtains and gazing out upon the sunny streets of Galveston. "We steal nothing, sir," he replied with an air off overstrained patience. "And may I suggest that you keep your loose tongue in check, Verdene."

Visibly shaken, the older man clutched his hat nervously and reasoned, "But, sir, this is a small, modest establishment I keep here. Surely you would prefer more luxurious surroundings. Why, just down the street there's the Tremont—"

"Which is far too large to be properly secured by my forces," Lafflin replied curtly, turing to stare icily at the inebriated Verdene. "Any further questions, sir?"

"Nay, Captain," the older man shuddered.

Lafflin smiled tightly. "Never fear, Verdene, we shall not keep you from your favorite pastimes. There are ample servants about, and heaven knows, you'll be of no use to us in your present condition."

Verdene's features twisted in a curious mixture of affronted dignity and relief. "Aye, sir," he mumbled, turning to leave.

"You'll be paid two dollars per day for each man quartered here," Lafflin continued. "Fair enough?"

The bulky man nodded without looking back as he hastily headed for the archway.

"Just a moment, Verdene!"

Verdene froze, then turned.

Lafflin nodded toward the three women standing nearby.

"You will, of course, pay these people for the services they render us."

Verdene squinted at the girls. "Begging your pardon, sir, but I don't know who the hell these wenches be."

Lafflin arched a black brow, staring hard at the three nervous women. "Interesting."

Gulping, Laurel quickly stepped forward, her blue eyes wide and entreating. "Surely, Mr. Verdene, you remember me," she said sweetly, taking the older man's arm. "I'm Laurel, sir. Why just last week you helped me make the funeral arrangements for my baby brother, Casper, and you gave me the position of—of upstairs maid. Don't you remember me, sir?"

Verdene's features contorted in confusion as he stared down at the lovely, innocently smiling girl. Obviously much affected by the young woman's beauty, he started to speak, then hesitated, finally sputtering, "Jesus, miss, I don't wish to contradict a pretty thing like you, but I ain't never laid eyes on you or them others before!"

Watching Jacob Lafflin's eyes narrow at this revelation, Laurel was swept by a chill of fear. But outwardly her appearance was cool, coy, as she preened, "Perhaps, Mr. Verdene, I should remind you of the circumstances of our meeting." Standing on tiptoe, she whispered a brief remark in Verdene's ear, then giggled.

As Laurel moved away from Verdene, smiling demurely, the rotund man turned a bright red, nervously jamming his thumbs into his vest pockets.

Watching them, Jacob Lafflin inquired testily, "Well, Verdene? Did you hire the girl or not?"

Verdene stared at his dusty brown boots. "I don't remember, sir."

Lafflin laughed dryly. "I had intended to ask you why you weren't fighting with your fellow Confederates, Verdene, but the reason seems obvious enough. By all means, get back to your cards, and—'' he paused, nostrils flared in distaste—"your whiskey."

Nodding miserably, the older man hastily took his leave.

As Verdene exited, Reba approached Jacob Lafflin, her dark brown eyes boldly studying him. "Do you and your men wish food, m'sieur?" she asked in a smooth tone.

Jacob Lafflin's features relaxed as he smiled back at the pretty woman. "Well, it's good to find at least one capable soul in this establishment. Aye, we could use some lunch directly."

Reba nodded, moving closer to the handsome Yankee. "*Certainement*, m'sieur. And if I can serve you—in any other way, please call me at once."

Lafflin chuckled as Laurel and Fancy exchanged amazed glances at the obvious sensual undertone in Reba's remark. His eyes sweeping Reba admiringly, Lafflin said thoughtfully, "I just might do that."

From the doorway, the sandy-haired Carter cleared his throat, causing Lafflin to turn from Reba. "Carter, gather the men and assign bunks—at least two men per room, mind you." Glancing at Laurel and Fancy, he added, "Makes it less likely the men will be surprised during their slumber."

"Aye, sir," Carter replied, turning and leaving the room.

Lafflin again directed his attention to Reba. "See to the food, then, girl." Nodding toward Fancy, he added, "And take this little brown mouse with you. She might be good for something."

"*Oui,* m'sieur," Reba replied, pulling the timorous Fancy from the room.

Now Laurel was completely alone with Lieutenant Jacob Lafflin; but, curiously, the tall Yankee did not seem to take any notice of her as he casually strolled back to the table, seated himself, and pulled a document from his breast pocket. He unfolded the parchment, studying it in frowning concentration.

Cautiously, Laurel approached the brooding Yankee. Moving around behind him, she peered over his shoulder and saw that he was studying a map of Galveston. She was leaning over closer, trying to make out some notations scribbled on the bottom, when suddenly, a strong arm reached out to grab her waist and she was pulled violently downward, into Jacob Lafflin's lap.

For a moment, Laurel was too stunned to speak as she looked up into pitiless dark brown eyes, at black brows knitted in anger. Then, feeling the muscular line of Lafflin's chest against her back and the bold, hard strength of his arm around her waist, it occurred to Laurel that her dignity had been affronted. "Why, you brute!" she spat, struggling to extricate herself from his lap even as she drew back her hand to slap him.

But his hands easily caught both of hers, his strong arms pinning her arms against her breasts in a familiar manner that made Laurel mindless with rage. Yet the more she fought him, the tighter his arms became, like relentless steel bands. While Laurel shrieked every obscenity she knew, Lafflin was silent; but she heard him chuckle softly as her struggles unwittingly caused his forearm to pull downward the bodice of her white frock; she cried out in impotent rage as his flesh contacted the creamy rise of her bosom.

His arms tightened and moved lower, uncovering the upper part of a firm young breast. Laurel gasped sharply, then grew speechless with shock. Chills swept through her body as she felt Lafflin's mouth on her ear.

"There," he murmured silkily. "Will you hush like a good child, or must I take further measures to silence you? I assure you, Miss Ashland, no one would dare come to your aid."

Though Laurel could not see Lafflin's face, his intent was obvious. Again, she struggled wildly—to no avail; much to her mortification, she felt the cloth of her bodice slipping even lower as Jacob Lafflin's arms clenched about her.

In that instant, Laurel realized that the man was playing a game with her, toying with her sadistically, as a cat would with a mouse. And she hated him for it. Yet what choice did she have but to acquiesce? She was no match for his brute strength; any moment her breasts would literally pop out of her gown and surely the man would then ravish her upon the dining room floor!

Realizing the hopelessness of her state, Laurel ceased all resistance, growing limp in his arms. Again, Lafflin chuckled, then whispered harshly, "Don't *ever* come up behind me again."

With this admonition, Lafflin summarily pushed Laurel off his lap. She uttered an incoherent cry as her rump contacted the hard wooden floor.

Laurel bolted to her feet, shaking her fist at the imperturbable Yankee. "Why, you—you—" she sputtered.

"Hush," Jacob Lafflin commanded without looking up as he again poured over the map of Galveston.

Laurel glared at the calm Yankee, the full impact of the indignity she had just suffered dawning upon her. Never had any man abused her so flagrantly. The obscene intimacy of his touch, the musky masculine scent of him—Laurel felt her heart pounding in her chest at the memory.

"If my father were here, sir, he would kill you for the outrage you just dealt me!" she spat at the Yankee.

"A pity that he's dead," Lafflin countered smoothly, still not looking at her as he crackled the parchment in an offhanded manner that infuriated Laurel. "Were he alive, I should not sleep a wink tonight for the fear of it."

Lafflin's sarcasm hit Laurel like a slap across the face, and she moved forward, defending stoutly, "I was merely trying to read the map that so interests you!"

"You read?" he asked with an air of boredom.

"Yes, of course! I told you I—I—"

"Ah, yes—you come from one of the finest families in the South," he cynically supplied. "Pray, hush, before you join your fine family in their present abode."

Laurel uttered a cry of dismay, her blue eyes widening at the dangerous undertone in the Yankee's voice. But he seemed to take no notice of her as his strong brown fingers traced a path on the map laid out across the table.

Laurel watched him, glowering, tapping her foot impatiently. A fine state of affairs she had gotten herself into! She groaned to herself. Even Mother Superior was easier to deal with than the blackguard who now held her captive!

Laurel's face lit up. Mother St. Pierre! Yes, perhaps she actually missed the old bat after all!

Laurel eyed the Yankee covertly. He seemed oblivious of her presence. If she could just ease out of the room, go find Fancy—

Warily, she took a step toward the archway.

"Don't," the Yankee said, his eyes still fixed upon the map.

Laurel obeyed him, her heart thudding in desolation. What did the man intend doing with her?

Presently, Lafflin stood up, carefully folded the map, and replaced it in his breast pocket. As he approached Laurel, she asked, "What are you going to do with me?"

Laurel could hardly believe the pitiful croak she heard was her own voice; she felt her face heating as Lafflin drew closer, his eyes full of amusement.

Lafflin took Laurel's hand and, with the attitude of a stern parent toward a willful child, said simply, "Come with me, Laurel."

Laurel gulped, letting Lafflin lead her into the hallway and up the dusty board steps to the second story of the hotel. They moved through the upstairs hallway, passing a guard stationed in the middle of the long corridor. The tall, wiry man saluted and said, "We saved the finest room for you, sir." Pointing down the hallway, he added, "Last door on the right, Captain."

"Thanks, Wilson," Lafflin returned, pulling Laurel along behind him.

Lafflin led Laurel into the large room at the end of the hallway. As Laurel stood watching him nervously, Lafflin inspected the surroundings—large, handsome, but dusty Chippendale furniture, including a full tester bed with knitted blue counterpane. Several oil paintings of the Gulf hung above walnut wainscotting, a market scene above the fireplace. A gold and blue braided rug on the floor gave the room a masculine flavor.

Opening a door, Lafflin glanced into a small room adjoining the bedroom. He then reentered the main room and strode to the window, opening it and sending in the balmy Gulf breeze.

Pivoting toward Laurel, he said smoothly, "It'll do, for the two of us."

"The *two* of us?" Laurel choked, blue eyes bewildered.

Lafflin laughed mirthlessly as he leaned against the tallboy, crossing one black boot over the other. "Surely you don't think I'm going to let you out of my sight, Miss Ashland. Not after hearing your bizarre tale downstairs."

Laurel's eyebrows shot up as she stood, hands on hips, glowering at the tall, handsome Yankee. "You expect me to—to—"

"I expect you to be my maid and to sleep in the anteroom."

Laurel bolted forward, shaking a fist at Lafflin. "Why, you ruthless, arrogant monster! I'll see you in hell first!"

Undaunted, the Yankee strode off. Passing the dresser, he traced a straight line across the mahogany with a fingertip. "This establishment is exceedingly dusty," he commented with distaste. Proceeding to a gold silk brocade wing chair, he seated himself, cooly studying Laurel's irate countenance. "Quit carping and come pull off my boots."

"Your—your boots!"

"Yes. How else are you going to polish them?"

Laurel could only stare at the Yankee in utter amazement.

"Don't tell me I've offended your sensibilities, Miss Ashland. Surely such tasks are not beneath your dignity since you've been employed as—what is it?—upstairs maid in this establishment."

"In that, sir, I had no choice!"

"Did you have a choice in the manner in which you obtained your position?"

"What do you mean?"

"What did you whisper to Verdene?" Lafflin asked nastily.

"I—I—"

"To be more specific, Miss Ashland, what other services may I expect you to perform?"

"Go to the devil!" Laurel cried, spinning about to exit the room.

But the Yankee was beside her in an instant, his hard fingers grabbing her forearm. "You'll do as I say, Miss Ashland, or I'll pack you off to Commander Renshaw for questioning."

Laurel's jaw dropped. "Wh—what are you saying?"

"I'm saying that your conduct has been highly suspicious, Miss Ashland. My orders are to take anyone suspected of spying to the commodore's flagship."

"S—spying?"

"Have you a speech impediment, girl?" he snapped, releasing her forearm. Moving off, he added, "Has it occurred to you that you are safer here with me than you would be elsewhere in the hotel, or on a ship full of love-starved sailors?"

"Safer with you?" Laurel scoffed. "How can you say

that after you just insulted my virtue with your presumptuous questions?''

Lafflin shrugged, his dark eyes boldly sweeping Laurel's figure. "I'll not have you propositioning my men."

That was the last straw. "Monster!" Laurel shrieked, diving for Lafflin, fingernails aimed for his throat.

But Lafflin grabbed her, pinning both her arms at the small of her back. As Laurel cried out, twisting to get free, his grip tightened, causing tears of outrage to spill from her eyes.

Realizing the futility of her struggles, Laurel quit fighting. She avoided his eyes as he leaned over and whispered, "Through with your tirade, dear?"

Laurel nodded desolately.

He released her; she straightened, feeling an ache across her shoulders. Seeing his smile of triumph as they faced each other, she lowered her gaze to the floor, biting her lip to hold back more tears, even as she thought of how she abhorred him.

"That's better," he soothed with a trace of sarcasm as he studied her downcast countenance. "A more fitting attitude for a maid."

Laurel said nothing, but inside, she felt as if the heartless Yankee had inserted a knife in her middle and was remorselessly twisting the blade.

"Now as to your attire," Lafflin continued. "Why the turban? Are you indeed a quadroon, as Carter suggested?"

Laurel looked up, hoping he could read the raw hatred in her gaze. "I told you I'm—"

"Spare me further lies," he interrupted tensely, moving toward her. His features were harsh, threatening, as he drew near enough to touch her. "Remember this, my dear. Your fate is in my hands—" his hand reached out, pulling loose the tie holding her turban "—entirely."

Laurel drew in her breath sharply as the turban slid from

her head and her luxuriant black tresses fell in silky waves about her neck and shoulders. Her face burned at the Yankee's impudence—had he stripped her naked, she could not have felt more abused.

But then she saw his eyes—and she felt naked indeed. Jacob Lafflin backed off, staring at Laurel awestruck, as if seeing her for the first time. Never had Laurel seen such a look in a man's eyes—a carnal, irrepressible need.

"Astonishing," he breathed, his eyes moving over her face and hair, his expression growing strangely gentle, tender. "Absolutely astonishing."

Laurel shivered, summoning all her courage as she warned, "Don't you dare touch me!"

The spell broke. Jacob Lafflin threw back his head and laughed until tears sprang to his dark eyes. "Touch you— why the hell do you think I would want to touch you?"

"Why the things you said, the look on your face—" Laurel stammered.

Still laughing, Lafflin returned to the wing chair. "Come here and take off my boots." Chuckling at Laurel's irate countenance, he added, "You flatter yourself if you think I would ravish you, Miss Ashland. If I seem amazed, it's simply because you're the ugliest wench I've ever laid eyes on."

Chapter Five

OCTOBER 10, 1862

"Our position is much that of a lone mountain lion surrounded by a pack of wolves," Jacob Lafflin said as he took a corn dodger from the cobalt blue ironstone platter Laurel offered him.

The dozen sailors were assembled in the dining hall for the evening meal. Laurel, Fancy, and Reba were busily serving the hungry men ham, sweet potatoes, and beans, as Jacob Lafflin instructed the men of their duties during the coming night.

"The island is literally surrounded by Confederates," Lafflin continued, cutting his ham. "They have infiltrated every cove of the bay, and several Confederate steamers are sitting in the Gulf, patiently awaiting our slightest inattention so that they may run the blockade." Glancing meaningfully at the men, he added, "With the curfew established, your duty will be to detain anyone caught roaming the streets at night, whether in Confederate uniform or not. Any person breaking the curfew must be assumed to be a spy—you may meet resistance with necessary force.''

A chill coursed through Laurel's body at Lafflin's last statement as the seaman named Wilson inquired of his captain, ''Does that mean we're to use our rifles, sir?''

Lafflin nodded. ''With discretion.''

''Aye, sir.''

As Lafflin assigned temporary patrol routes, adding that he would reconnoiter the city the next day in order to establish permanent paths, Laurel thought of the events of the day. She had, indeed, removed and polished Lafflin's boots and had fetched his bath. Then she waited miserably in the stuffy anteroom as Lafflin bathed himself, singing loud choruses of ''Beautiful Dreamer.''' Once Lafflin was dressed, he had forced her to sit upon a straight chair in his room while he again studied the map of Galveston. Though he refused to let her go look for Fancy or help with the cooking, he later ordered her to help serve at lunch. Afterward, he left to go report to Commodore Renshaw, leaving Carter in charge. Carter ordered her back to Lafflin's room, assigning a seaman to guard her. Going crazy with boredom, Laurel spent the afternoon tidying up the dusty suite and unpacking Lafflin's clothes.

Of course, Laurel's ire had built all day at the Yankee's callous treatment of her. So far she had found no way to get even with him. But now, as she caught the sandy-haired Carter boldly eyeing her, a plan occurred to her.

Leaning far forward, exposing the valley between her breasts, Laurel dropped three corn dodgers on Carter's plate, one by one. Doing so, she smiled at him dazzlingly, her forearm brushing his shoulder. Her overture was not lost upon the burly seaman, who, to Laurel's horror, reached out for her bosom.

''A handsome trinket—who you stole it off, wench?'' Carter asked with a wicked smile as he held in his hand the gold and sapphire brooch that dangled from its blue ribbon around Laurel's neck.

Laurel glared at the seaman. "That belonged to my great-grandmother. Take your slimy hands off it!"

Tossing the brooch back against Laurel's bosom, Carter quipped, "Ain't no baubles like that in Africa, sweetheart!"

The other sailors present laughed heartily, but all fell silent when Jacob Lafflin bolted to his feet. "You're dismissed, Carter," he ordered curtly.

"But sir, I ain't eaten—"

"Dismissed! Attend to your duties!" Lafflin barked.

"Aye, sir!" the abashed seaman said, getting to his feet. But he shot Laurel a venemous look over his shoulder.

Glancing from Carter to Laurel, Lafflin added menacingly, "You'd be in the brig this moment had it not been obvious that the girl was leading you on."

While Carter hastily took his leave, Laurel burst forward, her mouth open, poised to defend herself. But Lafflin pivoted hard to face her, pointing a threatening finger at her. "Girl, say one word and I'll have you locked in your room. Now go sit in the corner and quit shaking your fanny at my men!"

Uttering a cry of frustrated rage, Laurel noisily dumped the platter of corn dodgers onto the table, then stormed off to sit by Fancy in a darkened corner of the room.

For a moment, Laurel tried to calm herself as she eyed Lafflin stonily. Lafflin calmly instructed his men of their duties during the night, his impassive features betraying no hint of the intense incident that had just occurred.

"Miss Laurel, what the Lord's name you think you is doing?" Fancy hissed half-hysterically from beside her.

Laurel shrugged off the slave's remark.

"You is going to git us all kilt, what with your defying them Yankees! Why you do that, and tell all them lies?"

Laurel gritted back, "Because it's our duty!"

"Duty?"

"Yes! We're going to study their activities and report them to our own army."

Fancy's face contorted in horror. "You mean we is going to *spy*?"

Laurel clapped a hand over the black girl's mouth. "Lower your voice, stupid chit, or they'll hear you! Yes of course we're going to be spies." She bit her lip. "At least that's what I *think* we'll do." Watching Jacob Lafflin get to his feet, she quickly added, "Oh, to hell with it! This spying business is neither glamorous nor intriguing—in fact, it's downright dangerous! Quick, Fancy, tell me where you're sleeping tonight. I'm actually beginning to miss Witch St. Pierre!"

Fancy heaved a sigh of relief. "Now you is talkin'. I sleep in a cabin with Reba—out back, the other side of the kitchen."

Seeing Jacob Lafflin motioning for her to come, Laurel stood up, muttering under her breath, "I'll come get you when everyone's asleep."

Laurel tossed and turned miserably. The night had aged considerably and she simply could not rest in the stuffy, cramped little room Lafflin had assigned her. The cubicle did have a tiny window, but Laurel had been forced to close it to keep out mosquitoes, for her bed consisted of a tiny pallet with no mosquito netting.

She felt secure in her decision to return to the academy and face her punishment. Whatever Mother St. Pierre meted out, it could be no worse than being at Jacob Lafflin's mercy! How she hated the arrogant, conceited beast!

She detested him even more because, at the moment, Lafflin stood between her and escape. He slept in the next room and she must walk right past him to get to the hall, possibly awakening him. And what if he was not asleep in the first place? It would just be like the cad to lie in wait for her—after all, hadn't he asked her what *other* services he could expect her to perform?

Even if she did get past him and out of the hotel, she still would have to contend with the sailors patrolling the streets—men who had orders to shoot!

Laurel sat up, took her white dress from the chair beside her, and put it on in the moonlight. She donned her stockings and slippers, then carefully got to her feet. For long moments she stood with her ear pressed against the door to Lafflin's room. Hearing only silence, she was turning the doorknob when suddenly she heard a soft knocking sound coming from his room.

Someone was knocking on Jacob Lafflin's door!

Her heart racing, Laurel stood motionless, straining to hear. Silence—then the knocking sound again, louder.

This time, she heard the mattress springs groan in the next room, then shuffling noises, followed by a door creaking open.

"What the hell are *you* doing here?" she heard Lafflin mumble sleepily.

She heard a woman's soft voice murmuring something indistinguishable, then the door closing.

Seconds later, she heard the bed creaking, followed by laughter and a soft sentence in French.

French! Was Reba in bed with Jacob Lafflin?

With deepening horror, Laurel pressed her ear against the door and listened. She heard the unmistakable sound of Reba's throaty laughter, then Lafflin chuckling, then more French from Reba. Laurel had studied French at the academy but could not understand any of the words Reba was saying—though she assumed they were all filthy, having to do with the animal act the two obviously intended to perform.

Laurel was seething about this when she heard Lafflin

reply to Reba, *"Très bien, chérie."* More French! Where had the Yankee learned the language? A most peculiar man—aside from being a tyrant and a cutthroat, he was also an enigma!

Suddenly, there was silence—were they kissing?—then the mattress springs began to creak rhythmically, raucously. Laurel's face smarted with mortification. Were they actually doing it—copulating, only a few feet away from her? Oh, how could they? How could Reba be a traitor to the South, bedding down with a Yankee? And how could Lafflin stoop so low?

Laurel angrily threw herself on her pallet, overwhelmed by a feeling of betrayal she only half understood. But somehow, she felt Lafflin was doing this to punish her, that he realized she was awake, listening.

"Fat chance of me escaping now," she moaned. "Or should I walk right past them? Would they take notice of me or simply continue with their coupling?"

She paused, again listening as the rocking sound reached a crescendo. Then a woman's incoherent cry split the night—an animal wail, half pain, half ecstasy. A man's voice whispered soothingly, then silence.

"Monster! Monster!" Laurel hissed, pounding her fists upon the mattress as tears spilled, unheeded, upon her hands.

Laurel awakened in the silvery darkness. Her pillow was still damp from her tears and her dress clung to her, due to the unbearable closeness of the tiny room.

How long she had slept, she did not know. But no sounds emanated from the room next to her.

Getting to her feet, she cautiously cracked open the door to Jacob Lafflin's room. She could not see him or Reba—the bed was in a shadow. But she could hear him breathing deeply, regularly.

Holding her breath, she tiptoed into the dark room. She took tiny steps, feeling her way past the wardrobe, dresser, and chair. After what seemed an eternity, she reached the door to the hall. As she slowly creaked open the door, moonlight spilled into the room from the window at the end of the hallway. Laurel turned, staring at the bed.

Jacob Lafflin slept peacefully, alone. Evidently, Reba had served her purpose and had been dismissed, Laurel thought ruefully. Now Lafflin snored contentedly, his arms spread out across the mattress, his chest bare, the sheet draped across his middle. Lafflin felt her face heating as she realized the Yankee was doubtless stark naked beneath his thin covering. Was that how people performed the sexual act—removing all their clothing? Had Reba been naked also?

Laurel studied Lafflin's face. There was a tenderness about his relaxed countenance, a peacefulness that belied his earlier bullishness. The mouth that had seemed so firm and tight earlier had a gentleness to it now. Her eyes moved slowly down his neck to his chest, which was muscular, smooth, without hair. Was she losing her mind? For she had an insane wish to rush over, run her fingers over the smooth bronze of his skin, draw back the sheet—

Horrified at her wicked thoughts, Laurel quickly exited the room. The man was a Yankee traitor and she'd best get as far away from him as possible!

Closing the door, she started down the moonlit hallway. She must exit the building, find Fancy, get home—

Then suddenly, violently, she was grabbed about the middle. She tried to scream, but a large, fleshy hand smothered her mouth.

Oh God, what's happening? she thought hysterically. The hallway was deserted yet this person had materialized out of thin air, like a ghost—

As the man dragged Laurel into an alcove, she realized he

must have jumped out from the tiny nook. At least she hadn't lost her mind—

But her thoughts were squashed as she felt a pair of fleshy lips pressed against her ear. "Out looking for action, sweetheart?" a low nasal voice inquired. "Lafflin ain't man enough to satisfy the likes of you, eh?"

Laurel gulped as she recognized the voice of Chief Carter. The man had obviously been assigned guard duty inside the hotel. Mother of God, what did he intend doing with her?

"Don't worry, honey, old Abe'll fix you up fine," the sailor continued in a nauseatingly sweet voice.

Laurel struggled wildly as the burly man pressed his mouth against her cheek. But she was no match for him—his thick arms held her easily. He chuckled, filling her nostrils with the vile odor of whiskey; she was swept with revulsion.

While one hand still firmly silenced her mouth, Carter's other hand fumbled for her bosom, grabbing the cloth, then ripping downward.

A muffled scream rose in Laurel's throat as the sailor yanked at the tie of her chemise, his calloused hand roughly seeking her breasts.

She bucked like a frightened deer, but again, he chuckled, his hand moving audaciously from her breasts to her bottom, which he grabbed, pinching painfully. "Hush, you little whore," she heard him mutter smoothly. "If the captain finds you out, you'll be in one hell of a worse mess than you are now. Why, he'll have you tied to the post outside and shot."

Laurel froze.

"Aye, sweetheart," Carter continued in a ruthless whisper. "Real cutthroat, the captain is. I seen him give a man thirty lashes for not saluting. The man be half pirate."

Laurel's heart beat frantically. She obviously could expect

no help from Jacob Lafflin. But why wouldn't this brute let her go?

Her question was immediately answered as Abel Carter pulled her to the floor. Laurel flailed about, revolted, as he lowered his bulky body upon her. "There, sweetheart, spread your legs," he hissed. "I know you done it countless times before."

A sob died in Laurel's throat as she felt a hard bulge through the layers of clothing pressing relentlessly against her pelvic bone. Never had she felt more repelled—yet worse indignities awaited her as Carter's heavy legs drew hers apart.

Laurel struggled to no avail as Carter's hand groped beneath her skirts, sliding beneath her buttocks, then pulling downward on the cloth of her pantalets.

With rising hysteria, Laurel realized it was *really* going to happen—the man was actually going to unclothe her posterior, then ram her with the revolting instrument now pressing so obscenely against her underclothing.

Laurel made a quick decision—she preferred being shot at the hitching post. Her jaw clenched upon Carter's hand, her teeth cutting fiercely into his flesh.

"Bitch!" Carter hollered, drawing his wounded hand to his mouth. Then he drew it back and struck Laurel full across the face.

Laurel cried out, reeling from the vicious slap. She was thinking surely she would faint when she saw the moonlight-outlined sailor draw his hand back, poising himself for another blow.

But then, suddenly, the man was pulled from her. Laurel hastily covered herself as she looked up the tall frame of Jacob Lafflin. Yet her relief was mingled with terror, for even in the moonlight there was no mistaking the murderous light in Lafflin's eyes as he glared from Laurel to Carter.

"What the hell is going on here?" Lafflin demanded.

The darkness could not cloak the fear in Carter's eyes as he quickly defended, "The wench was seducing me, sir. Said she'd give me a roll if I let her out the back afterwards. I think she got a spy lover out on the streets t'night. 'Course I wouldn't of let her loose, sir. But you can't blame a man for taking his pleasure."

Laurel bolted to her feet. "Liar!" she hissed at the seaman. "You tried to rape me!"

Hard fingers grabbed Laurel's wrist as Jacob Lafflin pulled her alongside him. "Hush, wench! Your morals are not of the slightest concern to me!" Turning to Carter, he barked, "You'll meet me at first light in the dining hall, Carter, regarding disciplinary action I plan to take for this infraction. We all could have been murdered in our beds while you rutted!"

"Aye, sir," Carter mumbled humbly.

Gripping Laurel's wrist tighter, Lafflin directed menacingly, "*You*—come with me!"

Laurel choked back a protest as Lafflin half dragged her down the hallway and back into his room. He pulled her to the bed, ordering, "Sit down!"

Laurel's heart jumped into her throat as she sat listening to Lafflin moving about in the darkness. She heard a bang and a curse, then the room was flooded with lamplight.

"Look at me!" Lafflin commanded.

Gulping, Laurel looked up, hoping her trepidation was not betrayed on her face. But when her eyes locked with his, a spasm of fear gripped her features, for the rage on his face was horrible to see. Uneasily, her eyes moved down his figure—though his chest was still bare, she illogically wondered how he had donned his trousers so quickly.

"Why were you seducing Carter?" he demanded.

His remark hit Laurel like a potful of boiling water. Heedless of his ire, she sprang to her feet. "How dare you

say such a thing!'' she stormed, shaking her fist at him.
"The man was forcing himself on me!"

"Indeed?" Lafflin scoffed. He moved forward, then paused,
his brows knitting as his dark eyes examined the imprint of
Carter's hand on her cheek, then fixed upon her torn bodice.
Spotting the direction of his gaze, Laurel hastily pulled the
edges of cloth upward to cover her exposed chemise.

As he watched her, Lafflin's face twisted with conflicting
emotions. Then, surprisingly, his features softened. "What
were you doing in the hallway?" he asked gently.

The solicitude in his tone unnerved her. "I—I wanted to
go home," she stammered.

"Home?" he repeated in bewilderment. "To Tennessee?"

"I want my mother," she sniffed. And to her horror, she
burst into tears.

Filled with shame, Laurel turned away. But strong arms
closed about her, turning her, and she found her wet cheek
pressed against the hard satin of Jacob Lafflin's chest.

"Please, this is indecent!" she moaned, trying to push
him away.

"Hush!" he admonished. He pulled her with him to the
large wing chair, where he sat, then pulled her down upon
his lap, tucking her head under his chin.

Oddly, she felt unafraid, even comforted, being held thus.
The events, the fears, of the day seemed to close in upon
her and she sobbed loudly, shamelessly.

Once she quieted a bit, she felt his strong hand stroking
her hair. "There," he soothed. "What a strange wench you
are, Laurel Ashland. Either you know nothing of the ways
of men, or you know far too much." Lifting her tearstreaked
face, he asked her seriously, "Which is it, Laurel? Are you
wicked vixen or innocent maid?"

Looking up at him expectantly, she did not reply.

His dark eyes searched her face quizzically. "How old are
you, Laurel?"

His question was a blinding revelation; a wave of grief flooded her teeming mind. "I'm—I'm seventeen," she choked, "this very day! It's my birthday!"

With these words, she fell into renewed spasms of weeping.

"Your birthday? Seventeen?" he repeated in surprise. His fingertips gently stroked the blooming welt on her cheek. Gritting his teeth, he muttered harshly, "Carter shall pay for this! Why, you're little more than a child!"

"I'm not a child!" Laurel defended.

Lafflin smiled and Laurel sobbed her mortification, realizing the quavery soprano of her voice sounded just like that of a whining child.

Lafflin's hands reached downward, taking the two sections of ripped cloth at her bodice. Laurel stiffened as he tied the two ends together. "You may be young, Laurel Ashland," he whispered, a catch in his voice, "but remember this. You have the body of a beautiful woman. And you are safe only with me."

Laurel looked up at him, aghast, her tears frozen on her face. "Safe—with you?" she scoffed. "After what you and Reba did tonight in this very room?"

Lafflin grinned broadly. "Why, you little eavesdropper!"

"Eavesdropper! How could I avoid hearing the animal groans emitting from—" she paused, realizing her face was growing hot with embarrassment.

"Yes?" he prompted.

"Ooooh!" she cried, struggling to get out of his lap.

But his arms held her easily as he replied, "Never fear, Laurel, I've no desire to tangle with you. I've found maidens to be a hysterical lot and prefer a woman of experience. Besides, you'd doubtless fall in love with me, and I'd have to break your heart."

"Why, you insufferable cad!" she cried, clenching her fists at him, prepared to do battle.

His hands grabbed hers. "Careful, sweetheart. You're

bringing out the beast in me, and I just might make an exception in your case and give your name-calling its proper justification.''

The impact of his words sinking in upon her, Laurel grew still. Suddenly, she was exhausted. "Please, may I go to bed?" she asked in a small voice.

"No," he replied, again tucking her head beneath his chin.

"Why?" she wailed.

"Because I don't trust you. Either my arms shall hold you tonight—or ropes. Take your choice."

"But I'm so tired!"

"Then go to sleep."

"Here, with you? In this chair?"

"Would you prefer to sleep with me in my bed?"

"I see your point."

Her face pressed against Lafflin's bare shoulder, Laurel slept.

Long after Laurel Ashland fell asleep, Jacob Lafflin sat staring down at her lovely face. Again he asked himself the question he had pondered a dozen times during the past hour—why was he sitting here, making a fool of himself, holding a sleeping girl when he should be in bed, getting badly needed rest?

The answer hit him with the simplicity and sureness of a thunderbolt. She needed him. The girl was willful, hellbent upon getting herself in trouble. The thought of her being touched again by Carter—or even shot out upon the streets—was strangely unbearable. He must protect her.

From the moment he saw the girl this morning, he had shocked himself with his own behavior. First he had felt compelled to find out why she was there—in fact, everything about her. Then he had appointed her his personal maid, which was ridiculously inappropriate. To top it all off, he had threatened to throw one of his men in the brig for a casual flirtation with her—a totally disproportionate punishment, and he prided himself upon being fair. Why did she affect him so?

Even now, the mere thought of Abel Carter made him grit his teeth in anger as he stared at the fading welt on Laurel's cheek. Good, there would be no bruise. Why was it, then, that he had the intense desire to place Laurel gently on his bed, then take his sword and go run the bastard through?

Jacob took a deep breath, steadying himself, as he brushed a jet lock of hair from Laurel's forehead and intently studied her face. Long black eyelashes rested against porcelain cheeks, which were highlighted by a rosy flush. Her brows were beautifully arched, her nose delicate and straight. But it was her mouth that captured his attention—wide and smooth, wondrously shaped, just full enough to be perfectly kissable.

Mesmerized, he found himself leaning forward until his lips brushed hers. Pulling back, he drew in his breath sharply, feeling awed. How delectable, soft, sweet she was!

Laurel stirred in his arms, brushing her fingertips across her lips as if to wipe off the imprint of his mouth. He smiled to himself—even in sleep, she was defiant.

What a spitfire she was—an intriguing, marvelous challenge. Despite his bravado with her an hour earlier, he actually longed to take her to his bed. He sensed in her an innocence—was it too much to be hoped for?—and he longed to be the man to awaken her to sensuality.

Why not do it now? Just the thought of taking her to bed, undressing her, making love to her made a fire burn in his loins. Why he hesitated, he did not know—a few thorough kisses, and she would be willing enough.

What made him hold back? Was it her elusiveness? For the girl was certainly an enigma. She had boldly flung obvious lies in his face. He had no idea who she really was—whether black or white, friend or spy—

What if she were, indeed, a spy? What if he must someday capture her, imprison her, even kill her?

His arms tightened about her. No, the thought could not be borne! He must protect her, for he had sensed in her something so beautiful, so vibrant—

Yes, it was her spirit! Adventuresome, courageous, a glorious inner essence that simply must not be crushed! She must be shielded from the harsh realities of war!

Why? Because he wanted her. He wanted to have her as his very own, without crushing her spirit. Which meant she must come to him.

She must. And she would.

Jacob Lafflin leaned over, pressing his lips against Laurel's cheek. Until she was his, he would keep her from all harm. And he would let no other man touch her—ever again.

Chapter Six

OCTOBER 11, 1862

As the first rays of dawn filtered through the front windows of the Virginia House, Abel Carter stood alone in the dining hall, a half-bitter smile twisting his tight mouth as he watched his superior officer, Jacob Lafflin, trudge out of the room, shoulders slumped.

Carter had gotten off the hook with Lafflin—but Lord knows, it hadn't been easy! The seaman had schemed all night, carefully planning just the right words to use to convince his captain that the girl was, indeed, a whore. Seconds earlier, Lafflin had finally given Carter the benefit of the doubt, though only after much strenuous rhetoric on the seaman's part. It was obvious to Carter that the good lieutenant was dying to get into the girl's silken drawers himself!

As Carter pulled a flask of whiskey from his breast pocket, his jaw tightened in resentment. He glanced at a faded line across the upper arm of his uniform, where minutes earlier a stripe had been. Perhaps he was damned lucky not to be facing a court-martial, yet his excursion last night was not without price.

And *that* he would not forget. The little bitch would pay—pay in spades!

Carter uncapped the whiskey flask and took a long draw, his watery blue eyes narrowing as he thought of the eventual pleasure of his revenge.

No, Abel Carter would not forget—not for a long, long time!

Jacob Lafflin walked heavily up the stairs, his face stern, his brows knitted in brooding thought.

Had the girl made a fool of him? Last night he thought her to be quite the innocent, but his interview with Carter moments earlier had left him doubting.

What did he really know about Laurel Ashland? As Carter had pointed out, the girl had fed them obvious lies, had treated them with defiance, and had no doubt tried to escape the hotel last night. Hours before, Lafflin had assumed that Carter was completely at fault, that the seaman had tried to rape the girl—yet now he wasn't so sure. Just as Carter argued moments earlier, no one had dragged Laurel from her room and into the hallway last night. The only explanation that made sense was that Laurel had tried to escape, only to be caught by Carter. Then, when the girl tried to flirt her way out of the situation, her bluff was called.

And Lafflin couldn't really blame Carter on that score. As much as part of Jacob still wanted to kill his chief petty officer, he couldn't blame the man for being as much of an idiot about the girl as he, Lafflin, had been!

But no more! Laurel Ashland's game was up.

Jacob paused at the top of the stairs, nodding grimly to himself. Yes, the girl had made a fool of him. He was a proud man and would not stand for it. Indeed, he was in charge and could not afford to have his authority trifled with in this manner. He would teach Laurel Ashland a lesson or two and stop her shenanigans once and for all!

Laurel awakened in the half light. For a moment, she looked about the tiny room in confusion; then she sighed, remembering, recognizing her surroundings.

Her pallet had been moved into a corner. She frowned, pulling aside the mosquito netting, which hung from a peg on the wall above her.

She stood up, stretched, and yawned, taking deep breaths of the cool, salty breeze that drifted in through the room's small window. Evidently, Jacob Lafflin had realized her predicament in sleeping in the tiny room and had located a mosquito netting for her, she thought as she made up the bed. What a strange mixture the man was—half arrogance, half kindness.

Laurel felt a rush of blood to her face as she remembered how she had gone to sleep the previous night. The very idea—falling asleep, sobbing, against a man's naked chest! Of course, she had been saved from a far worse fate. Considering Abel Carter's treatment of her, she was, indeed, lucky to be still a virgin this morning!

Laurel eyed her torn, damp dress with distaste. Damn—she had no clothes to change into or any manner of getting fresh garments. For the dozenth time, she chided herself for her foolishness in staying with the Yankees at the Virginia House. Every moment that she stayed away from the academy made more sure and severe the punishment she would receive when she returned.

Should she tell Jacob Lafflin the truth? She shivered at the thought. Though she had seen a tender side to Lafflin's nature, she had also tasted his ruthlessness—he might well order her shot on a whim, as Carter insisted.

Hearing Jacob Lafflin moving about in the next room,

Laurel cast aside her thoughts. She drew back her hand to knock on the door, hesitated. Then, as if on command, the door opened and Lafflin stepped into the tiny room.

In the small, secluded space, his maleness was overpowering. He was clean-shaven, dressed in a neat blue uniform, his tight-fitting trousers tucked into shiny black boots, his sword hanging from his waist.

His expression was grim—his handsome features showing none of the softness of the previous evening. His eyes swept Laurel with distaste, sending a chill through her body. He seemed foreign, cold—a complete stranger compared with the gentle man in whose arms she had slept last night.

"Have you no sense of decorum, girl?" he demanded. "Change that filthy frock—it nauseates me. And do something with your moppish hair. You look like a whore after a busy night."

Laurel felt sleepy, confused—and the cruelty of his remarks hurt unbearably. "I'm sorry to cause you—gastric distress, sir, but I've no brush!" she retorted, feeling angry tears flood her eyes. "And I've no frock to change into!"

The Yankee threw his hands wide in exasperation. "Why not, pray tell?"

"B—because we lost all during the shipwreck—"

"Ah yes, the infamous shipwreck," he shot back sarcastically. Grabbing her hand, he tugged her into his room. "Jesus, what a bother you are," he said as if to himself. "I'm here to ensure the security of this island, not to play nursemaid to a dim-witted child." Turning on her, he ordered, "Don't just stand there—make the bed. You must be good for something."

"Oh!" Laurel cried, storming off to the bed, actually relieved to have something to do so he could not see the tears blinding her. She was yanking on the sheet when an odor—decidedly female—filled her nostrils, and she was swept with waves of nausea and revulsion. How dare he expect her to handle this tainted bedding!

Suddenly, she seemed possessed of a demon. She yanked the top sheet off the bed, rended the hem with her teeth, then ripped the muslin from end to end.

Hearing the tear, Jacob Lafflin bolted across the room. "What the hell—"

But Laurel stopped him in mid-sentence by throwing the remnants of the sheet in his face.

"Bitch!" Jacob Lafflin yelled, tossing the shreds aside and grabbing Laurel, shaking her with ungentle hands.

Finally, his anger abated. The room grew deathly silent as the two glared at each other. Then Lafflin drew a rough breath, snapping, "I should give you a hard spanking, you obnoxious little brat!"

Still recovering from the shaking, Laurel felt overwhelmed by his strength, bewildered by his fury. "Why are you so angry at me?" she asked. "After last night—"

"Forget last night. You'll not get me to play the fool again."

"Fool? What are you talking about?"

Lafflin strode off to the window, looking out, his broad back to Laurel. "I met with Carter a few moments ago and he convinced me that you were not altogether guiltless during your little excursion last night."

"And you believed him—over me?" she inquired indignantly, hands on hips. "You saw the welt on my face with your own eyes, damnit!"

Lafflin whirled upon her. "Carter did not escape last night's incident unscathed, either. That's a wicked bite you gave him, girl. I don't relish losing one of my best seamen to lockjaw from the likes of you."

"Lockjaw!"

"Carter insists you tried to seduce him in the hallway,

then changed your mind. You can't blame a man for giving a tease her just deserts.''

"Tease! I never—"

But Jacob Lafflin's bitter laughter interrupted her. "Girl, I'm not blind. As Carter just reminded me, I saw you leading him on at dinner last night.''

Laurel bit her lip, realizing she had engineered her own defeat. What could she say to make him believe her? They were from different countries, different worlds. Of course he would side with Carter.

A look of disgust filled Lafflin's features; Laurel realized he took her silence for an admission of guilt. He strode off to the dresser, snapping over his shoulder, "Next time, don't count on being rescued unless I desire a taste of your . . . carnal delights myself.''

His hateful remark tore at Laurel's insides. How dare he treat her so cruelly!

"Here," he said gruffly, turning and thrusting into her hand a tortoise-shell hairbrush with the gold letters J. L. on the handle. "Try to look like something less than the strumpet you obviously are.''

Uttering this final, penetrating barb, he turned and stormed from the room, slamming the door.

Feeling numb with shock, Laurel went to the dresser, looking at her reflection in the beveled mirror. Who was this washed-out wraith? Indeed, she looked pale as a ghost!

Not knowing how soon Lafflin might return and what further indignities he might heap upon her, Laurel pinched her cheeks, then began brushing her long tresses until they gleamed. She was frowning, longing for pins and ribbons, when Jacob Lafflin strode back into the room, tossing a diaphanous white shawl at her.

She turned, catching the crocheted wool. "Where did—"

"In the cloakroom downstairs. Now cover yourself, girl.

Perhaps you'd enjoy having half the island gape at your bosom, but I'll not have you sharing my horse so attired.''

"Your horse? What the devil—''

"Quit babbling, damnit. I've never heard such a witless parrot." He grabbed the shawl, quickly wrapping it about her neck and shoulders. "You don't think I'd leave you here to spy on my men—or worse?''

Evidently, the question was rhetorical, for even as she opened her mouth to speak, he scolded, "Hush,'' and pulled her into the hallway.

"But—but you arrived by ship!" Laurel gasped, struggling not to trip as Lafflin tore down the stairs two at a time, dragging her along behind him. "Where are you going to get a horse?''

As Lafflin's boots hit the downstairs floorboards, he stopped in his tracks, staring at Laurel as if she had lost her mind. "We might just try the stable across the street," he said with smooth, perfect sarcasm.

Chapter
Seven

OCTOBER 11, 1862

"Must you go so fast?" Laurel panted, struggling to keep her balance as the large brown stallion tore down the beach.

"Quit whining—we've much distance to cover," Lafflin retorted, clenching his legs against the horse's sides.

As they lurched into a more frenzied gallop, Laurel gritted her teeth, suffering in silence. From her position behind Lafflin on the saddle, she could not see his face to read his expression, and she dared not risk building his ire. Why Lafflin had insisted upon taking her on this reconnaissance expedition she did not know—though obviously, the man did not trust her and feared she was spying on his men. And he had cause, for she already hated him fiercely and fully intended to betray him at the first opportunity.

Laurel turned and looked at the ocean, trying not to think of the beating her bottom was taking as they bolted along. Lafflin was obviously an expert horseman, with well-developed saddle muscles; but it had been years since Laurel had ridden her pony at Brazos Bend.

A snowy gull flew over their heads, cawing raucously as it flew out into the Gulf. Laurel watched the gull until it melted into the misty blue horizon, then she followed the whitecaps back toward the shoreline, where the gray waves thudded upon coarse sand.

An hour earlier, Laurel and Lafflin had galloped through the business district of Galveston, finding it largely deserted, though Laurel had spotted a few businessmen opening their shops. She assumed the shopkeepers had stayed behind to protect their stores from looting and to sell goods to Galveston's population of free blacks and poor whites, for whom evacuation was an unobtainable luxury.

Now, they raced past deserted embattlements—large mounds of sand and driftwood where cannon had recently been. A week earlier, with the news of imminent Yankee occupation, the Confederates had left for the mainland, taking all their armaments with them. Lafflin was obviously checking the redoubts for any remaining munitions.

As they reached the west end of the island, the point jutting into San Luis Pass, Lafflin abruptly halted his horse. Dismounting, he pulled Laurel to the ground. "Stretch your legs," he suggested gruffly, then added sarcastically, "or perhaps you'd prefer to test out the currents—swim out and fetch in your trunk from the floor of the Gulf?"

Straightening her aching back, Laurel spat, "You're despicable!"

Lafflin shrugged, striding off toward the Gulf. Then he paused and stood scowling at the billowing waves, his fingers clenching upon the riding crop he held. Her curiosity piqued, Laurel approached him and saw that his brow was creased in a deep frown, his penetrating brown eyes fastened upon the horizon.

Glancing seaward, Laurel spotted the object of his

attention—a small white shape floating toward them. She couldn't resist bragging, "One of our steamers, no doubt—bringing the citizens of Galveston badly needed supplies."

Lafflin turned to Laurel, scowling. "Supplies, indeed. As low as she's sitting in the water, there's no doubt she's carrying munitions."

Laurel squinted at the horizon. "My word, Captain, you've surely the eyes of an eagle," she said with mock amazement. "If it's munitions, all the better. She'll supply our troops in the coves surrounding the bay, ensuring your defeat even more rapidly."

"You little fool," Lafflin replied, shaking his head. "More munitions simply means more death for your glorious boys in gray. The inevitable can only be postponed so long."

"Meaning what, Captain?"

"Meaning the North will win, hands down. We've got the South cut off. Almost the entire coastline is sewn up by our blockade—"

"And where is your awe-inspiring blockade now, Captain?" Laurel interrupted triumphantly, gesturing toward the Confederate vessel.

Without taking his eyes off Laurel, Lafflin inclined his head southward, while his lips curled in a cynical, victorious smile. "Behold the flagship *Westfield,* my dear."

Gasping, Laurel glanced over Lafflin's shoulder. She hadn't even noticed the heavily armed cutter approaching them from the south. Laurel knew the *Westfield* to be the commodore's flagship. The large steamer was formidable, and Laurel counted at least eight large guns on the vessel's deck.

Nodding toward the Confederate steamer, Lafflin commented, "If she's wise, she'll turn tail and run for Mexico." Lafflin was silent for a moment, then cursed, "Damn! She's going to run for the bay."

For what seemed an eternity, both were tensely silent as

they watched the two ships maneuvering for position near the pass. The *Westfield* was making for the pass, trying to cut off the Confederate stern-wheeler, which puffed laboriously toward the bay entrance. Suddenly, the *Westfield* fired. Laurel held her breath as she watched the cannonball hit the water close to the bow of the Confederate vessel. Though no harm was done, the booming sound split the morning air, creating screeching havoc in a flock of gulls flying overhead and making the brown stallion whinny nervously.

Then Laurel's heart seemed to cease beating as her eyes were captured by a more imminent peril—both vessels were now racing toward the pass, dead set on a collision course!

Suddenly, Laurel whooped with glee as the Confederate steamer made the pass, just cutting off the *Westfield*. She heaved a sigh of relief; but her elation was short-lived, for she realized the *Westfield* could easily chase the steamer into the bay, then blow apart the heavily loaded Confederate vessel.

She was pondering this new danger when she noticed a peculiar situation—the *Westfield* was no longer moving! Utterly confused, she turned to Lafflin.

"God's teeth!" he groaned. "She's grounded on the bar!"

Hearing this revelation, Laurel laughed until tears sprang to her bright blue eyes and she clapped her hands in jubilation. "So much for your indomitable navy, Captain!"

Lafflin spun about on his heel, teeth clenched at Laurel's effrontery. "Kindly wipe the smirk from your face, lady, before I scrub it off with seaweed!" he snapped, taking her arm and pulling her toward the horse.

Heedless of his ire, Laurel laughed her triumph as Lafflin released her arm and mounted his horse. "Do you wish to walk back?" he asked menacingly.

Looking at the endless, deserted stretch of beach ahead of them, Laurel sobered somewhat. But her eyes were full of amusement as she took the hand Lafflin extended toward her. Quickly, he pulled her onto the horse behind him, even as his hard-muscled legs squeezed the stallion's sides and the animal sprang forward.

"Where are we going at such a breakneck pace?" Laurel gasped, grabbing Lafflin's waist to keep her balance.

"I must get back to the *Owasco* so I can pull the *Westfield* off the bar."

"But won't the tide push them off tonight?" she asked sweetly.

"I doubt the commodore relishes spending the day stuck on the bar."

Laurel's dearly gained composure evaporated; she laughed giddily. "Ah yes—he does look a bit the fool, does he not?"

Lafflin's reply was to curse under his breath as he snapped the riding crop—in the process, stinging Laurel's thigh.

Biting back a cry of rage, Laurel gritted her teeth and scowled, thinking, all the way back to the hotel, of how she hated Lafflin.

Lafflin tugged Laurel into the Virginia House. She struggled not to show fear as they rushed past Chief Carter, who stood in the front hallway glaring murderously at Laurel. It was a look that promised revenge, Laurel reflected uneasily as she and Lafflin started up the stairway.

Once they were inside the bedroom, Lafflin announced, "I'll be gone the balance of the day. Wilson will be in charge of you—don't you dare move without his permission." Looking grimly at the floor, he then leaned over and gathered up the edges of torn sheet. "The first thing you will do is to repair the result of your little tantrum this morning, dear."

Taking the shreds of sheet, Laurel glowered at Lafflin. "The sheet—" she paused, flushing miserably. "The sheet must be washed, Captain."

His smile was humorless. "Indeed it must, dear, after you repair it. I'll instruct Wilson to take you to the washboard out back."

"You hateful beast!"

Lafflin sighed. "Your sharp tongue is becoming tiresome, wench. Why I have put up with you this long is truly a mystery." He rubbed his jaw thoughtfully. "I believe one of the men told me of discovering a nunnery on the south side of the island. Perhaps I should deposit you there and let the good sisters teach you a few lessons in humility and decorum."

Watching a deathly pallor spread across Laurel's features, Lafflin chuckled. "Why, lady, is it possible that the idea of leaving me fills you with regret? Perhaps I've been hasty." Nodding toward the sheet clutched in Laurel's hands, he added, "Once you've repaired the bed, you might just curl up and wait for me. That is, if you're not too tired from trying to seduce my men."

That did it! Something snapped inside Laurel at Lafflin's merciless gibe. Shrieking "Bastard!" she lunged for the Yankee.

But she was immediately caught in an iron grip, her hands pinned behind her. For a moment she struggled frantically, but then, glancing upward, she froze as she caught the murderous resolve in Jacob Lafflin's eyes.

When he finally spoke, his voice was ruthlessly soft. "You will find, wench, that I have ways of silencing your foul mouth."

Before Laurel could scream, Lafflin's lips descended to claim hers in a savage kiss.

As Lafflin's lips bruised hers, myriad emotions tore at Laurel's insides—shock, revulsion, fear. Yet as Jacob pulled her tighter against his hard frame and assaulted her mouth with his hot, demanding tongue, her initial horror was replaced by new, bewildering emotions. Funny little shivers coursed Laurel's spine as Lafflin's bold hands caressed her back, and a peculiar yet delicious yearning stirred in the forbidden recesses of her womanhood. The electric warmth of his chest seeped through the layers of cloth separating them, and the nipples of Laurel's young breasts tingled and tautened at the stimulation.

Lafflin seemed to sense Laurel's response—his arms relaxed somewhat and his kiss grew mellow even as it deepened, as if he would gentle her to the masculine taste and feel of him even while asserting his mastery of her senses. As his tongue tenderly probed and teased every recess of her sweet mouth, a mindless sob died in her throat and she found herself suddenly clinging to him, her arms tight about his neck. Forgotten for the moment was her hatred of him. She knew not why, but she wanted him to do with her that thing he had done with Reba—to make her cry out in that exquisite pain that was purest ecstasy . . .

Finally, the kiss ended. Lafflin backed away and stared at Laurel with brooding puzzlement, as if he had discovered through kissing her some new mystery that baffled him. Laurel's limbs shook as she stared back at him with distrust and confusion, an intense shame filling her as she realized what she had just done. How could she give herself to the enemy that way? Worse yet—how could she enjoy it?

As he saw her distress, a struggle crossed Jacob's features and his eyes softened in an emotion resembling remorse. "Laurel—" he began gently. "Laurel, I—"

He reached for her but she backed away, her mouth quivering as she eyed him with defiance and fear.

In return, Jacob scowled and cursed under his breath. He turned and exited the room, leaving Laurel still trembling as tears of self-loathing spilled from her eyes.

Laurel did, indeed, repair the sheet, using a sewing basket brought to her by Seaman Wilson. Afterward, she scrubbed the bedding and hung it up to dry in the sandy backyard of the Virginia House, while Wilson looked on awkwardly.

As she worked, Laurel contemplated Lafflin's remark about taking her to a nunnery. The man had knocked her completely off guard. Was it possible he knew she hailed from St. Ursuline's? Yet how could he?

No, she thought bitterly, the remark about St. Ursuline's was more likely a coincidence. Lafflin's kiss had proved he thought her to be not a saint but rather quite a sinner! She shuddered as she remembered the emotion-wrenching scene an hour earlier when Jacob Lafflin kissed her. Her mouth was still tender from his powerful assault. But most of all, her pride was badly battered due to the shameful behavior of her own body. She had discovered a new aspect to her nature—the fatal weakness of her own sensuality.

And she was sure Jacob Lafflin would use her vulnerability to his advantage!

Later, as Laurel lay huddled on the tiny pallet in the anteroom, she realized she was dealing with a dangerous man—a man who thought her to be a liar and a strumpet as well. While he was right about the former, his misconception regarding the latter filled her with a sick fear. Would he truly expect her to be curled up waiting for him when he returned?

Laurel turned, trying to find a comfortable position on the mattress. Her bottom ached unbearably after the long, hard ride by horseback. Laurel realized ruefully that Lafflin could not have chosen a better way to fulfill his promise of giving her "a good spanking."

Suddenly, the question crossed her mind—was that precisely what Jacob Lafflin had in mind when he insisted she accompany him on his ride? She certainly wouldn't put it past the sadistic villain! Tears of humiliation flooded her eyes at the thought, and she beat her fists upon her small pillow. "I hate you, Jacob Lafflin! I hate you!"

At length she ceased her tirade, placing her cheek against the damp pillow as the Gulf breeze swept in the tiny window, soothing her, and the distant sound of the ocean lulled her.

Yet as she thought of the days stretching ahead, she was swept by a wave of helplessness, hopelessness. She suddenly felt so very small—a tiny girl in a tiny room, cowering upon her pallet. Her body hurt, her heart ached, she longed to go home—

Home—to Brazos Bend. Home to the mother who saw to all her needs. Home to the older sister who listened to her every trouble. Camille was supposed to marry soon, when her beau came home on leave, according to a recent letter. But for all Laurel knew, she might have already missed the wedding. Oh, how she wished her entire family could be back together again! She particularly missed her dear father. Why did this damned war have to start in the first place? Why did she have to remain on this godforsaken island at the mercy of the despicable Jacob Lafflin?

Laurel drifted into a fitful rest, poignantly recalling the last time she was home on a visit, before this wretched conflict ever began . . .

"It's not fair!" Laurel cried. "Not fair!"

"Laurel!"

The plaintive plea of Laurel's mother was lost as the fifteen-year-old girl tore out of her parents' bedroom at Brazos Bend and headed for the stairs. "Mother can't do this to me—she simply can't, forcing me to return to those horrid nuns!" Laurel hissed to herself. "I've been imprisoned at that infernal nunnery for over a year already, and I cannot endure another second! Oh, why did Daddy have to leave yesterday for that silly secessionist convention? I'm sure he'd take my part in this!"

The girl took the stairs two at a time, intent upon seeking

support from her sister, Camille, who often worked on her trousseau in the parlor at this hour. Laurel well knew that she couldn't expect any help from her older brother, Charles, in this, since he was too close to their mother. With Daddy away, Camille was her only hope.

Laurel reached the downstairs hallway, then rushed for the front sitting room, only to pause, frozen, at the archway when she saw a young couple inside, locked in an ardent embrace. It was Cammie and her beau from a neighboring plantation, Trey Garrison.

A wave of anger, of jealousy, swept Laurel. Why was Cammie kissing her fiancé, unconcerned about her, Laurel? And why couldn't *she* be the older one, with her own beau, instead of being a mere schoolgirl, subject to her mother's dictates?

Yet as Trey released Camille and the pretty older girl turned to smile serenely at her sister, Laurel felt shame. Camille had never been anything but kind to her, and of course her nineteen-year-old sister had every right to choose a beau and later marry.

"Laurel, please come join us, dear," the golden-haired Camille coaxed.

When Laurel remained at the archway, biting her lip, her sister quickly came to her side and took her hand. "Darling, what is the matter? Are those tears I see?"

"Mother is forcing me to return to Galveston!" Laurel blurted as Cammie's blond-haired beau came over to join them. "She told me Charles will be taking me and Fancy back on Friday."

"But, darling, you know it's for your own good," Camille soothed. "Why, you've already learned so much at the academy. In a few more years, think of what a polished young woman you'll be."

"In a few more years, the sisters will have murdered me!" Laurel declared. Hearing Trey chuckle, Laurel turned to scowl at the handsome young man, arguing, "Besides, everyone says there's bound to be a war. You know that, Trey."

"Laurel, don't you think you're getting the cart before the horse?" Trey Garrison cajoled. "Texas hasn't even seceded yet. And even if there should be a war, you'll doubtless be far away from the conflict down there in Galveston."

"Amy Brewster got to leave already," Laurel wheedled to Camille.

"And didn't you tell me yesterday that that's because her family is moving further west?" Camille pointed out with an admonishing look. "There are still plenty of young women at the academy to keep you company." The older girl wrapped a comforting arm around Laurel. "Darling, please don't be difficult about this. Mother told me there's no safer place for you than a convent school. And with Daddy so involved in the political situation here, it will be such a comfort to her to know that your education is being provided for—"

"She doesn't love me!" Laurel railed, unheeding, pulling away from her sister.

Camille looked shocked. "Laurel! You know that's not true. Of course Mother loves you—we all do! That's why it's so important to us that you attend the academy, that you develop into the fine young lady we all know you are destined to become." Camille paused, slanting a devoted glance at Trey. "You'll never regret it, my dear, I assure you. Why, Trey never took notice of me until after I graduated from finishing school."

"Cammie, you know I was always smitten with you!" Trey insisted.

Meanwhile Laurel stared at the floor, fighting tears, too proud to acknowledge the truth of Camille's statements. "I bet I'll miss your wedding to Trey," she stubbornly maintained.

"Not if we can help it, darling," Camille soothed.

"I—I spent all yesterday afternoon helping you embroider napkins for your hope chest, Cammie," the younger sister sniffed, feeling extremely sorry for herself. "I stabbed myself at least a thousand times with the blasted needle."

"You were wonderful to help, dear," Camille warmly agreed.

Biting her lip hard, Laurel glanced up at Trey in a final, desperate attempt to get her way. "The Yankees could—could land at Galveston," she told him half wildly. "They could descend from their boats like—like barbarians and murder us all in our beds!"

Both Camille and Trey laughed at Laurel's melodramatics. "Laurel, even if there is a war, we'll beat the tar out of those Yanks in no time," Trey assuredly told the younger girl. "They'll never get as far as Galveston, much less Texas." Grinning, he wrapped an arm around each girl, then winked solemnly at Laurel. "Besides, if the Yanks were foolhardy enough to come to Galveston, why I'd simply be duty-bound to come down there, whip them all, and rescue you, baby sister. Wouldn't I, now?"

At this, Laurel actually blushed, smiling at her sister's beau despite herself . . .

Chapter Eight

OCTOBER 11, 1862

A distant thudding bludgeoned Laurel's senses. Her lethargy pressed away wakefulness; her eyelids were simply too heavy to lift.

Then the sound grew nearer. Laurel realized someone was pounding on the door to her room. Slowly, she sat up, then fell back, wincing with the pain the movement brought.

"Miss Ashland, open up, please. It's me, Wilson."

Grimacing sleepily, Laurel got slowly to her feet, her eyes smarting as she straightened her back. "Just a moment, Wilson," she called in a throaty whisper.

Laurel donned her ruined white gown, hurriedly tying the torn bodice as best she could. Then she opened the door and stepped, barefoot, into the next room.

Seeing her, the tall, lanky seaman smiled sheepishly. "Sorry to awaken you, miss, but the Captain just sent a messenger with this for you." He held out an envelope.

Wiping sleep from her eyes, Laurel stepped forward and

took the letter from Wilson. As she opened the envelope and took out a note, four gold coins jangled to the floor. Laurel watched, confused, as Wilson leaned over and retrieved the money. Watching Wilson straighten and extend a bony hand holding the gold, Laurel felt the color rushing to her face. Wilson looked equally distressed—a flush colored his jutting cheekbones and hawklike nose and his deep-set gray eyes avoided her embarrassed stare.

Laurel took the coins and turned to catch the afternoon light pouring through the window, relieved to have the awkward exchange over. Frowning, she unfolded the parchment and read Jacob Lafflin's note.

> Kindly purchase yourself decent clothing, befitting a proper maid. Wilson will escort you.
>
> Jacob Lafflin
>
> P.S.: Happy Birthday

Laurel crumpled the parchment in her hand. How dare the man humiliate her this way—sending her a messenger with money, as if some payment were necessary for her services! She had an overpowering desire to rush outside, run the several blocks to the harbor, and fling his gifts to the dark depths of the ocean.

But sanity filtered into her consciousness. What price would she pay for her defiance? Laurel bit her lip as she studied the gold. Doubtless, everyone thought the worst of her already—she could prove no point by disposing of the gold. Also, Lafflin was right—she desperately needed decent clothing. But why did the man present her with the gift in such a flagrant manner? He could have quietly given her the coin earlier; but no, he had to humiliate her in front of Wilson!

Studying the money more closely, Laurel scowled. Each coin boasted a gothic cross and strange lettering she could not understand.

"What manner of coin are these?" she questioned Wilson.

Wilson stepped forward and took the money from Laurel. After a moment, he whistled. "Spanish doubloons, girl. Quite old."

Spanish doubloons! However had Jacob Lafflin acquired them? "Will they be accepted by local merchants?" Laurel asked suspiciously.

Wilson laughed heartily, pressing the coins into Laurel's hands. "Gold is gold, miss. At present, these coins would be honored anywhere throughout your Confederacy."

Wilson was right. Duncan Carmichael of Carmichael's General Store eyed the gold doubloons on the counter with delight. Stuffing his pudgy hands into the pockets of his merchant's apron, as if to restrain himself from grabbing the money, he said charmingly, "Your wish is our command, lady."

Laurel glanced from Carmichael to his smiling wife, Maureen. The Carmichaels' ran the only general store remaining open in Galveston and, by all appearances, were doing a booming business. Several Yankee sailors milled about, eyeing jewelry and women's clothing. A young white couple dressed in shabby cottonades whispered in a corner, counting their money as they longingly eyed precious flour and lard.

"By the way, where did you get the coins, lass?" Carmichael continued, his shrewd green eyes fixed upon the doubloons. "You been digging for buried treasure hereabouts?"

Laurel looked confusedly from Carmichael to his wife. "It's rumored Jean Lafitte left a fortune buried in these parts," the amply proportioned Maureen put in sweetly. "Could it be you've discovered his secret hiding place?"

The sailors nearby inclined their ears expectantly as the Scottish couple studied Laurel intently. Laurel felt very much on the spot, but Wilson intervened, gruffly informing Maureen Carmichael, "There's much to be said for minding your *own* business, if you get my drift, ma'am."

Far from chagrined, the gray-haired matron seemed amused by the seaman's stern remark. Turning to her husband, she laughed, "Minding our *own* business, Mr. Carmichael! What a clever man this Yankee is!"

"Aye," Carmichael agreed, nodding sagely. "Maureen, do take the lass into the back room and outfit her royally. 'Tis a pretty penny we'll earn this day."

Moments later, in the musty back room, Maureen Carmichael went straight to business, taking measuring tape to Laurel as she prattled about the woeful state of the girl's clothing.

"Where do you hail from, lass?" she asked as she encircled Laurel's waist with the tape.

"From the island," Laurel grudgingly replied.

" 'Tis strange we've not seen you before."

'Tis not strange at all, Laurel thought to herself, remembering the strict rules at the academy, which forbade the girls journeying into Galveston except for emergencies. But she said nothing, hoping the Carmichael woman would take the hint and complete their transactions with a minimum of conversation.

Yet the woman's curiosity was insatiable. As she showed Laurel lacy pantalets, sheer chemises, silk stockings, she asked the girl one question after another. Gradually, the entire story was wrenched from Laurel: her leaving the academy with Fancy, the lies she told the Yankees, her present plight—everything. Not at all sure why she trusted the Scottish woman with these secrets, Laurel ruefully thought that Jacob Lafflin could have profited from a few lessons in interrogation from the sagacious woman.

Maureen Carmichael made no comment regarding Laurel's story as she showed the young girl ready-made frocks of dimity, gingham, muslin, and silk. "Most of these will need alterations—which I can complete in two days time, miss."

"You are a seamstress?" Laurel inquired with interest.

Nodding toward a dressmaker's form in the corner, Maureen replied, "Aye, I've near finished that frock for Milly Spencer." Moving closer to the figure, she held up a fold of gold satin, eyeing the tawdry, sequined gown with distaste. "Shameless, ain't it? I rue that the times don't allow a body to pick and choose who she is to sew for."

When Laurel continued to study the flashy garment with amazed curiosity, the woman added, "Don't tell me a decent girl like you craves the likes of this?"

"Oh no, ma'am." Smiling, Laurel shook her head. It was good to be considered decent after Jacob Lafflin's treatment of her.

Moving off, Maureen continued, "Now I've one frock which should be a perfect fit for you—you'll no doubt need to wear it home today. No offense, miss, but the gown you wore in must be cast to the rag bag."

Laurel nodded her agreement as she watched Maureen Carmichael take from the rack a beautiful blue and gold calico dress. "Wish I had something a mite more fashionable for you," the matron apologized as she held up the homemade garment for Laurel's perusal, "like one of them fancy hoop skirts. But here in Texas we have to settle for what we can get."

"Oh, don't apologize. I love it!" Laurel breathed, her eyes fastened upon the charming frock, her face glowing.

Moments later, as Laurel surveyed herself in the tall pier mirror, she realized Maureen had been right about the dress being a perfect fit. The gathered bodice was highlighted by ruffles interlaced with soft blue ribbon. Tiers of ruffles flounced from the waist and adorned the wrists of the fitted sleeves. As Laurel stood admiring herself, Maureen tied Laurel's ebony curls with a yellow velvet ribbon at the nape of her neck.

"Perfection," Maureen commented. "And I've just the finishing touch."

As Maureen swept out of the curtained doorway, Laurel continued to stare at herself in the mirror. Gone was the pallor that had whitened her cheeks that morning—the thrill of buying new garments sent a flush across Laurel's high cheekbones, and her blue eyes sparkled.

"Never seen eyes such as yours," Maureen commented as she stepped back into the room, carrying several boxes. "T'would call them sapphires, but they be brighter. Here, lass, see which of these shoes fits you."

Laurel's face shone with excitement as she went through the three boxes containing kid walking shoes. One pair was tan, one black, but her breath caught in her throat as she held up a pair of white high-topped shoes edged in navy.

"Aye, 'tis the one I'm hoping will fit you," Maureen told Laurel as she swept a gray strand from her forehead.

Laurel quickly donned the shoes, laced and tied them. But she frowned as she discovered they were a bit large.

"No matter, girl," Maureen assured her. "I can tell your heart's set on them, so we'll just stuff a bit of cotton batting in the toes. Besides, a youngster your age t'ain't through growing."

Maureen packed up Laurel's new undergarments, nightgowns, and toiletry items and told her when to return for her altered dresses. Then she placed a yellow silk bonnet on Laurel's head, tying the gold satin ribbon. "Can't have the sun ruining that peaches and cream complexion."

As they gathered up the various boxes, Maureen paused, taking Laurel's arm. "A moment, lass. When you're out the next time, have an eye out for Uncle Billy Hendley."

"Uncle Billy?" Laurel replied in confusion. Everyone in Galveston knew of the queer little man who owned a lucrative shipping business but was, unfortunately, physically deformed. Laurel had seen Uncle Billy once, when Sister St. Augustin was ill and Laurel had been granted the "privilege" of going to the central market for the day's produce. She remembered watching the bent little old man throwing coins to a collection of children. Despite his eccentricities, he had seemed a harmless, kindly sort.

Laurel tried to read the expression of the stolid matron standing across from her. "Why should I contact Uncle Billy?"

"Why, indeed, are you staying with Yankees, lass?" Maureen countered. Handing Laurel a stack of quilted lingerie boxes, she added, "When you spot Uncle Billy, take him aside and tell him your tale. He'll know what you should be doing with your Yankees."

Frowning thoughtfully, Laurel exited the dressing room.

As they traveled toward the Virginia House on the board walkways of Galveston, Laurel studied Seaman Andrew Wilson thoughtfully. When she had returned from the dressing room at the store moments earlier, he had looked stunned, then had recovered, giving her a shy grin and eyeing her new attire admiringly. Now, as they walked down Market Street, past the William Tell Hotel, Laurel thought of how she liked the tall, quiet seaman.

"Where's your home, Wilson?" she asked conversationally.

"Atlantic City, New Jersey, ma'am," he replied, shifting the large assortment of boxes he carried in his arms.

"You have family there?"

"Yes—a wife and two small boys," he replied, smiling warmly. "As a matter of fact, I received a letter just yesterday from my Bess. Seems Timmy—that's my youngest—

went crabbing for the first time and learnt for good which is the wrong end of the crab."

Laurel smiled, staring at Wilson with new interest. It was so difficult to think of this kindly man as the enemy. After all, weren't they all just people united in their love for their families?

"I know you must miss your people, as I miss mine," Laurel said sadly.

Wilson turned to her, his gray eyes filled with compassion. "Poor girl—the captain told me you be an orphan, and a recent one. My sympathies, miss."

Hearing Wilson's words, Laurel felt her spine crawling. She must be more careful—she'd almost let her background slip! Trying as it was, she must keep on her guard, for even this gentle man *was* the enemy. Recalling Maureen Carmichael's suggestion of a few moments before, she reminded herself of her purpose in staying at the Virginia House—doing anything she might to aid the South.

Casually slanting a smile at Wilson, Laurel suggested, "Tell me about your captain. Is he also from New Jersey?"

Wilson shrugged. "That I don't know, miss. The captain stays much to hisself. I do know he got a mother somewhere—seen him reading her letters whilst I was in his cabin once. Though he don't like to talk about her, neither."

"How do you know she's his mother? Did he say so?"

"No. But one time I seen him crating up wool blankets to send to her. A man don't do that for his sweetheart."

Laurel shook her head disdainfully. "Jacob Lafflin might. He's so inept."

They climbed the board steps to the Virginia House. Reaching for the door, Wilson inquired, "What's your interest in the captain, miss?"

"My—my interest?" Laurel stammered, flustered. Then, recovering quickly, she swept through the open doorway and replied graciously, "*Pity,* Wilson—strictly pity, and Christian charity."

Wilson chuckled while Laurel pleaded prettily, "May I go, now, to seek out my maid, Fancy? I haven't seen her all day and I'm truly worried."

Wilson nodded, but admonished, "Mind you don't leave the premises, though. You wouldn't get me in trouble with the captain, now would you, miss?"

Laurel's eyes danced merrily as she swept toward the dining room, murmuring, "Be assured, Wilson, I bear *you* no ill feeling."

Shaking his head and grinning, Wilson started up the stairs with the boxes while Laurel entered the dining hall.

After a quick glance about the large room revealed that no one was about, Laurel swept to the back door and opened it, carefully stepping down the wooden steps. She hurried across the yard, which was long and narrow, lined with oleanders and shaded by two large trees. Several outbuildings squatted on the sand; smoke curled from the squarish kitchen, mingling with scattered birdsong and whispers of cool gulf breeze.

Laurel swung open the heavy wooden door to the stone and shingle kitchen. Inside the warm room, half a dozen black women were busily preparing the evening meal—Reba was chopping cabbage, while another woman shelled beans just picked from the garden plot behind the kitchen; nearby, a grizzled old woman strained corned beef from a vat. The tantalizing aroma of cornbread seeped out from the stone bakeoven, mingling with the odors of garlic, pepper, and other spices strung across the ceiling.

Sister Suki turned, wooden spoon in hand, from the large kettle of broth boiling on the hearth. "Lizzy, get your hands moving wid them beans. This broth ready and you best cast them in or they be tough as sand pones this evening."

Spotting Laurel, she wiped her shiny face with her apron and beamed, "Why, hello, honey. What you need?"

"Fancy," Laurel replied, glancing about expectantly. She spotted the girl in a steamy corner, ironing sheets.

But as Laurel rushed toward her maid, a tawny hand reached out, grabbing her arm. Confusedly, Laurel looked down at Reba, who sat at the chopping table. There was venom in her honey-brown eyes as she asked, "How did you get the new frock, mam'zelle?"

Carefully disengaging Reba's fingers from her arm, Laurel replied with silky sarcasm, "Guess, Reba."

Smiling smugly, Laurel moved off toward Fancy, her retort to Reba filling her with perverse pleasure.

"Miss Laurel, you is a welcome sight!" Fancy prattled as Laurel got to her side. "I is most in my grave from all this work. I ain't never worked in a kitchen, Miss Laurel. You got to get me out of here!"

There was little sympathy in Laurel's eyes as she gazed at the nervous, sweaty Fancy. "Hush up, lazybones. Obviously, I've spoiled you shamelessly in the past. A few days' hard labor won't kill you."

"But, Miss Laurel—"

"But nothing!" Lowering her voice to a dangerous hiss, Laurel scolded, "How do you think *I* enjoy being slave to that insufferable Captain Lafflin—polishing his boots, scrubbing his sheets, and such?"

"Miss Laurel, you don't look like you suffering none."

Clenching her teeth, Laurel grabbed the slave's arm. "You have no idea of the indignities I've been forced to endure. But I've no time to go into that now." She looked about warily, then whispered, "Tell me, Fancy, are you allowed to go to the central market?"

"Yes 'um. I gone today wid Reba, but—"

"Hush and listen! The next time you go to the market, you must find William Hendley."

"Uncle Billy!" Fancy gasped, eyes wild. "Oh no, Miss Laurel! Reba, she say he possessed of bad spirits!"

Spotting several of the slaves looking curiously in their direction, Laurel warned, "Lower your voice, blast it! And don't you dare listen to Reba—ever. I'll not have her filling your head with her voodoo nonsense."

"It ain't nonsense, Miss Laurel. Suki tell me Reba were learnt by Marie Laveau in N'Orleans." Dark eyes growing huge, Fancy whispered intensely, "Reba a *mambo*, Miss Laurel!"

"I'm utterly terrified!" Laurel retorted. "Merciful heavens, Fancy, quit babbling and listen well. The next time you see Uncle Billy, you must tell him I wish to speak to him—"

"Oh no, Miss Laurel. I is scared of him."

Laurel grabbed Fancy's shoulders. "You'll obey me, you willful chit, or I'll pack you back to Mother St. Pierre."

At her mistress's words, Fancy's eyes grew wild with fear. The slave gulped hard, then said defeatedly, "Yes 'um," her lower lip quivering as she cast her gaze toward the floor.

"Good!" Laurel replied, her eyes lighting with triumph. "You'll speak with Uncle Billy, then—tomorrow, when you go to the market?"

Fancy nodded, shuddering miserably. "Yes 'um."

"Tell him I must see him at night—oh, tell him midnight. He can name the place. And mind Reba doesn't see you speak with him. I'd not put it past her to turn us in as spies."

"Spies!" Fancy repeated, her hand flying to her heart. "Is we sure enough spies now?"

"Not for long, the way you're telling everyone!" Laurel hissed back through clenched teeth. Suddenly, she looked down, exclaiming, "Good grief, Fancy—you're going to set the place afire!"

With a cry of dismay, Fancy lifted the iron from the sheet, looking crestfallen at the ugly smoking black scorch mark her carelessness had left. "Oh no, Miss Laurel. Sister Suki, she tell me what I burn, I pay from the wages them Yankees give us."

"Wages, indeed!" Laurel scoffed. "However would you take care of yourself without me, Fancy?"

Laurel turned and was moving toward the door when Reba again caught her attention. She had finished chopping the cabbage and now sat intently whittling a slender oak limb with a small sharp knife.

Laurel eyed Reba curiously as she thought of her warning moments earlier to Fancy. Reba could indeed do Laurel and Fancy much harm, especially if she were to inform Jacob Lafflin of where the two girls truly hailed from. In fact, Laurel was a bit puzzled as to why the dissolute woman had not already betrayed them. Honor among thieves, she supposed wryly. Reba, too, was at the Virginia House under false pretenses, and the Trinidad woman would also be in deep trouble if Jacob Lafflin were informed of her history as a voodoo priestess.

As if reading Laurel's thoughts and fears, Reba now put her knife down and slowly raised the carved stick with one hand while the honey-brown fingers of her other hand stroked it gently, in a gesture that seemed somehow obscene. Although the black woman did not even glance at Laurel or otherwise acknowledge her presence, Laurel somehow knew the brazen ritual was for her benefit.

Despite herself, Laurel was becoming strangely mesmerized by the display. Staring at the familiar snake amulet hanging from Reba's neck and again remembering Fancy's warning, she asked, "What are you making, Reba?"

Suddenly, Reba stood up and turned, looking down at Laurel scornfully. Although Laurel's gaze did not waver, she felt overwelmed by the sensuous power of the older woman—and the fanatic gleam in Reba's haunting yellow eyes was frightening, terrifyingly hypnotic.

Seeing a flash of silver, Laurel glanced quickly downward and saw Reba raising the small knife. Laurel watched, transfixed, as Reba brought the other hand up to the knife and quickly cut a slash across the tip of her middle finger. There was not a flicker of pain in the gold depths of Reba's eyes as blood oozed from the wound. She turned, took the stick from the table, and quickly cut an indentation in the wood, then filled it with blood from the gash. Extending the dripping stick toward the horrified Laurel, Reba spat upon the blood-smeared wood, then smiled cruelly, her amber gaze glowing with wanton, orgasmic languor.

Uttering a cry of rage mixed with revulsion, Laurel whirled and fled the building.

Chapter Nine

OCTOBER 11, 1862

Laurel was tearing in the back door of the hotel when rough fingers grabbed her arm. "Not so fast, missy!" a harsh voice growled.

Laurel turned to face the contemptuous gaze of Abel Carter. The sailor's broad, sea-ravaged face was contorted in an angry grimace, his lashless eyelids blinking rapidly over watery blue eyes.

"Unhand me!" Laurel demanded, trying to jerk away from his grip. But his grasp was like iron, and a smile of cruel pleasure twisted his fleshy lips at her helplessness. His eyes swept her new clothing with slow disdain.

"Earned yourself some new duds, did you, you little whore? Well hear this, slut. You'll be paying the price for getting me in trouble with the captain!"

Seeing the savage gleam in his eyes, Laurel struggled wildly, to no avail. "Let me go, you—you—" suddenly, she paused, noting a dark blue mark on Carter's faded sleeve—a rolling line where once, obviously, a stripe had been. Despite the dangers, she couldn't resist crooning victoriously, "Why, Carter, it seems you've paid the price already."

She immediately knew she had made a fatal mistake. Carter drew back his hand, ready to strike, his eyes crazed. Realizing that in an instant her face would be bashed beyond recognition, Laurel desperately pointed at Carter's feet and shrieked, "My God—a rat!"

Her exclamation caught him off guard for a fraction of a second and Laurel seized the opportunity, jerking away mightily, breaking his grip and bolting out of the room.

Carter stood stock still, staring at the floor, flabbergasted. Discovering no furry creature about his boots, he stamped his foot in anger. "Lying bitch! And I ain't even scared of rats!"

Fists clenched, he stormed toward the archway and stomped into the hallway. But he stopped as he saw Wilson hurrying down the stairs, looking quite alarmed.

"What happened to the girl?" the seaman asked as his boots hit the downstairs floor. "She almost knocked me down in the hallway, then ran for her room, locking the door."

"The wench saw a rat and lost her wits," Carter replied grimly. "What business is it of yours anyhow?"

"The captain asked me to keep an eye on her," Wilson replied defensively.

"Then be at it—go watch the wench!"

Carter gnashed his teeth in silent ire as he watched the tall, frowning seaman amble up the stairs. Then, cursing under his breath, Carter opened the flap on his breast pocket and was about to pull out a whiskey flask when he heard a knock at the front door. Annoyed, he strode to the door, throwing it open.

"Well I'll be damned—a nun," he said, staring at the tall woman dressed in a black habit.

The angular middle-aged woman raised an eyebrow in distaste as she stepped into the hallway. Her spectacled, steel-gray eyes surveying Carter coldly, she began, "*Bonjour, m'sieur,* I am Mother St. Pierre, of Ursuline Academy. I was told this establishment is the headquarters of the naval forces occupying this island."

"You been told right, lady," Carter replied with an air of boredom, taking the whiskey flask from his pocket.

Mother St. Pierre's eyes narrowed. "May I speak with your commander, m'sieur?"

"He ain't here." Heedless of the sister's presence, Carter threw his head back and took a noisy gulp of whiskey.

"Then, m'sieur, *you* must help me," the nun returned, her tone commanding.

Recapping the flask, Carter shrugged. "Maybe."

"This afternoon, the other sisters and I are conducting a door to door visitation of all homes and businesses still open in the city. Yesterday, one of our young women and her maid disappeared without a trace."

Carter glanced at the nun with sudden interest. "Escaped, you say? A young girl? Tell me what she looks like."

"*Oui,* m'sieur," Mother St. Pierre replied, nodding, evidently pleased to strike a responsive chord in the sailor. "The young woman I am seeking is taller than most girls of seventeen, slender, and delicately boned. Her hair is raven and quite long, and her eyes are blue—a vivid, rather startling color. Her complexion is quite fair, and she often wears a brooch of sapphires and—" Suddenly, Mother St. Pierre paused, a look of searching expectation on her face as she clapped her hands. "M'sieur, I see it in your eyes—a spark of recognition! Could it be—have you seen our Laurel?"

"Laurel?"

"*Oui,* m'sieur, Laurel Ashland. Where have you seen her?"

Carter realized he was on shaky ground. He could tell this woman the truth about the girl, but that would deny him his revenge. No, he decided, he wanted to keep the wench about for a bit. Giving the nun what he hoped was an ingratiating smile, he replied, "Sorry, ma'am, but I ain't seen your girl. It's just you described her so pretty—well, you know how it is, ma'am, a man being at sea and all, I'd love to see the likes of her, I would. But no, ma'am, I ain't."

Mother St. Pierre frowned. "You are quite sure?"

His meager patience exhausted, Carter mimicked sarcastically, "*Quite* sure." Then, with an air of dismissal, he again uncapped his flask, taking a hearty gulp of whiskey.

After he finished, he smiled smugly as he glimpsed the nun's black habit disappearing out the front door. Chuckling, he replaced the flask in his breast pocket. "Escaped from a nunnery, did you now, Miss Laurel Ashland? Be sure, I'll find a way to use the information to my advantage, missy."

Laurel tossed and turned fitfully. For over an hour she had struggled to get to sleep, but the night was uncharacteristically warm and humid, and the breeze a mere whisper.

For the dozenth time, she thanked God for the noble Andrew Wilson. Had he not been there that afternoon, she was sure Carter would have made mincemeat of her. Even now, it helped to know he was asleep down the hallway, for Jacob Lafflin still had not returned. Though perhaps she was feeling a false security—Carter's glare at dinner had been murderous. With all the other sailors out patrolling the streets, what would stop Carter from coming after her now? Would Wilson hear her if she screamed?

"Silly chit—the door is locked!" she scolded herself

aloud. She had indeed locked Jacob Lafflin's door before she retired, yet a terrifying image of Carter booting it open swirled in her mind.

Suddenly, she stiffened as she heard a distant scratching sound. In the still darkness, all her senses seemed intensified, and the sound had a frightening timbre, which set her heart pounding.

Beads of perspiration popped out on her forehead as she heard the door in the next room swing open with an ominous creak. For long moments she did not breathe as she heard a man's boots moving about the room in a soft, thudding cadence. The footsteps moved to her door, then stopped, followed by an electric silence. Laurel gasped with relief as she heard someone knocking softly. Of one thing she was certain—Carter would not knock!

"Laurel?"

Laurel recognized Jacob Lafflin's voice outside her door. His tone was mellow, almost caressing. A peculiar sense of expectation raced through her veins, but she did not answer.

The door to her room opened gently. She saw his features outlined in the pool of lamplight pouring in from his room. For a moment she stared up at his handsome, weary face, wondering at the strange tide of feeling within her, the warmth again building in the pit of her stomach. Then, fearing his eyes would adjust to the darkness, she closed her own.

In the quiet dimness, she heard him whisper, "Laurel, I'm sorry."

She opened her eyes. But he was gone, the door clicking softly behind him. She lay still, perplexed yet warmed by his words as she listened to the muffled sounds of him preparing for bed. Why his presence was so reassuring was something that baffled her utterly.

As she drifted off to sleep, she thought she heard a door opening, a man whispering, "No—not tonight . . ." Yet the words seemed to drift on the tide of her dream, which took her floating slowly homeward across the years...

The mambo danced to the beat of pagan drums, summoning the Loa. Tall, sultry, her yellow eyes glowed as her bronze limbs writhed to the rhythm. Her hair was caught in a turban of blood red, her arms and shoulders bared, her hips and breasts thrusting voluptuously against the vividly patterned sheath tied beneath her arms and extending just beneath the swell of her buttocks.

The snakes, black and slimy, rose up from the bowels of the earth. The priestess raised her arms toward the fiery heavens, moaning, "Bon Dieu, bon Dieu," as the creatures slithered up her thighs, wound themselves about her abdomen, arms, and neck. She twisted in orgasmic splendor, her eyes like burning sulphur, as the drum beat raced to a frantic crescendo. Suddenly, she cried out, then grew still, panting as the snakes slid away...

The mambo spotted the girl sleeping nearby, on the shore of a lake of coals. The priestess's eyes glowed with a fiendish, unnatural light as she approached the black-haired sacrifice. She circled the girl slowly, moving provocatively as the drums began a ritualistic beat and murmuring the chant, "*L'Loa vinie, li Grand Bon Dieu, L'Loa vinie, pour sacrifice.*"

Overhead, thunder roared, followed by blood-red lightning. Bon Dieu was ready for the sacrifice. The priestess pulled the stick and a small knife from her belt, getting to her knees to begin her work. Then she sat up, smiling cruelly as she wound a strand of ebony hair about the stick with fingers that dripped blood.

Her eyes closed in entreaty, the mambo raised the stick—the Loa directed her aim, above the sleeping girl's belly. She moaned the chant again and again, twitching spasmodically as the spirit took possession of her—"*Li Grand Bon Dieu . . . pour sacrifice!*"

Again, it happened—thunder boomed, lighting blazed across the sky—the voice of Li Bon Dieu. And the shaft of wood became a sliver of silver—long, slender, wickedly sharp—

With the blood-curdling cry of vengeance, the mambo lunged, ripping open the girl's belly . . .

Jacob Lafflin bolted awake as he heard Laurel's harrowing cry. He literally jumped into his trousers as he raced across the room, flinging open her door. The grayness of dawn revealed the girl on her knees, clutching her belly as she rocked to and fro, tears streaming down her face, screams of agony ripping from her throat. Overhead, a hard, ominous rain tried to drown out the girl's anguish, pounding the roof like a funeral cadence.

Jacob quickly squatted on the mattress beside Laurel, pulling the girl into his arms. "Laurel, what is it?"

But her shrieks became incoherent sobbing as she tried to pull away from him. "I'm—I'm dying!" she choked.

"Jesus Christ—you must be poisoned! I'll get a doctor!"

"No—don't leave me!" she panted convulsively, grabbing his arm, her fingernails digging into his flesh. But she immediately released him, grasping her stomach and screaming.

Jacob held her, feeling more helpless than he ever had in his life as he heard the girl's horrible cries of pain and felt the frightful jerking and heaving of her slender body. "Sweet Jesus, Laurel—don't die on me!" he begged. "Please don't die on me!"

As he uttered the words, a catch in his voice, he realized he could think of no thought more unbearable than that of losing the slender thread of life he held in his arms. He had seen men blown apart at New Orleans, had heard screams of agony worse than hers, yet never before had anything wrenched his heart like her piteous cries now did.

Suddenly, she seemed possessed of a stabbing pain so intense, she shoved him away and grabbed the pillow, clutching it against her belly as her awful cry—like a death wail—split the morning air.

But Laurel's grabbing the pillow revealed an object on the mattress. Thunderstruck, Jacob Lafflin stared at a small doll, clothed in blood-smeared cotton, lying on the pallet. Grabbing the image, he glanced, appalled, from the clump of black hair, tied with a tiny braid to the doll's head, to the large hatpin, deeply impaled in its belly.

Somehow he knew to pull out the pin.

Laurel dropped the pillow, her hands falling limply to her sides as her head fell back against the wall, a dizzying lassitude washing over her.

Her eyes locked with Jacob Lafflin's as they exchanged looks of stark relief mingled with utter amazement.

Chapter Ten

The door to the small frame cabin bolted open with a bang. The two black women inside jerked awake, jumping upright on their cots as they gathered bedclothes about them.

Jacob Lafflin's boots pounded a cadence that almost drowned out the rain as he stormed toward the wide-eyed Reba. "Explain this, you yellow-eyed whore!" He threw the blood-smeared doll atop the moth-eaten gray wool blanket covering the woman and stood shaking in his rage, dripping wet.

Fancy, in the other corner, gasped sharply, then threw a hand over her mouth as she stared horror-stricken at the doll, while Reba, emotionless, gingerly picked up the cotton-clothed image and stared up at Lafflin dispassionately. "What is it, m'sieur?"

Jacob Lafflin clenched his fists. "Don't lie to me, you goddamned voodoo witch! You know you put it under Laurel's pillow!"

Reba arched an eyebrow at the furious Yankee. "May I get up, m'sieur? It is difficult to speak with you shouting down at me."

In one quick motion, Jacob Lafflin leaned forward and yanked back the covers on Reba's bed. Fancy cried out in shock, for Reba's bronze body was now entirely nude against the stark whiteness of the sheet. But no emotion flickered in the grim depths of Jacob Lafflin's eyes as he gritted, "By all means, get up."

A cool smile played upon Reba's lips as she lazily got to her feet, stretching languidly. A vein jumped in Lafflin's temple as he stared at the tall, magnificently proportioned woman. Drawing a hard breath, he turned to Fancy. "Go fetch your mistress a hot bath—in my room!" he ordered.

Fancy jumped up, wrapping herself in a small, faded quilt. "Yessir! But I ain't dressed, sir!"

"Now!" the tall Yankee roared.

Her dark eyes like twin saucers, Fancy dashed for the door, pausing for a split second to grab her blue cottonade dress from a ladder-back chair before she ran out into the rain.

Lafflin turned back to Reba. Smiling provocatively, she slowly reached over to retrieve her white cotton shift from the floor, giving Lafflin a generous view of her voluptuous backside.

But suddenly, with an angry cry, Reba lurched forward onto the bed as Lafflin roughly shoved her buttocks with a black boot. "Answer my question, slut!"

Reba landed hard on her belly, then hastily rolled to her back, glaring up at Lafflin, yellow eyes now blazing with contempt.

Lafflin grabbed the voodoo doll from the floor. Shaking it at Reba, he demanded, "Explain why you did this to Laurel or by God I'll horsewhip you, you damned she-wolf!"

Regaining some measure of control, Reba gave Lafflin a

look of icy anger. She sat up, quickly threw her long legs over the side of the bed, and hastily bent over to grab her shift from the floor, gathering it up and pulling it over her head. As the folds of muslin fell about her, she said quietly, "I know nothing of the doll, m'sieur."

Throwing the doll down with a curse, Lafflin yanked Reba to her feet. "Liar! Laurel told me she saw you whittling it yesterday!"

The woman tried to disengage Lafflin's fingers from her arm. "Please, m'sieur, if you will release me, I can explain."

"Doubtless!" he shot back sarcastically, dropping her arm. Setting his arms akimbo, he growled, "Very well, whore. Explain."

Reba moved off to the flagstone hearth, picking up a small wooden box. Returning to Lafflin, she opened the small chest and handed it to Lafflin. Eyes coldly triumphant, she said, "Behold, m'sieur."

Lafflin stared, frowning, at the collection of tiny wooden dolls inside the box. The images were all brightly painted— children, animals, men and women, blacks and whites.

The Yankee looked back up at Reba, his deep-set dark brown eyes a mixture of ire, suspicion, and confusion. "Clothespins, m'sieur," the gold-eyed woman said smoothly, seemingly unperturbed by the heat of the Yankee's gaze. "I make clothespins and sell them at the central market."

Abruptly, Lafflin shoved the box back at Reba. "Which proves nothing."

Snapping the lid shut and walking back to the hearth, Reba said smoothly, "*Au contraire,* m'sieur. The clothes-pins prove that I did not make the *image.*" Calmly, she replaced the box on the flagstone ledge.

Lafflin stormed to the fireplace, grabbing Reba's arm and turning her violently. Holding up her right hand, he demanded, "And what do these slashes on your fingers prove? Admit it—you smeared the doll with blood!"

Reba slowly shook her head. "I frequently cut myself when whittling, m'sieur."

Lafflin dropped Reba's hand in disgust, his handsome face a study of clashing emotions. "I might have known you'd try lie your way out of it. If you didn't make the damned thing, who did, pray tell?"

Reba shrugged. "Someone put a curse on Laurel."

"Aha!" Lafflin exclaimed triumphantly. "You do know about voodoo."

"Why of course, m'sieur. Anyone who has lived in New Orleans knows of the ritual." Smiling tauntingly, Reba added, "As a matter of fact, Mam'zelle Laurel is quite familiar with the worship of vodun."

Lafflin scowled. "What do you mean?"

Reba laughed. "Ah, m'sieur, how the little actress has deceived you. Ask yourself this—what do you actually know of Laurel Ashland?"

"That she's a planter's daughter, just arrived from Tennessee," Lafflin snapped back. His jaw tightening, he added, "But why am I explaining this to you? It's none of your goddamned business."

Reba shook her head. "Laurel is not from Tennessee, m'sieur. I know that to be a fact because I have been acquainted with her for over three years."

"Indeed?" Lafflin scoffed.

"*Oui*, m'sieur. Like me, Laurel is a free woman of color. Her mother was a quadroon who lived on this very island with a white gambler who frequented the local grog shops. Her father was shot three years ago during a fight at the card tables, and her mother died a year later, of malaria."

"Just how the hell do you know all this?"

"Laurel and I have performed together at Taylor's, entertaining the gentlemen with chants and dances." Reba's yellow eyes gleaming venomously, she added, "But Laurel's best performances were held afterwards, m'sieur, for all gentlemen who could pay her price.''

Lafflin grabbed Reba's shoulders, giving her another hard shaking. "Enough, you lying—"

"It's true, m'sieur! It is Laurel who lied to you. She would say anything to gain your sympathies.''

"And why should she want to gain my sympathies?''

Reba smiled wickedly. "Your side appears to be winning, m'sieur.''

Cursing under his breath, Lafflin released Reba. "Jesus Christ, I don't know who to believe. Your tale is no more believable than hers." He turned and picked up the voodoo doll from the floor, then again shook the blood-smeared image at Reba. "I'm going to find out the truth, woman," he swore hoarsely, his eyes black with determination. "And by God, if you're lying, when you get the damned doll back, you'll walk bowlegged for a week!''

Reba merely stared at Lafflin impassively. "I have nothing to fear, m'sieur.''

Lafflin scowled, pointing the doll at Reba meaningfully. "We shall see.''

The Yankee hurried toward the door, the voodoo doll in his hand. As he grabbed the knob, he hissed between clenched teeth, "Don't claim you weren't warned, whore.''

The door slammed, sending cold moisture spattering into the room.

Reba smiled triumphantly, slowly returning to her bed like a sleek cat. She lay down, stretching luxuriously.

The story had been well worth contriving, she thought smugly, even though she had stayed awake much of the night to concoct it. Now Lafflin would not know who to believe, for Laurel Ashland had also lied to him, telling him she hailed from Tennessee.

But Reba was far more clever than the little blue-eyed brat. She was sure the Yankee would eventually believe *her* story—why else would Laurel have been dressed like a quadroon when he first met her?

Reba sat up and leaned over, pulling a hat box from beneath her cot. She squatted on the floor, opened the box, and breathed deeply of its pungent aroma. She had plans for Jacob Lafflin, plans that did not include the spoiled little bitch Laurel Ashland, she thought as she pulled out bottles of powder and bits of red fabric.

Reba smiled cruelly as she took a small pair of scissors from the box and began cutting squares of cotton. She felt sure she had planted the seeds of doubt in Jacob Lafflin's mind and that, at this very moment, Laurel was in deep trouble.

Actually, the story had not been that difficult to invent. There had been a girl once at Taylor's—a quadroon. But she had not been a gambler's daughter—instead, the gambler had been Reba's lover. That is, until the night Reba caught him in bed with the quadroon slut.

Remembering, Reba smiled, her yellow eyes glowing with vindictive pleasure. Then, too, the priestess had gone to work quickly to destroy her rival. Two days later, the quadroon girl had walked into the Gulf at dawn, never to return.

Reba laughed and sang a French chant about snakes as her nimble fingers prepared the *gris-gris* . . .

Laurel screamed as Jacob Lafflin burst into the room.

The Yankee's dark brown eyes fixed upon Laurel, who sat, nude, in the bathtub, her only covering her arms and the soapy water. Snapping his fingers, he jerked his hand toward Fancy, ordering, "Leave us."

Nodding vigorously, Fancy skitted out of the room, not even flinching as Laurel screamed, "No, Fancy! Don't!"

Lafflin strode to the door, slamming it behind the disappearing servant. Then he returned to the stunned Laurel, his face tight as he demanded, "Tell me who you really are, Laurel."

Laurel's face grew crimson with rage. "Captain, how dare you intrude—"

Jacob Lafflin took a hard step forward. "Tell me who you really are, you little liar, or I'll yank you out of that tub and beat the truth out of your naked hide!"

Laurel froze, looking up, horrified, at the handsome Yankee who glared down at her so menacingly, the damp clothing that clung to his limbs only emphasizing his ferocity. "You wouldn't dare!"

He nodded slowly, his dark eyes pitiless.

Laurel gulped. "I told you, Captain, that I'm a planter's daughter from Tennessee—"

"And Reba tells me you're an octoroon, that you've spent the past few years performing parodies of voodoo—and whoring!" His dark eyes accusing her, he asked, "Was that what your little demonstration was about this morning? a ruse to gain my sympathies?"

"That's preposterous!" Laurel sputtered, features aghast as she leaned forward in the bathtub, modesty forgotten in her outrage.

Jacob Lafflin's dark face colored and he uttered a hoarse curse under his breath as he glimpsed an immodest portion of Laurel's rosy flesh. Meanwhile, Laurel hastily covered her breasts with her arms, realizing her movements had exposed the upper part of her bosom to Lafflin's gaze.

Looking much like a man who had been hit in the stomach by a brick, Lafflin abruptly strode off to the wing chair, grabbing a black dressing gown. He returned to Laurel and threw the gown on the towel stand next to the tub. "Get out and cover yourself—we're going to talk," he told her gruffly, the uneven tone of his voice belying his sternness.

Laurel's jaw dropped. "Do you think I'm going to dress in front of—"

"Do you desire help?" Lafflin interjected, regaining his fierce determination as he glowered at her. He moved off toward the window, his broad back to her. "Be quick about it. My patience is not limitless."

For a moment, Laurel blinked at Lafflin's back in amazement. He stood tall and stubborn, every inch of him oozing muscle and virility as he gazed at the rain, his strong brown hands clasped behind him, his handsome profile fixed, merciless, as if carved from stone.

Laurel shuddered silently. Realizing her choices were indeed poor, she hastily stepped out of the tub, eyeing her adversary warily. Her limbs shook as she quickly rubbed herself dry with a towel. Then she swiftly donned the black robe, securely tying the satin belt. Frowning at the folds of material dragging the floor, she cleared her throat and said nastily, "I'm dressed, Captain."

Lafflin turned, his expression grim. Then, suddenly, his features seemed to melt. His anger faded, replaced by a stark look of animal lust, even more frightening in its intensity than his wrath had been. Throwing his hands wide in supplication, he groaned, "Jesus, Laurel—must you look like that?"

"Like—like what?" she asked uneasily, gulping as she watched his brown eyes grow even more desperate with desire as they raked her warm, blushing curves.

He moved forward, his eyes still devouring her. "So small and pathetic in my robe. Makes a man want to grab you and fill you up."

"Captain!" Laurel gasped, eyes wild.

He stopped within inches of her, gazing down at her with fiery, penetrating eyes. "Mother of God, I never thought I'd be jealous of a dressing gown!" He reached out, touching an ebony curl that rested upon her shoulder. She shuddered, and he let his hand drop to his side. "You should see yourself—the glow across your cheeks, the sunlight gleaming in your hair. And the smell of you—what is that? lavender? —Laurel, I could just eat you up!"

Laurel backed away from him, near panic. "Oh no you don't!"

Lafflin chuckled, rubbing his jaw thoughtfully. "You know, sweetheart, there's only one way to determine the truth in this matter—there, don't run off. Won't you listen to me?"

Laurel's backside contacted the edge of the bed, making further escape impossible for the moment. "Do I have a choice, Captain?"

Slowly, he approached her. She watched him suspiciously, her gaze moving from his assured, smiling face to the V on his chest—he had left his white uniform shirt partially unbuttoned in his haste to leave the room earlier and go find Reba, adding a roguish slant to his countenance.

He stopped before her, so close to her now that she could see the shadow of whiskers on his bronze face and smell the strangely exciting male scent of him. And, dash it all, there was something quite sensual about the way his damp black hair curled about his head. Laurel trembled as Lafflin's hands gently took her shoulders. As she looked up at him, his eyes changed perceptibly, taking on a deeper, more intense urgency. "Sweetheart," he said huskily, "I want to take you to my bed."

"*What?*" Laurel shrieked, yanking free of his grasp and bolting away from him. But he moved into her path, blocking her escape to the door. Like a pursued animal, she whirled, racing off to the far corner of the room until the walls forbade further movement. She turned, positioning herself in the corner, staring at him with the fierce yet frightened eyes of a trapped animal. "Don't you dare come closer!" she warned.

Jacob Lafflin stood perhaps ten feet away from her now, smiling at her cynically. "You know it's the only way to find out who's lying, Laurel. If you're telling the truth, you're a virgin. If Reba's telling the truth, you're a whore."

"And if I go to bed with you, I'll be a whore regardless!" Laurel spat.

Jacob Lafflin laughed heartily. "Girl, I admire your spirit." His eyes sparkling with amusement, he added, "And I do see your point. How about a sporting proposition, then? If Reba told the truth, I get your services any time I wish—upon demand. If you told the truth—well, hell, you're not bad to look at, Laurel. I'll marry you."

Laurel stamped her foot and clenched her fists in rage. "Oooh! You arrogant, insufferable—oooh! What kind of proposition is *that*? I'm the loser in any event!"

Lafflin stepped forward assuredly. "You know, dear, your options at the moment are rather meager."

Watching him approach, she pressed herself harder into the corner. Things were going wretchedly! Her spine crawled at the very thought of Lafflin's brazen proposal, yet perverse curiosity won out. "And just when were you thinking of staging this—this experiment?" she asked, her voice cracking.

Lafflin grinned devilishly. "As it happens, I've an hour free right now."

Laurel bolted out of the corner to face Lafflin, eyes blazing as she shook a fist at him. "An hour free! Go to hell, you arrogant bastard!"

Jacob Lafflin's face darkened in anger. "Damn your willfulness, Laurel!"

And he lunged for her.

She dodged him, screaming, "No! Don't you dare!"

But steely arms grabbed her, and she gasped sharply as the floor was swept violently from beneath her. Eyes grim, Jacob Lafflin carried Laurel, kicking and screaming, to the bed. "By God, Laurel Ashland, I'm going to get to the bottom of this!"

"The bottom! You foul-mouthed villain!" Laurel shrieked as Lafflin threw her onto the bed then landed squarely on top of her.

Lafflin's features were merciless as one of his strong hands pinned both of Laurel's into the pillow above her head. She struggled, revolted to have his body pressed so boldly against her own. Yet she was even more horrified by the reaction that stirred unwittingly within her—for inexorably, every inch of her that was female yearned for every inch of him that was male. Her heart hammered wildly and her face flamed at her wanton reaction. She bucked beneath him, but this only gave him the opportunity to slip his free hand beneath her bottom in the most appalling and intimate way. The ruthless hand then firmly arched her upward, melding her pelvis against the hard maleness of him, a great shaft that made Carter's instrument seem, by comparison, the tool of a eunuch!

Laurel cried out, but her savage anger could not conceal the pain and need of a woman aching to be filled, an unrestrained desire she felt with bright new shattering intensity in the most vulnerable recesses of her body.

Above her, Jacob Lafflin pulled back, a triumphant smile twisting his lips as his eyes strayed slowly down her body, pausing where their struggles had partially opened the dressing gown, revealing the delicate outline of a flushed young breast. Obviously aware of her response as he watched her bosom rise and fall quickly at his remorseless perusal, he uttered evenly, "Now, sweetheart, I'm going to kiss you."

Watching his head move slowly downward, Laurel froze for a moment in unspeakable panic as she realized he was aiming not for her mouth but for her breast! A small sob was wrenched from her as his lips burned the virgin flesh of her breast, further nudging open the gown, while below, the errant hand pushed her even harder against his burgeoning manhood.

At last, Laurel regained control, ire welling in her at this outrageous double assault upon her dignity and virtue. Desperately, she spat, "I might have known, Captain, that you would be no better than Carter—so vile and repulsive that you have to rape your women to sate your lusts!"

Suddenly, Lafflin's weight was lifted from her. She looked up to see him standing by the bed, glaring at her murderously. Chills coursed through her body as she watched the struggle on his face and saw the veins standing out on his clenched fists as if he were trying to restrain himself from killing her.

Then roughly, he yanked her up into his arms. His face was so formidable, his hands so hard on her flesh, that she could only gape up at him, her sapphire eyes huge, luminous with fear.

"The day will come when you will ask for my lovemaking, Laurel—nay, beg for it!" he promised hoarsely. "But for now you're a cold-blooded little bitch, badly in need of a warming!"

With these words, he strode forcefully to the bathtub, dumping her in with an explosive splash.

For a moment, Laurel was too stunned to react other than to shake tepid water from her face and hair. Then, watching Lafflin stride toward the door, she sputtered wildly, "I—I hope you're satisfied, Captain! The blasted water's cold, and—and you've *ruined* your dressing gown!"

Lafflin turned, eyeing her insolently. Then, seeing her plight, he struggled not to grin. "No matter. As it happens, sweetheart, I prefer lounging naked in my quarters." And he gave her a very wicked wink.

"Oh!" Laurel cried, throwing the sponge at him, then screaming her mortification as it landed, with a sloppy splash, against the closed door.

Chapter Eleven

Laurel could only hope that she spotted the sailor before he saw her. She ducked into the entrance of the Planter's Hotel on the Strand, pressing herself into the shadows near the door and silently praying that the darkness would conceal her.

Slowly, the sailor passed the hotel, his boots pounding out an ominous cadence. Laurel held her breath, her heart beating wildly as the seaman paused on the sidewalk then turned to stare in her direction. Moonlight etched the outline of his shoulders and glittered vacantly in his eyes, making him seem almost unreal.

His silvery hand moved to his waist, then paused. Laurel's heart seemed to jump into her throat; she felt as if her own pulse would strangle her as she watched the sailor fumble in the darkness to remove an object from his waist, then draw a suspicious, shadowy shape upward. Hearing scratching sounds, she closed her eyes and waited for the explosion, the bullet that would shatter her life.

As the interminable seconds passed, Laurel squinted open her eyes, just in time to see a flash of light in the darkness. For a moment she thought she would faint, so great was her relief as she watched the tall sailor light his pipe. He threw the match down; a puff of smoke wafted across her in the darkness. Then he lumbered off.

Giving the sailor time to move out of sight, Laurel then eased herself back onto the moonlight-washed walkway. As she raced along on tiptoe, she silently thanked God that the Galveston Gas Works had closed weeks earlier; with more light on the streets, the sailor surely would have spotted her.

Yet the darkness could be foe as well as friend, Laurel reflected uneasily. Dozens of gaping entrances yawned from deserted warehouses, while the hulking buildings spilled sinister shadows onto the sandy streets. What would she do if suddenly one of the Yankees appeared from an alcove or materialized from a shadow?

She bit her lip not to cry aloud at the very thought. This is sheer insanity! she thought to herself hysterically. Granted, after Jacob Lafflin's outrageous behavior yesterday, she was determined to gain revenge against him, determined to meet with Billy Hendley as Maureen Carmichael had suggested. But what if Lafflin discovered that she had left the hotel? What if Carter did? What if Maureen Carmichael was mistaken and Billy Hendley was actually a ruthless traitor who would turn her in to the Yankees without a qualm?

The darkness magnifying her fears, she crossed Twentieth Street and hurried toward the entrance of the William Hendley Building. The three-story structure was cloaked in blackness. Rushing up the steps on her toes, Laurel squinted at the brass plaque that read: "William Hendley and Company, Agents for J. H. Brower, New York."

Surprisingly, the building was unlocked. Laurel opened

the heavy oak door, grimacing as the hinges squeaked. Once inside, she pressed herself against the closed door and stood staring at the empty blackness.

As long, terrifying moments passed, her eyes could discern no pockets of light in the deep void. Finally, timorously, she croaked, "Is—is anyone here?"

Silence was her only answer. Cautiously, she moved forward, saying, "Hello. Is anyone—damn!"

Laurel crashed to the floor in the darkness, grasping her shin where the edge of a sharp object had jabbed her. Suddenly, she saw a pool of light in the distance above her. A high-pitched masculine voice inquired, "Who be there?"

Laurel gulped as a disembodied head and hand floated down the stairs toward her in the wavery light of a candle. The features of the face were gaunt and strongly etched, a muscle twitching in the cheek. "Johnny, get me pistol!" the apparition called up the stairs.

"Got it primed already, Billy," a deep voice boomed. "I'll learn them clay eaters to leave our wares alone!"

"No, don't!" Laurel gasped, bolting to her feet in the shadows. "Uncle Billy, it's me, Laurel Ashland. My maid, Fancy, told you I was coming!"

A tense silence followed, then William Hendley ordered, "Don't fire, Johnny, this may be the gal."

Laurel stood watching as the two vaguely defined figures moved down the stairs. Finally, Billy Hendley arrived at her side, his hand moving the slender taper he carried to within inches of her face. "There, gal, don't flinch, I'll not burn ye. It's just a look I'm wanting." He moved the light slowly over Laurel's figure. "By George, you don't look like no clay eater. You must be the one. And a pretty thing you are."

"Aye, Billy—a rare beauty," the invisible companion now commented. "She must be the one, 'tis true."

"Come—follow us up the stairs, gal."

Numbly, Laurel turned with the two men toward the stairway, wincing as another object poked her in the thigh. She started up the stairs but tripped on the third step, tottering to keep her balance. She gasped as a fleshy arm slid about her waist in the darkness, steadying her. "There, girl, don't be afeared," the deep voice soothed.

Laurel let the man help her up the stairs, then lead her down a long, narrow corridor on the second floor. Finally, they entered a room at the end of the hallway.

Laurel blinked at the brightness cast by several oil lamps as she stared at cluttered desks, at walls covered by enormous maps. But as she turned back to the door and at last viewed her two hosts standing side by side, her hand flew to her heart and she was stunned speechless.

Though she had seen William Hendley from a distance before, viewing his deformities at this close range was truly frightful. The man was tiny, shorter than Laurel, and was cursed not only by a hunched back, but also by a withered leg. One gnarled hand rested upon a walking stick, supporting Hendley's twisted frame. His face was long, angular, and weatherbeaten; his left cheek twitched spasmodically, the muscle tugging at the corner of his mouth, creating a sardonic grin.

Hendley's companion was an even more appalling sight—a monstrous hulk of a man. Laurel guessed this gentleman must weigh well over three hundred pounds. He was taller than Hendley and bald; tiny black eyes peeked out at Laurel, small slits squeezed between rolls of fat. Laurel's eyes moved downward, following waves of flesh down the man's neck and body. The unfortunate soul wore a white shirt and enormous brown trousers, obviously tailor-made. His huge middle was tied with a cord sash, his feet bulging from frayed slippers slit open to the toes to accommodate his swollen feet.

"Meet me partner, Johnny Sleight," Hendley now said, jerking his head toward his gargantuan companion.

"How—how do you do?" Laurel stammered, giving Sleight a frozen smile. She swallowed a hysterical giggle at the thought of such an elephantine man having the name Sleight.

"There, gal, take a seat," Hendley urged, pointing a knotty finger at a nearby leather chair.

Laurel started toward the chair, then winced aloud as her shin smarted painfully from the movement. She seated herself, rubbing her shin and frowning.

William Hendley limped across the room toward the oak swivel chair across from Laurel. While one hand rested on the walking stick, the other hand lifted the tails of his dark brown frock coat, and he eased himself into the chair with a groan. Frowning as he studied Laurel, he called over his shoulder, "Johnny, fetch the gal a cool cloth for her leg."

Laurel quickly looked up. "Oh no, sir, that's not really—"

But John Sleight interrupted her by booming, "Aye, Billy," and noisily padding out of the room.

"Where's your little maid?" Billy Hendley asked Laurel with a crooked grin.

"She's back at the Virginia House asleep, I assume."

William Hendley laughed an odd, rather hollow laugh. " 'Tis pleased I am to learn she's alive after seeing the likes of me. I've never seen such a skittish little mouse."

Laurel smiled thinly, trying not to betray her uneasiness. Then the door opened and John Sleight returned, carrying a white cloth. The floorboards groaned as he approached Laurel, handing her the rag. "Here, miss, wrap this about your shin," he directed.

Laurel held the wet cloth, staring at her two companions uncertainly. "Go on, gal," Billy Hendley urged, "else it swells till it won't carry you home this night."

Hearing this admonition, Laurel hastily raised the blue

hem of her skirt. But as she leaned over to pull down her silk stocking, she caught the greedy stares of the two men and paused.

John Sleight laughed heartily. "Don't be afeared, miss. Owing to our unusual physiques, Billy and I is confined to the bachelor life. Can't neither or us do more than look!"

And the two men fell into gales of laughter, John Sleight's hearty and booming, Billy Hendley's shrill and grating.

Noting their distraction, Laurel hastily pulled down her stocking, tied the damp rag about the tender spot on her shin, then smoothed down her skirts. An odd pair of coconspirators she had thrown herself in with, she thought with a shudder.

"Well, gal—so you're staying with the Yankees?" Billy Hendley asked, as Laurel straightened.

"Yes, sir. I—I wish to do all I can to help."

"Help with what?" William Hendley inquired with an enigmatic smile.

Laurel stared, confused, from Hendley to Sleight. "What Billy means is, which side you be on?" John Sleight questioned.

"Why, the South's, of course!" Laurel retorted indignantly. "What do you take me for?"

"There, miss, don't get your feathers ruffled," John Sleight soothed. "Many a gal in your position would warm up to the Yanks just for decent food and a place to lay her head."

"Food is not one of my worries!" Laurel shot back, then immediately regretted her hasty rejoinder to the corpulent Sleight.

But she needn't have worried, for both men again fell into spasms of hearty laughter, Sleight himself slapping his legs in glee, sending rolls of fat billowing outward. Laurel watched the bench upon which Sleight was seated sag under the weight of his mirth, and she feared at any moment the heavy seat might indeed snap.

Disaster was averted as the two men finally quieted and Billy Hendley directed, "Now, gal, tell us all about yourself and how you came to be staying in the bosom of the enemy."

Laurel quickly related her background to the two men, then told them of coming to the Virginia House and of her decision to spy for the South. The two listened intently, at times interrupting her to ask a shrewd question or two. Then they asked detailed information about the Yankees staying at the hotel—names, personalities, movements, everything Laurel could remember.

As Laurel finished her account, she realized that despite the curse of nature, her two companions were possessed of keen wit and great intelligence. As she ceased speaking, she looked at them expectantly, waiting for her instructions.

Both men were curiously silent for long moments, while Hendley's swivel chair creaked and Sleight breathed in shallow, laborious fashion.

Finally, Hendley spoke. "The one called Carter—he's the one you must watch the closest."

"Aye, he'll be doing his best to get you at sixes and sevens," John Sleight concurred. "I don't mean to be scaring you, miss, but the man sounds exceedingly dangerous. Best keep the corner of your eyes trained on him and do your best not to provoke him further."

Laurel nodded solemnly.

"Wilson will be your best best for information," Uncle Billy put in. "He's trusting and not too bright, and he seems to have taken a shine to you." Rubbing his stubby chin thoughtfully, Hendley continued, "But your captain—now he's a man you must handle most shrewdly, for he's doubtless nobody's fool." Eyeing Laurel speculatively, he inquired, "But then you're no dimwitted little chit, are you, dearie?"

Laurel shook her head, her blue eyes large and thoughtful.

"Consider this, gal," Hendley suggested. "Do you think over a period of time you might convince your captain that you've taken a fancy to him?"

"I—I don't know," Laurel replied, frowning.

Hendley smiled crookedly. "You're a very clever little girl. We've every confidence you can do it—eh, Johnny?"

John Sleight nodded his agreement, while Laurel glanced from one man to the other in perplexity. "Why do you want me to play up to the captain?"

"That would be best revealed in good time," Hendley replied.

Laurel's eyes narrowed. "Meaning you don't trust me."

Hendley shook his head. "On the contrary, gal. Should the Yanks decide to question you, 'tis best, for your own sake, that you've little to tell."

"Also, you might insinuate to your captain that you're disheartened about the loss of your family—that you feel abandoned, even betrayed," John Sleight suggested.

Laurel frowned. "Why?"

"Because we want Captain Lafflin to think you're crossing over to his side," Hendley explained.

Laurel laughed ruefully. "He'd never believe that!"

"He will if you're subtle about it, gal," Hendley insisted. The aging businessman grinned wryly and added, "In time you'll surely bewitch him with those huge blue eyes of yours."

Laurel felt her face heating. "Do you expect me to—to seduce Captain Lafflin?"

Hendley shrugged. "That is something only you can decide, gal." He leaned forward, lacing gnarled fingers as he continued intently, "But you'd best remember something, Miss Ashland. 'Tis not a child's game you're playing.

If that's what you're thinking, you'd best flee back to your nunnery. Your brothers in gray are delivering the ultimate sacrifice daily, so be assured, girl, that before the war is over, you may be losing much more than your virtue.''

Laurel gulped, looking from Hendley to Sleight, her eyes enormous, her face white as the true seriousness of the situation dawned upon her.

''Billy don't mean to be so stern with you, miss,'' Sleight put in, more gently, ''but the fact is, we've little use for a babe in arms—such might panic and squeal on the lot of us. When the time comes that we need you, you must be prepared to act like a woman, standing up for what you believe in, even putting your life on the line. If that be the case—well then, miss, we welcome you.''

Laurel nodded gravely. Frightening as it was, the two men were right—the business in which they were engaging was life and death, and there was no room for childish mistakes. ''My father and my brother are risking their lives daily for the Confederacy,'' she told the two men seriously. ''I can do no less.''

Both men nodded their appreciation. ''Fine, gal,'' Hendley commented. ''Keep your eyes and ears open then and report back to us in, say, a week—sooner if there's significant news. You can always pass me a note at the market—I'll be there each day.''

Laurel frowned. ''I'm not allowed to go out. I mean, I had to sneak out of the hotel to come over here tonight.''

''Then that's one of the first things you must change, gal. For now, you're the only informant we have living right there with the Yanks. You must find a way to keep us apprised of their plans and movements.''

Laurel nodded pensively.

William Hendley rose laboriously and extended a bony hand to Laurel. ''Come with us for a moment, Miss Ashland.''

Laurel hesitated, then stood and took the proffered hand,

forcing herself not to flinch as Hendley's hand grasped hers in a steely grip. She watched Hendley take the taper from the table, then let him lead her out of the room into the blackened hallway. She heard the floorboards squeak as John Sleight followed behind them.

As they started up a flight of very steep stars, Hendley's grip tightened upon Laurel's hand. Feeling the tension in his thin fingers and hearing the small groans he uttered with each step, Laurel realized how painful it was for the deformed man to climb the treacherous stairs. She held her hand firmly in his, trying to give him support without being too obvious about it, while she thought to herself that she had to respect Hendley's courage in the face of overwelming physical odds.

Soon, the little man creaked open a door at the top of the stairs, and the three moved out upon the roof of the building, into the cool October sea breeze. As they walked over to the edge of the platform, Laurel looked out upon the Galveston harbor. Leaning on the roof railing, she inhaled deeply of the salty night freshness and listened to the distant slapping of the waves against the jetties. She spotted several lights bobbing in the distance—Yankee ships anchored at the pier—and shivered with a chill which went much deeper than the coolness of the night.

"Not a pretty sight, is it, gal?" Hendley inquired from her side. "A man's homeland being occupied by the enemy."

Looking out at the harbor, Laurel admitted to herself that it was indeed a sobering scene. Hearing noises to her right, she turned to see John Sleight lighting a lantern.

"Johnny sends the signal this time each night," Hendley explained. "He once mastered a brig in the merchant marine."

"But won't the Yankees see it?" Laurel questioned, gesturing toward the Yankee ships in the harbor.

Hendley shook his head. "Johnny signals at an angle to the harbor."

Laurel watched Sleight send a message by opening and closing the door on the lantern. Long moments passed, but no return signal was visible from the mainland. "They're not replying to your message," Laurel finally commented, watching Sleight lay down his now extinguished lantern.

Billy Hendley turned to Laurel, his strongly etched features smiling in the wavery light cast by the candle. "They never do, gal. We can signal them at an angle, but ain't no way they can flash us back without being spotted from the harbor. But be assured that they're there, Miss Ashland. And pleased they are to have you aboard."

Chapter Twelve

OCTOBER 15, 1862

The moment of truth was approaching, Laurel thought uneasily as she tied a ribbon on the bodice of her blue calico dress. She had heard Jacob Lafflin moving about in the next room for several minutes now, and she knew that soon he would knock upon her door and she would find out for sure whether he had noted her absence during the previous night.

Laurel ran a hairbrush through her ebony curls, longing for a mirror. She glanced about her cubicle in distaste—there was no dresser and today, after she fetched her new frocks from Carmichael's Store, she would have to figure out how to squeeze them all onto the narrow clothes rack.

Laurel made up her pallet, then went to the room's small window. She squeezed her torso through the tiny opening and looked out upon the sunny, deserted streets of Galveston. Taking a deep breath of salty breeze, she was whistling at a passing dog when a deep voice behind her commented, "A fetching sight you make this morning, sweetheart."

Uttering a cry of dismay, Laurel disengaged herself from the window, hitting her head in the process. She turned, glowering up at Jacob Lafflin as she rubbed her smarting head.

Lafflin chuckled, and despite herself, Laurel had to silently concede that he looked quite dashing this morning in his immaculate blue uniform and shiny boots. "I must admit, Laurel, that my first inclination was to whack your fanny, but I thought better of it," the Yankee now teased.

Laurel's blue eyes shot sparks as she balled her fists upon her hips. "And to what do I owe this commendable restraint, Captain?"

Lafflin took one of Laurel's clenched hands. "Come into my room. I dislike conversing in a closet."

"And I dislike sleeping in one!" Laurel retorted nastily as she grudgingly let Lafflin lead her into his room.

Lafflin released her hand and turned to face her, his dark eyes filled with amusement. "You've no right to protest too loudly, sweetheart," he taunted, "since you've rejected the alternative to sleeping in the anteroom." He nodded meaningfully toward the bed.

Outraged, Laurel stamped her foot and whirled to leave, but Lafflin grabbed her arm. "Let's not tangle this morning, Laurel," he cajoled. "Actually, I—I came to get you in order to apologize."

"Apologize?" she reiterated incredulously, frozen in her tracks by his surprising remorse.

He grinned sheepishly, releasing her arm. "I had no right to stage that little seduction scene yesterday."

Laurel raised an eyebrow in amazement. "Attempted rape was more like it!"

He struggled not to smile. "Very well. Call it what you will." He sighed, gesturing resignedly. "But, Laurel—dash it all!—I find you irresistible."

"That's your problem," she replied ungraciously. "And I

must comment that you've had quite a change of heart, Captain, irresistible being a far cry from your calling me— what was it?—the ugliest wench you had ever laid eyes on!''

Lafflin snapped his fingers and laughed. "So that's it! You've yet to forgive me for my rather hasty judgment when we first met.''

Laurel strolled off to the dresser, casually straightening the white eyelet scarf. "Perhaps.''

She heard the soft thud of his boots as he crossed the room, and as she toyed with the toiletry items on the dresser, she could feel his gaze, almost as if his eyes were boring into the back of her head. She looked up; her eyes locked with his in the mirror.

"Laurel,'' he said seriously. "I'm leaving today.''

She turned, startled. "You are?''

He nodded. "I'm accompanying Commander Renshaw on a voyage along the coastline.''

She looked up at him, gulping—God, he was so very close to her now! For a moment she stared at him, transfixed, as she studied his dark, wavy hair, his fine expressive eyes, his classically etched face. The smell of bay rum wafted over her, making her treacherously want to reach out and touch the smooth bronze of his face.

Seeming puzzled by her absorbed stare, he cleared his throat. "I'm taking Carter with me. That way, you should be safe.''

Carter! The name of the hated seaman reminded Laurel of her purpose in staying at the Virginia House—to do all she could to aid the South against the barbarism of cutthroats such as the villainous sailor who now plotted his revenge against her. To that end, she needed to begin implementing William Hendley's suggestion, playing up to Lafflin in order to gain information.

For a moment, Laurel felt the intense discomfort of

conflicting emotions. Lafflin seemed almost human this morning—especially in his concern regarding her safety. Must she deceive him, betray him? Then, watching one of his bronzed hands play with the hilt of his sword at his waist, she quickly made her decision. He was the enemy, occupying her homeland. She must steel herself against his "kindness," and fight for her country, her family. After all, how did she know his attitude toward her wasn't spurred by an ulterior motive, to trick her into trusting him? Perhaps ultimately they sought to betray each other.

Her resolve strengthened but her exterior cool, Laurel asked Lafflin innocently, "What is the destination of your voyage?"

Lafflin shook a finger at her. "Oh no you don't, sweetheart. That's a military secret. Not that you'd tell anyone," he added sarcastically, "but I rue the thought of your fellow Confederates torturing you to gain the information."

Laurel scowled, flouncing off and seating herself upon the straight chair. "I was merely trying to be friendly," she put in defensively.

"Indeed?" he laughed, following her. "To what do I owe this heartwarming solicitude?"

"Perhaps I like you," she conceded coyly. Then, noting his incredulous grin, she added, "A little."

Lafflin sat down in the wing chair across from her, casually crossing his long legs. For an interminable moment he stared at her, frowning musingly as his eyes raked her figure, as if he were planning a brief diversion before he left on his journey.

Laurel felt her skin crawl. "What—what about Reba?" she asked, hoping to distract him.

"What about her?" he repeated.

"What are you going to *do* about her?" she questioned impatiently.

He shrugged. "She claims she didn't make the voodoo doll."

"And you believed her? You're going to leave me here alone, with her skulking about?"

Lafflin leaned forward, lacing long, brown fingers. "Laurel, that's something I've wanted to talk to you about," he said gravely. "Look, honey, I think you should leave this rather disreputable place."

"Leave! But I've nowhere to go!"

"Surely there's someone you can stay with," he reasoned. "A family on the island—"

"No, there's no one," she insisted.

He stood and strode toward her determinedly. "Then I'll take you to the nunnery and leave you there."

"No!" she gasped, eyes wild, bolting to her feet. "No, I—Jacob, I want to stay."

Jacob Lafflin stopped in mid-stride, his features softening. "Jacob," he repeated wonderingly, as if he'd never heard his own name before. "I like the sound of my name on your lips."

He drew closer to her and looked down at her earnestly, his face mellow, tender, as if she had caressed him by using his Christian name. Almost sadly, he said, "Laurel, if you must stay, you will have to be willing to take risks. There's a war going on—very real and exceedingly dangerous. Let's face it, Laurel—Reba is probably the least of your worries."

She nodded miserably.

Slowly, his hand lifted her chin and her eyes locked with his. She found herself quite shaken by his emotional gaze as he whispered, "Laurel, if I could, I would protect you with my life."

Laurel felt herself treacherously softening at the Yankee's sincere, ardent statement. Something deep, measureless, passed between them at that moment. They were bonded, just as they had been at the moment when Jacob discovered the voodoo doll—joined in mutual pain and need.

Jacob cleared his throat and went on unsteadily, "However, unfortunately, my duty lies elsewhere for now. Wilson will be here with you, but otherwise, I'm afraid you're on your own, Laurel."

"I know," she said heavily.

His eyes grew even warmer as he evidently noted the dejection in her tone of voice. "Could it be that you've softened toward me, lady?" His face moved slowly toward hers. "You know, Laurel, great danger may lie in the Gulf. Who knows if I'll ever see you again. Tell me, would you kiss me goodbye?"

She looked up at his expectant face, at eyes now darkened by passion. "Yes," she said, her lower lip trembling.

She closed her eyes, waiting for his mouth to touch hers, hoping that this time he would want no more than a chaste, polite kiss.

But the anticipated moment did not come. Instead, she heard him striding off angrily. Bewildered, she opened her eyes and saw him standing at the door, glaring at her.

When he spoke, his voice was tense, cynical. "Something I'll contemplate well during my absence is why you said yes to the kiss when you did not want it."

"But I—"

"Don't make it worse by lying!" he interrupted. He went to the dresser and took a blue sea bag from a drawer, then tossed it at her. "Have my clothes packed within the hour. I'll send Barnaby up for my bag."

"Oh!" Laurel raged, angrily flinging the bag onto the bed. "You're—you're exasperating! I'll pack your things with pleasure, for I can't wait for you to leave! I hope your ship gets blown apart and you drown and a tidal wave engulfs you—"

His hand on the doorknob, Lafflin paused, obviously

amused by her childish outburst. "Any more fond wishes, sweet?"

"And that you go straight to hell!"

"Perhaps I'll oblige you, sweet," he laughed, apparently enjoying himself thoroughly. His eyes sweeping her figure brazenly, he suggested, "See if you can manage to grow up while I'm gone, and maybe you'll get that kiss after all."

He turned and exited the room before she could think of a retort.

Laurel stormed about the room, gathering Lafflin's things. "He'll kiss me, indeed!" she fumed. "I should die of revulsion before his lips left mine!"

She threw open drawers, carelessly packing Lafflin's uniforms and toiletry items in his canvas sea bag. She supposed she should be grateful that the Yankee evidently took no note of her absence the previous night, but his audacious behavior still made her blood boil. Staring at his bed stonily, she hissed, "One thing's for certain, Captain. I'm not sleeping in the damned closet while you're gone! At least your absence will ensure me a decent bed! And I hope you stay gone forever!"

She stormed back to the dresser, yanking open the bottom drawer, sending its contents spilling upon the floor. But she paused, arrested, staring at two little red cloth sacks that rolled out from between two shirts. Bending over, she picked up one of the odd bags and smelled it, finding its odor pungent and vile. She was about to untie the cord on the tiny sack when she heard a knock at the door.

Standing up, the sack still in her hand, Laurel went to the door and let in Fancy. "Fancy, what do you suppose this is? I found it in Captain Lafflin's dresser."

Spotting the object, Fancy jerked away, her eyes enormous with terror as she croaked, "The devil's bones, Miss Laurel! Reba, she put the *gris-gris* on Captain Lafflin!"

"The *what*, Fancy? What are you talking about?"

"The *gris-gris*, Miss Laurel!" Fancy repeated, pointing at the object of her horror and backing away into the hall. "Reba done voodooed him! The *gris-gris*, it mean pow'ful bad, Miss Laurel. It mean death!"

Fancy fled, and Laurel dropped the bag as if it had burned her. Remembering her own cruel farewell to Lafflin, she was swept by a sickening wave of fear and shame.

"Oh no!" she gasped, her eyes fixed upon the appalling lump of evil. "May God protect you, Jacob!"

Chapter Thirteen

OCTOBER 25, 1862

The shining Gulf was peaceful, rocking the three Federal steamers toward their destination. Jacob Lafflin stood at the stern of the *Owasco*, taking deep breaths of the cool, salty morning breeze as he stared out at the wake carved in the waves by the flagship *Westfield* ahead of them.

. His eyes moving back to his own ship, Jacob watched some of his men trim sails and stone the deck, while others sat on the fo'castle hatch, singing to the accompaniment of a lone harmonica, "The Union forever, hurrah! boys, hurrah! Down with the traitor, up with the star."

Lafflin smiled tightly. It was good the men had their fun now, for soon enough they would be approaching Pass Cavallo and confronting the citizens of Indianola and, later, Port Lavaca.

Thinking of the imminent encounter, Lafflin stared moodily at the commodore's flagship tacking to the north of them. Why Renshaw wanted to capture the two Confederate

124

forts was truly a mystery—even if both villages surrendered, they had not sufficient troops to leave quartered there to secure the occupation.

At least there would be no Confederate navy at this confrontation, Lafflin consoled himself. Frowning, he remembered the battle of New Orleans the previous April—a long and bloody siege. The deck of the *Owasco*, painted white so the men could easily locate their gear, had run red with blood. At one point, a cannonball had torn in through a porthole, blowing apart a three-man crew in an instant, sending bits of human flesh flying all about the boat. It had been a long, brutal, bloody battle, but the United States Navy had prevailed, as it would today.

Distracted by a fluttering object in the distance, Jacob Lafflin took up the spyglass and gazed out toward Pass Cavallo. The telescope swept the wooden stockade Lafflin knew to be Fort Esperanza. He smiled as his eyes fixed upon the object that had distracted him—a huge flag, possibly three yards by four. Obviously homemade, the flag sported three enormous stripes of red and white. In the upper left-hand corner was a blue patch boasting a ring of six stars, with a seventh star at the circle's center. Beneath the large flag, militiamen scurried about the stockade, while nearby, a cast-iron lighthouse tilted precariously toward the bay, looking as if it might topple over with the slightest breeze. Noting the missing plates and lighting apparatus, Lafflin decided the Confederates must have tried to blow up the heavy iron structure—without success.

Lowering the spyglass, Lafflin thought of how he admired the Confederates' bravado. It was foolhardy of the Rebs to try to mount a land defense against the three heavily armed Federal boats. The pride and stubbornness of the Southerners would cost them dearly.

The thought of pride or rebelliousness brought Laurel to his mind. Jacob cursed under his breath. He'd been apart from the girl for almost two weeks now, yet instead of being able to forget her as he had hoped, he found himself thinking of her with increasing regularity. He would look into the blue of the ocean and think of her eyes, and at night, as he lay in his lonely bunk, the sound of the waves would seem to be her voice instead, whispering his name. Fears about her safety haunted his dreams—what if, in fact, she were in danger at this very moment?

Jacob had never given much credence to the idea of voodoo curses or the preternatural before, yet some strange, unexplainable things had happened on this voyage. One time, when he was descending the ladder into the hold, a step had broken and he had narrowly escaped a bad fall in the darkness. And another time, as he was walking the deck, a belaying pin had come hurtling down from the mast, like a wickedly swift iron club, narrowly missing his head. Yet when he looked up at the fore top, no one was there working the rigging. Peculiar. It almost made him wonder if there could be some truth to this talk of hexes, especially as he remembered the venom in Reba's yellow eyes when he chastised her, remembered the grudge she obviously held against Laurel as well . . .

Jacob scowled and chided himself for his foolish, even superstitious, thoughts as he started down the steps toward Carter at the forward mast. Would he let a couple of near accidents turn him into a hysterical woman? No, he'd be damned if he'd let the serving wench Reba intimidate him with her well-practiced act. And neither would he let clever little Laurel Ashland get her clutching hands on his heart. Hell, the girl had wished him ill with her parting breath. When he returned to Galveston, he would deal with the girl, settling the myth of her virginity once and for all. He would topple her from her pedestal, make her admit to the earthy, carnal nature she tried to conceal, bed her vigorously until he got her out of his system. He was sure that inside, she was no different from all the rest—a cold-blooded liar at heart. The sooner he called her bluff, the better. He would not be deceived again, used again, as he had been with Lucinda.

Lucinda. Damn, he hadn't thought of the bitch in years, he reflected as he passed a lifeboat strapped to the deck. It had been eight years earlier, when he had just turned nineteen, that he met the seventeen-year-old blond beauty. Creamy skin, guileless huge green eyes—she had smitten him utterly. Two month's after Lucinda's family had moved to St. Louis, she had given herself to Jacob in a reckless episode in the summerhouse behind the Missouri home of Jacob's family. Lucinda had cried great tears at their joining, bewailing the loss of her innocence, but Jacob had not been deceived—he had sported with his mother's personal maid since the age of fifteen, and he knew Lucinda's body to be that of a woman. The perverse ingenuity of Lucinda's scheme had been revealed to him two weeks later, when she and her parents had come to the Lafflin home, demanding that Jacob marry Lucinda, giving a name to the child she claimed he had fathered. Jacob's widowed mother listened patiently, throwing Jacob pleading glances, while Jacob hotly denied responsibility for the pregnancy, realizing the now-obvious outward curving of Lucinda's belly could not have been caused by their coupling a mere fortnight before. Indeed, he realized then that the only reason the bitch had given herself to him was to entrap him into marriage to give her bastard child a name. Ultimately, Jacob had settled the matter by finding two lads who both admitted to romping with Lucinda. He took the boys to Lucinda's home, then watched triumphantly as they told their tale, reducing the lovely Lucinda to tears and humiliation before her family. Jacob had loved the taste of vengeance and had savored it for years—to nurse the wound of her betrayal.

Remembering, Jacob now smiled grimly. Since that day

he had tasted many a woman, but none had filled him with more than the usual carnal satisfactions. And, by damn, Laurel Ashland would not be the first to get her clutching little hands on his heart! Or had she already? Why was it every time he was with her, he found himself saying things he hadn't intended to say, doing things he hadn't intended to do, wanting to protect her, to believe her?

"Looks like them Rebs is fixed to fight," a nasal voice commented, drawing Lafflin out of his thoughts.

Jacob Lafflin turned to Carter at the foremast. "Aye. You'd best call the men to battle stations and have an eye out for the commodore's signal."

Lafflin took a deep breath while Carter relayed his captain's order, at mid-ship, to the boson's mate, who then piped out the call for battle stations. Jacob watched several men scurry to their positions at the various guns, while powder monkeys brought up powder and cannonballs from the magazine. As the *Owasco* made toward the pass, following the commodore's lead, a Confederate cannonball suddenly boomed forth from Fort Esperanza, creasing the bow of the *Westfield*.

At Lafflin's side, Carter whistled. "They do got guts, them Johnny Rebs."

Lafflin nodded grimly, then raised the spyglass, examining the *Westfield*. The wound was high and shallow—she would not be taking water. Studying the vessel more closely, he paused, catching a flurry of signal flags from the deck. After a few moments, he informed Carter, "We're to back off out of their range and bombard them. Come about and follow the *Westfield*."

Carter grinned greedily as he shouted the order to the seaman at the wheel, who maneuvered the *Owasco* into a due east heading. Jacob watched the other two Federal boats take position across from Point Cavallo. Then, raising the spyglass, he caught the commodore's signal to open fire.

"Now they're going to get it," he stated flatly, relaying the commodore's order to Carter.

The resulting onslaught was deafening, as the guns of all three Federal ships opened upon Fort Esperanza. Within minutes, the fort was thoroughly riddled, wood splintering in every direction. Jacob Lafflin smiled humorlessly as he observed the Confederate flag being lowered by the panicky militia, then watched the evacuation of the fort, a steady stream of men, munitions, and horses fleeing through the western gate of the structure.

The skirmish had ended. Unwittingly, Jacob thought again of Laurel. "A brief show of bravado and you, too, shall surrender, lady."

The next afternoon, Captain Jacob Lafflin again stood at the foremast of his ship, awaiting the order to do battle. The *Owasco* and the *Clifton* lay anchored a half mile off Indianola, in Matagorda Bay, while the *Westfield* was tied at the village's wharf. Leaning upon the ship's railing into the cool breeze, Lafflin stared moodily out at stark clapboard storefronts squatting on flat sand. A strange sense of unrest had haunted him all day. From the first moment he viewed Indianola, he had been filled with a peculiar sense of familiarity, as if seeing an old friend after a long absence. Yet as he stared at the neat rows of homes and stores, he found the buildings incongruous, an alien invasion upon the bleak October landscape, almost negating his feeling of *déjà vu*. The town seemed, somehow, displaced. He smiled grimly. No doubt the town would soon *be* displaced—blown to the winds and the depths of the Gulf.

Lafflin had watched the drama unfold all day. First, the *Westfield* had steamed into the harbor, waving a flag of truce. Then a delegation of four men from the village had boarded the steamer. An hour later the Confederates left, their departure followed by furious activity within the village. The women and children boarded wagons and left, while the men manned the redoubts, priming the cannon. Obviously, the citizens of Indianola had refused to let the Federals take possession of their town peaceably.

Lafflin smiled bitterly. The barbarous chivalry of war, the code of the gentleman, allowed the women and children time to evacuate before the men blew each others' brains and entrails to kingdom come.

Lafflin watched the *Westfield* steam out of the harbor. As she approached the other two Federal gunboats, she lowered the flag of truce and drew the colors. Lafflin raised the spyglass and read the flag signals ordering the bombardment. His men had been ready for almost an hour, standing at general quarters, tensely watching the vignette unfold. All that remained was for Lafflin to give the order to do battle, which he now did. "Open fire!"

The other two gunboats also opened fire, pelting the small German settlement with a black hail of cannonball. The fire was answered by the Confederates batteries, but, unfortunately for the Confederates, the shoreline embattlements lacked the range of the heavily armed gunboats, and round after round of the Confederates fire fell short, splashing harmlessly into the bay.

The fighting was brief but furious. Buildings flew apart; militiamen filled the streets, scurrying about without purpose. Lafflin winced as he watched an elderly gentleman collapse beneath a barage of flying glass and wood.

Soon the outmatched opponent capitulated; a white flag was hastily drawn up the courthouse pole, and across the decks of all three gunboats, the order rang out—"Cease fire!"

The three Federal vessels steamed back into the harbor, tying up at one of the two fingerlike wharves projecting out into the bay. The sailors on the *Owasco* were the last to disembark, and by the time Lafflin stepped ashore into the town, he found men from both other boats moving about busily, gathering provisions and tending to the wounded Confederates.

With a peculiar detachment, Lafflin watched two blue-clad sailors lift the elderly gentleman from the pile of rubble Lafflin had watched descend upon the man. The old man was dead, his face a bloody pulp, beyond recognition.

As Lafflin watched one of the sailors yank a watch and chain from the corpse, ripping the old man's gray suit, he was filled with a sense of outrage. "Leave it be, sailor," Lafflin commented, pointing threateningly at the seaman. "We're not corpse mongers."

From his position squatting on the sand near the corpse, the sailor scowled up at Lafflin from beneath the brim of his white cap. "Aye, sir," he grunted grudgingly. Then, tossing the watch upon the body, he added ungraciously, "The glass is broken anyhow."

Throwing the sailor a look of contempt, Lafflin strode off, dodging piles of rubble as he eyed the desolation. Moving toward the west end of town, he spotted David Winston, aide-de-camp to the commodore, approaching from the other direction. "Afternoon, David. Tell me, why did Renshaw order the bombardment?"

The tall, blond lieutenant turned and fell into stride with Lafflin. "The citizens of Indianola denied the commodore beef."

Jacob Lafflin shook his head in perplexity. "No doubt in a day or two we'll all steam back out across the bar and the citizens of Indianola shall reclaim their village, giving this entire episode no purpose, save gratuitous devastation."

David Winston nodded sadly. "But don't count on our retreat being quite that hasty, Jacob. Renshaw has informed me that we're to first take several villages along the bay, including Port Lavaca, where, I understand, they are in the grips of a yellow fever epidemic."

"Damn. And if I know the Rebs, the fever will serve only to kindle their ire. They've got courage, I'll grant them that."

"Aye," Winston agreed as two seamen carrying a sack of cornmeal passed them on the narrow walkway. Frowning, he added, "And just between you and me, Jacob, something about these skirmishes troubles me as well."

"Yes?" Jacob prompted, turning to his companion with keen interest.

Winston looked about warily, as if to assure himself that no one could hear them. "It's like you were saying—gratuitous devastation," he admitted in a low voice. "There's no logic to it—bombarding villages we cannot possibly occupy." He shrugged. "Who can make sense of war anyway? What matters is the surrender, not the means by which it is accomplished, however cruel that may sometimes seem."

Winston's statement—"What matters is the surrender, not the means by which it is accomplished . . ."—hit home hard with Jacob Lafflin. Was that his goal with Laurel? Did he wish to degrade her in his mind to justify his ultimately plundering her body?

"Hey, friend, let's cheer up," David urged, his mood abruptly jovial as he playfully punched Lafflin on the shoulder. "A far cry this is from our days at Annapolis, when our biggest worry was which pretty little thing we would bed next, eh, Jacob?"

Lafflin smiled tightly, murmuring, "Aye," as they rounded a corner. But as they turned northward onto a street of modest, dog-trot homes, Jacob Lafflin froze in his tracks, his eyes arrested by a form lying sprawled in the street. His face whitening, he gasped, "Laurel!"

He raced toward the girl lying face down upon the coarse sand. Silky black curls cascaded from her head, catching the afternoon light. The girl's white frock was garishly bloodsoaked from a wound in her back that still oozed. Her legs sprawled out at unnatural, rakish angles, one shoe missing from a silk-stockinged foot.

Lafflin knelt, turning the girl over. She was, of course, not Laurel. But nonetheless, he felt angry tears burning his eyes as he gazed at the small, cherubic face, so peaceful in death, saw the hand-embroidered Confederate flag sewn to the bosom of her gown, viewed the small ivory-hilted dagger clutched tightly in her delicate hand. Gently sweeping sand from the girl's lifeless face—which was, strangely, neither warm nor cold—he questioned inanely, "Why didn't you leave with the others, sweetheart?"

Laurel would not have left either, he thought desolately. This could have been her—so brave, so defiant. Jesus, what if Laurel were in similar peril at this very moment? he thought with a shudder. What if Reba had indeed attempted to harm her? Damn, he should have strangled the yellow-eyed witch before he left!

He heard David Winston clear his throat and say lamely, "I sent a sailor searching for her kin."

Lafflin's head jerked up as he glared at his friend with revulsion mixed with disbelief. "You *knew?* That's right, you came from this direction. And you left the girl here, in the street?"

Winston's face fell. "Were she my child, I should not want the enemy touching her."

Lafflin shot Winston a look of contempt. "I suppose there's some sense to your rather bizarre reasoning."

Jacob removed his blue jacket and started to cover the girl with it, but David admonished, "Don't, Lafflin. 'Twould be like shrouding her with the Union Jack."

At his friend's words, Jacob hesitated, then, realizing that Winston spoke the truth, he instead folded the jacket, carefully placing it beneath the girl's head. He felt he should afford her some symbolic measure of dignity, however futile it all seemed.

Then Jacob Lafflin did a curious thing. He carefully disengaged the girl's fingers from the small dagger. Then, with infinite care, he cut the blue threads tacking the small Confederate flag to the girl's bosom. Frowning, he tucked the flag into the waist of his blue trousers.

"Why did you do that?" his puzzled companion inquired.

Lafflin stood, shaking his head slowly. "I don't really know."

Just then, a sailor and a tall, gaunt middle-aged man rounded the corner. Uttering a cry of infinite anguish, the tall civilian raced for the lifeless figure, falling to his knees in the sand, then screaming up at the sailors, "Bastards! You've murdered my Betsy!"

With distaste, Lafflin tossed the dagger into the sand beyond them. Nodding toward the dead girl, he muttered, "The price of a side of beef."

All at once, Jacob could abide no more, his disgust becoming almost a physical thing. He strode away from the grisly scene, calling over his shoulder, "Help the man bury the girl, David."

Lafflin continued past the edge of town, his feet having a purpose his mind could not comprehend—escape, or discovery? Then he saw the lake, and he knew.

It began as a tiny slit near the bay, then wound about in cornucopia fashion. "Powder Horn Lake," he murmured.

That was why the buildings had seemed foreign! They had not been there—not before!

On Lafflin marched. To hell with Renshaw, he thought. To hell with the war! He would take all the time he needed, explore every inlet and curve outlining the lake, much as he would explore a woman—until he found the spot, the *very* spot, where he had lain upon the sand two decades earlier.

It would hurt, he knew—ripping open a scarcely healed wound, rendering it raw, gaping again. Yet he must find the place—he was drawn to it, like steel to a magnet. He would rest upon the sand, his eyes closed, as the memory sprang to life again in his mind.

And he would hear again the voice, the words, that twenty years previous had changed his life irrevocably.

Chapter Fourteen

NOVEMBER 6, 1862

The night was star-strewn and cool as Laurel Ashland moved quietly down Water Street. She was tempting fate, she knew, with this midnight excursion along the channel, but her mind was deeply troubled and it was essential that she do some hard thinking before she returned to the Virginia House.

Moonlight washed her hair with silver as the breeze toyed with her cascading curls. The sound of waves slapping against wharves was monotonous, lulling, as she swept past quiet, shadow-strewn warehouses.

Moments earlier, at the Hendley building on the Strand, her plans with Billy Hendley and John Sleight had been finalized. Hendley had just received word that Colonel Debray, commander of the Confederate land forces at Virginia Point on the mainland, approved of their idea and would aid them in every possible way. All that now remained was to wait—wait until Jacob Lafflin returned. Then it was up to

Laurel to make the first move—to take that first very dangerous step.

Laurel shuddered. Success or failure of the Confederate mission rested squarely upon her shoulders. " 'Tis the best performance you'll ever give, girl," Billy Hendley had informed her solemnly.

Idly, Laurel kicked a small seashell out of her way as she proceeded down the dark street. To think a few weeks earlier she had been a carefree schoolgirl with no responsibilities, few worries. Now she had charged full-blown into adulthood, into danger. She smiled morosely. She had only herself to thank, for she had chosen this perilous adventure—nay, demanded it.

She glanced up at the moon—it was full and bright and seemed to mock her from the star-dotted void of the sky. Somewhere beneath that same moon were her loved ones. She thought of her mother and sister, Cammie, at Washington-on-the-Brazos. Had Cammie indeed married Trey Garrison on his last leave? And what of her father and her brother, Charles, who had also joined the Confederate brigade from Washington when the war began? Were Daddy and Charles staring at the same moon, in some cold, miserable Confederate encampment hundreds of miles away? Were they even alive to know the moon was there?

Blinking back a tear, Laurel moved to the intersection of Water Street and Fifteenth, where she viewed a familiar sight—the ruins of Jean Lafitte's Maison Rouge. Laurel had visited what remained of the pirate's fort once before, with one of her classes from the academy. Laurel's history teacher, Sister Mary Joseph, had seemed quite taken with the legend of the French rogue who had set up headquarters on the island in 1817. Laurel remembered how the usually solemn sister glowed when she spoke of the mysterious Lafitte. Somehow, Sister Mary Joseph managed to get permission from Mother St. Pierre to take the girls to view the ruins. There, Sister Mary Joseph had poignantly related the legend of Lafitte burning Maison Rouge before he left Galveston, following the death of his wife, Madeline Rigaud.

Now, Laurel gazed solemnly at decaying shell, a crumbling foundation that was the only evidence that the pirate had ever visited the island.

As she climbed stone steps to the deteriorating foundation, she wondered absently if Sister Mary Joseph secretly thirsted for a life of adventure—to be abducted by a handsome rake, taken to sea, ravished in a pirate's bunk...

A chill coursed through Laurel at the thought. She gazed longingly at the ships bobbing up and down in the harbor, lights twinkling slightly in the mild night wind. What if one of the vessels were Lafitte's schooner, come back to Galveston from another age, come to rescue her from the troubles of her present plight, from the demands of adulthood?

Laurel closed her eyes and felt the gulf breeze stroking her face with whisper-soft fingertips. It was a cool, balmy, altogether dreamy night. Letting her inhibitions evaporate with a deep sigh, she conjured up an image of the pirate Lafitte. He was tall, swarthy, dark-haired, his black eyes gleaming lustily. His billowing white shirt was rakishly open to his waist, revealing his sun-bronzed chest. A wickedly sharp dagger was clamped between smooth white teeth and he sported a moustache, black and devilishly trim.

Sleek and sinewy, Lafitte now moved through Laurel's vision, striding steadily, remorselessly toward her, a brazen message in his eyes. He would brook no denial, play no game with words. He would snatch her up into his hard arms, whisk her away to his ship and, heedless of her protests, claim her body as his own while the Gulf gently rocked their bed...

"Laurel?"

Slowly, Laurel opened her eyes and saw him approaching. His hair was streaked by shimmering silver, his features

softened by moonlight, his eyes glittering with a mysterious
light. Could it be? Had her dream caused him to materialize
before her? Would he now take her away?

"Laurel, what are you doing here?" The voice was now
tense, distressed.

The spell shattered; Laurel recognized Jacob Lafflin moving across the decaying foundation toward her. The Yankee
was dressed in his navy uniform, his physique even more
tight and muscular than she remembered, his skin an even
deeper bronze.

"So you've returned," she mumbled. He looked very
tired, she noted.

He paused, close to her now, his dark eyes troubled as he
adjusted the cap on his head. "Damn, Laurel. Don't you
know it's dangerous to be about this time of night?"

She shrugged. "I couldn't sleep."

Lafflin glanced about at the ruins of the fort. "Why did
you come here, to Lafitte's former headquarters?"

Laurel glanced at Lafflin with new interest. "You knew
about Lafitte?"

"Of course, who doesn't? Every man of the sea is
familiar with the life of the French privateer."

Laurel moved away from Lafflin toward the edge of the
foundation, gazing out at the meagerly lit harbor. "Was
your voyage successful, Captain?" she asked, with a trace
of bitterness.

He did not reply, but moved toward her, his boots scraping the shell. Taking her shoulders, he turned her. When he
spoke, his voice was edged with impatience. "You haven't
answered my question, Laurel. What are you doing here?"
Then, in a harsh tone strangely tinged with anguish, he
added, "Do you know you could be shot, out alone after the
curfew?"

Laurel backed away from his touch. Looking up at his
impassioned face, she felt herself treacherously softening

toward him. He had been gone for over three weeks, and despite herself, she had to admit that she had missed him, that his presence now was definitely a comfort to her. Fighting her appalling weakness, she asked in a voice she hoped would sound scornful, but which, instead, merely sounded resigned, "Where does the danger lie, Captain?"

Hearing him curse softly under his breath at her words and watching him move even closer, she reacted in fear and blurted, "If you must know, Captain, I was hoping Lafitte would come to this spot tonight and take me away from all this!"

He paused then, and she waited, her face tilted defiantly, for his reply. Curiously, he was silent, frowning, for long moments, as if considering her provocative remark carefully. Then he said flatly, "Lafitte is dead, girl. But I'm not." Hoarsely, he asked, "Would you let a pirate make love to you, Laurel?"

And he crushed her against him.

His mouth was hard, bruising, as if he could not get enough of her, and her own lips, too numb to react, yielded. She felt his tongue push past her teeth, boldly, deeply into her mouth, and she was horrified by the traitorous sensations raging rampant in her body at his assault. When his hand reached for her breast, she momentarily recovered, flailing at his back with her fists. But he took no note as one of his fingertips teased a young nipple through the cloth of her dress. The sensations aroused by his touch were potently erotic, titillating; she shuddered with desire and surprise and his mouth abruptly moved to her cheek. Raining her face with kisses, he whispered, "Easy, love, easy."

She was touched by his words and by his soft, sensuous kisses, and all at once she found herself wanting to drown in him. Her hands moved to encircle his body tentatively, then caressed the corded muscles of his back as she half sobbed his name.

He kissed her again, more demandingly, and she let herself relax and enjoy the heat and taste of his mouth as she curled her arms around his neck. His reaction to her softening was almost violent—his arms clenched about her waist, until she felt a part of him. Her senses became ignited, reeling dizzily—and even the thudding of the surf seemed obscured now by the mad pounding of her heart. Oh, she thought desperately, he could not go on kissing her like this, squeezing her essense into his, or surely she would faint!

His kiss ended; they both gasped for air. "Laurel, I missed you—Jesus, I missed you so!" he breathed, burying his face against her neck, his voice shaky with emotion.

His lips sent powerful waves of feeling through her body, and she realized suddenly that she had also missed him, *really* missed him. It was not Jean Lafitte that she desired, but this man that she wanted, needed fiercely. In a barely audible voice, she whispered, "I missed you too, Jacob."

He groaned and his lips sought hers again. He tasted her mouth in a more leisurely, thorough way, enticing her tongue with his while his hands reached down, cupping her buttocks, fitting her against him. She was appalled yet strangely captivated, fascinated by his boldness as she felt the hard length of his maleness pressing against her—it seemed somehow so natural, so right—

Suddenly, she ached unbearably to be one with him, to be filled with his heat. She wanted to give herself to him even though he was all male, strong, and hard, and she realized if she gave him her consent, he would proceed relentlessly to accomplish their coupling, whether hurtful to her or not.

He drew back, then, and stared down at her, a glaze of passion in his eyes. As if reading her thoughts, he whispered, "Laurel, I want to make love to you." He took her hand. "Sweetheart, come with me down to the sand."

He leaned over and kissed the top of her head, and again, he seemed to know her mind as he warned gently, "Be very sure before you answer, darling, for if I take you in my arms again this night, I'll hold no quarter.''

Laurel's hand trembled in his as she realized that she indeed wanted no quarter held. He moved back slightly to wait for her reply, and at that moment, moonlight gleamed savagely on the brass buttons of his uniform. The reflection, symbolizing his allegiance, jarred her deeply, and suddenly, the passionate web he had woven about her shattered. Gulping, she looked up into his eyes—smoky brown eyes smoldering with desire for her now, but the eyes of her foe, nonetheless. No, this man was not a mythical pirate come to take her adrift on a wave of fantasy—this man was the enemy, a man she would ultimately betray, a man who might kill her!

"No!" she cried, wrenching herself away from him and fleeing across the crumbling foundation.

Tearing down the stairs of the ruined home, she heard him call her name in the darkness behind her; but she did not hear him following her.

Nonetheless, she tore down Water Street like one pursued, heedless of the dangers, bolting past gray, hulking warehouses, listening for the sound of footsteps, which never came. At length, she realized he would not pursue her, and she slowed her pace. It occurred to her, sinkingly, that her frantic escape was merely an attempt to flee her own feelings . . .

Later, when she was safely in her bed at the hotel, she thought again of her encounter with Jacob Lafflin. It seemed unreal now. Had it not been for the slight bruise on her mouth where his lips had been and the lingering sound of his voice, she might have dismissed the entire episode as a waking dream.

Chapter Fifteen

Laurel sat quietly in the darkness. Soon, the sun's first amber rays would steal through the tiny window of the anteroom and the time would arrive for her to leave.

Never in her life had she attempted anything this dangerous. One mistake, one misstep, and she might well be dead within the hour. Oh, how wretched was this war, to bring people to the perilous undertakings such as she must soon perform!

Stretching forward on her pallet, Laurel folded her arms across raised knees, her eyes fixed pensively upon the still-gray window. She wore the best of the frocks she had purchased at Carmichael's—a pale gray-blue silk with straight, elegant lines, complemented by long, fitted sleeves and by two dozen mother-of-pearl buttons traveling down the bodice. Unquestionably, the sand would ruin the hem of the Sunday frock; but the color was necessary to obscure her in the half light through which she must travel.

Taking hairpins from a tin cup near her on the floor, Laurel began securing her black tresses atop her head, thinking as she worked of her meeting with Jacob Lafflin two nights earlier. Even now, the memory of his words— "Would you let a pirate make love to you, Laurel?" sent a haunting chill down her spine. What had shaken her more, though, was her own response to his passion—the feeling of being transported, of wanting to yield to the primal twist in her belly. It made approaching the task at hand exceedingly difficult.

So Laurel thought instead of the way Lafflin had treated her since their happenstance rendezvous—with cool contempt, as if the midnight episode had never occurred. In fairness to him, however, she had to admit that he had been frantically busy since his return. Things had not gone well in Galveston during Lafflin's absence, if the black grapevine was correct. Rumor had it that several Confederate soldiers had been sighted in the city while Lafflin was gone. In fact, during one nocturnal episode there was a brief exchange of gunfire between blue and gray, though no one was injured.

Admittedly, there was great tension among the Federal troops, a sense of imminent confrontation with the Confederates, confirmed by Commodore Renshaw's appearance at the Virginia House the previous day. Laurel shuddered as she remembered serving tea to the tall, spare Union commander. Renshaw, Lafflin, and Captain Law of the *Clifton* had been seated in the dining hall when Laurel brought in the coffee and johnny cake.

Laurel remembered Renshaw tasting the johnny cake, then commenting with distaste, "Cornmeal again, I note. I wonder if the Texans prepare anything without it."

Without thinking, Laurel had burst forward, saying boldly, "Sir, your blockade has made flour an unobtainable luxury!" She snatched up Renshaw's dish. "Do forgive us for offending your delicate palate, Commodore!"

Abruptly, Renshaw had looked up at Laurel. Piercing gray eyes, partially obscured by bushy black brows, had fixed upon her coolly. Laurel immediately regretted what she knew was a foolish outburst, but couldn't think of what to do without losing face. Meanwhile, the commodore nodded toward Lafflin and inquired, "Who is the impertinent wench?"

Renshaw's voice held a grating quality, an edge of annoyance that made Laurel further lament her reckless remarks. Instinctively, she turned toward Lafflin. His dark brown eyes held anger, entreaty, and something else—a cloud of fear! Surely he was not afraid? she asked herself confusedly. But, yes, he was afraid—for her!

A slow tingling began in Laurel's toes and traveled upward, until it suffused her entire body. While her heart thudded ominously, she heard Lafflin reply with studied smoothness, "She's one of the maids." He added with emphasis, "A quadroon."

"Is she now?" Renshaw had replied slowly, his eyes gleaming with an emotion Laurel couldn't name—amusement? Vengefulness? "I suppose it would not do to incarcerate the girl, since it's our charge to free the Africans."

At this remark, Captain Law, a man of average appearance, had laughed loudly and a bit nervously. Laurel, however, was too stunned to react as she stared at Renshaw apprehensively. The man seemed lost in thought, as if pondering a method to punish Laurel for her effrontery.

Laurel suddenly realized that if she valued her hide, she'd best lay aside her pride and her temper. She hastily replaced the commander's plate, her gaze demurely cast downward as she murmured, "I must apologize, Commodore. I spoke out of turn."

Just as Renshaw opened his mouth to reply, Jacob Lafflin said hoarsely to Laurel, "Leave us, girl. We've important matters to discuss!"

Though his words to her were harsh, his deep-set brown eyes seemed to add, "Please."

Remembering her hasty retreat from Renshaw's scrutiny, Laurel now wondered if she would see the man again before the day was out. If she was caught, there was no doubt in her mind that the Yankee commodore would order her execution without batting an eyelash!

A narrow shaft of sunlight threaded its way through the small window of the anteroom, shining in Laurel's sapphire eyes, now large with fear. She took a turban from her lap and tied it tightly about her head, wondering numbly if it would hurt to die. The question brought to mind the morning several weeks past when she had awakened with the excruciating pain. Her mind had rebelled since that day, forbidding thought of the harrowing episode, but now her fears brought the incident freshly to her mind, and she recalled once more, even half felt, the frightful, wrenching pain that had made her pray for death.

Yes, it would hurt to die, hurt horribly, she decided with a shudder. But it was a risk that must be borne if she was to do her part in this tragic war. She must cast aside her romantic feelings for Jacob, betraying him and all he represented. After all, had not the man betrayed her twice already, by siding first with Carter, then with Reba? Indeed, for all his kissing her and saying he missed her, he might be the very one to take her life this day!

Frowning, Laurel stood up, taking her reticule from the peg on the wall. Inside the blue velvet bag was the letter William Hendley had given her two nights previous, the letter that had lain pressed against her bosom inside her dress even as Jacob Lafflin kissed her. She drew open the bag, feeling the crisp parchment one last time. Satisfied, she drew the strings, then reached for the door.

The door creaked open, and she tiptoed into Lafflin's room. She glanced at the bed but saw only deep shadows beneath the canopy. The curtains were drawn tightly across the window, making the room exceedingly dark; Laurel almost tripped as her toe caught the edge of the braided rug. Gulping, she moved forward quickly, before she could lose her nerve. Then her leg met the edge of the straight chair full force, and she crashed to the floor.

Before she knew what was happening, she was dragged, roughly, to her feet. Her heart beating fiercely, Laurel gazed up at the shadowy face of Jacob Lafflin. How had he arisen so quickly?

A pinprick of light, from where the sun pierced the drapes, shone on his bronze chest. But otherwise, the darkness obscured his nakedness—and his rage, Laurel added to herself uneasily.

"Up a bit early this morning, aren't we, sweetheart?" he gritted in a voice thick with sleep.

Her throat feeling strangely constricted, Laurel could not answer.

He released her and leaned over into the deep shadows near the floor. "By all means be seated, Miss Ashland," he said, with mock cordiality as he righted the chair. "Do let's have a chat."

Laurel half gasped as Jacob's ungentle hands pushed her shoulders downward until her buttocks contacted the hard wood of the chair. He moved off then, and she caught her breath, trying to steady herself. She heard a soft rustle of cloth, followed by the dull scrape of a match. Her eyes moved instinctively for the light, and she watched Jacob Lafflin approach her in a pool of lamplight.

He had donned his trousers, but was otherwise still unclothed. His bare feet moved soundlessly, slowly, across the woven rug, as if he were savoring her moments of discomfort. The wavery light made his features appear harsh, sinister, despite the opaque sleepiness in his eyes, the ruffled appearance of his dark, shiny hair.

Placing the lantern on the small tea table that separated the room's two chairs, Jacob then sat down in the large wing chair. He drew a finely shaped hand through his hair, combing it away from his eyes. Then, with dispassionate thoroughness, his eyes swept Laurel's figure. As he examined her shoes, her dress, the reticule clutched in her hands, the turban binding her hair, his brow grew deeply creased.

The silence that ensued was electric. Finally, he said with soft cynicism, "Well, I'll be damned. What are you up to this time?"

"Up to?" Laurel repeated in a cracking voice, her blue eyes wide and guileless.

"I know of no sunrise *fêtes* being given this day," he said with silky sarcasm. "And doubtless, you're not so elegantly attired merely to fetch my breakfast. Which brings to mind the obvious question." He leaned forward, his stare icy. "Who are you going to meet, and for what purpose?"

"Why Captain, I've no idea what you're talking about," Laurel replied innocently, her nervousness betrayed by fingers that fidgeted with her reticule.

Lafflin nodded toward her lap. "What's in the bag you clutch so protectively?"

Laurel gulped, her eyes the frightened eyes of a cornered animal. Suddenly, she bolted to her feet, diving for the door. But Lafflin was beside her in an instant, grabbing her roughly even as she screamed out and flailed at him. He wrestled her to the floor, trying to disengage the reticule from her clinging fingers; but she gripped the bag as if it were her very heart that he was trying to wrench away. "No! Let me go!" she choked in a voice thick with indignation and fear.

But his powerful body pressed her to the rigid floor, and his hands held her wrists in steely bands, tightening relentlessly. Wildly, she jerked her head upward, trying to bite his face. With a quick motion of his head, he managed to dodge her sharp teeth, looking thunderstruck as he gritted his own in tenacious resolve and cursed under his breath. Determinedly, he transferred both of her wrists to an even tighter vise in one of his large hands, and then, with his free hand, he ripped the gray turban from her head so violently that she cried out as her hair was yanked. Yet worse pain awaited her as his strong fingers tangled themselves in her hair, twisting a large clump of locks unmercifully until her head was held immobile beneath his cold, pitiless gaze. Staring up at her formidable opponent as the battle of wills continued, Laurel found Lafflin's image blurring by the tears that sprang to her eyes, due to the tormenting pain in her wrists, her scalp, exceeded only by the unbearable pressure of his hard male body bearing down upon her, until she thought her backside would become fused with the solid, unyielding floor beneath her.

What demoralized Laurel the most was the fact that Lafflin could have easily snatched the reticule from her weakening fingers. Yet instead, he opted to play out the game, forcing her to choose to release the bag through her own volition, capitulating to his will entirely.

At last, Laurel could take no more. Her humiliation complete, she released the reticule and averted her face from him in shame.

The bag slipped from Laurel's fingers; she felt Jacob's weight leaving her and heard him moving off toward the light. Cautiously, she rose, just as he turned to hold up the letter and give her a look of disgust. "It's addressed to Colonel Debray, the Confederate commander," he said, accusation and disbelief in his voice.

"Is it, now?" she countered with a bravado she did not feel as she rubbed her smarting wrists and touched her tender, aching head.

In two strides, Lafflin was beside her, again pulling her to the straight chair and pushing her down. "Goddamnit,

Laurel, quit playing the empty-headed belle. You're in deep trouble this time—indeed, you could be shot for much less!''

Laurel felt her insides rearranging themselves at the Yankee's sobering remark. Yet her eyes were coldly disdainful as she goaded back, ''Don't you keep your pistol in the top bureau drawer?''

In reply, he cursed under his breath, turned on his heel, and marched off toward the dresser, making Laurel regret her cold contempt. Her heart thudding in fright, she watched him yank open the bureau drawer. He removed not a gun, but a knife—which was, under the circumstances, little consolation to her. Slowly, he returned to Laurel's side and stood staring down at her, his expression remorseless as he balanced the weapon across the fingers of one hand while his other hand still held the letter. He held the knife almost playfully, toying with it as if he were a knife-thrower trying to impress his audience before he threw his weapon deep into its target. That he was relishing, slowly savoring Laurel's discomfort could not have been more apparent—or more horrifying.

Then, just as Laurel was ready to abandon her pride and plead for her life, he raised the hand holding the letter, turning it over. Laurel was too relieved to be angry as she watched him gingerly push aside the letter's waxen seal with the sharp tip of the dagger.

In the silence of the room, the crackling sound made when he opened the envelope seemed almost deafening. He placed the envelope and the intact waxen seal on the tea table, then strode off toward the window and opened the curtains. He unfolded the parchment, held it up to the light, and studied the letter in frowning scrutiny. After interminable moments, he turned to Laurel. ''So Debray and his staff are to come to Galveston. We'll want to give them a proper welcome, now won't we? I'm sure Commander Renshaw will want to personally attend the *tête-á-tête*."

"I—I don't know what you're talking about!" Laurel replied, her voice rising.

Raising a black brow, Lafflin read in a grating tone, "'We shall await you and your staff on the tenth at noon in the central market, from there to repair to a place of security to finalize our plans. Kindly appear in civilian clothing, and identify yourselves by wearing oleander blooms in your lapels.'" Lafflin glanced at the bottom of the page, then looked up at Laurel, demanding, "Who is W.H.?"

Laurel shrugged. "I have no idea."

"Undeniably," he replied testily. Rubbing his jaw, he continued, "So the conspirators shall gather in the central market. Rather open and obvious, don't you think?"

"Also providing countless avenues of escape!" Laurel shot back. Then, with a cry of dismay, she clapped her hand over her mouth.

"Aha!" he exclaimed, giving her a nasty, triumphant smile. "You do know all about this little intrigue."

Laurel set her arms akimbo and stared off defiantly at an oil painting of the Gulf.

Lafflin rushed to her side, his hard fingers turning her chin, forcing her to meet his determined gaze. "Who wrote the letter, Laurel?"

Laurel met his gaze steadily, her blue eyes gleaming with scorn. "That information you shall never gain, Captain, not even if you kill me!"

Above her, his hard, muscular physique was menacing as rage blazed in his brown eyes. Laurel caught the musky scent of him and it seemed only to magnify his ruthless masculinity as he replied evenly, "Frankly, dear, that's a distinct possibility at the moment."

Despite her wildly beating heart, Laurel's tone was reckless as she retorted, "So be it."

Jacob cursed and strode away from her, seating himself in the wing chair. Taking the envelope from the tea table, he carefully folded the parchment and replaced it in the envelope. Then he stood, picked up the waxen seal and strode off to the dresser. Laurel heard the hiss of a match; then the smell of sulphur wafted over her. She strained to see what he was doing, but his broad back blocked her view.

He turned and moved back to her side, extending a bronze hand holding the letter. "I must apologize for keeping you from your mission, lady," he said with heavy sarcasm. "By all means, be about your business."

"Are you out of your mind?" Laurel gasped, blue eyes incredulous.

"Who are you to deliver this letter to?" he asked nastily.

"That's none of your goddammed business!"

Laurel tried, too late, to bite back her hasty retort. But the damage was done. Jacob's eyes blackened and, with a curse, he tossed the letter on the tea table and hauled Laurel to her feet, his fingers digging into her arms. "Listen to me, Laurel! You'll deliver this letter now, or I'll take you straight to Renshaw!"

Laurel sobered, her face turning white. "Jacob—you wouldn't!"

He nodded slowly. "Frankly, Laurel, after your rather thoughtless behavior yesterday, I fear the commodore relishes getting his hands on you. And don't take for granted that he'll be satisfied merely by ordering your execution."

"You—you mean?"

"Yes. I doubt Renshaw would be the least bit concerned for your safety after he turns you over to his men to be guarded."

A tense silence ensued. Finally, in a small voice filled with shame, Laurel said, "I'm to watch for a rowboat at dawn on the beach near Nineteenth Street."

Lafflin released her, glancing off toward the window.

"Which means we've no time to lose." He hurried to the dresser, opened a drawer, and pulled out a shirt, his pistol, and a spyglass. He quickly donned the shirt, tucked the pistol into his waist, then moved off to the bed. Sitting down, he laid the spyglass by his side, then pulled on his boots. He stood up, the spyglass in his hand, his tone threatening as he informed Laurel, "I'll be watching you from a distance. You are to give whoever comes ashore the letter, and say nothing. I repeat—*nothing*." Touching his pistol, he added coldly, "Cross me, Laurel, and you may risk death, indeed."

Half an hour later, Laurel stood on the cool November beach, clutching her wool shawl about her with one hand, while her other hand held the reticule in which lay the letter. She could almost feel the heat of Lafflin's gaze at the back of her head as she looked stonily at the billowing surf and felt the cold, misty gulf spray on her face. As she watched a tiny rowboat move into view, she shuddered silently, hoping she would get through the next few moments alive. Lafflin's threatening words still seared her brain—that if she didn't do precisely what he had commanded, he would shoot her or turn her over to Renshaw. Would he really kill her if she spoke with Colonel Debray's men?

The rowboat grew closer, and Laurel stood motionless, her skirts flapping about her as she made out the darkly clothed figures of four men in the small boat. The boat bobbed over the waves, moving closer, until it was within twenty yards of the shore. Then a long-legged man dropped to his waist in the surf and waded in.

He was young and blond and rather reminded Laurel of Cammie's beau, Trey. She felt a tightness in her throat as he drew to her side and stood before her wet and shaking, hugging himself with his arms. Oh, if only this man could be Trey, come to rescue her as he promised! But he wasn't.

"Morning, ma'am" the soldier said.

She did not reply, but nervously drew open her reticule, pulling out the envelope and handing it to him. The boy took the letter from her and stuffed it in the breast pocket of his dark brown shirt.

He looked up at her, his expression puzzled. "Any other message, ma'am?"

She shook her head vigorously, turned, and walked away from him. As she approached the row of frame buildings marking the beginning of Nineteenth Street, she glanced over her shoulder, catching the soldier's image as he ambled through the surf toward the rowboat.

Laurel was starting down the board walkway, breathing a sigh of relief, when steely fingers grabbed her, pulling her into the recessed entrance to a feed store.

Jacob Lafflin pressed Laurel's squirming body hard against the oak door to the store. "A fine performance," he commented dryly. "You should be proud of yourself."

"Proud?" she spat, giving him a scornful look. "Are you proud of yourself for making me do it?"

His dark eyes narrowed. "You made a choice, Laurel."

"Choice? Should I have chosen to be killed—or worse?"

He shrugged. "Under the circumstances, offering your life for your principles would have been commendable."

"I think you're disappointed that you didn't get to kill me!" she spat.

"No, I'm not disappointed," he conceded, releasing her.

He turned and started back toward the hotel. She followed him, seething inside. First, the monster had bludgeoned her into doing his bidding, then he had the audacity to chide her for bending to his will!

For a few moments they walked in tense silence, the sound of their footsteps echoing down the deserted streets.

Then, abruptly, Jacob stopped, turning to Laurel and pulling a small piece of cloth from his breast pocket.

"Here," he said, grabbing Laurel's hand and pressing into it a small Confederate flag. "For you."

Laurel looked down at the small piece of embroidered fabric in confusion. "Why are you giving this to me?"

"At Indianola, I took it off the body of a young girl who died rather than run from what she believed. You might wish to keep it in memory of this noble occasion."

Laurel gazed up at him, appalled.

"She—the girl—rather reminded me of you," he added ruthlessly, his finely chiseled jaw tight.

His words were like daggers in her heart as she gazed at the flag and thought of the dead girl who gave her life for the Confederacy. "Why did you give this to me, Jacob?"

His reply was barely audible. "Perhaps—perhaps because I'm disappointed in you."

He turned and strode off into the gray, dismal morning, leaving her to stare at the small precious flag through the blur of her tears.

Chapter
Sixteen

NOVEMBER 10, 1862

Laurel tiptoed down the stairs in the semidarkness of dawn. She felt edge and exhausted after a sleepless night—Jacob Lafflin had never come to his room, and she had lain awake much of the night wondering what he was up to.

Her nerves had been on edge anyway, because Lafflin had kept Laurel under guard and locked in his room ever since the other morning, when he had surprised her en route to her spying assignment. In fact, she had dispaired of being able to sneak away for her assignment again this morning; yet when she had awakened from a half sleep thirty minutes earlier, she had discovered Lafflin's room empty and unlocked, with no guard in the hallway. Already late, she had dressed quickly, not questioning her good fortune.

Reaching the downstairs hallway, Laurel now lowered the hem of her yellow gingham frock and moved silently through the shadows toward the front door. Yet suddenly, she cried out in fright as a hard hand grabbed her arm, spinning her about.

"These sunrise rondezvous are getting rather tiresome, sweetheart," Jacob Lafflin informed her sarcastically.

"What are you doing here?" Laurel gasped, gazing up at the tall Yankee.

In reply, Lafflin pulled her into the dining hall, toward a small table upon which were placed a coffee pot and two cups. Holding out a chair for her, he said smoothly, "I'm waiting for you, dear."

Stunned, Laurel sat down, blinking rapidly as she watched Lafflin seat himself across from her and pour two steamy cups of coffee. His dark blue uniform was uncharacteristically wrinkled, his face unshaven and lined with weariness.

Taking the hot cup of coffee from Lafflin, Laurel struggled not to fling the scalding brew in his face as she remembered how he had deliberately shamed her two mornings previous. Yet she knew to show hostility would defeat her purpose at the moment. "You've been waiting for me all night?" she asked in mock amazement, casually sipping her coffee.

He laughed ruefully. "Hardly. What I've been doing all night is none of your goddamned business, to quote your pet phrase. But I have been waiting for you for perhaps a quarter hour. I must say, dear, that your sense of timing is not very imaginative." As he sipped his own coffee, his eyes fixed upon the tiny flag pinned upon the bosom of her gown. "May I compliment you on your—patriotism, Miss Ashland."

Laurel noisily put down her coffee cup and glowered up at Lafflin. Ever since her confrontation with Lafflin two days earlier, she had worn the tiny Confederate flag as her banner, to symbolize to him that she refused to accept the degradation he had tried to heap upon her. She was about to issue a sharp rejoinder to his sarcasm when the back door to the dining hall opened and Reba entered the room, carrying a cobalt-blue crock covered with a white cloth, two earthen-ware bowls and spoons. Spotting Laurel, she stopped in her tracks, throwing the younger woman a murderous glare. "M'sieur, you did not inform me that your guest for breakfast was to be—a woman," she said defensively to Jacob Lafflin.

Lafflin turned to scowl at Reba impatiently. "Put down the cereal and quit meddling in matters that are none of your concern, wench!" he barked.

Reba moved forward, her yellow eyes sullen, her mouth petulent as she placed the crock and the bowls on the table top. Laurel, noticing her chagrin, gave the older woman a poisonous smile.

Reba spun about to leave as Jacob Lafflin uncovered the crock, took the serving spoon, and inquired of Laurel, "How hungry are you this morning, sweetheart?"

Laurel's jaw dropped. "Surely you don't expect me to eat that slop! I'm sure the witch poisoned it!"

Surprisingly, Lafflin chuckled as Reba spun about to face her accuser, brown hands on her hips, gold eyes blazing.

"Did you poison the gruel, Reba?" Lafflin asked.

Reba quickly moved forward, like a sleek cat preparing to pounce. She grabbed the full serving spoon from Jacob Lafflin, raised it to her lips, and quickly consumed a large mouthful of the yellow cereal. Then, in a gesture of con-tempt, she shoved the spoon deep into the crock, whirled, and left the room, slamming the door with a resounding bang.

Jacob Lafflin grinned as he served up a heaping bowlful of the corn mush. "Females!" he groaned, handing the steaming gruel to Laurel.

When she did not take the bowl, Lafflin placed it in front of her. "Dig in."

"Are you out of your mind?" Laurel spat back incredulously.

"You expect me to eat this after that—that snake woman just licked the serving spoon!"

Jacob Lafflin laughed, shaking his head. "My, you are a snob, aren't you, sweetheart?" Giving her a nasty smile, he added, "Do think twice before you refuse my generous hospitality, Miss Ashland, for at the moment, nothing would give me greater pleasure than to shove your lovely pink and white face into this cereal crock."

Laurel gaped at Lafflin in astonishment, her blue eyes enormous, but he merely nodded back meaningfully.

Uttering a cry of frustrated rage, Laurel grabbed her spoon and began shoving the gruel in her mouth. In a voice gravelly from the corn mush, she muttered defiantly, "That she-devil is probably outside spitting out her poison at this very moment!"

"Doubtless," Jacob sarcastically concurred, taking a large bite of the gruel himself.

For a few moments, they ate in silence. Laurel grudgingly admitted to herself that the corn mush was quite good; as she downed the last of her coffee, she began to feel calmer.

Jacob Lafflin put down his spoon and leaned back in his chair. "Where are you going this morning, Laurel?"

"Nowhere," Laurel replied, adding contemptuously, "and when I fail to show up, today's meeting in the central market will be called off."

"Not true," Lafflin countered. "The Confederates officers will attend. You've ensured that, by delivering to them the letter from your coconspirators."

Laurel shrugged, saying mysteriously, "Perhaps someone will warn the officers before they arrive at the market."

"Perhaps," Lafflin agreed, smiling and showing his teeth. "But it won't be you."

A tense silence followed. Finally, Laurel threw her hands wide in exasperation. "Oh, this is ridiculous! You already know our officers are coming—their capture is guaranteed. Very well, Captain. I'm to go to the Tremont Hotel this morning, to obtain a letter from—a friend. Then I'm to meet the Confederate officers in the market at noon, leading them to a place of safety so they may meet with—representatives from the town.''

"Where will this meeting occur?" Lafflin asked.

Laurel's eyes rolled heavenward as she retorted condescendingly, "That information is in the message waiting for me at the Tremont, of course. My—friends thought it best we delay the decision regarding the meeting place until the last possible moment—to keep the enemy from gaining the information.''

"Shrewd," Lafflin agreed amiably.

Laurel glared at the Yankee through narrowed eyes. "It really makes no difference what's in the letter now, Captain, since I have no intention of going to the market and aiding you in your—plot. When the officers discover there is no one there to lead them to the meeting, they'll simply leave.''

"Will they, now?" Lafflin inquired silkily. "How far do you think they'll get with bullets in their guts?''

Laurel's eyes grew huge, but she said nothing.

Jacob Lafflin got to his feet, circled the table, and stopped in front of Laurel. He placed one brown hand on each of her shoulders and looked down at her, his features hard and unemotional. "What a little fool you are. Jesus, I rejoice that you're' not fighting on our side, else you'd have already lost the war for us. Do you realize you've given me all the information I need, that I now hold all the cards? All I have to do to capture the Confederate officers is to surround the market at noon. And all I have to do to find out where the spy ring is waiting for them is to go to the Tremont Hotel and get the letter.''

"They might not give you the letter," Laurel said hopefully.

Lafflin laughed shortly, released Laurel, and moved off

toward the window. Moving aside the curtain and gazing out at the quiet street, he said dryly, "You're undoubtedly the most inept group of spies I've ever come across. Putting all your plans down on parchment, like a group of schoolboys. Indeed, you've spoon-fed us everything we need to know."

Laurel drew herself up haughtily and stared at Lafflin in stony silence.

Lafflin returned to her side. "Your one remaining decision, dear Laurel, shall be the manner in which your fellow Confederates will be captured," he said, his tone menacing.

"What do you mean?" she asked suspiciously.

"Whether they shall be taken alive or dead."

"You bastard!" she gasped.

A spark of anger blazed in Jacob's eyes at Laurel's invective, yet then those same brown orbs narrowed in implacable resolve. "You'll not find a bunch of saints winning this war," he told her coolly. Tilting her chin so that she met his determined gaze fully, he added, "Hear this well, Laurel. If you follow through on your plans precisely and lead the officers from the market to the specified site, I give you my word, I'll try my best to capture them and the others alive. But if you cross me and give warning, I'll order my men to fire at will. And I can't promise that they'll exclude you—or any bystanders who may become inadvertently involved—from the exchange."

"You're despicable!" Laurel spat. Then, in a voice laced with hostility, she demanded, "Anyway, why should I trust you?"

"Why should I trust you?" he countered.

For a moment Laurel was silent, her face a study of warring emotions. Then she let out her breath in a ragged sigh and said bitterly, "Very well, Captain, you have a deal. You seem to hold all the cards at the moment. May I go fetch the letter now?"

Lafflin pulled Laurel to her feet. "No. You may go

straight to your room. I'm going to awaken Wilson to watch you, then I'll find that little maid of yours and send her for the letter.''

"As you wish, Captain," Laurel gritted.

Sweeping about to leave him, Laurel heard him call after her, "Shall we seal our bargain with a kiss, sweetheart?"

Laurel whirled upon him, her eyes shooting blue sparks. "Certainly, Captain, that's exactly what you must do!" Gesturing toward the back door, she added sweetly, 'I do believe there's a pig penned up near the kitchen. By all means, go seal our bargain with a kiss—that is, if you can convince the pig to tolerate you that long!"

Laurel spun about disdainfully and left him. But she heard the sound of his deep laughter all the way up the stairs.

Chapter
Seventeen

Laurel and Fancy stood at the center of the market. Laurel was outwardly calm as she held an empty wicker basket; Fancy's dark eyes seemed to dart in every direction at once as she nervously twisted her fingers and waited with her mistress.

Half an hour earlier, Lafflin had come to Laurel's room, informing her that she was to go to the market with Fancy, then lead the Confederate officers to the site chosen for the meeting. Though he didn't show her the letter Fancy fetched from the Tremont, he informed her that the meeting was to be held at the courthouse on Twentieth Street.

Laurel glanced about intently, looking for any gentleman sporting an oleander blossom in his lapel. Her search was fruitless; indeed, the market had a deserted air this morning. Most of the stands were closed; those few remaining open were manned by a few blacks selling fish and produce. The customers consisted of three shabbily dressed negroes and a bent old white woman, dressed in a faded calico gown and wearing a huge slat-bonnet.

"Here, make yourself useful," Laurel told Fancy, shoving the basket at her. As the girl took the basket, Laurel adjusted the white turban on her head and pulled her wool shawl more tightly about her. She wrinkled her nose as a cool breeze swept over her. Even on this rather chilly morning, the odor of fish in the market was pungent and quite unpleasant.

Laurel turned, eyeing Fancy with distaste. "Fancy, you look like a refugee from a slaughterhouse this morning," she complained, studying the girl's red-stained apron. "What have you been doing—butchering pigs? You might have at least removed that nauseating apron!"

"Miss Laurel, I don't like the sound of things this morning," Fancy replied nervously. "First, Captain Lafflin, he send me to fetch that letter. Then later he come get me whilst I is chopping chickens and he tell me I go wid you to the market. He say if'n we make one wrong move, we is worse off than the chickens!" Sighing heavily, her bosom heaving, Fancy reached into the huge pocket of her blood-spattered apron, her trembling black hand grasping an object and raising it upward slightly, to reveal to Laurel the handle of a butcher knife. "I tell you, I don't like the sound of things this morning, Miss Laurel."

Eyes wide with astonishment, Laurel gazed at her with new respect—Fancy was demonstrating much forethought and ingenuity this morning. As the servant hastily concealed her knife, Laurel spotted a tall man dressed in black crossing the street to enter the market. She grabbed the basket back from Fancy, and her breath caught in her throat as the gentleman drew closer. The bearded man smiled and tipped his hat at Laurel. As she noted that he wore no flower in his lapel, he walked off to a fruit stand and began examining vegetables.

A few moments, later, a second man, similarly dressed, entered the market. Laurel recognized J. W. Moore, who was the acting mayor of Galveston. One of the most prominent citizens of the town, Moore was a patron of St. Ursuline's. On occasion, Laurel had seen Moore visiting there, conferring with Mother St. Pierre.

As Moore approached the two girls, his gait surprisingly lively for a man who must be in his mid-sixties, Laurel smiled as she spotted the lilac oleander bloom in his lapel.

Moore paused before the two girls, tipping his black silk hat at Laurel, his fine eyes sparkling with amusement Then, winking at Laurel, he pulled the flower from his lapel, depositing it in the basket she held. "For you, pretty lady," he told Laurel, his voice carrying a silky timbre of culture and wit.

As Moore moved off toward a fish stand, Fancy asked confusedly, "Why he do that?"

Laurel did not reply as her bright blue eyes noted the presence of two more darkly clad gentlemen in the market. Within a few moments, four more men arrived—all wore black, and three sported oleander blooms. One by one, the men stopped to greet Laurel, then went about their business in the market.

"Ain't never seen so much black 'cept at a funeral," Fancy commented in befuddlement.

Again, Laurel was silent as she fingered the four oleander blooms now in her basket—lilac, white, pink, and blood red . . .

Jacob Lafflin stood in the dusty front office of the deserted *News* Building, gazing out at Market Street. Andrew Wilson stood beside him; in the hallway to their left, a dozen sailors awaited Lafflin's command, holding rifles with bayonets affixed and whispering to one another in strained tones.

Soon the Rebs would be coming—just as Lafflin thought they would.

"Are you sure they'll march this way, sir?" Wilson asked his commander.

Sweeping dust from the window through which he gazed, Lafflin nodded. "It's the most logical approach. However, I've men stationed on the streets to the north and south of us, just in case they've decided to change directions since we got our last report from the scouts."

Wilson nodded while Lafflin, his eyes fixed upon the street, grew tense. "This may be news now."

In the hallway to the left, the front door of the building opened noisily. Within seconds, a young sailor bolted into the room, his face flushed as he panted for air. "Sir, they're within two blocks of us!"

Lafflin nodded. "Good work, sailor. You may join the others."

As the boy left the room, Lafflin drew the sheer panels to obscure them from the soon-to-approach Confederates. Then he and Wilson tensely watched the street. They had not long to wait, for soon a long gray line of men moved into view. The soldiers were led by a tall officer wearing an elegant uniform with tails, a sword at his side, a plumed gray hat on his head. The rest of the platoon followed him, carrying rifles and wearing ragtag gray uniforms and a mismatched assortment of caps.

"Got us outnumbered three to one, sir," Wilson whispered from Lafflin's side. "But we got the advantage of surprise."

"Aye," Lafflin concurred, watching the line of perhaps forty men move into full view. Then suddenly his gaze darted to the intersection east of them. "Blast! Here comes one of the brave citizens of Galveston. An unwelcome complication."

Wilson and Lafflin were rigidly silent as a young gentleman dressed in a white frock coat, dark trousers, and wearing a brown panama hat came around the corner from Twenty-first Street onto Market. Spotting the platoon of Confederates soldiers, he stopped in his tracks.

The Confederate officer, seeing the young man, ordered his troups to halt. Then he approached the gentleman and started a conversation with him, pointing at the young man's clothing as he spoke.

"The Confederate major is no doubt curious as to how this able-bodied young man escaped conscription," Lafflin commented to Wilson in a low voice heavy with irony.

Wilson nodded. "A dandy, by the looks of him, sir."

Though Wilson and Lafflin could not understand the conversation from where they stood, the building animosity between the two men was obvious as the exchange grew more animated—both were now shouting and gesturing angrily. Suddenly, the Confederate officer reached out to grab the younger man's arm, and the boy dodged him, running off and screaming, in a voice that could be heard even where the Yankees stood, "Help! Murder! Police!"

Jacob Lafflin shook his head, smiling cynically at his companion. "What the lad lacks in courage he makes up for in bravado."

Out on the street, the Confederate soldiers looked about in confusion, talking nervously among themselves as the disgruntled officer returned to his men. The major's sharp command of "Attention!" was met with instant obedience. But then a loud bell began clanging to the north of them and the Confederate soldiers again became noisy and disorderly.

The bell continued to ring interminably. "Some idiot's obviously set off the fire alarm," Jacob Lafflin commented in disbelief.

Just then, three men—obviously citizens of the town— came racing around the corner from Twenty-first Street. Suddenly, one of the Confederate soldiers stepped out of line, raised his weapon, and fired. A citizen fell to a heap on the street.

"Jesus!" Wilson gasped. "Have the Rebs lost their wits, sir?"

"That appears to be the case, Wilson, " Lafflin replied grimly, watching with perverse fascination as the two gentlemen and the Rebel officer pored over the body of the wounded, elderly man. The other soldiers milled about nervously as the boy who had fired began backing away.

"The old man who was shot wore a cap similar to that of our soldiers—that's the only sense I can make of it," Lafflin commented.

As the two Yankees watched, the three men who had been examining the body sprang to their feet. One of the citizens shook his fist at the young Confederate soldier and screamed, "You little bastard! You killed Rohledder!"

The young soldier looked about in alarm, then panicked, throwing his rifle to the ground and racing off, pursued by the two other citizens and the Rebel commander.

Jacob Lafflin laughed his amazement as he looked at the confused Confederate soldiers who remained standing in the street, minus their officer. "I don't know why we bothered to come out this morning, Wilson. Looks like the Rebs are perfectly capable of engineering their own defeat."

"Aye, sir," Wilson concurred.

Then a curious thing occurred. Though the fire bell had ceased ringing, the troops out on the street suddenly panicked, racing off in the direction their commander had taken. "What the hell—" Jacob Lafflin muttered.

Then he saw the cause of their fright. A detachment of Union troops, led by Commander Renshaw and Captain Law, was marching briskly toward them from the east, and they were now within a block of the *News* building. As Lafflin watched, Renshaw gave the command to pursue the fleeing Confederates. The Yankees gave chase, firing at the men in gray.

Inside the *News* building, Lafflin inquired of his companion, "Well, Wilson, shall we help our boys bid the Rebs farewell?"

Wilson nodded his agreement, and he and Lafflin hurried to the foyer, Lafflin issuing crisp orders to his dozen men to pursue the Confederates and fire at will.

Seconds later, they were out on Market Street, chasing the Confederates with the others. The men in gray returned only scattered fire as the Union soldiers chased them down and picked them off one by one.

Jacob Lafflin squeezed the trigger on his Colt Navy and watched one of the Rebs fall to the street, a bright patch of red obliterating the gray back of his jacket.

While Lafflin hurried on, recocking his pistol, his eyes were filled with bitter anger. It didn't sit well with him, shooting men in the back—a soldier deserved a better death than that. But it was the Reb commander's fault, for losing his head and deserting his men.

Lafflin paused, raised his pistol, and squeezed off another round. In front of him, a Confederate soldier jerked spasmodically, then fell forward, a crimson blot upon the sandy street . . .

In the market, panic ensued when the fire bell began to clang. All of the customers in the market, including the eight gentlemen who had recently arrived, dashed for the various exits. But before anyone could leave, dozens of Yankee soldiers streamed into the area, seemingly materializing out of thin air.

Laurel glanced about wildly as the men in blue poured out of every building in the vicinity. "Damn! There must be a hundred of them!" she gasped.

The Yankees encircled the citizens in the market, closing

in. Though Laurel and the eight black-clad gentlemen from the town struggled not to betray their trepidation to the Yankees, all of the blacks shook with fear, and the old woman in the slat-bonnet fainted.

Laurel watched, horrified, as Commodore Renshaw came forward, along with Captain Law and Seaman Carter. The bell continued to peal unmercifully as the commodore's piercing eyes fixed upon Laurel and a meaningful, victorious smile twisted his lips. Turning to Carter, the commodore said briskly, "Seaman, take these citizens to the Virginia House and hold them there under arrest."

While Carter said, "Aye, sir," and began selecting men to help with the surveillance, J. W. Moore called out to Renshaw, "May I ask the reason for our detention, sir?"

Renshaw turned to Moore, his brow furrowed. Before the commodore could reply, the fire bell ceased its din; for a moment, Renshaw delayed his remarks, carefully watching the reaction of his uneasy captives during the ominous silence that followed.

Finally, Renshaw told Moore, "You and these others are being arrested for spying."

Upon hearing the Yankee commander's devastating charge, the captives uttered in unison a cry of dismay, and the old woman whom Fancy had just helped to her feet tottered and grasped her chest, hanging on to Fancy for support. Renshaw, ignoring the citizens, turned to Captain Law, issuing addition crisp orders. Within seconds, Renshaw, Law, and most of the soldiers had left the market, leaving the citizens at the mercy of Abel Carter and about ten other seamen.

Laurel felt her skin crawl as she met the hateful gaze of Carter, whose water blue eyes were fixed upon her now, as if he were devising a thousand methods for dealing her a slow and agonizing death. The burly man's eyes now gleamed with what looked to be a perverse realization; he nodded meaningfully toward Laurel, an evil smile upon his cracked lips. Carter then ordered the citizens and blacks to form a single line, and the somberly silent group of captives left the market, flanked on either side by rifle-toting sailors. Laurel and Fancy were at the end of the line; Carter followed them, and Laurel could almost feel his hard gaze boring into her head.

As they turned a corner, Laurel was suddenly grabbed about the waist. Before she could cry out, Abel Carter dragged her back around a building, pulling her toward the door to a warehouse. "We got some business to finish, wench," he growled.

"No!" Laurel screamed, realizing his intent and kicking and screaming, digging her heels into the board walkway. But her cries were drowned out by the sounds of gunfire, which now came pelting forth from somewhere to the west of them. Laurel desperately realized that the soldiers in charge of the other civilians could not hear her screams. Would they care if they could?

Holding the squirming girl firmly about the waist, Carter kicked open the flimsy side door to the warehouse and dragged Laurel into the dark, musty-smelling interior. They had no sooner gotten inside when Fancy bolted in behind them. "You let Miss Laurel go!" the girl screamed at Carter, reaching for the pocket of her apron.

With a curse, Carter tossed aside his rifle and threw Laurel to the floor; for a moment, her mind spun in blackness as the breath was whisked from her lungs. Then consciousness returned, just in time for Laurel to watch Carter fling Fancy against the wall as if she were a sack of potatoes. An awful cracking sound came forth as Fancy's head banged the wall; then the slave collapsed into a limp heap in the shadows.

Laurel sprang to her feet, reeling, her head spinning crazily. "Oh my God—Fancy—"

But Carter grabbed her violently before she could move

toward Fancy. His arm clenching brutally about her middle, he snarled, "Hush, whore! I'm going to use you in ways you never dreamt of!"

And he threw her to the floor in the darkness.

It was the nightmare of the night at the hotel, only worse—for this time there was no Jacob Lafflin to rescue her, and Fancy was surely dead! Carter's heavy weight pressed down upon her, threatening to crack her ribs. The sadistic Yankee ripped the Confederate flag from Laurel's bosom and shook it in her face, threatening, "When I'm through with you, bitch, I'm stuffing this down your throat—and I hope you gag on it!"

Laurel tried to cry out, but Carter smothered her lips with a savage kiss, the rough texture of his mouth like cracked leather on hers and tasting vilely of soured liquor. Swept with revulsion, Laurel clawed at the seaman's cheek with her fingernails and felt the wetness of his blood on her fingertips. He cursed and drew back, and Laurel noted with vindictive satisfaction the wicked stripes now staining his cheeks. "That was a mistake, whore!" he growled ferociously, his eyes seeming to glow fiendishly in the shadowy void. Gesturing toward his rifle off to the side of them, he continued vengefully, "When I'm through with you, slut, it's my rifle I'm stuffing down your throat, and blowing your guts to the four winds. Think of that while your legs is spread!"

Carter's fleshy hand slapped her hard across the face—not once, but again and again, until her flesh grew numb and she lost count of the vicious blows. As consciousness grew elusive, she felt her clothing being ripped. Her breasts felt the cool shock of air inside the warehouse, then her pantalets were shredded, her legs brutally spread.

Instinctively, the muscles of Laurel's thighs tightened and clenched as her body anticipated the searing pain of rape. She felt something hard and repulsive push hurtfully against her most intimate parts, then a shrill, horrible scream echoed through the deep cavern of the warehouse. Hazily, it occurred to Laurel that the voice she heard was not her own, yet in her dazed state, the realization seemed meaningless.

"Miss Laurel—get up, please!" a hysterical voice insisted.

Laurel opened swollen eyelids, gazing up at the blurry image of Fancy. "Fancy, you're alive," she moaned weakly.

"I ain't for long if'n you don't get up, Miss Laurel!" the girl squealed fretfully, tugging on Laurel's arm.

With Fancy's help, Laurel got shakily to her feet. She tottered as the younger girl picked up Laurel's shawl from the floor, covering her mistress's gaping bosom and rearranging Laurel's torn clothing to preserve as much modesty as possible. Hearing a moan to her left, Laurel turned and saw Abel Carter lying prone on the floor next to them, blood oozing from his back, a butcher knife protruding from his shoulder. "Fancy, you—you saved my life!" Laurel gasped. And my virtue, she added ruefully to herself.

"Yes'um," Fancy said, tugging at Laurel's hand. 'Now we is running!"

As the two girls turned to leave, Fancy swayed, almost collapsing. Laurel steadied her with an arm and noted the blood staining the black girl's turban at the back of her head. "Why that bastard Carter! Come on, Fancy, let's get out of here and tend your wound."

Ignoring the now screaming man on the floor, the two girls quickly exited the building, entering the cool, sunny street. Instinctively, Laurel headed for the academy. It was the most logical place to go, she thought to herself, for surely death or imprisonment awaited them back at the Virginia House. Laurel pulled Fancy along by the hand, glancing worriedly at the bloody lump protruding from the younger girl's turban. They reached the corner and were turning south when Laurel's body ran full force into the muscular frame of a man.

Oddly, she had almost expected him to be there. Hard arms closed about her, and she looked up at his face—at implacable features that showed no hint of mercy, at dark, pitiless eyes. Her heart thudded in desolation.

"The game is up, sweetheart," Jacob Lafflin said.

Chapter
Eighteen

The anteroom was shadowy and still, the curtains drawn. Laurel sat alone, leaning against the wall, looking as limp and tired as a rag doll. After they returned to the hotel an hour earlier, she had changed her clothing and bathed her face but then had collapsed upon her pallet, the deepest dread filling her mind as to what would happen next.

For as Jacob Lafflin was leading the girls back to the Virginia House two hours earlier, they had once again passed the warehouse, and Lafflin had heard Carter moaning. Laurel shuddered as she remembered the look of bewilderment on Lafflin's face as he gazed at the wounded seaman. He had then given the girls a hard, appraising stare; his dark eyes had been emotionless as he studied Laurel's disheveled appearance and swollen face.

Laurel wondered what lies Abel Carter might be telling Jacob Lafflin at this very moment, if indeed Carter was even alive now. For the sailor had bled copiously as two seamen carried him back to the hotel.

Laurel stiffened as she heard muffled, angry voices coming from downstairs. Was her fate being decided at this very moment? And what of poor Fancy and the citizens of the town who were now in the dining room under guard?

Laurel longed to be with the others. She thought unkindly that Jacob Lafflin must have taken devious pleasure in leaving her alone in the anteroom with Wilson standing guard outside. At least the prisoners in the dining hall could comfort one another; Laurel's sole companion was the devastating fear running havoc in her mind.

Suddenly, Laurel jerked upright as she heard the door open in the next room, then footsteps slowly approaching her door. Her heart pounded so hard, she feared it would burst from her chest as she realized the next few seconds would reveal whether she lived or died.

Shakily, she got to her feet, praying that her features did not reveal her terror and that her legs would not collapse beneath her as her eyes fastened upon the door to her room, watching the knob turn ever so slowly . . .

Jacob Lafflin started up the stairs, feeling exhausted. The scene with Renshaw had been difficult. But he had done his best; now came the unpleasant task of dealing with Laurel.

At the top of the stairs, he paused. Could he go through with it—tell Laurel what he knew he should? Perhaps he shouldn't. No, he had no choice. He couldn't just let it pass this time; there was too much at stake.

He moved slowly toward the door, nodding at Wilson and saying softly, "I'll take over."

For a moment, he stood watching Wilson amble off. Then he turned to the door, his face lined with sadness. "Damnit, Laurel, why did you do it?"

He opened the door to his room and started wearily across to the anteroom. His face was tight, controlled. For her own good, he would not let her see his anger—or his disappointment . . .

Laurel twisted her fingers nervously as Jacob Lafflin opened the door to the anteroom. "Good afternoon, sweetheart," he said.

His tone was heavy with cynicism, his eyes flat and cold; Laurel realized with sinking desolation that she was in deep, deep trouble.

Jacob took a step toward her, reached out, and grasped her hand. "Pray join me in my room, Miss Ashland."

Numbly, she followed him, looking at his broad back as she heard him murmur, "My dear, your hand is like ice. Something troubling you?"

He took her to the straight chair, his strong hands gently pushing her down. Then he strode through the shadowy light to the window, drew back the curtains and pulled up the sash, flooding the room with a chill breeze and bright afternoon sunshine.

He came back to her and she blinked up at him, staring at the coppery halo the sun had cast about his head. She searched his face, the familiar classically handsome lines, but saw only tight weariness and a sadness approaching resignation. She shivered, drawing her shawl tightly about her.

"You've been a very busy little girl today," he began with deceptive smoothness. "Let's see—lying, spying, attempted murder."

Laurel gulped. "What do you mean?"

Lafflin shook his head and laughed ruefully. "Isn't it a bit late for more lies, dear? Shall I give you an account of your activities during the past few weeks?"

"Can I stop you?" she countered bitterly.

"No."

Lafflin moved off and seated himself in the wing chair

across from her. Rubbing his jaw, he mused thoughtfully, "Where shall I begin? At the beginning, I suppose. For some weeks, Miss Ashland, you have been meeting with fellow spies from the city—probably at night. You and your cohorts devised a scheme. By allowing us to intercept your 'correspondence,' you would convince us that the Confederate officers from the mainland were coming to Galveston on this day and assembling in the central market, from thence to be led to a place of safety where they could meet with the spy ring from the city. Then, instead of sending Confederate officers to the market today, you dispatched a collection of elderly gentlemen, respected citizens of the town, who were all above reproach. To add to the confusion, you designated in one of your letters that each of the 'officers' should wear an oleander bloom in his lapel. Then you had half the civilians arrive without the flowers while the others removed them." He paused. "Am I correct so far, dear?"

Laurel yawned with a feigned disinterest she far from felt. "A tale of fiction, Captain, and a boring one at that. But I do suppose there's no silencing you."

"You suppose correctly. The purpose of your intrigue, as we saw it, was to lure Union soldiers and officers into the vicinity of the market at noon. Confederate soldiers, arriving by boat on the west side of the island, would then converge upon the market, hopefully surrounding and capturing the Union troops and their officers."

Twisting the fringe of her shawl, Laurel did not reply.

"I, of course, knew all along that you were trying to deceive us," Lafflin continued casually. "Actually, dear, your performance was rather amateurish—like that morning you deliberately stumbled about in the the dark, then so conveniently saw to it that I received the most helpful letter."

Laurel's head shot up, her wrath spurring her to abandon further pretense. "You mean you knew—that very morning—

about our ploy, and still you—you humiliated me out on the street that day, when you gave me the flag?''

He smiled bitterly. ''I had to convince you that I believed you were turning traitor to the South.''

She bolted to her feet, shaking her fist at him. ''You bastard!''

Raising a black brow at her, Lafflin replied with cool contempt, ''Careful, dear, you're in serious trouble already. And have you no curiosity about what actually transpired today, and the fate of your friends downstairs?''

Laurel sobered instantly. Her face paling and her legs buckling beneath her, she collapsed upon her chair.

''That's better,'' Lafflin said. ''Since we saw through your scheme, we decided to station troops in the various buildings surrounding the market. My detachment was assigned the task of reconnoitering the streets in search of Confederate troops as they entered the island and moved toward the market. If we spotted Rebel activity, we were to allow the soldiers to pass through, then attack their flank, forcing them to march into the central market. We would then converge upon the Rebs, trapping them, just as they intended to trap us.''

Her eyes growing huge, Laurel was silent.

Jacob laughed humorlessly and shook his head as he crossed long legs. ''Such were our plans. What actually happened today was the most farcical military maneuver I have ever witnessed. While approaching the market, your gallant boys in gray spotted a young man from the island whom they desired to conscript. He, however, did not share their zeal and scurried away, setting off a general alarm. In the ensuing panic, one of your most prominent citizens was shot by a Confederate soldier.'' Again, Jacob shook his head. ''It seems we Federals must protect the Confederate citizens here on the island from being rescued by their own kind! At any rate, following the ignoble act by the panicky Reb soldier, he and the balance of the Confederates soldiers fled the island, but not before we managed to kill a good two dozen of them.''

Laurel sighed heavily as Lafflin said what she was thinking. "So all your plotting was for naught, dear. Now all that remains for us is to punish the offenders."

Laurel blinked rapidly, staring at Lafflin intently.

Jacob uncrossed his legs and leaned forward, resting his elbows on his knees and lacing long brown fingers as he continued to speak in an unemotional voice. "I'll end the suspense, dear. The citizens from the town will be released— much as Renshaw wanted to clap them all in irons or worse, I convinced him that punishing a group of geriatics would only outrage the enemy and encourage more of this type of activity. Though obviously some of the gentlemen in the market returned here from the mainland just to participate, there was the convenient confusion about who wore the damning oleander blooms—which tipped the scale in their favor somewhat.''

Laurel heaved a sigh of relief. Though Billy Hendley had recruited the men and she knew none of them personally, other than Moore, the idea of the genteel oldsters suffering would have filled her with debilitating guilt under the circumstances.

"Don't relax yet, dear," Lafflin warned, his expression stern. "We have yet to speak . . .'' his voice trailed off ominously.

"Yes?" Laurel croaked.

"Of you." He took a sharp breath, then plunged on. "Laurel, it grieves me to tell you this, but you will be shipped north as soon as there is a ship available. There, you will be tried for spying.''

"Oh my God!" Laurel gasped, her hands flying to her face.

Lafflin sat back in his chair and gestured resignedly. "I urged the commodore to be lenient, but Renshaw was adamant on that point. You see, he has known of your activities all along."

Laurel's composure cracked as she stared at Lafflin with naked fear. "He—he's known all along? Then if—if I'm found guilty—"

Jacob cleared his throat, looking quite uncomfortable now. "You'll be imprisoned, or..." his voice again faded, and he averted his gaze from hers.

Laurel drew her hands through her hair and stared mutely at the floor, her mind splintering.

"Actually, you're the lucky one," she heard Lafflin say. "You, at least, have a chance. You might consider poor Fancy."

"Fancy!" Laurel's head shot up. "Oh my God. Fancy—I hadn't thought—" She gulped convulsively, then blurted, "Jacob, please, you must do something! Carter tried to rape me again! Fancy saved my life! Surely Carter will admit that, if—oh, Jacob, is he still alive?"

"He's alive." Jacob stood, moving slowly to her side and looking down at her, his expression sad, almost kind. "And I'd tell you what he had to say about the incident, but I'm sure you can guess, dear."

Laurel nodded desolately. "Fancy only wanted to save me!" she half sobbed, her voice small and pathetic.

Jacob reached out and stroked Laurel's cheek gently, fingering the shadow of a welt that marred her porcelain skin. His voice was sincere as he whispered, "I believe you, dear."

The awkward moment ended; Jacob tore his gaze from Laurel's and cleared his throat. "Laurel, I'm sorry, but it's out of my hands. Whatever her reason, Fancy is guilty of attempted murder of a Union soldier.''

"And?" Laurel choked, looking up at him with her heart in her eyes.

"And she faces the firing squad at dawn."

Chapter
Nineteen

Laurel stood, with Wilson, facing the closed door to the room in which Fancy was imprisoned. She reached for the lock, then hesitated, a million thoughts swirling through her agonized brain. Were they actually going to shoot—kill? —Fancy tomorrow morning? Might this be the last time she ever saw her servant? Was there naught she could do to save the girl?

Laurel tried to steady herself. It was absolutely imperative that she not let Fancy see the torment she was feeling.

Miserably, Laurel remembered her last words with Jacob Lafflin in the room upstairs. "Fancy will lose her mind when she finds out about tomorrow," she had told him desperately.

Lafflin had sighed, giving Laurel an understanding look, along with a gesture of compassion. "Don't tell her, then," he had suggested. "Let the poor soul have a peaceful night."

Lafflin was right, Laurel reflected unhappily. Naught could

183

be accomplished by telling Fancy of her fate. And though
Laurel despised Jacob Lafflin as the bearer of the tragic
announcement, she had to admit to herself that it was
human of the Yankee to let her have some time alone with
her servant.

Behind her, Wilson cleared his throat nervously. "Miss,
are you ready to go in?"

Laurel nodded shakily, her eyes apprehensively fixed
upon the dark oak door before her.

Smiling lamely, Wilson drew back the bolt and swung the
door open with a labored creak.

Laurel entered the small, musty, shadowy room, and the
door squeaked shut behind her. She spotted Fancy sitting on
the floor in the far corner, propped up against the wall like a
rag doll, her outline just revealed by the dismal light
filtering through the small, dusty window above her—an
opening too tiny for either of them to crawl through, Laurel
noted with dismay.

"Miss Laurel!" the slave whispered hoarsely, struggling
to get to her feet.

'Don't you dare get up, Fancy!" Laurel scolded, shaking
a slim finger at the slave. "With that nasty bump on your
head, you'll surely swoon."

"Yes 'um," Fancy replied, sighing gratefully as she
gingerly stroked her bandage-wrapped head.

The gesture wrenched Laurel's heart as she moved across
the narrow room. Fingering the dusty sleeve of a great coat
that hung from the long rack lining the wall, Laurel commented
with distaste, "The Yankees are surely the cruelest of
captors, stuffing you away in the cloakroom like this."

"It don't matter, Miss Laurel," Fancy commented
resignedly. "I is pleased to be away from Reba."

"I'll bet you are." Laurel seated herself on the floor
beside her servant, wrapping her arms about her knees as
she turned to gaze at the girl. Fancy still wore the blood-

spattered apron she had hidden the knife in earlier—the knife she had used to save her mistress's life. The thought filled Laurel with a surge of pride, followed by a sick welling of sorrow and fear. Fancy's devotion to her mistress, her heroism, meant she would lose her own life tomorrow. It just wasn't fair!

Laurel continued to study the younger girl. Funny, she thought with a shiver, now that she was about to lose Fancy, it was as if she were seeing her for the first time, at last considering her an individual, a person. She gazed intently at Fancy's face, noting the clear, youthful cocoa-colored skin, the large, expressive dark brown eyes, the impish, upturned features. Fancy's milk-white teeth now nervously bit her full lower lip—the slave's only betrayal of what must surely be her terror at her present plight.

Why, she's just like me! Laurel suddenly thought. She has feelings, thoughts, fears in her head just like I do! We could be sisters. She's just like me—only her skin is black.

A wave of shame swept Laurel as she thought of her callous treatment of Fancy over the years. The girl had never been more than a pet, a toy to Laurel, and whenever the slave had failed in the slightest to please her demanding mistress, she had invariably received the full brunt of Laurel's hair-triggered temper.

Laurel again remembered the day when she was five years old and had dressed up her two-year-old black baby doll in the finest hand-embroidered baby clothes, dangling bracelets, beads, and rings from the child and nicknaming her Fancy. Why, even the poor girl's name wasn't her own, and since Fancy's family was only too happy to have her brought up in the big house, she had spent her entire short life as the exclusive possession of a spoiled, willful young planter's daughter.

A short life, indeed—grievously short at the moment! Thinking of the morrow, Laurel felt tears welling in her eyes and choked back a sob, grateful for the darkness that cloaked her trepidation and grief.

"Miss Laurel, is you all right?" Fancy asked.

Laurel blinked at Fancy through tears. "Y—yes," she choked.

"Them Yankees, they whip you for what you done?" Fancy asked fretfully, her brow puckered in a frown.

Fancy's last question was too much for Laurel. The black girl, with her life hanging by a thread, was concerned only for her mistress! With a cry of anguish, Laurel fell into convulsive weeping. Oh God, how could she live without her Fancy? Her companion. Her sister.

"Miss Laurel, what the matter? Them Yankees going to whip you later?"

Laurel shook her head and sobbed loudly. After a moment, overwhelmed by the excruciating flood of feelings she was experiencing, she turned to the slave, clutching the younger girl in her arms. "Oh, Fancy, Fancy, you saved my life," she moaned, holding the younger girl tightly. "You saved my life and I've never done a damn thing for you—except to cause you grief."

For a moment the black girl was silent, her face pressed against Laurel's shoulder. Finally, timidly, she asked, "Miss Laurel, what them Yankees going to do with us? Is we in real bad trouble this time?"

Laurel's arms instinctively tightened about the slave. At last, the question had come. Bless her heart, Fancy knew something was amiss and could hold back her own trepidation no longer.

"The Yankees are madder than a hornet's nest, but they'll get over it," Laurel lied, her voice shaking. She pulled back slightly and gazed down at Fancy's troubled face. "Oh, Fancy, your bandage is all askew," she lamented, eager to change the subject.

Laurel sniffed and wiped her tears with her sleeve as she

reached out to right the white bandage slipping from
Fancy's forehead. But as her hand contacted the bump
at the back of Fancy's head, she gasped, her stomach
knotting violently in reaction. "Merciful heavens, Fancy, that knot is huge—and the bandage is soaked with
blood!"

"I be all right, Miss Laurel," Fancy assured her mistress.
"Though I got a headache big enough to fell an ox, and
sometimes this here room move up and down. Wilson, he
bandage my head and he say better it bleed than keep the
poison stuffed inside."

"Well, I won't let you bleed to death!" Laurel retorted
vehemently. As she uttered the word *death*, she felt her
heart thud sickeningly. "Never mind what I said, Fancy,"
she continued distractedly, now struggling to hide her apprehension and to reassure the girl. "Your head will heal in a
few days' time."

Suddenly, Laurel gasped as her soothing words had just
the opposite effect upon her. Fancy's wound would never
heal, she realized, her heart pounding so it threatened to
constrict her throat. The doomed girl would go to her grave
bearing the very knot she received saving her mistress from
rape.

And what if—horror of horrors—the soldiers aimed for
Fancy's poor, wounded head tomorrow?

The thought was Laurel's undoing. She seemed to die
inside, and again began weeping, weeping her heart out.
She leaned forward, pounding her fists upon the floor in
agony and frustration. "Not fair..." she gasped convulsively,
hurting her hands with her unrestrained violence. "Not
fair..."

"Miss Laurel! What is it?" the distraught Fancy asked,
trying to grab Laurel's hands while the older girl's bones
were still intact.

With a tortured gasp, Laurel jerked upright, throwing her

arms about the slave, holding on to Fancy as if she were clinging to dear life itself.

Rocking to and fro, Laurel held her friend. Over and over, she moaned, "Fancy... Fancy..."

Chapter
Twenty

NOVEMBER 10, 1862

"Laurel."

Laurel looked up to see Jacob Lafflin leaning over her, frowning.

"Laurel, it's getting late. You'll have to leave now."

Unsteadily, Laurel blinked and looked about at her surroundings. Feeling Fancy's weight pressing against her, she glanced down to see the girl's peaceful, sleeping face nestled against her shoulder. Carefully, Laurel reached for an old gray coat that lay in a heap in the corner just beyond her. She gingerly shifted the wounded girl, slowly lowering Fancy to the floor and placing the makeshift pillow beneath her head.

Watching Laurel, Jacob Lafflin quickly knelt down beside her, helping her stretch Fancy out into a sleeping position. "We were both so exhausted—I can't even remember falling asleep," Laurel muttered as they worked.

Jacob stood up, took a coat from the rack, and spread it over the sleeping girl. Then he straightened, extending his hand toward Laurel. She gritted her teeth and shot him a contemptuous look but accepted his assistance nonetheless, too tired and defeated to protest.

Quietly, they left the now dusky cloakroom. As they entered the hallway, Laurel spotted Wilson nearby, leaning against the wall. Seeing Lafflin, the seaman instantly drew himself erect and came forward to bolt the door.

Scowling deeply as she watched Wilson, Laurel whirled upon Lafflin. "Why is Fancy locked in that disgusting cloakroom?" she demanded.

Lafflin shrugged. "Renshaw's orders."

A chill swept Laurel's spine at the mention of the feared commodore, but she straightened reflexively and looked Lafflin straight in the eye as she commanded, "Fancy must be moved from that filth immediately, and her bandage changed at once."

Though Laurel expected a fight from Lafflin, surprisingly, the Yankee did give a bit. Looking over Laurel's head, he said to Wilson, "Change the girl's bandage when she awakens." He added flatly to Laurel, "Sorry, dear, but I can't have Fancy moved. The commodore wouldn't hear of it."

Laurel opened her mouth to issue a retort but thought better of it. At least Fancy's bandage would be changed. She'd best not press her luck at the moment.

Again turning to the seaman, Lafflin ordered, "Take Miss Ashland back upstairs, Wilson. Barnaby's waiting there to guard her."

As Wilson replied, "Aye, sir," Jacob Lafflin strode off toward the dining hall. But Laurel rushed after him, clutching the blue sleeve of his uniform. "Jacob—wait!"

He turned to her, his features softening somewhat as he heard her use his given name.

"Jacob, please, I must talk with you!" Laurel pleaded, her eyes huge with desperation.

Lafflin studied Laurel intently for a moment, then sighed. "Very well, Laurel," he conceded gruffly, taking her arm. "But it must be quick."

As they started past the archway to the dining hall, Laurel heard the sound of men laughing. She turned and saw Commodore Renshaw inside, conversing with Captain Law and several other officers. Seeing the blue-coated commodore conversing so casually with the other men as if he had not just heartlessly ordered Fancy's execution, Laurel froze, glaring at the commodore, her young face tight with hatred, her eyes cold with scorn.

As if he felt her icy gaze, the black-haired commander began to turn in his chair. But Jacob tugged on Laurel's arm, yanking her out of sight before a confrontation could occur. In strained silence, the two started up the narrow, shadowy stairs.

Upstairs near Lafflin's door, a young, red-headed seaman greeted them. "Afternoon, Captain."

"Good afternoon, Barnaby," Lafflin greeted the spare, freckle-faced young man as he opened the door to his room.

Once they were inside, Lafflin turned to Laurel, a patient, weary look on his face. "All right, Laurel—what is it?"

Gulping nervously, she walked off across the shadowy room, pausing to finger the coverlet on the tester bed. Then, as if touching the bedding had burned her, she hastily turned to face Lafflin, her calico skirts swirling about her, her delicately featured face twisted in a look of entreaty.

"Jacob, is there nothing you can do for Fancy?" she asked, her heart in her voice.

He shrugged, but eyed her sympathetically as he replied, "I told you, Laurel—that decision was Renshaw's, not mine."

"But have you no influence over him?"

Frowning unfathomably, Lafflin was silent.

"Surely you could change his mind," Laurel continued

persuasively, "tell him how utterly remorseful we are, Fancy and I."

"Are you?" he asked.

"Are we what?" she replied, taken aback.

He gave her a hard look. "Are you remorseful?"

Laurel met his gaze, inwardly struggling with herself. "No," she said at last.

"I thought not."

Laurel gulped as she looked at her stern adversary. This was going wretchedly! Half-choking, she begged, "Jacob, please! You can't just let them kill my Fancy!"

Lafflin drew closer to her, his tanned features hard. "Laurel, has it occurred to you that there is a war going on? That lives are lost every day, people shot for crimes much less serious than the ones you and Fancy committed?" Coldly, he continued, "You and Fancy spied on us, Laurel— you aided our enemy. What is it you expect of me? Should I pretend none of this happened?"

A sickening fear gripped Laurel. "You mean you could help us but you won't?"

"That's not what I said, Laurel," Jacob replied guardedly.

"But do you deny it?" she demanded, her voice surging.

She watched him intently, studying the tense emotion on his face. Then, slowly, he replied, "No, Laurel. I don't deny it."

An electrifying chill coursed through Laurel's body at Jacob's words. Never had she realized so strongly that she stood face to face with her enemy. Oh, what foolish games she had played—games of idle curiosity, of petty revenge. Why had it never occurred to her that she was grievously, fatally outmatched? There was no place for pity, for compassion, in this war—and certainly none in Jacob Lafflin's heart at the moment! Now Fancy was the loser and would pay with her life for her mistress's reckless intrigues!

Laurel fought a rising sense of hopelessness. Was there

no bargaining with this Yankee? Was Jacob Lafflin truly as cold and ruthless as he appeared at this moment, standing across from her, all male and muscle, with booted foot spread, arms firmly akimbo, chin firm and resolute, eyes like hard black diamonds?

"Jacob," she said with a sudden welling of courage. "Let me be shot in Fancy's place."

"What?" he exclaimed, so astonished that his arms fell to his sides while his features grew incredulous.

"Let me face the firing squad tomorrow in Fancy's place," Laurel repeated, her blue eyes wild with despair.

Lafflin shook his head. "Laurel, you've lost your mind."

"Surely Renshaw could be persuaded—"

"Your heroics impress me, Laurel," Jacob interrupted, "but you're not facing reality. Renshaw might be persuaded to shoot the both of you tomorrow, but not to let Fancy off. After all," he reminded her grimly, "Fancy stabbed a Union soldier."

"But she did it to save me!" Laurel cried, clenching her fists. "Fancy had nothing to do with the spying, Jacob, nothing! It was all my idea—she only followed my orders today—"

Lafflin silenced her by raising a broad hand. "Then doubtless you deserve her punishment. The fact remains, however, that the knife was in Fancy's hand. Which means she'll be executed. And you—" he eyed her resignedly— "you get the far worse punishment, my dear. You get to live with the guilt."

With these damning words, Jacob Lafflin turned to leave her. But Laurel rushed after him, pleading, "No, Jacob, please!"

Lafflin turned to her, his black brows knitted in irritation. "Laurel, I'm already late for the officers' meeting."

But she grabbed his arm, hysteria rising in her like bile as she realized he would do naught for Fancy. "Damn the officers' meeting!'' she hissed, stinging tears flooding her eyes. "I'll not let you leave me until you promise me you'll save my Fancy!"

And, much to her humiliation, she began sobbing convulsively.

Laurel dropped Lafflin's arm and drew her hands upward to hide her face. She felt completely broken up inside, utterly defeated. Then she felt Lafflin's arms encircle her gently, drawing her close. She hated him, yet there was no fight left in her to push him away.

Once she quieted a bit, Lafflin tilted her tear-streaked face with a long, brown finger. Numbly, she stared up at his shadowy face, at his dark brown eyes, now earnestly fixed upon her. "Does the wench mean that much to you?" he asked softly.

"Never so much until today," Laurel said, "when I realized—" she paused, choking, as the truth at last splintered her brain "—when I realized that I—I love her!"

And she wept heartbrokenly against Lafflin's chest.

Jacob Lafflin stroked her hair comfortingly. "You really have suffered today, haven't you, sweetheart?" she heard him ask sympathetically. "I had no idea that the wench meant so much to you."

Feeling his oddly tender touch upon her hair and hearing the solicitude in his tone, Laurel clutched at a last, desperate hope. Looking up at Jacob with all pride abandoned, she said, "Jacob, save Fancy, and—and I'm yours."

Jacob Lafflin stiffened, studying Laurel with shock and disbelief. "Laurel, do you realize what you're saying?"

She nodded, gulping.

"Are you actually promising me the use of your body if I intervene and save Fancy's life?" he queried in amazement.

Again, she nodded.

He paused, studying her intently for an interminable moment. "For how long?" he finally asked. His expression was growing decidedly cool, and Laurel realized incredulously that he was actually acting insulted by her offer!

Laurel would have loved to tell him to go straight to the devil, but concern for Fancy made such rashness out of the question. Steeling herself against the intensity of his gaze, she replied, "For as long as you want me."

Jacob Lafflin whistled. "My, you are desperate," he said, a trace of bitterness in his tone.

"Jacob, please, just save Fancy. I'll—I'll do anything you want!"

"Anything?" Jacob scowled and released her. Walking to the window, he parted the curtains and raised the sash, flooding the room with dusky light and a chill late afternoon breeze. He turned to her, his expression constrained, unreadable. "What makes you think I want you?"

Laurel flushed crimson. Oh, he was truly being a bastard about this! But, again remembering Fancy, she blustered, "You—you've kissed me, Jacob, and you've told me you wished to get me into—into your bed, and—"

"And?" he prompted.

"And I know you want me!" she finished defiantly.

He strode back to her side, looking down at her speculatively. "You're right, Laurel, I do want you," he admitted. "And it's quite possible that I might have some influence over Renshaw in Fancy's behalf, or even possibly in yours. However, I do not find the circumstances of your offer very—appealing."

"What do you mean?" she asked, glowering at him.

He placed his hands on her shoulders. "Meaning I have no desire for a cold-blooded little martyr in my bed."

Totally exasperated, Laurel threw off his hands. "God in heaven, Jacob, will you give me no help in this?" she asked, her voice a mixture of humiliation and frustration. "Will you not meet me halfway?"

"Will you meet me halfway?" he countered.

"What do you mean?"

"Will you come to my bed willingly?"

Laurel threw her hands wide in entreaty. "Jacob, what did I just offer you?"

"You offered me the use of your body," he replied. "That I can get from any whore." His gaze slowly swept her figure, his eyes taking an odd, glittering intensity as they paused at her now heaving bosom. "I want to make love to you, Laurel—slow, passionate love. And I desire your full, uninhibited cooperation every step of the way."

Now he looked her straight in the eye, his silent, unabashed message so loud it made the blood thunder in her ears even as her entire body burned in mortification.

Mentally reeling, Laurel lowered her gaze to the floor and stammered, "Jacob, I—I haven't—I don't know what you expect."

He drew closer. "I don't expect you to know," he half growled, reaching out to encircle her waist possessively with his arm.

Timidly, she looked up at him and was again seared, pierced, by the heat emanating from his expression. Shuddering, she whispered, "Jacob, what is it you want from me?"

At this, he smiled—a slow, sensual smile. "Willingness," he said meaningfully.

"Jacob, damnit, I'm willing!"

He drew her scandalously closer. "Then prove it—kiss me," he demanded.

"You bastard!" she hissed.

"Steady, Laurel," he warned, his eyes the cunning eyes of a savage animal that has caught its prey and is savoring the ecstasy of devouring it. "Don't forget about Fancy."

She stared up at his clever, cynical face. Every fiber of her being ached to murder him. But if playing the whore would save Fancy's life, by God, she would play the whore!

Before she could lose her nerve, she threw her arms about his neck and pulled his face down to hers. Hesitantly at first, she pressed her mouth against his. Then, remembering her mission, she kissed him hard, thrusting her tongue through his lips, past the smoothness of his teeth and deep into his mouth.

He groaned and returned her kiss with a fierceness that frightened her, his teeth cutting into her mouth, his tongue audaciously exploring every texture and recess of her mouth. At last their lips parted and his mouth moved to find the pulse on her neck, even as his hands moved assuredly down her spine, grasping her hips, pulling her against his rising desire. As his mouth moved further downward, she cursed herself for wearing a dress with an open neckline, as the roughness of his face—indeed, his unrestrained hands upon her posterior—aroused in her desires she feared to name or feel.

His mouth now nudged inside the boat neckline of her dress, kissing the top of a young breast, tickling devilishly. "Laurel, Laurel," he breathed, his lips slipping inexorably lower.

How it happened, she did not even know—but all at once, her dress and chemise were pushed aside and his mouth was firmly attached to her breast, sucking as if he would draw her into his very being. Laurel's eyes grew huge as amazed blue ponds, and she was grateful that Jacob couldn't glimpse her guileless horror. While his mouth worked its possessive power upon her breast, his tongue teased and tantalized the nipple with the tormentingly delicate touch of a master. Riotous sensations stirred in the deepest recesses of Laurel's womanhood, and she was hard pressed not to cry out with the sheer intensity of it. Some primitive instinct urged her to run her hands through Jacob's thick black hair, to pull his head more firmly against her, but she somehow resisted. Yet she could not suppress the strange yet glorious tingling that now suffused her entire body, making her light-headed and languorously close to total emotional surrender.

Pausing, Jacob again murmured, "Show me how willing you are, Laurel."

Laurel felt unnerved, yet wildly titillated, by Jacob's words. God in heaven, what else did he expect of her? Hadn't she just abundantly demonstrated precisely how willing she was?

Her question was promptly answered. As Jacob's loins moved provocatively against her hips and he took one of her hands and insinuated it between their bodies, she realized exactly what he wanted her to do. Summoning all her will, she did his bidding, sliding her hand downward until he groaned violently, his mouth abruptly leaving her breast to attack her mouth in an even more savage kiss.

By now, Laurel could feel such tension in Jacob's body, such hard readiness, that she doubted she would survive another minute with her maidenhead intact. Indeed, Jacob now pulled back slightly, studying Laurel's face intently, as if to gauge her readiness.

Hell, why not? she thought to herself. There was nothing to be accomplished by postponing the inevitable. Burning to be one with him even as she hated his very guts, she smiled up at him dreamily.

"Jesus, " he whispered back, his expression strangely that of a man hit in the stomach with a brick.

Yet at that very instant there was a timid knock at the door, followed by Barnaby's calling out shrilly, "Sir, Commodore Renshaw is holding the start of the meeting for you."

Cursing under his breath, Jacob broke their embrace. "You're willing," she head him utter, his voice strained and unsteady, as he turned and started for the door. Pivoting to give her a last look, which confirmed the terms of their bargain so explicitly and irrevocably that Laurel again found herself blushing profusely, he murmured, "I'll see what I can do about Fancy."

Chapter
Twenty-one

NOVEMBER 10, 1862

In the dining hall, five officers sat at the table in a haze of cigar smoke. Jacob Lafflin wore a scowl on his face. Renshaw was droning on about security on the island and today's attempted Confederate takeover, and Jacob found his mind straying toward Laurel.

He was really being hard on the girl; he knew that. His original intention had only been to shock some sense into her, to make her squirm for a few hours until she thought better of her reckless activities. In fact, when he realized just how distraught she truly was about Fancy, he was prepared to let her off the hook right away. Yet then she had surprised him by offering herself to him. He had been a scroundrel to play her along at that point, he knew. But by damn, he never could resist tangling with her—Jesus, she was in his blood! Now he was trapped in his own web, caught between his desire for her and his sense of honor. Doubtless, the honorable thing to do would be to tell her the truth. Did he really want her to come to him under less than honest circumstances?

Yes, dash it all, he wanted her under any circumstances! His need of her was tearing him up inside. And another emotion plagued him—stark, almost physical fear. Every time he remembered that pitiful child lying dead on the street back in Indianola, and imagined Laurel in similar straits, the fear became unendurable. He was endlessly torn between wanting to make love to her and wanting to beat the willfulness out of her hide. The girl had almost gotten herself raped—killed—by Carter that morning. Somehow she must be made to see reason—even if it meant scaring the living hell out of her! He wanted to protect her, and at the same time, he wanted her bound to him, he wanted his baby growing inside her. Sometimes he thought he couldn't live through another day unless he made her his, entirely his. If he lost her now, he was sure he would lose his mind—

"I repeat, Captain Lafflin. Do you agree with my assessment of the situation?"

Snapped out of his thoughts, Jacob stared blankly at Renshaw and the other officers. Then he recovered, saying, "Yes, Commodore. I agree wholeheartedly." Agreeing with the commodore's point of view was always a welcomed response, he added to himself ruefully.

Suddenly, Jacob smiled. Perhaps he should agree with what Laurel offered as well. After all, there was one surefire way to protect her. And it might even mean an honorable way out of this dilemma...

Upstairs, Laurel paced Jacob Lafflin's room in a swirl of calico skirts. Night was falling, and the Yankee still had not returned from his conference with Renshaw. Yet she had heard smattering of raucous laughter drifting up from below.

Evidently, the officer's meeting had turned into an evening of revelry.

Suddenly, Laurel stiffened as she heard a key scratching into the lock out in the hallway. She stood motionless waiting, her hands tightly twisted together, her heart filled with hope and terror.

The red-haired boy named Barnaby entered the room carrying a napkin-covered tray. "Evening, ma'am," he said shyly in a half-shrill, still boyish voice. "The captain had this sent up for you."

Barnaby placed the tray on the tea table near the wing chair. Turning and nodding to Laurel politely, he said, "Hope you enjoy your dinner, ma'am."

Laurel stepped forward. "Barnarby?" she asked tentatively.

Now near the door, he pivoted, looking flustered.

Laurel flashed him a dazzling smile. "It is Barnaby, isn't it?"

"Yes, ma'am," he said nervously, shifting from foot to foot.

Laurel nodded toward the tray. "Won't you share my supper, Barnaby? I'll bet you're famished, standing alone in that dark, dismal hallway all these hours."

"Oh no, ma'am, I already ate." He paused, color rising in his young, naïve face. "Besides, ma'am, the captain ordered me to guard you."

Demurely, Laurel lowered jet eyelashes as she said innocently, "But, Barnaby, what better place to watch me than right here in this very room?" The dark lashes now fluttered upward as she gave him a devastating smile.

Across from her, Barnaby gulped and stammered, "W—well, ma'am, I do suppose—I do suppose you got a point." Then his thin, freckled face puckered in an embarrassed frown as he inquired in an unsteady, rising voice, "But, ma'am—you ain't thinking of bolting on me, are you?"

Laurel giggled in her best imitation of the empty-headed

belle. "Why, Barnaby, perish the thought," she teased. "A little old thing like me taking on a big, strong example of manhood such as you?"

Barnaby was smitten; he gave Laurel a cockeyed grin and flushed vigorously, blinking rapidly in betrayal of his giddiness. "Well, ma'am, I guess—"

"Barnaby, do have a seat," Laurel said graciously but imperiously, gesturing toward the straight chair across from the wing chair.

Not giving him a chance to back out, Laurel gracefully seated herself across from him. Studying the young man, who was now stiffly perched on the edge of his chair, she found Barnaby reminded her of a nervous bride—half eager anticipation, half dread.

Scrutinizing him more closely, Laurel decided Barnaby must be about two years her junior. Physically, he was as yet no prime specimen. He was scarcely taller than Laurel and decidedly on the thin side, his blue shirt and trousers hanging loosely about him even as he sat.

Meeting Laurel's frankly curious stare, Barnaby squirmed and reddened even more brilliantly, his hot face now vying with his bright hair. "Ma'am, your dinner's getting cold."

She smiled. "So it is."

Laurel removed the cloth from the tray, glancing with little interest at the plateful of chicken and dumplings, which smelled potently spicy, tickling her nose unpleasantly rather than enticing her. But the full goblet of wine sitting beside the food caught her attention. She looked up at Barnaby curiously, raising a finely arched black brow.

"Ma'am, the captain sent the wine up for you. Seems they brought in a cask of port from the *Clifton*."

"Indeed?" Laurel bit her lip, frowning thoughtfully as she stared at the rose-colored brew. Had Lafflin sent it up through kindness, to soothe her fears regarding Fancy's fate? Or did he seek to dull her senses, easing her struggles when he later came to demand his due for ensuring Fancy's safety?

Laurel decided on the latter explanation. She didn't trust Lafflin at all, either. What was to keep him from assuring her Fancy was safe, then claiming her virtue, only to ruthlessly allow the execution to take place later on?

Considering her options carefully, Laurel raised the glass, her face a coquettish mask as she graciously extended the wine toward Barnaby. "Won't you have this, Barnaby?" she asked sweetly. "I'm quite unaccustomed to spirits."

"Oh no, ma'am, I couldn't!" Barnaby blustered, shaking his head adamantly at the proffered brew. "The captain would have me flogged if I touched a drop whilst I was on duty."

Laurel sighed, replacing the glass upon the wicker tray. Idly, she fingered the heavy ironstone plate holding the chicken and dumplings. Then, with an irritable sigh, she picked up her fork and took a desultory bite of the dumplings. But as the peppery stew contacted her tongue, tears sprang to her eyes and her hand flew to her throat. Hastily, her other hand grabbed the wine, and she took a hearty gulp, then choked and sputtered as the wine, combined with the wickedly seasoned food, scalded her throat unmercifully going down. "My God!" she gasped wildly, her voice almost dissolved by the pandemonium unleashed in her gullet, "Did Captain Lafflin order me poisoned?"

Barnaby grinned. "I heard one of the men say the cook put heaps of cayenne in them dumplings tonight."

"Surely an understatement," Laurel moaned hoarsely, fanning her face vigorously, her eyes enormous and tear-filled.

Barnaby shook his head and smiled sheepishly.

Bringing the wineglass once again to her still-burning lips, Laurel eyed Barnaby steadily and inquired raspily, "Tell me, Barnaby, does the captain have you flogged often?"

The boy shifted uncomfortably and stuttered, "I—I beg your pardon, ma'am?"

"Didn't you tell me Captain Lafflin would have you flogged if you accepted this wine?" She took a sip, shuddering, but found the burning sensation was easing into a strangely pleasant warmth. "What other outrageous injustices does he impose upon you?"

Barnaby twisted his frail, freckled hands in his lap. "Ma'am, I told you the captain would have me flogged if I drank the wine because them be the rules regarding a sailor on duty. But Captain Lafflin ain't never ordered me whipped, ma'am, because I respect him too much to disobey him."

"I see," Laurel replied, an unmistakable trace of disappointment in her tone. She took another sip of port, now thoroughly enjoying the heat spreading through her veins, uncoiling her nerve endings. Smiling flirtatiously, she asked, "Barnaby, if I may be so bold, how old are you?"

"Fifteen, ma'am," came the reply.

Laurel took an angry swill of wine, then set the goblet down, scowling. "And this captain you say you respect has conscripted a—a virtual child like you into this life of toil and drudgery?"

"Oh no, ma'am," Barnaby denied vehemently, now springing to life, eyes full of devotion. "The captain, he saved my life!"

"He *what*?" Laurel demanded, disbelief in her tone.

"Oh yes, ma'am," Barnaby explained earnestly. "Three years past, me and my folks was moving south from Maryland, when our ship capsized off the coast of Florida. Out on the cold seas in a rowboat for three days, we was. Then the captain, he rescued those of us what made it."

"Oh, Barnaby, how perfectly ghastly!" Laurel sympathized, taking another hefty swig of port. "And—and your parents?" she inquired, her voice becoming slightly slurred. "Were—were they saved, too?"

Barnaby shook his head and stared miserably at the floor. " 'Twas a boiler explosion that capsized the ship, ma'am. My folks was instantly killed."

"Oh, Barnaby!" Laurel cried, her face crestfallen. Upending her glass and gulping the rest of its contents, she then commented ruefully, "I do understand, dear Barnaby. I, too, am an orphan."

"You are, ma'am?" Barnaby questioned in trusting amazement, his fawnlike eyes large.

"Aye, Barnaby," Laurel concurred dramatically with an extravagant gesture of grief. "My parents and b—baby brother died soon after our ship capsized, off San Luis Pass." She sniffed meaningfully.

"My deepest sympathies, ma'am," the artless Barnaby replied. "When was it you lost your folks?"

Before she risked getting herself caught in a lie, especially considering her not too alert state of mind at the moment, Laurel threw her hands to her heart and cried melodramatically, "It pains me too greatly to discuss it, dear Barnaby." After an emphatic pause, ostensibly to control herself, Laurel went on with forbearance, "Now tell me about Captain Lafflin's monstrous treatment of you, my friend. Do the scars stripe your back like the furrows of a savagely plowed field?"

Barnaby was horrified. "I told you, ma'am. The captain ain't never had me lashed. He been more like a father to me since he pulled me from the sea. He made me his cabin boy and got old Pearson to learn me my studies." Barnaby's young face glowed as he continued, "The captain said if I apply myself, he might someday get me into Annapolis, where he gone."

"*Went*, Barnaby," Laurel corrected automatically. "If you desire to go to Annapolis, you must use proper English."

Barnaby grinned broadly. "Yes, ma'am. That's what Pearson tells me."

Laurel distractedly fanned herself with her napkin, feeling distinctly warm. "Though if I were you, Barnaby, I shouldn't place much stock in anything Jacob Lafflin says. The man is an accomplished liar!"

Barnaby's pale eyebrows flew up, and his soft brown eyes widened. "Oh, ma'am, you mustn't say that! What proof you got that the captain lies?"

Laurel opened her mouth to document her claim, then frowned in consternation. Barnaby had a point, she realized grimly. And her thinking was becoming decidedly on the muddy side. "Well," she managed. "Considering Captain Lafflin's other glaring character flaws, we may as well assume the worst."

Barnaby chuckled while Laurel, still scowling, reflected dismally that she was not having much success in wooing the young cabin boy to her side. Her eyes swept the wicker tray, lingering with disappointment upon the now empty wine goblet, then fixing upon the offensive chicken and dumplings. Her eyes narrowed momentarily; then she quickly glanced upward, her gaze fastening upon Barnaby, who now looked blissfully contented, slouched in the ladder-back chair.

Gritting her teeth, Laurel grasped her fork, stabbing a large, doughy dumpling. Taking a deep breath, she quickly raised the fork to her mouth, stuffing the contents inside. She gulped down the peppery dumpling in one swallow, then bolted to her feet, coughing and choking.

"Barnaby, I shall wretch!" she gurgled, hunching over in her distress, clutching her stomach. "Water—water!"

Laurel heard Barnaby utter a cry of dismay and bolt to his feet. His boots tapped out a wild, thudding cadence on the rug as he raced for the water pitcher atop the dresser.

Laurel tiptoed up behind Barnaby just as he was pouring water into a glass. Then an awful cracking sound split the quiet of the room.

"Poooor Barnaby," Laurel mumbled as she stood holding the two pieces of the now broken ironstone plate.

Barnaby lay at her feet, unconscious, chicken and dumplings all over his face and head. Looking exceedingly guilty, Laurel knelt down beside him, wiping up the flecks of dough and chicken spattering his countenance as best she could. Gingerly, she fingered the vein protruding from his thin neck, sighing gratefully as she felt the pulse. "Sorry, Barna-bly," she stuttered, hiccuping. "You'll have one devil of a headache tomorrow, but with Fancy's life hanging by a thread, I had no choice."

Laurel got to her feet, then tottered as the room tilted. Damn! Whatever had possessed her to consume the entire glass of port? She definitely needed her wits about her if she was to rescue Fancy, yet she was becoming dizzier by the moment!

Carefully stepping over Barnaby, Laurel stood at the dresser, splashing cool water on her face. She shivered and stared at her flushed face, at her lusterless, slightly droopy eyes. "Heaven help me," she groaned, her diaphragm again going into a raucous spasm.

Laurel walked unsteadily to the door, cracking it open. Cautiously, she peered out into the dark, rambling cavern of the hallway. Good, no one was about.

Just as she left, she sheepishly glanced over her shoulder at the still unconscious Barnaby. "Believe me, Bar-Blarnaby, I bear you no ill will," she said with slurred sincerity.

Once she was in the dark hallway, Laurel slowly closed the door, then tiptoed tipsily toward the stairwell, feeling her way along the wall and trying to keep her balance. As she started down the steps, she heard the sound of loud, bawdy voices drifting up from below. She crouched low as she neared the bottom of the stairs, seating herself on the last step so she could gaze through the wooden spindles at the sailors assembled in the now smoky dining hall. She scrutinized the men carefully, hoping the shadows would conceal her in her vulnerable position, less than ten yards from the Yankees.

There were five officers in the dining hall gathered about one of the round tables, playing poker. Jacob Lafflin sat with his chair tilted, scowling at his hand, a smoking cigar hanging from the corner of his mouth. His uniform was uncharacteristically askew, his face bright and animated. Next to Lafflin sat Renshaw, and, beyond him, Captain Law. The other two men Laurel did not recognize, though their bars indicated they were of similar rank to Jacob's. On the floor near Lafflin sat the cask of port and half-empty wineglasses cluttered the table.

Suddenly, a hoot of victory came forth from Lafflin, chorused by a howl of outrage from the other officers. Laurel watched Lafflin stretch forward, gathering the currency cluttering the center of the table.

Seizing her opportunity, Laurel dashed around the stairwell, crossing the hall. She pressed herself against the wall beyond the archway, just out of sight of the Yankees. For a moment she stood frozen, her heart racing, as she prayed that no one had seen her.

"Well, Lafflin, it seems you are gathering all the treasures hearabouts," she heard an officer comment. "How long is it you've been bedding the girl?"

Laurel's eyes grew huge with fright mixed with affront. Were they talking about her? Had they spotted her? Or was the man's question merely a bizarre coincidence?

"How long?" she heard Lafflin banter back drunkenly. "Long enough!"

This comment brought gales of laughter from the other officers. Meanwhile, the assumed subject of this verbal abuse silently gnashed her teeth and clenched her fists. Was Lafflin talking about her, specifically? If so, why was he bragging to the others that he had bedded her?

Remembering Fancy, Laurel scolded herself for her petty resentment at such a critical moment. In any event, she promised herself, if her mission was successful, she need not concern herself with Jacob Lafflin ever again!

Stealthily Laurel started down the dark hallway, tottering slightly as she moved, then biting her lip to sharpen her senses. Tentatively, she peered around the corner leading to the cloakroom. Thank heaven, Wilson was not about! Not pausing to question her good fortune, Laurel dashed on tiptoe for the door, her trembling fingers grasping the latch.

Suddenly, violently, she was grabbed from behind and whirled about against a man's hard chest. "Thought you could sneak by me, didn't you, sweetheart?" Jacob Lafflin asked in a throaty, indistinct voice, his dark form menacing above her.

"I—I—" Laurel hiccuped convulsively as her petrified mind fought blankness. "I just wanted to tell Fran—Fancy good night."

"You're drunk," Jacob accused.

And his mouth descended upon hers.

He clutched her tightly to him as he kissed her so hard, so ruthlessly, that tears sprang to her eyes. His tongue ravaged her mouth, his own mouth tasting heavily of wine and tobacco, mixed with lust. Laurel was swept by waves of dizziness and revulsion mixed with inevitable, traitorous desire.

At last, abruptly, Jacob released her. "Jesus Christ," he groaned.

Laurel gasped for her breath, the oxygen stabbing her constricted airways as Jacob's presence and his insulting kiss spurred her to reckless rage and unthinking desperation. Frantically grabbing the latch to the cloakroom, she shoved Jacob's body with her own, hissing venomously, "Get out of my way, you drunken monster! I'm getting Fancy!"

But Jacob laughed, his steely fingers easily prying Laurel's hand from the latch. He threw back the bolt and kicked open the door to the tiny room. As Laurel's eyes wildly searched the shadowy, narrow enclosure, Jacob said, "Behold, sweetheart!"

The room was empty!

Terrified, Laurel whirled, attacking Lafflin with both fists at once. "You goddamned bastard! What have you done to my Fancy?" Tears of outrage and total physical fear streamed from her eyes as she screamed at him and flailed at him with all her might.

Lafflin grabbed Laurel's fists. "Be still, damnit! Fancy's out back asleep in Reba's cabin!"

Laurel froze.

"Renshaw rescinded the order," Lafflin continued in a hoarse voice, eyeing Laurel meaningfully.

"You mean?" Laurel gasped.

"Fancy's safe abed," Lafflin reiterated, then added with a nasty smile, "Which is precisely where you're going, sweetheart, though I'll not promise you'll be safe!"

With these audacious words, Lafflin quickly bent over, grasping Laurel tightly about the knees. Before she knew what was happening, she felt herself being hefted, like a sack of potatoes, and thrown across Lafflin's shoulder. Momentarily, Laurel's world went black as the breath was knocked from her lungs. Then she came to, the blood rushing to her face, waves of nausea sweeping her as Lafflin's shoulder cinched her stomach and he staggered down the hallway.

As they reached the archway leading to the dining room, Lafflin paused, evidently to bow before the officers assembled, for Laurel's entire body heaved forward, then jerked backward again as Lafflin straightened.

Wanton laughter swelled from the dining hall as one of the officers yelled, "Quite a little hellcat you're taking to your bed tonight, eh, Lafflin?"

"Oh, I'll have her purring soon enough, " Lafflin slurred back.

A roar of mirth boomed from the dining hall at Lafflin's reply, while Laurel, outraged, beat upon his back with her fists.

In reply, Jacob slapped her hard on the derriere, much to the delight of the drunken officers. Then, Jacob turned and staggered for the stairs, starting up determinedly but wavering precariously on the third step. Laurel's heart skipped a beat as she thought for a terrifying instant that they would both topple back downstairs. "Put me down!" she demanded hysterically.

Undaunted, Lafflin administered another hard, resounding whack on Laurel's bottom and barked, "Hush, wench!"

Laurel sobered, inwardly still enraged by Jacob's arrogance, but realizing that further resistance could send her toppling down the stairs head first.

Laurel suffered in silence as Lafflin climbed to the top of the steps, then groped his way down the black hallway upstairs, banging her head against the wall twice. Then, he booted open the door to his room and they crashed inside.

Laurel felt herself being abruptly righted, and she struggled to keep her balance as her feet hit the floor. She blinked about the room in fear and bewilderment, then sighed in dismay as she saw poor Barnaby, still passed out upon the floor.

Meanwhile, Lafflin strode over to the young seaman, scowling at the unconscious boy. Cursing under his breath, he jabbed the boy in the side with his boot. Barnaby reflexively flinched, but did not awaken, while Laurel cried, "Jacob—please, don't!"

Lafflin turned to Laurel, his dark, handsome features thunderous. "Your doing, doubtless?" he inquired icily.

Miserably, Laurel nodded. "But, Jacob, it wasn't his fault—"

"Silence!" Lafflin interrupted nastily as he stormed to the dresser and poured a glass of water. Turning to Barnaby, he summarily tossed the water in the boy's face.

Choking and sputtering, Barnaby awakened, then hastily sat up, staring about the room in befuddlement. "Why, Captain, sir," he said, spying Lafflin. "What happened?"

"That, you should be telling me!" Lafflin replied grimly, leaning over and roughly pulling the boy to his feet. Yanking the confused young man toward the door, he continued disgustedly, "I should have known better than to send a boy on a man's mission. You'll be fined a week's wages for this!"

With this severe pronouncement, Lafflin threw open the door and propelled Barnaby into the hallway, while the distressed boy said lamely, "Aye, sir!" and disappeared into the shadows.

As Lafflin shut the door and returned his attention to Laurel, she chided irately, hands on hips, "Jacob, how dare you be so hard on the poor boy—I told you it was my doing!"

Lafflin pointed a finger at Laurel and warned, "Laurel, never, never try to interfere between me and one of my men. Another word and I'll take it out on your tender little rump!"

"Oooh!" Laurel sputtered indignantly, remembering all too well the power of his broad hand upon her delicate backside.

Lafflin strode forward, his gait menacing. "I should give you a hard spanking anyway, you little witch. I was sure you would have learned your lesson by now. But no, you had to make a fool of me tonight. I told you I would intervene in Fancy's behalf, but what do you do? Bash Barnaby over the head and tear off to save Fancy yourself, thus sabotaging my intricate maneuvers to save the hides of both of you." He paused, his dark eyes narrowing. Then a slow smile tugged at the corners of his mouth. "But no matter. We've a bargain, you and I, don't we?"

Laurel's heart thudded desolately. "Y-yes," she quavered. "You mean you're demanding—" her voice trailed off.

"Satisfaction," he supplied, his eyes perusing her figure boldly. "But don't despair, Laurel. I'll not take you this night. Tonight I'm so damned angry that I'd probably rape you."

She gasped, but he only drew closer, cupping her chin with his hand as he gazed down at her fiercely. "Nay, I'll not force you, Laurel, and let you play the martyr, keeping your pride intact. I'm not letting you off that easy. When I make love to you, there will be no barriers between us—not liquor, not pride. You shall give yourself to me completely, holding nothing back."

Laurel jerked away from his touch. "Aye, I'll hold nothing back—because I feel nothing for you!" she retorted, too infuriated by his audacious remarks to control herself, even for Fancy's sake. "You—you only want to humiliate me!"

"Perhaps," he conceded. "But you've played the virgin queen long enough, dear Laurel. I'd say it's high time you were taught a measure of humility, albeit it means a thorough taming at my hands."

"I hate you!"

He chuckled. "We shall see," he murmured, his soft tone decidedly ominous. Leaning over, he gave her a quick, hard kiss, like the fleeting but final sear of a brand. "Tomorrow. After we're married."

Chapter
Twenty-two

Laurel stood beside Jacob Lafflin before the altar of Trinity Episcopal Church. Next to Lafflin stood Seaman Wilson; behind them, on a hard pine pew, sat Fancy and Barnaby.

Laurel shivered slightly and clutched the bouquet of pale pink roses Jacob Lafflin had brought her this morning as she solemnly listened to Father Eaton, the Episcopal priest, who was now giving them a sound sermon on the sanctity of marriage.

Laurel glanced furtively at Jacob Lafflin. Her husband-to-be looked impassive, emotionless, yet devastatingly handsome in his brass-buttoned dress uniform. He seemed a distant, inscrutable god this morning—all hard sinew and deep bronze skin, his dark face handsome and imperious, even as prisms of light filtered through the windows, dancing shimmering highlights in his black, wavy hair.

Laurel returned her attention to the tall, blunt-featured parson, who now looked her straight in the eye and entoned, "And you must remember, Laurel Ashland, that your husband's word is your bond. In all matters, you are to consult and obey his wishes.''

The hell I will! Laurel vowed silently, defiantly. But outwardly, she granted the stern, black-clothed parson a half smile, then demurely lowered her gaze toward the floor.

Laurel studied the miniature red roses gracing the skirt of her dress. The white eyelet gown, with its sprinkling of embroidered flowers, was the closest thing she owned to a wedding gown and was the obvious choice this morning, when Jacob Lafflin dragged her off to become his bride.

Jacob Lafflin's bride! How insane it all was! For the hundredth time, Laurel's mind recalled the bizarre conversation she had had with the drunken Lafflin the previous night. She had been fully prepared to sacrifice her virginity for Fancy's freedom, but when Lafflin demanded that she become his wife, she had been utterly appalled.

"Jacob, you've lost your mind!" she had gasped.

He had shrugged, his features grim. "We're getting married tomorrow."

"Jacob, our arrangement has nothing to do with marriage!" she insisted.

"Didn't you tell me I could have you for as long as I wanted you?"

"Yes, but—"

"Are you reneging on our agreement?"

"No, I'm—"

"My, my, Laurel," he had scolded, shaking his head. "If you're still determined to dictate terms to me, perhaps some punishment is in order for today's escapade."

Laurel had stared at him, aghast. "Jacob, you don't mean—"

He nodded implacably.

Giving him a gesture of supplication, Laurel had cried, in bewilderment, "But, Jacob, why do you want to marry me?"

He laughed bitterly. "You're quite an adversary, Laurel. To ensure a victory for our side, I think it best to find a method to keep you off the streets at night."

Laurel flushed hotly. "You think making me your wife will ensure my loyalty?"

He raised an eyebrow at her and returned flatly, "Oh, I plan to persuade you to our way of thinking."

"Never! Never!" she had hissed.

His face darkened in anger. "Hellcat!" he growled. Grabbing her arm, he had ordered roughly, "Get your stubborn little carcass to bed before I change my mind and have you shipped north. Perhaps a few months of deprivation in a cold northern prison would make you come to regret your willfulness."

Laurel's eyes grew huge, her delicately formed face white. "Jacob, you wouldn't!"

"The devil I wouldn't!" he thundered, a murderous gleam in his eyes. "Now get the hell to bed!"

This morning Laurel had waited to hear again from Lafflin, the moments in the tiny anteroom spent in greatest trepidation. Over and over, she had hoped, prayed, that Lafflin would awaken in charge of his senses and disclaim his drunken follies of the previous night. But soon after sunrise, Lafflin had peered into her room, saying gruffly, "Be dressed and waiting for me by mid-morning. I'm going to find a parson."

Things had happened so very fast, Laurel had not time to think. But she well knew Lafflin was dangerous, unpredictable, and that to cross him now could mean disastrous consequences for both her and Fancy. Yes, she was trapped by him—totally, irrevocably trapped . . .

"Miss Ashland, I said are you ready to repeat your vows?"

Laurel's attention was jerked back to the present as she

felt all eyes upon her. "Yes, Father," she whispered to the unsmiling, gray-haired parson.

As the pastor turned to a bookmark in his prayer book and cleared his throat, Laurel scowled at him sideways. Her last, futile hope was that Lafflin would be unable to find anyone to marry them on the island. Yet only blocks from the hotel, Lafflin had found Father Eaton, at Trinity Episcopal, who informed them before the service that he hoped their union would be symbolic of the ceasing of hostilities between North and South. At any rate, Laurel added to herself dismally, Lafflin could have gotten Renshaw or Captain Law to marry them had no parson been willing.

All too soon their vows were repeated, and Laurel found herself staring at a plain gold band on her hand. Evidently, finding the ring was also part of Lafflin's mission this morning, she thought dolefully.

Then Laurel was pulled into Lafflin's arms, and he kissed her briefly, possessively. She trembled, and he pulled back slightly and whispered, "You're shivering, Mrs. Lafflin."

Mrs. Lafflin! Hearing her new name made Laurel again shudder. "It's cold in here," she replied tonelessly.

"Indeed it is. Shall we depart to warmer surroundings, my love?"

The cynical gleam in Jacob's eyes left no doubt as to his intention. Luckily, at this point Wilson turned to congratulate the newlyweds, and Laurel was spared her new husband's subtly meaningful gaze for the moment.

The parson was thanked and given a gold piece by Lafflin, then the small party proceeded down the aisle of the church and out upon the sunny, cool streets of Galveston.

Laurel blinked at the brightness and took deep breaths of the crisp, salty breeze to steady herself. She and Jacob led the entourage, while Wilson, Barnaby, and Fancy followed at a discreet distance. As their feet tapped out a cadence on the sidewalk, Laurel avoided Jacob's eyes, rubbing her arms to warm the gooseflesh patterning her flesh beneath her thin eyelet sleeves.

"You should have worn a shawl, sweetheart," Jacob admonished, drawing closer and wrapping an arm about her waist.

Laurel stiffened at his touch, at the long steel of his sword pressing into the softness of her side, a symbolically brazen reminder to her of his virility, of his ruthless intention—and of her total vulnerability! Her stomach rearranged itself. "Please, Jacob, I'm fine," she lied weakly, trying unobtrusively to push him away.

"Sweetheart, you must grow accustomed to my touch," he replied smoothly, drawing her firmly closer, making her bite her lip in silent frustration. They passed a run-down looking hostelry, and Lafflin nodded at the black lad sweeping the front porch. "Almost home," he murmured significantly, smiling at Laurel.

Laurel's eyes were fixed like hard blue diamonds on the walkway before them as she tried not to let her husband's gibes rattle her. Yet as they entered the Virginia House moments later, Laurel's composure was close to cracking, especially since Wilson, Barnaby, and Fancy immediately disappeared into the rambling structure, leaving Laurel totally alone with her new husband in the cool front hallway.

Laurel thought she detected a glint of sympathy in Jacob's eyes as he wordlessly took her hand and lead her toward the stairs. She was far from consoled, however, and became even more unnerved as they passed the archway leading to the dining hall. For just inside the doorway was Reba, her tall, magnificent figure motionless, oozing an evil that could only come from a demonic presence as she glared at the newlyweds with the wild, rabid eyes of a she-wolf.

Laurel stopped in her tracks, mesmerized by the malevolent gaze of the bronze-skinned woman. Then Jacob tugged

Laurel's arm firmly, leading her off as he said casually, "Morning, Reba."

They climbed the steps in tense silence. Upstairs, as they arrived at Jacob's door, he frowned at Laurel's strained face and scolded softly, "Forget that yellow-eyed witch. Time to think about pleasuring your new husband."

"B—but Jacob—"

Laurel's protest was obliterated as Jacob suddenly swung her up into his arms, kicked open the door, and carried her inside. No sooner had the door been shut, her feet planted upon the floor, than she was pulled hard into her new husband's embrace and kissed very thoroughly. The cold chill of fear was replaced by the heat of mortification, especially as his hand boldly caressed a breast through the cloth of her gown. Though she hated to admit it to herself, his touch definitely warmed her blood!

"Jesus, you look beautiful today!" Jacob finally breathed, his eyes languorous, almost as if he were in a dreamlike state, as he pulled back to stare down at her in wonder. His hand reached out to toy with an ebony curl that rested upon her shoulder. "Your blue eyes have never looked brighter, and your skin is literally glowing. Is it the flush of expectation, love?" He pressed a long brown finger against her open, indignant mouth. "There, sweetheart, don't say anything hasty, else I'll be forced to smother your protests. I'll not let anything spoil this perfect day." His eyes swept her figure caressingly. "I love the dress—even the high neck, the demure little collar." The hand that had played with her hair now caressed her neck near the curve of her jaw, and she fought back a shudder as his fingertips moved lower to touch the first mother-of-pearl button on her gown. "All your treasures shall be mine alone to enjoy."

Laurel blinked at the unveiled desire in her husband's eyes, then abruptly whirled and moved away from him. Her heart thudded as she heard him approach from behind her;

she stiffened as his strong hands grasped her shoulders. Then his hands moved to the front of her dress and his deft fingers began unbuttoning the frock. She began to die by inches.

Surprisingly, he murmured, "I want you to get undressed, sweetheart, and go to bed. I know you didn't sleep at all last night—I heard you sobbing. I would have gone to you, but frankly, I didn't trust myself."

His tenderness was nerve-shattering, and she knew he must now detect her physical trembling. Having unbuttoned the first few buttons on her gown, his hands moved to her hair, gathering her heavy tresses and piling them upon her head, raising gooseflesh on her spine. He pressed his lips on the back of her neck; she swayed, half dizzy, as his warm mouth provocatively tickled her sensitive flesh. "No more sobbing alone on your cold little pallet," she heard him soothe. "I have duties to attend to now, sweet. But when I return, I expect to find you asleep—in my bed. There shall be no tears for you tonight, love, none save the tears of first becoming a woman—and Jacob Lafflin's wife."

He smoothed down her hair about her shoulders, then abruptly left her.

Laurel gazed in perplexity at the closed door, the empty room. Hardly the denouement her mind had conjured for the little vignette enacted this morning.

But suddenly Laurel found she was too tired to care why Lafflin had granted her this reprieve, too numb to worry about what he would do when he returned. She removed her gown and carefully hung it in the armoire. Then she stared at his bed, struggling with herself for a moment. Finally, she walked over and pulled back the coverlet. At least the sheets were fresh—and the bed looked too soft and heavenly to resist. Sitting down upon the sheet, clad in her chemise, she removed her silk stockings and white satin slippers, then tiredly sank onto the mattress, covering herself with a quilt to shut out the morning chill.

What a curious mixture of moods Jacob Lafflin was, she thought wearily. Last night he had been angry, cruel. Yet today he was the picture of the solicitous—and amorous— bridegroom.

What of tonight?

Long-eluded sleep overtook Laurel before her mind could ponder the question.

Chapter
Twenty-three

NOVEMBER 11, 1862

Laurel ran down a blazing, endless street as hulking buildings, sinister and misshapen, leered at her. She must find Fancy—her mind was exploding with the sound of her servant's distant, awful cry.

On she raced, drawing closer to the piteous wail of her friend. Then she heard him behind her, the horrid sound of his boots scraping the sandy street as he moved. She ran faster, gasping for breath, her lungs bursting as she now heard the sickening cadence of Fancy's head being banged against a wall, accompanied by the wrenching screams of her servant.

"Fancy!" Laurel cried. "Oh my God, Fancy! You saved my life! I must find you! I must—"

But suddenly, violently, he grabbed her, throwing her to the ground. "I got unfinished business with you, whore!"

Struggling with the man, Laurel looked about wildly, seeking help, but instead she saw a yellow-eyed priestess approaching, dangling an awful, spitting serpent just inches from her eyes. "L'Loa vinnie!" the mambo hissed.

The man brutally spread Laurel's legs, and she waited for the inevitable dual death. She suddenly realized that Fancy's screams had ceased. Yet the distant bludgeoning of her servant's head continued, now like the sound of wood pounding pulp . . .

"Laurel!"

Laurel jerked awake, looking around the lamp-lit room in terror, then spotting Jacob seated next to her on the bed.

"Laurel, what is it?" he asked, placing a comforting hand on her shoulder. "You were screaming like demons were chasing you."

"Jacob!" Laurel threw herself into his arms, sobbing. "They were—oh, Jacob, it was horrible! Someone was k-killing Fancy, and Reba shook a snake in my face and Carter was trying to r-rape me—"

"Easy sweetheart!" Jacob soothed, pulling Laurel protectively into his lap. His face creased with distress, he tenderly stroked her disheveled hair. "Darling, it was only a dream."

But Laurel sobbed and trembled, clutching Jacob desperately, pressing her face deep into his shoulder. "J-Jacob, when you were gone at sea, Reba hid this awful *gris-gris* in your dresser, and Fancy said it could mean Reba wanted you d-dead—"

Jacob's arms tightened about her, and Laurel was unable to see that his features had paled. "That yellow-eyed witch!" he growled. "Forget about Reba, Laurel. I'll see that she remembers her place."

Laurel looked up at him, her pink mouth trembling. "But Jacob, Reba has these awful, wicked powers. Fancy said so!"

Jacob grasped Laurel's face in both his hands, looking down at her sternly. "Laurel, Reba's powers can harm you only if you believe they can. Do you understand?"

She gazed up at him in perplexity. "No."

He sighed. "Sweetheart, Reba works her charms largely through the power of suggestion. Simply refuse to believe her spells will work and avoid looking into those catlike eyes of hers, and you'll be safe."

"Jacob, you make it sound so simple!"

"It is." Protectively, he tucked her head beneath his chin, stroking her back with a strong hand. "Laurel, I'm your husband now. I vowed to protect you today. Don't you believe I will?"

"Yes," she conceded. "But—"

"But nothing. Forget Reba. Forget the dream."

Laurel shivered. "Jacob, Fancy was . . ." her voice trailed off, then she whispered tonelessly, "In the dream, Fancy was dead."

"Mother of God," Jacob muttered. "If I had known how much the wench meant to you—"

Abruptly, Jacob shifted Laurel out of his lap and stood up, walking to the wing chair and taking his black velvet dressing gown from its position folded on the arm. Carrying the robe, he came back to her, his brow furrowed. "Laurel, Fancy is safe. Absolutely safe. Will you please believe it?"

Looking up at him, she nodded solemnly.

He looked down at her almost lamely now, his dark eyes troubled. For a moment, she was sure he was about to say something quite important. Then he extended the dressing gown toward her and said gruffly, "Here. Put this on."

Laurel blushed as she finally realized the sight she must pose, clothed only in her thin chemise, her long, slim legs bare upon the sheet. Had she lost all sense of modesty in her all-consuming fear? And what must Jacob think—indeed, feel—now? Gratefully, she accepted the robe and donned it.

She was about to tie the sash when Jacob reached out, pulling her to her feet.

His eyes swept her figure; he chuckled as he looked at the hem of the robe dragging the floor. Pulling the folds about her, he tied the sash, a look of thoughtful amusement in his eyes. "How very small you are in my robe. Makes me wish my arms were surrounding you now instead. But I suppose it wouldn't be proper not to feed you first."

Laurel flushed and struggled for a reply as Lafflin strode off toward the tea table. "Quite a sleepyhead you are," she heard him say softly. "You slept the clock around, my dear. No matter—you'll be busy tonight." He turned, extending a brightly wrapped package toward her and grinning. "You should see your eyes—huge, round, like a lamb for the slaughter. I'm not planning to eat you alive, dear." He winked wickedly. "Well, not quite. Now, quit gaping at me and open your present."

"Present?" Laurel quavered. Biting her lower lip, she moved forward and took the round ribbon-graced package from Lafflin.

Jacob strode off assuredly, seating himself in the gold wing chair. Patting his lap, he said silkily, "Come here."

His intent was obvious. Laurel started for the ladder-back chair across from him, purposefuly steering a circuitous path about him. But she did not sidestep him widely enough, for a long, blue-clad arm shot out, grabbing the black velvet of the gown. Uttering an incoherent cry, Laurel found herself yanked into Lafflin's lap, present and all.

"Open your present, dear," he repeated calmly.

Laurel had half a mind to beat him over the head with the box, but the dangerous undercurrent in his tone made her think twice. Angrily, she tore the blue velvet ribbons sealing the round box. Tossing aside the top of the container, she gasped as she looked at the contents—yards and yards of the finest white Belgian lace.

"Jacob! Where—"

"That's quite a story, my love. I ransacked every shop still open in the city to find the lace, then somehow managed to locate a *couturière*—a withered little black lady, who spent the balance of the day sewing the gown and wrapper for our wedding night."

Her face awed, Laurel held up the gossamer garment. Row after row of intricate lace was sewn together lengthwise to create the gown. Thinner strips of lace formed the shoulder straps, plunging deeply to form the V of the bodice. A length of pale blue satin ribbon, overlaid with lace, secured the bodice empire style beneath the breasts.

Laurel felt her face heating as she envisioned her breasts clad in the gauzy gown. But as she glanced downward, she was even more horrified, for the sheer garment was slit open on either side, from beneath the arms to the hem.

"This gown leaves little to the imagination!" she commented ruefully.

Jacob's hand fastened upon Laurel's thigh, and she could feel the heat of his intent even through the thick folds of velvet. "That's the idea, sweetheart. Besides," he chuckled, "you do have the wrapper."

Laurel held up the equally filmy wrapper, which opened down the front, with only one tiny ribbon closure at the neck. "Scant consolation," she said dryly.

Jacob laughed, gently prodding Laurel to her feet, then rising to stand beside her. "Go put them on."

Laurel's eyebrows flew up. "Surely you don't expect—"

"I do," he replied, eyeing her levelly. "Most assuredly. And you'd best hurry. The men are coming up with our dinner. You'd best dash for the anteroom before they catch you in my dressing gown."

"The men?" Laurel repeated in consternation. "Whatever—"

"Oh, I have a few more surprises in store for you,"

Lafflin replied mysteriously, giving her a devilish grin. "Now, go on. Hurry."

"Very well," Laurel grumbled, taking the box and departing to her tiny cubicle.

Inside the anteroom, Laurel gratefully pressed herself against the closed door, sighing deeply. She looked about at the vacant blackness. At least she would not have to glimpse herself in the scandalous gown. Oh dear, was she really going to wear it? Damn if only the window were not so small, she could crawl out upon the roof and—

"Laurel?"

She shuddered as she heard Jacob's soft voice outside her door. Would the man give her no peace? "Jacob, please. Give me time!" she called out irritably.

"Laurel, I want my robe."

"Your robe?" she repeated, her voice rising. "Jacob, I had hoped to wear it during dinner. There's a chill in the room and—"

"Splendid. Then I take it the sight of me naked during dinner will not distress you, sweet?"

With commendable haste, Laurel tore off the robe, cracked open the door, and wordlessly handed it to Lafflin.

As she closed the door, she heard the sound of his soft, cynical laughter. Bastard! she seethed to herself. She'd be damned if she would parade before him half naked!

Laurel groped about in the darkness, locating the rod where her clothes were stored. God in heaven—it was empty! Again and again, she ran her fingers over the smooth, cold wooden bar. Dash it all, Lafflin must have had her clothes moved to the other room while they were being married! Now she had no choice but to wear the gown and wrapper and naught else.

While Laurel stood silently fuming, she heard a distant knocking sound, then the door to Lafflin's room opening. Straining to listen, she heard the deep timbre of men's voices and the scraping and bumping sounds of furniture being moved. All too soon, silence returned—a deafening, meaningful silence.

Presently, she heard soft footsteps approaching her door. "Sweetheart, all is ready," Jacob whispered through the wood, his voice deceptively smooth. "I shall now sit down and enjoy a leisurely glass of wine—after which I shall come into the anteroom and dress you. Or undress you. Whichever seems most expedient."

Cursing under her breath, Laurel yanked off her chemise and undergarments, then donned the diaphanous gown and wrapper. Angrily, she threw open the door and stepped back into Jacob's room. But the scene that greeted her there made her gasp with astonishment.

The room was in semidarkness, the only light being a candle glowing softly on a small, round table. The unfamiliar table had evidently been brought in by the men, along with the crocks of food, the plates and glasses and wine decanter now placed atop it.

"How very beautiful you look, sweetheart.'

Laurel's attention was captured by Jacob Lafflin, who now stepped out of the shadows wearing the black dressing gown. The robe was loosely tied, the open lapels revealing the bronze of his chest, his bare limbs beneath the robe's hem suggesting that he wore nothing beneath. Studying him, Laurel felt her mouth becoming suddenly dry, her knees weak.

He moved closer, his dark eyes soft, almost dreamy, glowing in the candlelight. With infinite care, he perused every inch of her lace-draped body from her toes to her hair, his gaze drawing a flush up her skin as if she had, indeed, been seared. "Angel," he whispered. He reached out, touching her hair; then his hand dropped and he entwined his fingers with hers. "Come here. Your hair is a mass of tangles, darling."

Numbly, she let him lead her to the dresser and stood gazing blankly at her shadowy reflection in the mirror as her husband took the hairbrush and ran it through her disheveled curls, sending chills through her body. Jacob completed the task with the greatest gentleness, then laid aside the brush and took her hand, leading her to the small table.

As they reached the feast laid out for them, the smell of freshly baked fish wafted over Laurel, and she felt a distinct wave of nausea.

"Sweetheart, you're shaking—I must light a fire in the grate later," Jacob said worriedly. Then he chuckled, turning her toward the wing chair, which was now placed on one side of the table. "Come sit in my lap, and I'll see that you're warm and fed."

Laurel's heart lurched into a frantic rhythm as she envisioned herself pressed against Jacob's body, clad only in her flimsy garments. What horrified her more was the thought of Jacob's robe slipping open even further!

"I'm not a child, Jacob—I'll feed myself," Laurel replied in a defiant, shrill voice, firmly disengaging his hand from hers and moving toward the ladder-back chair.

Quickly, Jacob circled the table, drawing the chair back for her. "You're right, of course, sweet. You're not a child, but a wife—or you will be shortly."

Now seated, Laurel stared at her plate, hoping the shadows would mute the flaming color in her cheeks.

Jacob took his seat across from her and busied himself serving them both oyster stew from a steaming crock. Then he poured two glasses of port from a crystal decanter.

"I take it the officers did not finish off the cask last night?" Laurel inquired, taking a sip of the strong wine.

Across from her, Jacob smiled sheepishly. "About last night . . ."

"Yes?" she prompted, eyeing him coolly.

He took a deep breath. "I wish to apologize for last night, Laurel."

Laurel's young face grew tight, her eyes cold. "Do my ears deceive me, sir? The saintly Jacob Lafflin admitting he was wrong?"

Lafflin scowled at her. "You're not making this easy for me, Laurel."

"Do you think last night was a garden party for me?" she demanded nastily.

"*Touché,*" he conceded. He leaned forward, his dark eyes serious. "Last night—well, I was drunk, Laurel. Sometimes I get mean when I'm drunk. When I saw you out and realized that you did not trust me to see to Fancy's wellfare . . . well, I'm sorry I whacked you and gave you such a hard time."

"I see," she commented stiffly. Nodding toward his glass of port, she reminded him ungraciously, "You're drinking tonight, Jacob."

"Aye. But I'll not get drunk. This night is far too important to me."

"Is it now?" she inquired, hoping he could not hear the quiver in her voice, as her trembling fingers grasped her wine goblet. She drew the glass to her lips, took a hearty gulp, then grimaced as the wine coursed its familiar burning path down her throat. "I suppose you had the port sent up to ensure my cooperation?"

He shrugged, dipping his spoon into his bowl of stew. "It should make things easier for you."

Abruptly, Laurel put her wineglass down, pushing it aside. "Jacob, why did you marry me?"

"Laurel, eat your dinner," he replied, taking a bite of the stew.

"Not until you answer my question."

"Eat your dinner, and perhaps I'll tell you."

Sighing angrily, Laurel picked up her spoon, taking a bite

of the oyster stew. Surprisingly, the soup was quite good, the oysters tender and succulent, the broth rich and creamy.

For a few moments the two ate in silence. Then, abruptly, Jacob asked, "Laurel, have you given any thought to the vows you said today?"

Taken aback, Laurel stared at him blankly. "What do you mean?"

"To love, to honor, to obey," he repeated meaningfully, his words stabbing at her with their impact.

"Jacob, I had no choice—"

"Wrong. You had a choice."

"To let Fancy be shot and myself imprisoned?" she argued, her voice cracking. "*That* was a choice?"

He sighed. "It's a moot point," he admitted. "At any rate, you said the vows. What I wish to know is, will you honor them?"

"Jacob, what do you expect of me?" she cried, tossing down her spoon with a clang. "You have my life now in exchange for Fancy's. What more do you want?"

"Your loyalty," he said, gazing at her steadily. "And, perhaps—your love."

"Love?" she repeated in amazement. "Whatever makes you want my love? You certainly don't love me!"

His handsome face darkened. "Correct. I certainly don't love you. I'm too smart to let a little schemer like you get her hands on my heart."

"As for loyalty," she continued, ignoring his flash of temper. "Jacob, I'm a Southerner. Do you actually expect me to side with the North, to forsake my family?"

"I'm not asking you to forsake your family. Only to stand by your husband."

Laurel uttered a sigh of raging frustration. "Jacob, it's impossible. We're enemies—"

"No!" he shot at her, reaching out and grabbing her hand over the table. "We're man and wife now, Laurel, and we shall never, never again be enemies! Do you want to know the real reason I married you?''

His words were so intense, his eyes so dark with outrage, Laurel could only murmur faintly, ''Why?''

''Because I could not bear the thought of seeing you dead!''

''D—dead?''

''Yes! As I told you once before, when we occupied Indianola, there was a young girl who looked much like you, dead upon the street. All the way home, the thought of that pitiful child haunted me. And I vowed, 'This will never happen to Laurel—*never*!' ''

Laurel gazed at her husband in awe, as if she had never seen him before. His voice was tortured, grim, his eyes too anguished to leave any doubts in her mind. He really meant what he was saying—he had married her to protect her, to keep her safe. At this, she felt a treacherous softening in her heart, and stared down at her lap in bewilderment. Could it be she had deep feelings for this Yankee?

Jacob tugged on her hand, and reluctantly, she gazed back up at him, hoping he could not read her feelings in her eyes.

''Laurel, do you realize the dangerous game you've been playing—intrigue, betrayal?''

''Jacob, I'm a Southerner,'' she whispered miserably.

''You're Jacob Lafflin's wife! And if you continue with your shenanigans, I may not be able to save you next time. Sweetheart, the South is going to lose—and your death would be senseless.''

Now angry, Laurel tossed off her husband's hand and hissed, ''The South will win!''

''You little fool! Goddamnit, Laurel, you will listen to me! You will obey!''

She shook her head stubbornly. ''No!''

Now his eyes were murderous. ''You will, if I must first

beat the stubbornness out of your hide or tie you to the bed, or . . . or otherwise ensure that you are incapable of moving."

"You—you would overwhelm me by brute force?" she bristled.

Now, amazingly, he grinned. "Of course."

Curiously, instead of being enraged, Laurel felt the horrible tension between them evaporate at his roguish remark. Heaven help her, he was a charming scoundrel, sitting across from her with triumphant dark eyes glittering, obviously savoring the delight of her undoing!

Laurel felt as if she were about to plunge off a cliff into dark, dangerous territory. Breathing far more rapidly than she wished to, she grabbed her spoon and attacked her soup, all the while avoiding Jacob's devilish eyes. The balance of their meal passed in tense silence; once Laurel's stomach was full from the stew, she sipped her wine and played with her poached redfish and fried vegetables.

Just as they finished, Jacob excused himself and walked off into a blackened corner of the room, where the tallboy stood. He stepped back into the wavery light, carrying a small white cake. "Suki baked it in honor of the occasion."

Looking up at this symbol of her union with a man who was almost a stranger to her, Laurel could not hide the apprehension on her face.

Sighing as he set the cake atop the table, Jacob seated himself. "Cheer up, sweetheart. This is our wedding night, after all, and should be a joyous occasion. What I said before—well, I was simply trying, in my inadequate manner, to explain to you that I would rather make love to you than kill you."

Laurel studied him with some alarm. "Would you kill me, Jacob?"

His expression was unreadable. "What do you think, dear?"

Laurel bit her lip. "I think I want a piece of cake, Jacob."

A smile tugged at the corners of his mouth as he took the knife and cut her a wedge of cake, carefully placing the slice on her bread saucer.

As he served himself cake, Jacob said thoughtfully, "Laurel, I'm twenty-seven years old—time for me to settle down, have a family of my own. That is if I manage to survive this war." Looking up at her intently, he continued, "If I don't make it, it would be a comfort to think I might leave an heir behind."

Laurel was not impressed. In fact, the mention of children—a possibility she had not considered before—sent a distinct shudder coursing up and down her spine. Taking a bite of the sweet white cake, she sniffed. "I'm to be a brood mare, then?"

"Do you think I'd have children with just anyone?" he growled.

"Perhaps. As a matter of fact, you know next to nothing about my upbringing. At one point, as I recall, you told me you thought me part black."

"And what if you were?" he countered flatly.

Laurel glowered at Lafflin and took a gulp of wine to wash down the cake. Quite an odd man she had married, she mused to herself.

All too soon the last crumbs of the cake had been consumed, and Jacob murmured meaningfully, "Time for bed, Laurel."

Laurel's head shot up, and she looked at Lafflin with stark fear. Suddenly, she was all frightened little girl. "Jacob, will you give me more time?" she begged, her voice frail and brittle.

A glimmer of sympathy flickered in his dark brown eyes, then faded. "You've made me wait long enough already, Laurel, and by damn, I'm not letting you out of my bed to go spy on the streets tonight. Do you really think I can lie next to you all night without making you my wife?''

Miserably, she shook her head.

He stood up, then took her hand and pulled her to her feet. "It won't be so terrible, love.''

Slowly, she was drawn into his arms. His hand caressed her hair and her face contacted the hard satin of his bare chest. "This is your first time, isn't it, Laurel?''

Mutely, she nodded.

His arms tightened about her as he breathed almost reverently, "It is as I thought. Tell me, sweetheart, do you know what's going to happen?''

She tilted her head toward him, her face burning. "Jacob, I spent much of my childhood playing near a barnyard.''

He chuckled softly. "This will be rather different, love.''

Drawing apart from her slightly, he untied the bow on her wrapper, removing it from her shoulders. She stood still, struggling not to shiver; but when he reached for the satin tie securing her gown beneath her breasts, she shuddered and sidestepped him.

"Easy, love," he admonished, pausing for a moment to study her curves through the lace fabric of her gown. "Easy," he repeated, but now the word came as a groan, and in one fluid stride, he reached her, sweeping her up into his arms.

Laurel's heart raced wildly as he carried her to the bed and laid her upon the cool counterpane. But as Jacob untied his robe, she gasped in distress. "Jacob, the candle!''

"It'll burn itself out, sweet.''

"N-no I mean the light—''

"Is there not sufficient light, love?" he teased. And he threw off his dressing gown.

Laurel's eyes grew huge as she saw Jacob, now totally naked, standing next to the bed. In the soft light, he was all glowing bronze and magnificent sinew, a tall god with glimmering brown eyes and burnished black hair. Looking downward, she felt her heart thud as she glimpsed his manhood—already swollen, standing ready. Never had she seen a man thus!

The mattress sagged as he got in beside her. Pulling her gently into his arms, he breathed, "Oh, Laurel, how I have waited for this!"

Despite her fears, her resentment of him, the caressing tone of his voice warmed her, leaving no doubts in her mind as to his sincerity. Rogue that he was, Jacob Lafflin did care for her, did want to protect her, in his way. She had expected cruelty, cynicism, tonight. Instead, her new husband was showering her with sweetness, gentleness—which left her feeling bewildered and overwhelmed.

But Laurel did not have long to consider her new feelings, for Jacob cupped her face in his hands and kissed her soulfully. His lips were ever so warm against hers, and his mouth tasted sweet from the cake and wine. His tongue teased her lips until she softened, opening her mouth to him. He drew her closer and encircled her waist with his arm, and the friction of the sheer lace separating his warm flesh from hers was powerfully erotic. But as his fingertips traced a delicate pattern up and down her spine, she realized that it was ultimately his tenderness that was her undoing.

When the kiss ended, he whispered softly, "Don't be afraid, Laurel. We've all night—and I'll not take you until you're ready."

She was at the point of opening her mouth to ask, what if she was never ready? But then he kissed her again, and she knew, as she began to melt deep inside, that she would indeed be ready—and soon!

He kissed her lips, her cheeks, her eyes, her hair, then his mouth moved to nibble on her ear, his warm breath sending delicious shivers through her body. As his tongue stole inside her ear, tickling in sweet torment, her breath quickened, and small, involuntary moans escaped her mouth.

He responded to her utterances by kissing her ardently, and a primal need began to stir between her thighs, making her ache to be penetrated by the wonderful hardness that now pressed against her. After a long, provocative moment, Jacob pulled back. Laurel's cheeks were flushed, and both were rapturously breathless now. He reached out and untied the bow beneath her bodice. "Sit up, sweetheart."

She did as he bid, trembling as she scooted up against the headboard. Slowly, he removed her gown, tossing it upon the floor. Instinctively, she clutched her breasts to hide her nakedness. But his hands grasped hers, pulling them away from her as he drew her once more to a supine position on the sheet. Then he knelt above her, pressing her hands into the mattress as his eyes examined her from head to toe, pausing to study her breasts, then moving lower, to fix, for an electrifying moment, upon the mound of soft hair where her legs were joined.

Laurel found that her husband's eyes kindled a more desperate need in her than his lips had moments earlier. The ache between her thighs became a fierce, restless yearning, demanding the hard fire of consummation. Like a wanton hoyden, she wanted to open her thighs to him, demand he take her quickly. What was happening to her? she wondered wildly. Where was her self-control?

Practically nonexistent! For now, Jacob drew a teasing finger up her body, beginning at her toes and sliding inexorably higher, pausing at strategic points on her body to torment her flesh in slow, circular patterns. Long before the bold finger reached Laurel's breasts, she was near panting with the intensity of the stimulation, losing control fast. Forgotten was her shame, her naked powerlessness before her husband and adversary. Her entire body grew alive with sensation, and as his fingertip reached a taut nipple, she cried out with exquisite torment. He quickly looked upward, his glittering eyes locking with hers, and despite the triumph in his gaze, she found herself moaning, "Jacob...oh, Jacob!"

"Steady, love. Wait for me," he teased. Yet he grasped her in his arms almost violently, and the sensation of his naked body pressed hard against hers made her shiver in intense pleasure. He rolled on top of her and looked deeply down into her eyes even as the sensation of his muscular chest flattening her breasts, along with his hard manhood probing against her lower belly, made her light-headed. At last he kissed her, his lips hot and trembling upon hers. She clung to him dizzily, brazenly sliding her tongue into his mouth, and he responded passionately, clutching her so tightly and possessively that she thought she would drown in the exquisite sensations rippling through her body.

After a moment, he whispered, "Touch me, darling."

Tentatively, she ran her hands over his back and felt gooseflesh rising on his skin as she caressed the smooth muscles of his spine.

He groaned and his lips moved lower, leaving her face to kiss the hollow of her neck. His hands cupped and kneaded her breasts; his mouth followed. When he teased each swollen nipple in turn with his tongue in a provocative, sensuous rhythm, she thought she would lose her mind. She moaned and shifted, the ache between her legs becoming a twisting pleasure. Soon, Jacob's mouth continued its trail of fire down her stomach, his tongue pausing to tease her navel.

As his mouth moved even lower, Laurel stiffened, realizing that he had no intention of stopping. Almost involuntarily, her thighs clenched against this new invasion, but Jacob's strong hands slid between her legs, parting them as he soothed, "Relax, sweet."

Now Laurel cried out in ecstasy as Jacob's mouth sent

shockwaves of exquisite rapture ripping through her body. Her hands grabbed his hair, twisting, tugging, as he drew her to the edge of a riotous explosion. But he held her there, just eluding consummation.

"Jacob," she pleaded, half sobbing. "Jacob."

He got to his knees and gazed down at her, his eyes full of passion and longing. "Laurel, give me your hand."

Stretching partially upright, Laurel obeyed him. Without shame, she let him place her hand upon his smooth, swollen manhood. "How can it be so soft," she breathed wondrously, "yet so hard?" As the shaft grew even more rigid and engorged in response, she added, "And so large?"

"No larger than what I feel for you." He laughed softly, pushing her shoulders to the mattress. "Close your eyes, love."

Ecstatically, she did as bid. She felt his hand between her thighs, his fingers preparing her for his entry. She did not flinch as his touch grew bolder, penetrating her flesh—the sensation was distinctly pleasurable, though vaguely hurtful.

Tenderly, he readied her as she lay twisting in rapture from his touch, swimming in glorious sensation. She moaned in delight when his fingers were replaced by the smooth, round tip of his manhood.

She was not prepared for the pain. At first there was a sharp jab as he met the hard wall of her resistance. Laurel's eyes flew open, and she stifled a cry. She tired to pull back, but her efforts only added to his ardor and forcefulness as his hands slid beneath her, holding her still as he renewed his assault. Laurel bit her lip and thought wildly that surely he would not continue to try to join himself with her this way. Surely it was impossible—

He did the impossible. Groaning her name, he pierced her maidenhead, then slowly drove himself deeply inside her. Tears spilled from Laurel's eyes as she felt split apart by the hard, hot shaft and wondered how such a soft, seemingly gentle implement could behave so brutally.

Jacob lowered himself upon her, kissing the tears on her cheeks. "There, there," he soothed. "The worst is over, darling."

Tenderly, he kissed her mouth, until her stiff, resisting body relaxed somewhat. He rocked against her gently for a moment, letting her adjust to and savor the sensation of his complete penetration. A deep heat, a delicious friction, began to build in the core of her until at last she began to accept, indeed to welcome, his unyielding invasion of every recess of her womanhood. He hooked his arms beneath her knees and drew himself to a kneeling position, locking his gaze with hers, as he began to move inside her slowly, gently. The pain was still there, vaguely—but now the hurt felt good, so very good! Laurel stared up at Jacob in awe as she realized that this—this was what she had waited for.

His movements grew more rapid, and Laurel found herself instinctively arching to meet him, panting as he drove her toward ecstasy. She found herself wanting more, more, more... yes, she wanted it all! She became completely open to him, letting him fill her to the hilt, meeting his thrusts with a power of her own, which propelled them both to greater heights of sense-shattering rapture. The lovers transcended physical limitations as their entire universe became the voracious need to devour, to fuse, to become one... "Yes! Yes!" Laurel moaned, a million white-hot shards of ecstasy exploding in her head.

In one last, powerfully deep thrust, Jacob collapsed on top of her, his lips smothering her startled cry of joy and pain. "Laurel—Christ, how sweet you are!"

Laurel kissed him back passionately, letting his warmth and strength blot out all else. Entwined thus, the two drifted off to sleep as the tiny, distant candle flickered and died...

*   *   *

Laurel awakened in the darkness, shivering. During his sleep, Jacob had rolled off her, though one arm was thrown possessively across her stomach. Carefully, she removed his arm, then sat up in the still, cold blackness, the movement bringing a twinge of pain and a flood of memories. Beside her, Jacob's hard-chiseled, muscular form was just visible in the dim moonlight.

He was her enemy. Yet now she was his. He had taken her, joined his body to hers in a strange, almost brutal ritual—the memory of her utter capitulation now made her shudder in mortification. She felt branded, physically and emotionally, bonded to him more by her unconditional response than by the primitive, intensely intimate nature of the act.

Why had she let him take her this way? Why had she surrendered without a fight, opened her body to his plunder, let him have her, hurt her . . . anything he wished?

She stared at his handsome, peaceful face, at his hair shimmering with moonlight. Unwittingly, she reached out, stroking the silky texture of his hair. "God help me," she murmured through her tears. She leaned over, gently pressing her lips against his until she tasted the saltiness of her own tears. She pulled back and he stirred slightly, smiling in his sleep.

Sitting upright once more, she closed her eyes to blot out his image. But she could no longer obliterate her feelings—

She had loved it! God help her, she had loved it! His touch, his kisses, his filling her—she had wanted it all, wanted it fiercely!

Why? Because she loved him! God help her, she was in love with Jacob Lafflin!

It could not be! Surely it was impossible! How could she love a man yet hate him at the same time?

She did! She did!

Stifling a sob, Laurel got to her feet and donned her gown

in the darkness, crossing to the anteroom. Once inside, she closed the door and knelt beside the tiny window, pressing her face against the cool glass to gaze out at a thousand cold stars in the black sky.

The sky would never be the same again. Last night, she had gazed at it as a girl. Now she was a woman—a woman in love.

And a traitor. A traitor to her family, to the loved ones who, somewhere, slept beneath the very same stars.

She poignantly thought of home. God, how she longed for her mother and her sister, Camille. For all Laurel knew, Cammie might also be a married woman at this very moment. How it would help to have someone to share these feelings with!

No, no, she realized with a sob, it wouldn't help at all. Even if Camille were married, she wouldn't be experiencing the agonizing pain of loving a man who was her enemy!

Laurel turned, crawling to her tiny pallet in the corner. She threw herself down and curled up into a ball of pain, shivering violently in the cold, muffling her sobs with a pillow. This was something she must face alone. There was no one who could help her . . .

Yet at that very moment, the door to the anteroom opened. Gasping, Laurel turned to gaze up at Jacob, who stood in the doorway, his magnificent nakedness outlined by the moonlight, his features rigid with determination.

Wordlessly, he crossed to her, lifting her from the pallet up into his arms.

Laurel's heart thudded as they reentered Jacob's room and approached the bed. As he lowered her upon the sheet, she managed a weak, "No, Jacob . . ."

Useless. In an instant he was beside her, his deft hands raising her gown to her neck, his warm, demanding lips capturing hers . . .

Chapter
Twenty-four

NOVEMBER 12, 1862

While Laurel at last slept in her husband's arms, Fancy lay wide awake in the small cabin she shared with Reba behind the Virginia House. Her eyes were dilated with fear in the darkness as she strained to watch Reba dress in the quiet room. Fancy wondered wildly where the woman could be going at this time of night. Did Reba mean Miss Laurel harm now that Miss Laurel was married to Captain Lafflin?

Reba stood outlined in a pool of moonlight near the window, and Fancy watched her from her shadowy cot as Reba finished donning a simple cottonade dress and matching turban. Taking a cloak from the rocking chair, Reba quietly slipped from the cabin.

Fancy bolted to her feet in the darkness, stumbling about for her clothing. She dared not light the taper lest Reba spot her from the yard. She literally sprang into an old calico dress and worn shoes, then wrapped a moth-eaten wool shawl about her shivering shoulders.

Leaving the cabin, Fancy grimaced as the hinges squeaked,

then shuddered silently in the chill of the porch. Her eyes desperately searched the yard, and she spotted Reba on the side of the Virginia House, already near the street.

Fancy braced herself, her teeth chattering, her eyes apprehensively sweeping the tree-lined yard. Night was not Fancy's favorite time. She had always feared the dark, had always taken seriously the warnings from her forbears about ghosts and bad spirits waiting in the trees to snatch at her as she passed. Nonetheless, Fancy charged heedlessly into the cold shadows of midnight, smothering her own terror as the wind and the moonlight played savage tricks upon her mind, making the trees sway and rustle and shimmer like lurking phantoms.

Now panting, Fancy reached the street just as Reba turned the corner. For a moment, Fancy paused, struggling with mixed emotions. Wherever Reba was going, it was away from the Virginia House and Miss Laurel. Perhaps she should return to the safety of her bed. She shivered and drew the shawl more tightly about her. There were Yankees about this night—Yankees with guns and orders to shoot!

Yet Fancy's feet seemed to have a will of their own, and she found herself following the Trinidad woman. Fancy knew in her heart that Reba wished Miss Laurel harm, that she might be sneaking forth this very night to plot her evil against Fancy's mistress. Fancy remembered the wildness in Reba's eyes earlier that day, when they returned from the wedding—that look told her that Reba would have no peace until her rival, Miss Laurel, was dead!

The young slave followed Reba through a maze of twists and turns along the Galveston streets. Luckily, there were no sailors patrolling in the area they walked. Things were quiet, ominously quiet, and very dark.

At last, Reba reached her destination—the very warehouse where Carter had tried to rape Miss Laurel! Fancy paused and watched Reba approach the door of the huge frame building. Immediately, a tall, husky black man stepped out from the shadows. Reba spoke with him briefly, then he opened the door to the warehouse for her. Yellow light spilled briefly out upon the board walkway, then Reba melted into the blackness.

"Oh no, what I going to do?" Fancy whispered to herself from her position in the shadows of a building across the street. "How I get in there past that man?"

As if in answer to Fancy's question, three blacks came around the corner toward her. Fancy ducked into the deeper darkness of a doorway as two men and a woman came into view, whispering quietly to one another. Watching the group pass, Fancy summoned all her courage, then fell into line behind them, moving with them across the street.

It was all almost too easy for Fancy. The foursome approached the door to the warehouse, then again, the big man stepped from the darkness. The woman murmured, "Evenin', Jesse," and the door swung open as if by magic, letting the three pass, with Fancy trailing in behind them.

Once inside the rambling, vacant structure, Fancy immediately spotted a damaged, solitary bale of cotton off to the side and dashed for cover behind it. Peeking over the bale, she quickly took in her surroundings. The huge room was lighted by lanterns, candles, and a small bonfire at the center of the shell floor. About ten Negroes, people Fancy had never seen before, were gathered near the fire. All were simply dressed, in faded muslins and cottonades. A jug of wine was being passed, and the talk was animated.

Fancy now noticed a small, rickety table off to the side of the bonfire, on which were placed half a dozen lighted black candles and a cracked white porcelain bowl. Fancy gulped as Reba went to the table and placed several hand-carved images upon it. Something evil was about to happen, she thought to herself.

Yet Fancy was even more horrified as she observed Reba moving off to a shadowy corner of the warehouse and picking up a dirty rag from the floor. As the woman shook out the bit of cloth, Fancy's eyes grew enormous. "That Miss Laurel's turban," she muttered hoarsely to herself. "She leave it the day we here wid Carter."

Fancy wondered half-hysterically why Reba had picked up the cloth. Her question was quickly answered as Reba returned to the center of the warehouse and placed the turban on the table next to the images. Oh Lord, did Reba know it was Miss Laurel's? Fancy wondered in fright. How could she?

Fancy was distracted from her thoughts as a couple entered the building, the woman carrying a basket that jumped and jerked about in her hands as if it had a life of its own. Fancy realized with a wave of physical fear that there must be some kind of living creature inside the basket, which the woman now placed upon the table.

With the arrival of the couple, the group of blacks gathered in a circle, with Reba seating herself in the center, between the table and the fire. A grizzled man produced a small drum made from an animal hide stretched on a wooden frame and began pounding out a native cadence with his hands. At this, the blacks started swaying, chanting, and singing. The mumblings were strange to Fancy—words like *Li Bon Dieu, L'Loa,* and *Damballah.*

Reba murmured her own chant, which Fancy assumed was French. The priestess's eyes were closed in entreaty, her face twisted with concentration. Once in a while, Fancy would hear Reba mutter Miss Laurel's name or Captain Lafflin's name—and her heart skipped a beat each time!

The wine was freely passed as the chanting continued. The pounding of the drum grew wilder, and the blacks began to cry out, clap, and lurch about on their haunches. All at once Reba's eyes opened, and a tumultuous cry went up from the blacks. Fancy clapped a hand over her mouth to keep from screaming out, for never had she seen a human being look more crazed. Reba's eyes were rabidly yellow, possessed, fiercely fixed, like the eyes of a demon. The blacks began chanting, "Mambo, mambo, mambo . . ." as Reba slowly rose up, like a spectral presence, and went to the table. Now Reba stood before the group with arms outstretched and gold eyes oozing evil, and unrestrained cries came forth from the blacks in the circle—a few seemed to go into some kind of state of their own, sprawling about on the floor, jerking and tearing at their clothes, their eyes rolling insanely. Hearing a sound to her right, Fancy jumped and noted that even the guard was now caught up in the ceremony and stood in the open doorway, watching with awe-faced fascination.

Turning back to Reba, Fancy thought her heart would leave her body as she watched the priestess take Miss Laurel's turban and wrap it about one of the images. "Oh no, oh no," Fancy whispered desperately to herself. "She going to voodoo Miss Laurel!"

Laying aside the cloth-wrapped image for the moment, Reba turned her attention to the chipped porcelain bowl, positioning it at the center of the table. Then she picked up the quivering basket, unfastened the top, reached inside, and pulled out a live chicken!

The drumming reached a crescendo, as did the shrieking and moaning of the blacks. Reba raised the live chicken above her head, then slowly lowered the flapping, screeching bird. Fancy felt compelled to scream out her own horror as she watched the priestess bite the chicken's head off, her teeth quick and cruel, blood dripping from her mouth and down her chin. More blood now gushed from the bird into the porcelain bowl, then Reba tossed aside the chicken's body, picking up the image and dipping it in the blood. Meanwhile, the headless chicken, still jerking with life, flapped its way through the Negroes and across the bare floor, only to land on the bale of cotton, squarely in front of Fancy's nose!

By now, the blacks were in such a riotous, convulsive state that not even the guard at the door noticed when a young black girl fled, screaming, into the night.

Chapter
Twenty-five

NOVEMBER 12, 1862

When Laurel awakened, the room was flooded with sunshine. Jacob was next to her on the bed, perched on his elbow as he gazed down at her, his brown eyes glowing, mellow. "Good morning, darling."

"Good morning," she replied. Unwittingly, she found herself studying his body. Though from the waist down he was covered with the sheet, his bronze torso was bare, and shamefully, Laurel remembered pressing her lips against the nipples on his chest. Glancing upward, she studied the heavy shadow of whiskers on his face, and felt her own face heating as she remembered how his beard had burned her stomach deliciously in the rosy shadows just before dawn.

In all, they had made love three times the previous night. Each time Laurel had given herself fully, let herself be consumed in passion by her new husband even as she brazenly devoured his body with her own.

Remembering her treason, Laurel slowly scooted away from Jacob, turning her back on him, pulling the sheet high about her neck. In an instant, a hard, warm arm slid about her waist, and she felt the muscular length of his naked body pressing against her back.

"Jacob," she shuddered as his other hand pushed aside her hair and his lips contacted the back of her neck. The hand at her waist moved lower, contacting the cleft between her legs.

"Jacob, please—no," she moaned even as she throbbed and ached inside and felt the hard rising of his desire behind her.

Jacob chuckled softly, his teeth nibbling her ear in exquisite torment. "Sore, darling? Did I do you in last night?"

Mutely, she nodded.

He quickly turned her to face him, and his mouth sought hers. Pressed against the smooth, muscular satin of his body, Laurel felt herself going weak and liquid inside and wanting him again.

Yet he drew back then, gazing down at her with thoughtful longing as his fingers stroked her cheek. "Quite a whisker burn I've given you, sweetheart. Or is it the glow of desire I see on your face, Laurel Lafflin?"

Gazing up at her husband, Laurel fought hard to squelch an urge to throw her arms about his neck and pull his mouth down to hers once more. "It's—it's a whisker burn," she lied, grimacing in mock distress.

Jacob chuckled, then sat up, throwing his long legs over the side of the bed. "You'd best get up, sweet—while you still can."

Jacob went to his dresser and made preparations to shave while Laurel sat up, clutching the quilt about her. Furtively, she glanced about the room, spotting her gown and wrapper, twin heaps upon the braided rug. With a wary glance confirming that Jacob was lathering his face, Laurel darted out of the bed, quickly grabbing the two items, then returning to the safety of the quilt.

As Laurel struggled to don her gown yet keep her body concealed with the quilt, she heard Jacob laugh softly. "Your modesty comes a bit late, don't you think, sweetheart?"

Looking up, she met his laughing gaze in the mirror over his dresser. The mirror! She had forgotten about it, yet surely he must have been watching her the entire time. He now stood with the razor pressed against his face, a devilish smile lighting his face and eyes. Yes, he had definitely seen her utterly unclothed!

"Don't you have duties to attend to?" she asked crossly.

"No, sweet. Sorry to disappoint you, but Renshaw gave me the day off, to spend with my bride." He gave her a wicked wink.

Laurel shuddered, then busied herself donning the gown and robe. She was about to get out of bed when a knock sounded at the door. "Yes?" she heard Jacob demand rather testily.

"Captain, we have brought madame's bath," came the voice from the hall.

Laurel gasped, her bright blue eyes widening. "Reba!" she whispered, looking at Jacob in some alarm.

Calmly, her husband turned from the dresser, wiping his clean-shaven face with a towel. Taking his dressing gown from the chair and quickly donning it, he crossed to the door and opened it.

Laurel pulled the covers up to her neck as Reba and Fancy entered the room, pulling along a tin bathtub. Despite Reba's disconcerting presence, Laurel felt herself warming as she saw Fancy, especially after the terrifying dream yesterday. It was so good to know the girl was safe, even though poor Fancy looked skittish and frightened as a rabbit as she pushed the heavy tub past Jacob Lafflin.

"Fancy!" Laurel called out, smiling brightly. "Come sit on the bed and let me check your wound."

Fancy spotted her mistress and took a step forward, then hesitated, furtively eyeing Jacob Lafflin.

"It's all right, Fancy," Jacob said.

As Fancy approached the bed, Laurel looked up to smile at Jacob. But her husband's brow was furrowed, his lips tightened in an inscrutable frown.

Shrugging, Laurel turned to Fancy, who was now seated beside her. She removed the girl's blue cottonade turban and examined the knot on the back of her head, noting with relief that the swelling was almost gone and a scab had formed. The wound was no longer bandaged, and there were no signs of infection.

"Good," Laurel murmured with relief, securing the turban once more upon Fancy's head.

"Fancy, we must fetch the water," a venomous feminine voice hissed.

Laurel looked up at Reba, who stood across the room, her hands on her hips. A chill gripped Laurel, for the tall, bronze woman's eyes were so intense, so full of hatred, that her gaze seemed to burn the younger woman, like a yellow fire. Laurel would have immediately turned away, but as usual, Reba's gold eyes cast their haunting, captivating spell, and Laurel felt almost mesmerized by a hypnotic evil force.

Remembering Jacob's admonition not to look Reba in the eye, Laurel managed, with an effort that was almost physically painful, to unfasten her gaze from Reba's. "By all means, Reba, do fetch the water," she directed her, attempting a sarcastic tone, but sounding rather apprehensive instead.

The two women left, returning several times with steaming buckets of water and filling the tub. On the final trip, neither woman carried water. Fancy brought a breakfast tray covered with a linen cloth, and Reba carried clean sheets and towels.

"Madame, if you would, I must change the bed," Reba told Laurel, her tone soft poison.

Reluctantly, Laurel rose from the bed, catching Reba's contemptuous look as she studied Laurel in the sheer gown and wrapper. Reba strode to the bed, tore back the covers, then gasped, cursing softly in French.

Scowling, Laurel whirled, then felt her face heating as she spotted the streaks of dried blood on the sheet. Reba now glared at Laurel with unveiled malice, her yellow eyes wild, rabid.

Despite her embarrassment regarding the sheets, Laurel found the situation with Reba irresistible and gave her a haughty, triumphant smile. Ignoring Laurel's victorious gaze, Reba turned, ripping the sheets off the bed with a vengeance.

Suddenly, Jacob laughed. Laurel pivoted to face him and saw her husband sitting in the wing chair, a look of cynical amusement in his eyes as he sipped his coffee.

Thankfully, the two black women soon left, and Laurel was once again alone with her new husband. Tapping her foot in irritation as she stood with arms akimbo, Laurel testily inquired, "Why is Reba attending us?"

Jacob shrugged, uncovering a crock of cereal on the tea table. "Yesterday I informed her that she is to assist Fancy when needed. As I told you last night, sweet, I'm going to see that Reba remembers her place."

Laurel's features twisted in incredulity. "But must you rub her nose in it?'

He laughed dryly. "Must you? That was quite a devastating smile you gave her just now, Laurel."

Laurel scowled at him, yet the corners of her mouth puckered in betrayal of her amusement.

"Take your bath before the water becomes cold," Jacob said.

The bath! Laurel glanced with distress at the steamy tub, which she had almost forgotten. "You—you expect me to undress in front of you and—'' her voice trailed off as she felt the color rise in her face.

Slowly, he nodded.

"Why, I couldn't," she sputtered. "It's—it's unthinkable!"

He shrugged, standing up. "Then I'll have the bath."

Laurel balled her fists and dug them into her hips. "I'll not let you have my bath!" she replied stubbornly, her jaw firmly set.

Jacob hooted with laughter and came to her side. "What a willful, spoiled little chit you are, Laurel Lafflin," he teased. He reached out, untying the bow on her wrapper.

"What—what are you doing?" she demanded.

"Helping you undress," he said wickedly, taking the wrapper from her shoulders. "Jesus!" he groaned, his dark eyes sweeping her lace-clad figure.

Watching his hand reach for the bow beneath her breasts, Laurel jumped backward. "Turn around. I'll—I'll undress myself."

Jacob shook his head, his eyes dancing with merriment. "Sweetheart, your coyness at this point—"

"Please, Jacob," she begged breathlessly.

He shrugged. Turning his back to her, he conceded, "Very well, Laurel, play the blushing bride today. But I must warn you that this sort of maneuver will not be long tolerated in our marriage. In case you hadn't noticed, I intend our relationship to be quite uninhibited."

Oh, she had noticed. Laurel quickly undressed and got into the tub, her face hotter than the steamy water. She sat down, stretching deliciously. But then she screamed as her toe contacted a slimy creature near the foot of the tub.

"Laurel, what is it?" Jacob was at her side in an instant as Laurel bolted to her feet and jumped out of the tub, sending a wave of water spilling onto the floor.

"Laurel?" Jacob demanded, staring at her in consternation.

Heedless of her nudity, Laurel stood shivering as she mutely pointed at the foot of the tub, her blue eyes wild.

Jacob quickly bent over, pulling up the sleeve of his dressing gown and fishing in the tub for the object of Laurel's terror. Seconds later, the culprit was discovered, and Jacob held up a dead creature by its tail.

"You certainly are a squeamish thing," Jacob told Laurel. "All this hysteria over a dead lizard."

Laurel grabbed a towel from the tub handle. "Reba did it!" she hissed.

"Doubtless," Jacob agreed. He went to the window, opened it slightly, and disposed of the ugly creature. Returning to Laurel, he scolded, "Finish your bath, sweet. Your teeth are chattering in the cold of this room."

Laurel shook her head. "My teeth are chattering with terror, Jacob! I know Reba means us both harm!"

Jacob threw his hands wide in exasperation. "Laurel, I told you I'd deal with Reba. Anyway, it was only a damned lizard. Get back into the tub."

Laurel gulped, staring at the bath in fear. "No!"

Jacob came to her side, ripping the towel from her body. "Laurel, you're becoming irrational. Get back into the tub and stay there until I get a fire going. Otherwise, I'll find another method of warming you—and quickly!"

With a gasp, Laurel dashed for the tub, quickly sinking into its warm depths. She shuddered, slowly, tentatively stretching her body out. Relieved to find no other terrors lurking in the warm water, she took the soap and began to enjoy the ritual of bathing. Meanwhile, Jacob lit a fire in the grate, taking the chill out of the room. Then he returned to his chair and sat eating his breakfast as he studied his wife thoughtfully.

Laurel avoided his gaze, scrubbing herself with a cloth and lavender-scented soap, luxuriating in the soothing water.

After a few moments, Jacob stood up and came to her

side, smiling down at her tenderly. He reached out, toying
with a damp, ebony curl resting upon her shoulder. "Your
hair is soaked, sweetheart. You should have pinned it up."

"Hm," Laurel sniffed. "I was not about to give you
further opportunity to attack me."

Jacob grinned. "Attack you—now, that's a fascinating
idea." And he began untying his robe.

"W-what are you doing?" Laurel croaked.

"What does it look like I'm doing? I'm going to take a
bath."

"Not with me, you aren't!" Frantically, she reached for
the towel hanging on the tub handle.

But Jacob was faster than she, grabbing the towel and
smiling down at her tauntingly. "Suit yourself."

"Jacob, please give me the towel," she entreated, trying
to cajole him even as she struggled not to clench her teeth at
him.

He laughed, dangling the towel just out of reach. "You
can't expect to use the towel while you're still in the tub,
Laurel."

Miserably, she stood up. His eyes moved slowly, burningly
over her rosy, glistening flesh. Laurel bit her lip, feeling her
body flood with color, but was determined not to shiver
from his gaze.

After a moment he cursed softly under his breath, then
quickly wrapped her with the towel. Laurel literally jumped
out of the tub and dashed off for the wardrobe, hearing his
deep laughter behind her. She opened the doors to the
armoire and stood staring at the interior, finally selecting a
rather prim rose-colored wool frock, grateful that Maureen
Carmichael had insisted Laurel buy at least two winter
dresses. She dashed to the dresser and grabbed undergarments, then returned to the relative privacy provided by the
open armoire door, dressing quickly. Buttoning her bodice,
she heard a slosh as Jacob got into the bathtub. "You

certainly aren't particular, using somebody else's bath,'' she called out ungraciously.

"Laurel, if you're carrying anything, I'm sure I've caught it by now."

Laurel slammed the wardrobe door with a resounding bang and faced her husband with eyes blazing. "Bastard!" she shrieked, clenching her fists at him. Gesturing toward the bed, she demanded, "What could I possibly be carrying after I came a virgin to your bed?"

Jacob shrugged, a musing smile on his face as he drew a sponge down a muscular arm. "You asked for the comment, sweet. Besides, why must you assume the worst? People do carry other diseases—let's see, diptheria, measles—"

"That's not what you were insinuating, and you know it!"

He chuckled, winking at her. "Come here and kiss me."

"Go to hell!"

She stormed off to the dresser, clenching her teeth as he laughed behind her. Angrily, she grabbed the hairbrush and began attacking her disheveled coiffure. As Jacob had pointed out, her hair was quite damp, and she began pinning it up to keep it from clinging to her neck. But as she finished the task, she suddenly gasped as her gaze met Jacob's in the mirror above her.

He stood directly behind her, his black hair glistening and tousled, his skin glowing from the bath. Smiling at her reflection, he wrapped his arms tightly about her waist. She shivered. For, even through her clothing, she could tell that he was very naked, and very ready!

"Sweet, I can't abide it when you're angry with me," he murmured, pressing his lips against her neck, sending shivers up and down her spine. His hand reached around her for the buttons on her frock. "I must make amends—and quickly."

"Jacob—I—I'm not angry with you anymore," she lied

in a quavering voice, fighting the appalling melting sensation deep within her that was aroused by his touch.

"Hmmm," he mused, his mouth pushing aside the collar of her frock. "I'm not convinced." Slowly, he began turning her, his lips moving around her neck.

"Jacob, I prom—"

He kissed her. At first her lips trembled in apprehension beneath his, then she relaxed and opened her mouth to him. He tugged at the buttons on her dress and said huskily, "I like it when you dress so demurely. Makes me feel like a lecherous old scoundrel ravishing a schoolgirl."

"But you are a lecherous old scoundrel ravishing a—"

"Hush." He kissed her again, and before she knew what was happening, her clothing began to fall from her piece by piece. She stood compliant, mesmerized by the taste and motion of his tongue deep inside her mouth. Soon she was totally nude, pressed against his warm, electrifying nakedness, even as his hands clutched her bottom, pulling her hard against the proof of his desire.

He pulled back slightly then, staring down at her. She saw the raw need in his eyes and knew there would be no denying him.

"Don't you think we've played this game long enough?" he asked softly.

He swept her up into his arms and carried her to the bed.

"Jacob, I shall not be able to rise from the bed," she protested weakly as he lay her down.

"That's the idea, sweet."

He lowered himself on top of her, hungrily kissing her even as his strong legs drew hers apart. "You little flirt," he groaned, planting kisses all over her face. "You've been leading me on all morning, tantalizing me with your breasts, your legs, not to mention your delectable little fanny, your kissable mouth, and those huge innocent blue eyes."

"Jacob, I didn't—"

"Tell me you didn't want this!" he demanded, surging into her tender flesh, searing her with his suddenness.

Laurel bit her lip; but her body yielded, welcoming his pleasure. Sensing her softening, he began to move inside her, and Laurel soared in the sensations his deep, hard thrusts kindled in her. "Yes, I wanted it," she moaned, "wanted it so bad—"

He kissed her, penetrating quickly and powerfully, and she wrapped her legs around his waist. He became hard steel dipping into liquid fire—again and again and again, until they melted into each other.

Chapter
Twenty-six

NOVEMBER 12, 1862

Despite Jacob's assurance that he would spend the entire day with his new wife, he was called away that afternoon to meet with Renshaw aboard the *Westfield*, giving Laurel a brief but needed respite. She felt exhausted, overwhelmed by new emotions—her passion, her love for Jacob Lafflin. A brief nap helped somewhat to soothe her tired mind, then she dressed and sought out Fancy, hoping to distract herself and possibly reassure the younger girl.

Speaking with Fancy proved, however, to be little comfort to Laurel. She found the servant in the tiny cabin the girl shared with Reba, behind the Virginia House. As Laurel entered the one-room structure, she spotted the slave sweeping the gray, splintery floor with a straw broom.

"Come on, Fancy, take a few minutes to catch your breath," Laurel said, taking the broom from the younger girl's hand.

She pulled the reluctant girl out upon the cabin's rickety porch, and the two sat down upon the steps, taking deep breaths of a breeze scented of sea and autumn as scattered leaves blew about them. "How are you doing, Fancy?" Laurel inquired of her servant. "You looked scared as a mouse in a trap this morning when you brought my bath."

The younger girl's lower lip trembled at Laurel's question, and she stared at her mistress with frightened, cocoa-colored eyes. "I is scared, Miss Laurel. Scared for you."

"For me?"

The girl nodded. "Reba been in a vi'lence ever since you and Captain Lafflin married."

"A—a violence?"

"She been arantin' and ascreamin'—words I don't understand. They is French, I think, but I know they is bad. I don't know what she plan to do to you, but it evil."

Laurel shuddered, remembering Reba's poisonous glare both yesterday and today. Here, she thought she and Fancy were safe at last—yet the worst might be yet to come!

"Tell me more, Fancy."

The younger girl bit her lip and twisted her tattered white apron with nervous fingers. Finally, she said haltingly, "Miss—Miss Laurel, I ain't wanting to scare you, but Reba, she voodooed you and Captain Lafflin, too."

"Voodooed? Explain that, Fancy."

Now it was Fancy who shuddered, avoiding the older girl's eyes. "Miss Laurel, last night, Reba, she leave, and I follow her. I think maybe she try to hurt you and Captain Lafflin."

"Oh, Fancy!" Laurel exclaimed, placing her hand over the black girl's, deeply touched by her devotion.

"Anyhow, she don't go to your room. Miss Laurel, you remember that big dark place where Carter, he try to have his way wid you?"

Laurel shivered and drew her white wool shawl tightly about her. "You mean the warehouse? I wish I could forget."

Fancy nodded. "The warehouse. That where Reba gone."

"Oh, Fancy! You shouldn't have followed her! My God, with the curfew—"

"I all right, Miss Laurel. But it you—it you—" Fancy's speech trailed off, and her face twisted in fear and pain.

Laurel distractedly brushed a wind-blown black lock from her eyes and studied the frightened girl intently. "Tell me what happened in the warehouse, Fancy."

Fancy began to shake, her chest heaving, tears welling in her eyes. "They voodooed you, Miss Laurel—Reba and them others. They was a bunch of strange folks there I ain't never seen before—I sneak in that warehouse and watch them from behind a bale of cotton. They dance and they sing, they light black candles, and—and they all say your name and Captain Lafflin's name and scream and beat a drum. And some, they act real bad, Miss Laurel—they eyes is crazy and they roll on the floor, atearin' at their clothes." Her own eyes now wild, Fancy expostulated, "I ain't never seen such sin! Then, Reba, she—she have your turban, Miss Laurel, and she wrap it round one of them things she whittle and then she—she kill a chicken wid her bare teeth and dip that doll in the blood—and—"

"Stop!" Laurel cried, too horrified to hear any more and deeply concerned about the state Fancy was working herself into. She wrapped a protective arm about the younger girl. "Oh, Fancy, how horrible for you to have seen that!" She squeezed Fancy and added, with a conviction she wished she felt, "You must try to forget it, Fancy. Jacob says Reba's spells cannot work unless you believe in them."

But Fancy shook her head vehemently. "Oh no, Miss Laurel. Reba, she taken by bad spirits. She see things ain't no one else can see."

Laurel stiffened. "What do you mean?"

"Your turban, Miss Laurel. I tell you, Reba have your turban. She take it from the floor of the warehouse last night. It there ever since we there wid Carter. How she know it there, Miss Laurel? How she know it yours?"

Laurel's frightened eyes locked with Fancy's. How indeed? she wondered.

That evening, as Jacob and Laurel sat upon the bed eating chicken legs and sipping wine, she told him about her conversation with Fancy. "I'm really concerned, Jacob," she concluded. "And I know Fancy is petrified with fear."

"Easy, sweetheart," Jacob admonished. "I warned you not to be hoodwinked by that voodoo malarky." Nonetheless, he frowned broodingly. "Perhaps we should let Fancy sleep in the anteroom from now on, where she'll be closer to you."

Laurel's face lit up. "Oh, Jacob, do you mean it?"

He nodded, his expression grimly determined. "I may even be able to persuade dear Reba to take her bag of tricks elsewhere." Looking down at Laurel, he added ardently, "But not right now. Tonight I have plans for you, my sweet, so you'll have to wait till morning to get Fancy moved and settled."

"Thank you, Jacob." Even as Laurel tried to sound sincere and casual, her voice cracked, for his meaning was not lost on her. She scooted away from him, smoothing her negligee demurely about her, then drawing her chicken leg to her mouth and chewing nervously.

Jacob observed her with amusement. "Getting enough to eat, Laurel?" His smile was wicked as he stared meaningfully at the chicken leg clamped between Laurel's teeth.

She blushed profusely as the salacious symbolism of his words dawned upon her. Hastily withdrawing the chicken leg from her mouth, she put it on her plate on the bedside table.

Jacob laughed softly and took her wineglass from her hand, reaching over her to place it on the night table, along with his dishes. Stroking her cheek with his fingertips, he inquired, "Don't you think it's about time for dessert?"

Laurel's eyes widened. "Jacob, surely you can't mean—again—"

Almost roughly, he pulled her into his lap, tucking her head beneath his chin. "Sweetheart, we're married, and I intend to make love to you every single night—except, of course, when nature dictates otherwise—so you may as well learn to accept it."

Laurel colored hotly at her husband's bluntness even as he pulled her even closer, until her cheek contacted the smooth skin of his chest where his robe was open, while her nose was tickled by the black velvet. "Do you know how happy you've made me, Laurel?" she heard him ask, a catch in his voice.

Laurel remained silent as his hand caressed her hair, afraid to give him further encouragement.

"I want to know more about you," he continued softly.

She grew rigid in his arms. "Why?"

"You're my wife, silly goose," he laughed.

Laurel crawled off his lap, sitting beside him against the headboard. "What do you want to know?" she asked suspiciously.

"Tell me about your life in Tennessee, for instance."

"Tennessee," Laurel repeated slowly, struggling to sound calm even as her heart pounded thunderously. She turned and stared at the window. "I can't talk about it, Jacob. It's too painful."

"Let's see—as I recall, you lost your father, mother, and baby brother to malaria following your family's shipwreck off San Luis Pass," he said, a trace of sarcasm in his tone. "Correct?"

"Y-yes."

"Where are they buried?"

"I beg your pardon?" Laurel turned to him, her eyebrows flying up.

"I said, where is your family buried? Is it in the Episcopal Cemetery off Broadway?"

"Why does that interest you, Jacob?" she asked in confusion. "And how do you know about the cemetery?"

"I passed it last week. Are they buried there, Laurel?"

"W-why yes," she stammered.

"Then we'll go there soon."

"Whatever for?"

Jacob looked incredulous. "Don't you ever visit their graves, to weed, leave flowers, and such?"

She shook her head in bewilderment. "No, I should be ... desolate to be reminded of the tragedy."

Jacob frowned, looking unconvinced. "Laurel, I think it's time for you to grow up a bit and consider your responsibilities to your kin. It's downright disrespectful to do otherwise. You should at least go pay your respects to them."

Laurel blinked rapidly and bit her lip. "Jacob, please. I'm not ready for that yet. Don't force me to do it right now!"

"Very well," he conceded. "But we shall go someday soon. Or I'll go alone and see to the duty for you."

Laurel stared at Jacob blankly.

Solemnly, he took her hand. "Have you thought of the importance of honesty in a marriage, Laurel?"

"Honesty?" she croaked.

"Yes. Lies can destroy a marriage." His tone was accusing, his eyes dark with suspicion and hurt.

Laurel was silent, frozen with fear.

Jacob dropped her hand, then tilted her chin with a finger. "Laurel, if there's anything you wish to tell me, I would suggest you do so—now. I promise I'll not punish you in any way. But if you wait until later . . ." his voice trailed off ominously.

"Yes?" she asked tremulously.

"I'll beat the deceit out of your hide," he said smoothly, adding, with a nasty smile, "to begin with."

Laurel gulped as she met his piercing gaze.

"Well, Laurel? Is there anything you wish to tell me?"

Laurel hesitated, feeling cowed by the intensity of his perusal. A near-fatal weakness swept her—why not tell him all, start anew? Then reason intervened, reminding her of his prior ruthlessness, of how she had to marry him to ensure Fancy's safety. No matter what she told him, he would surely use it against her—and if she admitted to him that she stayed at the Virginia House to spy on him, he might well expect her to do the same thing for him, betraying Hendley and the others. No—even though she loved him, she would not turn traitor for him. Besides, if she told him all she had done, and intended, he would surely beat the deceit out of her hide—now!

Summoning all of her bravado, she said, "Yes, Jacob, there's something I wish to say. Tell me of *your* family."

Jacob shrugged, scowling. Finally, he said, "There's not much to tell."

"Don't you have parents? Brothers and sisters?"

Jacob's dark brown eyes narrowed. "I'm an only child, and my father is dead."

"Oh, I'm sorry, Jacob. When did he die? And what was he like?"

"That, I prefer not to discuss."

Laurel tilted her head in puzzlement. "But didn't you love him?"

"What else do you wish to know?" he countered testily.

Laurel sighed. "Well, where your mother lives, for one thing."

"Pennsylvania." He added thoughtfully, "You'll meet her, one day soon."

"I will?"

Jacob took her hand. "Yes. I plan to arrange passage for you back east."

"You do?"

Suddenly, Jacob laughed, shaking his head. "What a parrot you are. You should see yourself, Laurel—your blue eyes like saucers, your face a picture of utter astonishment." More seriously, he continued, "Yes, Laurel, I plan to send you to my mother as soon as possible. You're not safe here."

"I'm not?"

Slowly, he shook his head. "We have it on good authority that the Rebs will try to retake Galveston—it's only a matter of time. When the battle occurs, I want you far away."

Laurel frowned. "What if I don't want to go?"

Jacob raised a black brow. "My dear, I'm not offering you a choice."

Laurel disengaged her hand from his and stared moodily at her lap. "So you expect me to sit out the war in—what is it?"

"Pennsylvania."

Laurel looked up angrily. "Jacob, why? I still don't know why you married me in the first place! Surely sooner or later you'll tire of this—this bedroom intimacy! Why must you send me back east to wait for you, against my will? I know you don't care for me!"

Jacob's eyes grew black, his brows thunderously knitted. "Laurel, don't presume to tell me my feelings!" he warned, his voice a dangerous hiss.

"It's true!" she raged at him, tears now in her eyes. "Your interest in me is—is purely physical. It's demeaning!"

"Demeaning?" he roared through clenched teeth.

"Yes! I paid for Fancy's life with my body. Sooner or

later, the debt must be considered repaid. Surely you cannot expect me to pay with a lifetime—''

"Indeed I do, my dear," he replied stonily, his anger now cold rage.

"It's not fair, Jacob!" she cried, clenching her fists. "One day you must let me go—"

"Never!" he vowed, pulling her closer, almost violently. "You're my wife, Laurel Lafflin, and you delude yourself if you think I'll ever let you go!"

He kissed her; she moaned as his hand slipped inside her wrapper, cupping her breast. "Is this demeaning, Laurel?"

Desperately, her lips sought to silence his.

But his hand gripped her chin, forcing her to meet his gaze as the fingers of his other hand continued to caress her breast. "Is it demeaning?" he repeated. He kissed her again, fiercely, then insisted, "Tell me, Laurel."

"No, it's heaven," she choked, throwing her arms about his neck.

Later, Laurel lay awake in the darkness, listening to the even sound of Jacob's breathing. She had given herself to him completely again. All barriers between them—their enmity, the war—had dissolved with his first kiss.

A tear trickled down her cheek. Loving was hell, she decided. She felt like a child who, having burned her fingers on the stove, went back again and again, endlessly prolonging the torment. Her love for Jacob was indeed almost physically painful, for the burden of her guilt, her betrayal, was unbearable.

Tears now streamed down her face. As she had done the previous night, she leaned over and pressed her mouth against Jacob's. Then she lay back upon her pillow, staring dismally at the blackness above her, shuddering silently to keep from sobbing aloud, wiping her tears with the sheet. Mere days before, she had been a lighthearted girl, now she was experiencing all the feelings, all the pain, of womanhood. She had been free, and now she was in bondage—more emotionally than physically—to a man she should hate. Worse yet, her husband intended to send her off alone to an alien place she knew nothing of, a place peopled solely by her enemies.

God in heaven, how she hurt inside. There was no wounding like this . . . this love, and there was no stopping it now.

She stared at Jacob's shadowy form through tears. He was so good for her. He was so bad for her. There was no solving it. She was doomed . . .

Chapter
Twenty-seven

NOVEMBER 12, 1862

Laurel jerked awake in the middle of the night. Instinctively, she reached for Jacob in the darkness, yet the mattress beside her was empty! Her heart thudded ominously—something was wrong! Where could he be?

Sitting up, she glanced about the room, but saw only darkness splashed with pools of moonlight. Was he in one of the blackened corners of the room? Or had he left her? And why?

Suddenly, with a low creak the door swung open. Laurel fearfully sank back against the pillows, straining to see. But the door was shrouded with blackness, though now she heard the soft thud of footsteps approaching the bed.

"Jacob?" she whispered.

The figure stepped into a shaft of moonlight near the bed. Laurel's heart lurched—it was a woman! Reba!

Moonlight contorted her face in sinister proportion, and her eyes gleamed with a white-hot, wanton light. But Laurel's eyes soon left the woman's face as she watched

Reba raise a small, sharp dagger. Oh God, Laurel thought wildly, it was the terror of the nightmare come true!

While Laurel watched in silent panic, Reba laughed a low, bitter laugh. "No, madame, it is not your husband—he evidently has tired of your services. It is I—L'Loa—come to cut out your heart!"

As Reba hissed the words, a maniacal light sprang into her eyes, then she raised the dagger and lunged for the bed. Horrified, Laurel dodged the descending blade, waiting for the sound of the dagger ripping the mattress. But the feared impact did not come—instead, Laurel heard a woman's low scream. She looked up, gasping, to see two figures now struggling in the shadowy light.

Jacob! It was Jacob! He was there all the time!

Laurel's heart pounded with relief mixed with a new wave of fear, for Jacob and Reba were now struggling for the knife! As the two fought, hands clenched upon the dagger, Reba's mouth clamped down upon Jacob's fist; Laurel heard him yell with rage and pain. Oh God, she must help him!

Laurel stood up, intent to help Jacob subdue Reba, who was now clawing, kicking, and screaming like a wild animal. Grabbing for Reba's hand, which still held the wicked dagger, Laurel heard Jacob order hoarsely, "No, Laurel!"

At the same time, Reba's other arm flew backward, striking Laurel hard on the chin.

Strangely, Laurel heard the awful cracking sound of her head hitting the bedpost just before everything went black . . .

"Jacob, I love you."

"I love you, Laurel."

They were floating upon a calm emerald ocean, lying naked upon a glass raft. As the waves sweetly rocked them, Laurel looked down through the glass and saw a sunken ship on the ocean floor sprinkled with gold dubloons, while huge, fantastic sea creatures swam about, their scaly bodies an assortment of rainbow colors seen vividly through the crystal-clear water.

"Oh, Jacob—it's so perfect," she whispered.

"Not as perfect as you are, my love."

She turned to look up at him, at the bronze of his skin against the blue of the sky. "Oh, Jacob, I love you," she breathed, tears in her eyes. "Make love to me, darling."

He laughed, his dark eyes sparkling with joy. Perched above her on the iridescent raft, he took her wildly, the turbulence of his movements in striking contrast to the tender, rocking motion of the waves. As they drew to the crest of a smooth, mighty green wave, he pulled her upright and they climaxed together, soaring in riotous rapture even as they slid ever so slowly down the face of the gentle wave.

Her lips trembling, she sought his mouth. But suddenly, his eyes grew crazed, and he screamed, "No, Laurel!"

She tumbled backward as if thrown by some terrific force. Her head cracked against the glass raft, her entire being exploding into a million shards of exquisite pain . . .

"Laurel?"

Laurel blinked at the light, looking up to see Jacob sitting beside her on the bed.

"Jacob!" she cried, tears springing to her eyes. "You're safe!"

She struggled to sit up, then fell back as her head throbbed painfully.

"Easy, sweet. That's quite a crack on the head you took." He grinned, reaching out to stroke her cheek, his hand loosely wrapped with a bandage. "You and Fancy."

Despite his teasing tone, Laurel could see the tension etched upon his face, and she could feel his fingers tremble as he stroked her cheek. "Reba?" she asked, her voice quivering, the pain surging unbearably at the back of her head.

Jacob looked down at her, his own face streaked with anguish as he viewed her suffering. "She's gone, Laurel."

"Gone?" Laurel repeated.

"Dead." His voice was toneless.

"Dead," she repeated woodenly. She looked about, her eyes apprehensive. "But where—is she—"

"At the undertaker's. Wilson took her there after we cleaned up."

"Cleaned up—you mean, the knife . . ."

Jacob nodded. "It was her or me."

Laurel looked about the room as if still unconvinced that the danger had subsided. The effort seemed to make her eyes hurt, even. "Jacob, the rug is gone," she finally managed.

"Aye. I'm afraid it simply wasn't salvageable after . . ." his voice trailed off and he cleared his throat awkwardly.

"Oh, Jacob, how horrible it must have been for you!"

He half shrugged. "I've seen much worse, Laurel." He reached out, gently caressing her hair as he whispered intensely, "Had it been you, though, love—that I could not have borne."

His voice was near cracking, his eyes strangely glazed. Laurel stared up at him in wonder. Could he really mean what he said? A dizzying wave of tenderness swept her.

Resisting her softer nature, Laurel tore her gaze from his and blurted, "How did you know Reba was coming? I mean, you were hiding when she entered the room, weren't you?"

He nodded. "I heard someone scratching at the door as if trying to force the lock with a knife. I knew I couldn't very well defend you from the bed, so I waited in the corner." He sighed, gesturing resignedly. No further details were necessary.

The uncomfortable silence was broken by a sharp knock at the door. Jacob hastily stood. "That will be the surgeon from the *Westfield*."

"Surgeon?" Laurel croaked.

"Yes," Jacob called over his shoulder, as his boots banged the bare floor. "I sent for him immediately—I'm quite worried about you, if you haven't as yet surmised it."

The door swung open and Jacob called out, "Good evening, Lieutenant Atkins."

Laurel heard a gruff voice reply, "Commander Renshaw sends his regards, Captain."

The doctor was a bald, middle-aged man who spoke tersely but had gentle hands and keen, thoughtful eyes. He examined the bump on the back of Laurel's head, then cleaned and bandaged it. Finally, he gave Laurel a generous dose of laudanum, leaving a small bottle with Jacob in case she should need more later.

"She'll doubtless have headaches for several days, and may have visual disturbances as well," the surgeon informed Jacob, closing his black bag. "Anything else—vomiting or convulsions, for instance—and you call me back at once."

"Of course," Jacob replied.

Atkins headed for the door. "Keep her still in bed for several days. Otherwise, she might go dizzy on us and take a tumble down the stairs." He reached for the doorknob, then turned to eye Jacob quizzically. "You two are newlyweds, are you not?"

Jacob smiled. "Aye."

"Then mind what I said, Lafflin. *Undisturbed* rest for several days. Understood?"

"Understood," Jacob repeated, grinning. "Thank you, Doctor."

As Jacob returned to the bed, Laurel found his stride seemed strangely slow, her vision of him oddly distorted.

The medicine seemed to make her feel groggy and rather sad, though the pain in her head had eased somewhat.

Jacob sat down beside her, worry creasing his brow. "Feeling better?"

She nodded sleepily. "He was a rude man, that doctor," she said.

"What do you mean?"

She yawned. "Do you know he didn't say a single word to me? He might at least have said, 'Good evening, Mrs. Lafflin.' "

Jacob chuckled. "So you're beginning to like the sound of your married name."

Laurel leaned forward and showed him the pink tip of her tongue, then grimaced with the pain the movement caused.

"Be still," Jacob scolded. He kissed her quickly. "Hush, now, and we'll get some rest."

He rose and extinguished the lamp, and she listened to the sounds of him undressing in the darkness. Moments later, the mattress sagged as he got in beside her; but he did not reach for her.

"Jacob, what is *L'Loa*?" she asked.

For a moment he was silent, then he replied, "*L'Loa*? I think it represents some sort of voodoo god."

Laurel shivered. "Reba said she was *L'Loa*! Oh, Jacob, she really thought she was possessed, and she nearly—"

Abruptly, Jacob reached for her, and her gowned body contacted his naked form. "Hush, darling. It's over now. No need to fret."

"Oh, Jacob, we could have both been killed!" Laurel suddenly wailed. And, much to her mortification, she fell into hysterical sobbing.

Jacob held her and patted her back while Laurel wept loudly, inwardly appalled that she had so little control over her emotions. Was it the medicine? For all her inhibitions were gone, and she was literally pouring out her feelings against her husband's heart.

"There, there, sweetheart. Don't cry," he soothed. "Why don't you tell me about your dream instead."

"My—my dream?" she stammered, her tears forgotten for the moment.

"Yes. You kept moaning while you were unconscious. Did you have a dream?"

She stiffened. "I dreamt I fell back and cracked open my head."

He kissed the top of her head. "No doubt because of the injury you received. Poor darling." He added in a low, almost wicked tone, "But what else did you dream?"

"What do you mean?"

"Well, the way you were moaning, I did wonder . . ."

"Jacob!" she whispered, embarrassed.

"You dreamt we were making love, didn't you?" he asked, his dark eyes taunting her in the shadowy light. "Making passionate, violent love."

"Oh, Jacob!"

"Easy, love, don't get excited," he teased. "Remember the doctor's orders." His hand slid beneath her gown, stroking her bare leg, while he buried his face against her throat. His voice was thick with emotion as he murmured, "To think that I nearly lost you. Let me just lie here and hold you, darling. It is enough."

This time it was Laurel who took the initiative, who raised her gown and pressed her eager nakedness against her husband. "No, Jacob, it's not enough," she whispered, her lips desperately seeking his even as her head pulsated painfully.

"Laurel, the doctor—" he scolded, his voice shaking.

"It's not enough, Jacob."

And she fastened her mouth on his.

*   *   *

An hour later, Jacob lay awake in the darkness, watching Laurel sleep, his heart full of tenderness but his mind troubled. He would never tell his wife what had actually transpired when Reba died tonight, that the voodoo priestess had cursed him with her final breath even as her yellow eyes glowed with a maniacal light that he at last recognized was not of this earth.

Chapter
Twenty-eight

NOVEMBER 30, 1862

"Jacob, must we go through with this?" Laurel demanded crossly, shivering as she clutched her black cloak tightly about her.

Beside her in the small buggy, her husband nodded grimly, clucking to the nervous chestnut horse pulling them through the cold, windy streets.

"Jacob, the skies are black. Surely a storm is brewing in the Gulf—and it's so damn cold!" Laurel shuddered as the buggy rocked on its springs in the wind. "Just look at the trees! They're practically bending over backwards!"

Her husband shrugged as they passed the public square. "I told you weeks ago, Laurel, that you must face up to your responsibilities to your loved ones."

Laurel gritted her teeth to stop their chattering and sank deeply into the seat. She and Jacob had been married for two and a half weeks now, and she had long since recovered from her injury suffered the night after their wedding. She still shuddered when she remembered the incident, though, and Fancy hadn't helped, either, warning her mistress that Reba's evil might not have entirely died with her. Laurel recalled the day after the priestess's death, when she had remarked to Fancy how grateful she was that at least the voodoo had now ended. But the younger girl had responded by violently shaking her head. "Oh no, Miss Laurel, I still worried," the frightened servant had warned her mistress. "Reba pow'ful bad. She put the curse on Captain Lafflin. It mean death!"

Remembering her servant's dire prophecy, Laurel bit her lip. The thought of Jacob coming to harm distressed her more than she could have dreamed possible weeks earlier. Though she rarely saw him during the day now, he always came to her side at night—and she forgot the past, the future, indeed the war itself, as she gave herself to him in love. In many ways, he was still a stranger to her. No words of love had been spoken between them, yet in the dark, sheltered confines of their bedroom, two people had never been more intimate.

Laurel sighed. Obviously, the honeymoon was over. She had known from the beginning that it was inevitable that reality intervene, that they must face up to the war going on about them, to the natural enmity they shared.

Today, obviously, Jacob had decided to force her hand— to make her produce the "erstwhile family" of which she had spoken. As if to properly prime her conscience, he had taken her to early church beforehand; at Trinity Episcopal, Father Eaton had orated a stern sermon on the importance of honesty. Had Jacob bribed him? she wondered.

She shivered as Jacob abruptly asked, "Have your cohorts informed you of the build-up of Confederate troops in the area surrounding the bay?"

Laurel was stunned by Jacob's remark. "My—my cohorts?" she questioned. "Just when could I have seen them? You've kept me rather occupied, you know."

"I haven't been with you every minute," he replied, his voice strangely tense. He sighed and worked the reins, turning the buggy onto Broadway. "I'm sorry, Laurel, I shouldn't take things out on you. It's just that the situation here has really heated up."

"It has?"

They now approached the large, windswept Episcopal Cemetery. As the chestnut trotted toward the iron picket gate, Jacob nodded and said, "I'm afraid I shall be having night duty from now on, Laurel. Last night two of my men were wounded by Confederates while on patrol. Even now, they are being attended on board the *Westfield*."

"I'm sorry, Jacob," Laurel murmured. She was indeed sorry and could understand Jacob's mixed feelings toward her this morning, for it may well have been one of her fellow spies who helped Confederate soldiers sneak onto the island last night! Though mere months before she would not have felt a flicker of sympathy at a Union soldier's being wounded, she could not now help but feel partially responsible for the incident. What hell it was to be torn between her love for her husband and her loyalty toward her country!

Laurel realized that she had been living in an artificial environment—in a magic world filled with wine, easy laughter, and lovemaking—while all the time, grave dangers existed outside the Virginia House for her new husband. A twinge of disappointment swept her that Jacob would be leaving her side at night, along with a new wave of fear for his safety. "Jacob, you will take care?" she asked in a small voice.

Jacob pulled the chestnut to a halt, then alighted. He looked up at her, devastatingly handsome in his dress uniform and brass-buttoned cloak. "Should you be disappointed at my demise, love?" he asked, extending his arm.

Laurel frowned and bit her lip. "Yes, Jacob."

He was silent as he assisted her to the ground. Her eyes

searched his face, but his dark features were unreadable. As she stood shivering in the cold wind, he opened the cemetery gate and motioned for her to enter, at last saying, "My new duties pose quite a problem—you, love."

"Me?" She tentatively edged forward.

"Yes, you. Perhaps I should tie you to the bed while I'm gone each night."

Now inside the cemetery, Laurel whirled to face him, glowering at him as he closed the gate. "Jacob, you wouldn't!"

"Wouldn't I?" Casually, he came to her side and took her arm. He gave her a hard, appraising stare, then turned to the cemetery with a sweeping gesture. "Behold your family's final resting place, my love."

Laurel gulped, the blood racing in her veins. His tone was consummate sarcasm, leaving no doubt in her mind that he utterly dismissed the story of her coming to Galveston from Tennessee. Laurel gazed about the unfamiliar cemetery in bewilderment—cold stone crypts and marble headstones stared back dispassionately. Good Lord, what was she to do? Had she been caught in her own web at last?

"Laurel, don't you think it's about time you told me who you really are?" her husband asked, his tone dangerously soft.

Laurel turned to him, her eyes enormous. "You—you don't believe me? I mean, about my family?"

He shot her a glance of disgust. "What kind of fool do you take me for? I can't watch you anymore at night, Laurel. So either you give me some straight answers—now—or I'll have no choice but to keep you locked in our room from now on."

"Locked in our room? You wouldn't dare! Surely you don't think I was responsible for your men being wounded last—"

"Damnit, Laurel, I don't know what to think!" he cut in,

grabbing her by the shoulders. "Don't you realize you've played a game with your very life? Jesus, I'd hoped to have you on a ship bound east by now, but unfortunately, there will not be a suitable vessel in the vicinity until early next year—and that may be too late."

His tone was intense as he spoke, his eyes filled with frustration. A cold wind burned Laurel's face, yet it was not as harsh as her husband's voice as it continued to lash at her ears. "How do you think I will feel, patrolling the streets at night, wondering what the hell kind of trouble you may be getting into? I want you to tell me who you really are, Laurel, and what you have been up to—now!"

He shook her as he spoke, and her teeth chattered as lightning flashed in the overhead skies, followed by the ominous boom of thunder. Never had she seen Jacob this filled with desperation. Haltingly, she found her voice. "Jacob, I told you you can't force my loyalty!"

"But I can sure the devil beat the truth out of you!" he growled.

His threat of physical violence filled her with righteous indignation. "The truth is that my family is buried here!" she railed back without thinking.

Releasing her, Jacob glared down at her in stony silence, looking so enraged that for a moment, Laurel feared he might indeed strike her. Then, grabbing her arm, he propelled her forward and ordered curtly, "Show me!"

Laurel stared at the sea of alien graves, her heart sinking, her bravado wearing thin. Slowly, she moved forward across the prairie grass while the wind blew gritty sand in her face and bent the bushy oleanders lining their path.

Laurel left the trail and proceeded through rows of tombstones, hearing Jacob's footsteps behind her. She glanced at each marker with desperate hope, praying for a miracle, inanely wishing the Ashland family plot would somehow materialize out of thin air.

After a moment she heard Jacob remark with disgust, "Laurel, you're wandering in circles. Where the hell are the graves?"

"I don't remember, Jacob," she offered lamely. "I was crazed with grief at the time—"

Again she was grabbed and whirled about to face the thunderous countenance of her husband. "Damn you, cease your lies or I'll have my belt to you, here and now!"

She stared up at his relentless visage, her heart sinking. Her hand had been called; the game was up. "Jacob—" she began, her voice breaking.

Then all at once, she saw it! Just beyond her husband's shoulder, on a small rise to the south of them, was a neat row of three wooden crosses!

"Jacob—there!" she exclaimed, pointing, her face full of amazement and forlorn hope.

Scowling, he pulled her with him to the crest of the rise. She shivered as a shaft of lightning hit earth to the east of them, illuminating the landscape. As thunder once again roared, Jacob said suspiciously, "These graves are old—sunken and covered over with prairie grass."

"It's been a while, Jacob," she said.

"Not that long."

"Jacob, nothing lasts long in these parts—the salt air and all..." she tried to explain, her voice trailing off.

Jacob looked unconvinced, grimly studying his wife's uneasy face. "Tell me, my dear, which one is the child?"

"The—the child?"

"Your baby brother—Casper, wasn't it?"

"Ummm—" Desperately, she pointed. "That one."

Jacob's dark eyes darted toward the center cross as he murmured sardonically, "A rather large grave for a child, wouldn't you say, Laurel?"

"I—well, when they all died, I was distraught, Jacob.

I—I paid the blacks to dig three graves but neglected to mention that one was for a child.''

Jacob looked like a keg of dynamite ready to explode. "My dear, at this moment I could cheerfully strangle you.''

"It's true, Jacob!'' Laurel cried wildly. "They are my family!''

"The devil they are!'' he growled. "Tell me, who buried them?''

"Who?'' she gasped, turning white.

"Which undertaker?'' he demanded.

Laurel felt light-headed. "I—we—I—''

"Or did you simply have the blacks slap together three pine boxes as well?'' he snapped. Abruptly, he strode toward the center cross, saying with cold triumph, "Ah, I see there is something carved on the wood—perhaps your undoing, my love.''

Laurel's heart seemed to cease beating as she watched her husband kneel down by the cross, closely scrutinizing the writing on the wood. "Damn!'' she heard him curse. "The writing's faded. Perhaps one of the others—''

But then suddenly, explosively, rain began to fall. Laurel uttered a gasp of alarm as the hard, cold droplets pounded her face. "Jacob, please, we must leave!'' she yelled through the thunderous din.

Again cursing, Jacob stood up and rushed to her side. They raced through the graveyard, soaked to the skin. Reaching the buggy, they climbed inside and left the cemetery in grim silence, broken only by the nervous neighing of the horse and the angry pelting of the rain.

Surprisingly, Jacob headed not for the Virginia House, but for the harbor area of Galveston. "Where are you taking me?'' Laurel finally asked, sinking deeply into the seat and drawing her cloak tightly about her. The cover of the buggy was scant protection in the driving rain, and her feet were becoming soaked.

"I must make sure the *Owasco* is tightly secured," Jacob replied tersely. "It looks like a fierce tropical storm is brewing."

They had now reached the wharf area, and Jacob left the buggy in a deserted shed, then he and Laurel dashed across the street and out upon the wooden dock, climbing the gangplank to the *Owasco*. Jacob exchanged brief greetings with the guards patrolling the ship, then he and Laurel boarded. On deck, even with Jacob's arm tightly around her, Laurel fought to keep her balance as they walked the rocking ship. She was surrounded by blackness, illuminated only by flashes of lightning, while thunder continued to assault her ears. Laurel caught vague glimpses of ropes, masts, and lifeboats, then Jacob was helping her climb down a shadowy stairwell.

Below, he guided her through the darkness to a cabin. Inside she stood shivering, the floor rocking beneath her as he lit a lantern. Glancing about in the wavery light, Laurel spotted a desk cluttered with maps and charts, a narrow bunk covered with a coarse woolen blanket, and a chest with a cushion on top of it. The cabin was small, and above them was a brass-framed skylight, its latticework of reinforcing bars making Laurel feel imprisoned, trapped.

Jacob went to the chest and drew out a white shirt. "Here," he said gruffly, handing it to her. "Put this on and wait in my bunk else you'll catch your death in those wet clothes. I'll go inspect the ship."

Laurel glanced at the shirt, not wanting to accept anything of his, her face revealing the struggle between her pride and her intense physical discomfort. Her teeth began to chatter.

Jacob forced the shirt into her hand. "Put it on. I'm sending Pearson down shortly with a hot brick and orders to dry your other clothes in the galley. And believe me, Laurel, Pearson is not the type to take any nonsense from you, though he might well take the clothes from your back should you practice your usual stubbornness.''

Jacob left her, and after groaning her frustration, Laurel did as he bid, undressing and donning the shirt, then climbing into his bunk. She had to admit to herself that he was displaying a solicitous attitude, she thought as she clutched the covers tightly about her, still shivering in the cold dampness that seemed to permeate the very hull of the ship. She glanced about at the tiny, austere room. So this was Jacob Lafflin's private domain, she thought to herself. There was nothing there that indicated anything of Jacob's personality—no belongings, no portraits of loved ones. In fact, the most personal thing in the entire room was the male scent of him, which permeated the pillow and blanket.

A knock now sounded at the door and Laurel called out, "Yes?"

A tall elderly man entered the room, carrying a bundle, which was obviously a hot brick wrapped in a towel. "Pearson, ma'am," the dungaree-clad man told Laurel. "The captain told me to fetch you this."

Pearson went straight to the bunk, matter-of-factly lifting up the blanket and depositing the bundle by Laurel's bare feet even as she watched in amazement. As he tucked in the covers, she noted that he was surprisingly brown and muscular for a man with pure white hair. At last, Pearson turned and fully faced Laurel, his diamond-hard blue eyes staring out from a leathery face. "Stay put now, missy, and you'll cease your shivering shortly." He turned and picked up her clothing from the floor. "I'll be bringing down gumbo to warm your innards directly."

Laurel nodded, saying, "Thank you," as the seaman left the room. She placed her feet upon the towel-wrapped brick, and a delicious warmth spread through her. Curled up in a cocoon of comfort, the rain beating a lulling cadence on the skylight above her, she slept . . .

"Time for lunch, Laurel."

Groggily, Laurel looked up to see Jacob seated beside her on the bunk. His hair was wet, curling about his face, though he wore a dry shirt and trousers.

She sat up, pulling the wool blanket up to her chin, then glancing upward at the skylight. It was still raining relentlessly. "Did you get the ship secured?" she asked.

He nodded. "We may as well wait out the storm here. I've a feeling it will let up before nightfall. Then I'll take you back to the Virginia House."

Jacob stood up and went to his desk, then brought back two steaming bowlfuls of gumbo. They ate the delicious shrimp and vegetable stew in silence, and Laurel was feeling safe and warm, lulled into a false sense of security, when Jacob took away their dishes, then turned to her, and said solemnly, "Laurel, we've unfinished business to discuss."

He once again seated himself beside her on the bunk. His hand stroked her cheek and his eyes grew pensive, intense, as he said, "Sweetheart, I want us to have so much more than what we have in bed."

Laurel felt herself blushing and stared down at her lap. "Jacob, I—"

"Not that our lovemaking isn't good," he continued, lifting her chin with his hand. "It's heavenly, in fact. But I want us to be close in every way, not just physically."

Looking up at his soulful, tormented face, Laurel could not doubt him, and for a moment, she could almost believe he loved her. But then reality intervened, and she sadly shook her head. "What you want is impossible, Jacob."

"Why?"

"Marrying you was not a matter of choice for me. We're

from different worlds. I'll always be a Southerner, and you'll always be a Yankee.''

His eyes darkened as a surge of rain pounded the skylight above them. ''Laurel, you see things too much in black and white. Life is rarely that simple. For instance, what makes you so certain that I'm a Northerner?''

''Jacob!'' she exclaimed, totally taken aback. ''What are you saying?''

''I'm saying that I just might be almost as much of a Southerner as you are.''

Her face whitened. ''You must explain that statement!''

He sighed and stared off at the desk. ''It's not easy for me to talk about this, dear wife, but I suppose if we're to be truly intimate, one of us has to make a beginning.'' He turned back to her. ''Laurel, even though I'm fighting for the Union, my roots are in the South. My parents met and married in Charleston, South Carolina. Later, my family moved to Missouri, a slave state, where I was raised.''

Laurel was horrified and confused. ''But—but you said your mother lives in Pennsylvania!''

He turned to her. ''She does, now. I moved her there after the war broke out, for her own safety. Missouri's governor wanted secession, and it's been all the Federal troops could do to maintain order there since the war began. I didn't want my mother caught in the middle of such bitter fighting.''

Laurel scowled for a few moments, absorbing Jacob's words, then asked incredulously, ''You mean you come from a Southern family, yet you sided with the North?''

He sighed. ''I attended Annapolis, Laurel, which made my career with the United States Navy inevitable. And there were other reasons for my choosing allegiance to the Union.''

''Yes?''

He turned to eye her steadily, a struggle gripping his features. At last, he announced, ''Laurel, my father was the privateer Jean Lafitte.''

Her eyebrows flew up. "Surely you jest! Lafitte never had a family!"

Jacob shook his head. "Oh, but he did. For the last twenty years of his life, when most people thought him dead, Jean Lafitte lived quietly as John Lafflin—businessman, model citizen, and father."

His tone was bitter, and Laurel shook her head in disbelief. "It cannot be. Lafitte could not have been your father. He was—he would have sided with the South!"

Jacob laughed cynically. "So you're back to determining loyalties again, setting up battle lines? Does nothing else matter to you, Laurel? Actually, you're right—my father would have sided with the South. In fact, he frequently spoke to me of his opposition to abolition, years past, when the controversy first ripened. Unfortunately, he died before he could put his beliefs to the test."

"You sound bitter, Jacob," Laurel commented. "If what you say is true, I would think you would be proud to have such a famous man for a father."

"Infamous is more like it," Jacob returned grimly.

Laurel's eyes flashed with disappointment. "But if Jean Lafitte was indeed your father, then you betrayed him by siding with the North!"

"Betrayed!" Jacob repeated caustically. "A rather strong word, my dear. Anyway, why are you so quick to defend my father?"

Taken aback, Laurel flushed and turned away. But two large hands grabbed her face, turning her to meet her husband's irate countenance. "That night at Maison Rouge, you were thinking of him, weren't you?"

"I—" Laurel stammered, flustered, trying to turn away.

But Jacob's strong hands held her face immobile even as his searing gaze burned her. "You dreamed of lying in Jean Lafitte's bed—go on, admit it!" he accused.

Backed in a corner, she lashed out at him. "All right, I'll

admit it—I dreamed of it for years and years, ever since I first saw Maison Rouge! I wanted to go with him out on the seas, to leave this island—''

"Aha!" Jacob said triumphantly. "So you have been here for years—you didn't just arrive from Tennessee!"

Laurel's face whitened with horror. Oh God, what had she done? Luckily, though, Jacob seemed preoccupied with her fantasy of Lafitte, for he continued hoarsely, "And how does it feel to know you have lain in the bed of Lafitte's son instead?"

Hurt and bewildered, she railed at him with all the venom she could summon. "It feels degrading to know I have slept in the bed of a traitor!"

The hands that had held her face abruptly dropped, and Jacob stood, turning his back to her and cursing under his breath. "Damnit, Laurel, must you be so rigid in your thinking, so literal? Would it never occur to your parrot brain that there just might be a reason for my shifting loyalties?" He turned to her, his eyes filled with challenge.

Laurel shook her head, glaring up at her husband. "A traitor is a traitor. The reasons are of no consequence."

A mask closed over his features at her savage words. Only his eyes revealed his brutal desire to retaliate. "I was a fool to expect you to understand," he said, each word a curse. "Besides, if I shared my motives with you, you might have to reciprocate and tell me why you married me."

"Jacob, what on earth are you talking about?" Laurel demanded, throwing her hands wide in exasperation. "The reason I'm your wife could not be more obvious. I married you to save Fancy—"

But his cold laughter interrupted her. "Fancy was not in danger," he stated flatly.

The words hit Laurel like a vicious blow. Mentally reeling, she whispered, "Jacob, what are you saying?"

"Do you really think I would have let Fancy be shot for defending you against Carter?"

She could only stare at him blankly, utterly appalled.

"Do you know Carter is at this moment sitting in the stockade at New Orleans?" he continued.

She shook her head in bewilderment. "Jacob, you said Renshaw thought I was spying—"

"He did. But the commodore is not a monster—he's willing to listen to reason. I'm surprised you haven't figured that out by now."

Laurel was totally bewildered by these revelations. "Mother of God, Jacob! Quit toying with me! Tell me what really happened!"

He studied her curiously for a moment, as if amazed that he had to explain anything to her at all. "Very well," he said at last. "The truth is, Laurel, that Renshaw did want you and Fancy punished following the incident in the market, to set an example for the Galveston community. But I talked him out of such action, pointing out that you had been providing us with information all along. I even implied that you had crossed over to our side." He smiled. "Actually, you were such an inept spy that you did help us considerably. Anyway, when I reminded Renshaw that Carter had indeed tried to rape you and told him of the numerous disciplinary problems the seaman had presented in the past, the commodore decided to go easy on you and Fancy and get rid of Carter." Jacob stared at Laurel meaningfully. "In other words, my dear, I got you and Fancy off the hook."

Laurel shook her head, her mind exploding with Jacob's perplexing statements. "But Fancy and I were locked up all day—"

"My doing," Jacob said. "To teach you a lesson, Laurel. I thought a few hours spent bemoaning your sins might whip you into line."

She sputtered, "Then you—you lied when you spoke to me—"

"Let's say I postponed telling you the truth, for your own good. Actually, I was planning to inform you that very night that Renshaw had relented, but then you really played into my hand, offering me all the delights of your lovely young body. I accepted your offer because I knew there was little hope of keeping you out of trouble without my personal supervision, and besides—" here he smiled wryly "—I'm only human, sweet."

Laurel was appalled. "You monster!" she hissed, clenching a fist at him. "You put me through holy hell and let Fancy suffer needlessly—"

Jacob shook his head. "Fancy never suffered. As you may recall, I'm the one who insisted you not tell her."

Realizing he was right, Laurel stared at him speechlessly for a moment. Then she recovered, bolting out of the bunk and facing him with eyes blazing, heedless of the fact that she was clothed only in his shirt. "What about the agonies you put *me* through? My God—when I thought Fancy was to be shot, I died a thousand deaths—"

"Good," Jacob retorted, his brown eyes immutable. "I'm deeply grateful if I made you think twice about the dangerous game you were playing. Jesus, Laurel, how do you think I felt after you almost got yourself raped—and killed—by Carter? And have you even considered what might have happened to you and Fancy had I not been there to intervene with Renshaw? I find it most ironic that you don't hesitate to blame me for Fancy's life being in jeopardy when it was in fact you who put the girl in peril!"

"That's a lie!" Laurel screamed, now flailing at him with her fists, more enraged than ever because she knew he had spoken the truth. "Damn you, Jacob Lafflin! Damn you! You told Renshaw I turned traitor for you! How could you?"

He grabbed her fists and said with cold anger, "Oh, I told Renshaw you were most cooperative—in every way. Why do you think he let you continue to stay at the Virginia House? Why indeed do you think he consented to our marriage? I told him you were carrying my child, so of course he agreed that I should do the honorable thing.'"

For a moment, she froze. Then, as the impact of his words splintered her brain, she shrieked, "Monster! I hate you! Oh God, how I hate you! To think that I married you for no good reason at all! You let me grovel before you like a common whore! You had my body, but that was not enough—you took my life too! You used me, you humiliated me! Why did you marry me, Jacob? Why?"

Had she not been in such a rage herself, she might have seen the bitter pain in his eyes caused by her words; she might have even been wise enough to take them back. Yet she was mindless with ire, beyond retracting anything.

Jacob yanked her closer, his hurt, vengeful eyes raking her scantily clad body with a murderous resolve as he replied hoarsely, "Why? Isn't it obvious?"

Realizing his intent, she began fighting like a wildcat. But he was out of control now and quickly wrestled her down upon the bunk. "Would you like to experience firsthand how a pirate takes his woman?" he demanded, yanking open the shirt.

Powerless beneath him, she spat, "I'll bet you're not half the man he was!"

Her words poured salt on a wound. "Not half?" he roared. Without preliminaries, he claimed her body with his. "Are you saying that I'm not man enough to satisfy you, Laurel Lafflin?"

Her answering moan told him that her rash declaration was a lie. Of course she had known before she ever spoke the angry words that he was more than man enough to satisfy her, but now that meaning was driven home inexorably as he held her hips in a vise and penetrated again and again, branding the deepest recesses of her womanhood with his hot tool. The punishment he inflicted was more emotional than physical, and she realized as he hurt her that she had hurt him too, hurt him terribly, that perhaps the cruelest thing a woman could do to her lover was to compare him to another. And she wondered why knowing she had wounded him brought her no joy.

When at last he collapsed on top of her, both were near tears. Ironically, the rain abated, and a pinprick of sunlight threaded its way through the skylight above them to shine into Laurel's pain-filled eyes.

Chapter
Twenty-nine

DECEMBER 1, 1862

Laurel crept down the dark streets of Galveston. She had managed to escape the Virginia House through a combination of coincidence and good luck. True to his word, when Jacob left to patrol the streets that night, he had not only locked her in their room, but had stationed a guard outside her door. However, she had awakened in the middle of the night to hear Barnaby snoring out in the hallway. Some patient work with a letter opener had jimmied the lock, then Laurel had tiptoed past the sleeping lad. She knew she was taking a terrible risk leaving like this—Barnaby might awaken or, worse yet, she might be captured by her husband or one of his men while she was out.

Yet risks meant little to Laurel now, she was so filled with a vengeful resolve following her scene with Jacob on board the *Owasco* yesterday. For now, her hatred of him blotted out all positive feeling. The man was a traitor, and to her mind, his cruel deceptions had ruined her life. She was now willing to go to any length to get her revenge, to hurt him as brutally and irrevocably as he had hurt her.

She turned onto the Strand, shivering in the coolness as she traversed in the shadows of buildings. Just a couple more blocks, and she would reach her destination. Then she could inform Hendley and Sleight of her desire to do something—anything—to hurt the Yankees and, most particularly, Jacob Lafflin!

Laurel was within a block of the Hendley Building when all at once, crazily, the calm of the night burst into pandemonium. A long succession of gun blasts boomed out from the harbor area, and cannonballs and grape whizzed over Laurel's head, shattering in the city beyond her. Appalled and terrified, she dashed for the protection of the Hendley Building, passing one store front just before a cannonball ripped through it, shattering glass and fragmenting wood.

Laurel cried out her dismay and tore onward. The deafening din continued, and she could also hear loud voices from the harbor area, though she couldn't make out any words. At last, she reached the entrance to the shipping agency and pounded on the door for dear life. "Oh, please, please let me in!" she cried, heedless of the fact that she might be heard by Yankees. Suddenly, she heard a strange jangling sound; then a shape lurched out of the shadows and she was grabbed violently by a man!

Laurel would have screamed, but he clamped a hard hand over her mouth, a hand smelling of dirt and sweat. "Hush!" the stranger growled in her ear, holding her tightly.

Struggling with the man, Laurel felt the hardness of a gun barrel pressed between them and wisely decided to cease further resistance. Yet she could not control an involuntary flinch each time another round sailed by, exploding in the streets to the south of them.

Just when Laurel thought she could take no more, the

door to the Hendley Building opened and the two were quickly pulled inside.

"Up the stairs with ye!" Billy Hendley ordered shrilly. Without pausing for further words, he, Laurel, and the stranger dashed for the second story.

Upstairs, they raced for the office, and inside, Hendley pushed Laurel down beneath the cover of a massive oak desk. Everything happened so fast, Laurel did not even get an opportunity to glance at the man who had materialized out upon the Strand to grab her.

For long moments Laurel held her ears and prayed, as the horrible "Whiz—boom! Whiz—boom!" continued. Several rounds exploded quite close to the Hendley Building, but miraculously, the structure did not sustain a direct hit.

At last, there was silence—a deathly silence. Cautiously, Laurel crawled out from beneath the desk. The first person Laurel saw was John Sleight, seated upon his bench near the door. "Hello, missy," he greeted her with a calm smile. "An exciting night of it we're having, eh?"

Laurel straightened, untying her black bonnet, which had slipped down about her neck, the ribbons constricting her breathing. Staring at the unruffled Sleight, she was at first amazed that the man had not sought some sort of protection from the onslaught. But then she realized there was no place for the gargantuan Sleight to hide.

"Tom Barnett, what the devil is going on?" Laurel heard William Hendley ask behind her. Laurel turned to watch Hendley converse with a tall, rough-looking man clad in a flannel shirt, dark trousers, and dusty boots with enormous silver spurs—no doubt the source of the jangling Laurel had heard down on the street. The man looked to be in his thirties, though discerning his features was difficult, considering his face was covered with a scruffy beard. Laurel noted a long bowie knife sheathed to Barnett's waist, a black felt hat with an embroidered star upon it in his hand.

Near him, leaning against the wall, was the double-barreled shotgun Laurel had felt wedged between her and Barnett out upon the Strand.

Instead of answering Hendley's question, the man turned to study Laurel, his eyes twinkling. Laurel gulped as she recognized the look of a man long without female companionship. "Hendley, you old snake, why in blazes is this pretty little thing beating at your door?" he asked, nodding at Laurel.

"The gal's been helping us out, spying on the Yanks quartered at the Virginia House," Hendley replied curtly. "Now tell me what in thunderation is going on down by the harbor, Barnett!"

Barnett chuckled, rubbing his stubby jaw as he turned to Hendley. "I was scouting near Kuhn's wharf when a Yank sentinel ordered me to halt."

"And?" Hendley prompted impatiently.

"And I told the bastard to go straight to hell," Barnett replied, grinning broadly. "The son of a bitch fired at me, wouldn't you know, so I gave him one of my barrels. Missed the blue-belly too, by damn. That's when the Yank steamers in the harbor opened up on us."

John Sleight laughed uproariously at Barnett's tale, but Hendley reprimanded rather sarcastically, "Well, well, Tommy. It seems congratulations are in order. You've single-handedly managed to turn half the guns of the Federal navy upon the citizenry of Galveston!"

Barnett was undaunted as he picked up his shotgun. "Thanks for the cover, old man. I'd best make for the mainland before the Yanks think to block off the bridge." He turned to Hendley. "Any message for Debray?"

Hendley shook his head. "Nay. I'll leave it to you to explain this fiasco to the colonel."

Barnett shrugged and started for the door, pausing to give Laurel's figure one last, thorough perusal. "Damned pretty little baggage.'' He winked at her. "Hope I didn't burn your ears with my heathen language, miss. T'warn't no harm meant.''

And he ducked out the door.

Laurel sighed heavily. Everything had happened so fast, it all seemed almost unreal now. She stared at her two companions. Hendley wore a brown suit, Sleight a dark shirt and trousers. As usual, viewing the two bizarre-looking men made Laurel half shudder. She tore her gaze from them and nodded toward the door. "Who was he?'' she asked.

"Who do you think, miss?'' Hendley countered, his cheek jerking as he frowned crookedly. "You're shivering, gal. Be down with ye by Johnny near the stove. 'Twill be a while before it's safe for you to take your leave.''

As Laurel moved toward the bench near the iron stove, Sleight directed, "Here, gal, give me your cloak and bonnet.''

Laurel did as she was told, taking her black silk bonnet from the desk top and handing Sleight the bonnet, her cloak, and gloves. She seated herself, watching Sleight stand and strain to hang her outer clothing upon a coat tree in the corner of the office. Then, breathing rapidly and shallowly, he returned to seat himself beside her, the bench groaning with his weight. She smiled and moved into the corner to allow him more room.

"Well, gal, you've chosen one devil of a night to be out,'' Hendley commented, scooting up in a leather swivel chair, joining the intimate scene by the stove. "To what do we owe the honor of this nocturnal call?''

"I'm here to help of course, sir,'' Laurel replied, eyeing Hendley solemnly.

"Help with what, gal?'' Hendley asked, shooting Sleight an amused glance.

"With the Confederate invasion—what else?'' Laurel inquired stoutly.

Hendley's beady eyes narrowed. "You've knowledge of that, miss?"

Laurel's patience was wearing thin. "The Yankees have knowledge of it, for heaven's sake." Watching Hendley and Sleight exchange startled glances, she continued, "I mean, they're expecting an invasion, considering the Confederate build-up on the mainland. Let's not play games, Mr. Hendley. Look what happened tonight. And I understand there was a skirmish two nights past, as well."

Hendley nodded shrewdly. "And just what is it you intend to do about it all gal?"

"Whatever you wish—anything to help," Laurel replied with a sweeping gesture.

Hendley's eyes fixed suspiciously upon Laurel's left hand. "Miss, isn't that a wedding band you're wearing?"

"Why—why, y-yes," Laurel stammered, lowering her gaze to the floor. "You see, I married Captain Lafflin."

"The Yank?" Hendley asked in disbelief. An ominous silence followed, then Hendley said gravely, "Forgive my bluntness, miss, but I fear we must question your loyalty, you having bedded down with the enemy, pledging your troth and all."

Laurel looked up miserably. "Sir, in that I had no choice."

"No choice, you say?" John Sleight interjected with interest. "Explain that if you will, miss."

Laurel looked at Sleight, her eyes bright with bitterness. "After the market incident, Captain Lafflin told me that my maid was to be shot. So I—I talked him out of it as best I could." She blushed her discomfort.

"You mean for that you walked down the aisle?" Sleight inquired, his gaze stern.

"Should I have allowed my maid to be shot?" Laurel countered indignantly.

Again, the two men were silent.

Laurel glanced from Hendley to Sleight and saw the suspicion etched in their features. Obviously, the two could not comprehend her feelings for Fancy. "Gentlemen, you must believe that I truly hate Captain Lafflin!" she told the two men vehemently, through clenched teeth.

Hendley and Sleight exchanged meaningful glances, then Hendley sighed and said, "Aye, gal, I believe you may be telling the truth. Unhappily, though, there's little you can do for us at the moment. After the disaster at the market, Johnny and I decided not to involve you again."

"Surely you don't think I was responsible for our defeat then!" Laurel bristled, leaning forward to glare at Hendley. "The Yankees may have seen through our scheme, but I assure you, I played my part to the hilt!"

Hendley's hunched shoulders shrugged.

"Mr. Hendley, had I turned traitor as you seem to be implying, you and Mr. Sleight would hardly be at liberty now!" Laurel reminded Hendley hoarsely.

"Billy, the girl has a point," John Sleight put in, in a placating tone. "Go easy on her."

"Very well, Johnny," Hendley conceded. Turning to Laurel, he said halfheartedly, "Miss if you hear any interesting tidbits, do come see us again. We're particularly interested in whether the Yanks plan to quarter additional troops on the island."

Laurel nodded solemnly. "I'm not having much luck gaining information from Captain Lafflin, but there's a young cabin boy assigned to guard me now and I may be more successful manipulating him to our purpose. It won't be easy, since I bashed him one good on the head a few weeks past, but I think I can play up to him."

"Good. Give it your best, gal. Other than that—" Hendley paused, gesturing resignedly. " 'Tis a waiting game we'll be playing."

"I see," Laurel murmured, frowning pensively. Turning

to Sleight, she inquired, "Are the Confederates coming to liberate Galveston?"

Sleight shot Hendley an inquiring glance, and the latter nodded slowly. "Yes, miss," Sleight informed Laurel. "Though we're not at liberty to say when."

"I understand," Laurel replied gravely. Her blue eyes sparkling, she continued with vengeful pleasure, "Just knowing our men are coming to defeat the blue-bellied beasts will shed a bright beam of hope upon my forlorn existence!"

Chapter
Thirty

DECEMBER 25, 1862

It was several weeks later and near midnight when Laurel left the Hendley Building, braving the icy, windy streets of Galveston.

She headed south toward her destination, a home near the intersection of McKinney and Twenty-first Street. William Hendley had given Laurel an urgent message regarding Federal troop movements, with orders to deliver it to that address before returning to the Virginia House.

As always when she was gone from the hotel, Laurel wondered if her absence had been noted. On the five occasions when she had sneaked out during the past month, her luck had held remarkably. Barnaby was still under order to guard her, but he invariably fell asleep outside her door, and forcing the frequently jimmied lock had become quick work for Laurel. Yet she realized that each moonlight excursion brought her closer to possible—and perhaps inevitable—capture.

Today was Christmas Day, but Laurel was almost oblivious to the fact. What was foremost in her mind, and in the minds of other Galvestonians, was the fact that last night, three hundred and fifty Federal troops had landed at Kuhn's wharf. The Yankees were now barricaded in the harbor area, which was part of the message contained in Hendley's note. There was no longer any doubt that the Federals expected a clash with the Confederates, and soon.

All in all, it had been a most dismal Christmas for the citizens of Galveston, not only because of the heavy Federal forces landing, but also because provisions were now so scarce, due to the blockade, that the citizens had been forced to seek rations from the enemy. Renshaw had magnanimously issued necessities to all who came to him, yet it was a degrading and dispiriting position for the townspeople to be placed in, as Hendley had pointed out that evening.

Laurel almost never saw Jacob, and when she did, they behaved as strangers to one another. When Jacob was not out on patrol, he was helping Renshaw erect batteries off Pelican Spit. He came to the Virginia House only to eat irregular meals and to catch a few hours' sleep.

At least Jacob's being occupied left Laurel free to carry out the duties assigned her by Hendley and Sleight. True to her promise, she had ingratiated herself further with Barnaby, gleaning much useful information from the boy. Consequently, she had been able to inform Hendley and Sleight of the expected transport of Federal troops weeks earlier.

The coming of heavy ground forces made sense, not only because the Federals expected a Confederate invasion, but because the Yankees were rapidly losing control of the city from within. Confrontations with Confederate spies were growing frequent, since Rebel scouts now visited the city freely at night, riding across on the bridge from Virginia Point, even as the Federals fired at them ineffectually from the harbor. Yes, a battle between the two sides seemed not only imminent but inevitable.

What impact would the coming clash have upon her marriage to Jacob? Laurel wondered as she turned onto McKinney. Would she at last be free of him afterward? Did she want to be free of him?

Weeks earlier, after her disastrous scene with Jacob aboard the *Owasco*, Laurel had been immutable in her resolve to betray Jacob Lafflin. Yet now that she had taken action against him, she found she felt no sense of vindication, but rather that she was becoming increasingly torn between her wounded pride and her romantic feelings for Jacob. Though finding out about the lesson he had tried to teach her galled her to the core, at the same time she had to grudgingly admit to herself that he had gone out of his way to protect her and Fancy. And the very thought of him in danger during the coming battle filled her with a panic approaching desperation. What if what Fancy said was true and Reba's spell remained to dog his steps? Oh, what hell it was to love him and hate him all at once!

Laurel tried to push these unhappy thoughts from her mind as she hurried down the tree-lined street in the inky darkness, stumbling a few times on the walkway. No lights were allowed in the city now—and no one dared disobey the Yankee dictate, for even though the Union gunboats had been silent since the Barnett incident, in the past the Federals had gone so far as to fire upon slaughterhouses where butchers did their nocturnal work.

Laurel paused to scrutinize a number on a cottage in the darkness and realized she was within two houses of her destination. She hurried on on tiptoe, then quickly climbed the steps to a dark, rambling Greek Revival home. She knocked on the door even as the wind howled about her and the trees rustled. Despite her wool cloak, her bonnet, and gloves, the cold seemed to penetrate to her very bones.

She knocked again and was about to despair of her
mission when the door creaked open. She gasped, staring at
the vacant blackness, for no light, not even a candle, was
visible.

"Who goes there?" a deep, suspicious voice inquired.

"I've—I've a letter from William Hendley," Laurel blurted
through chattering teeth. "Are you Mr.—"

"Never mind who I am, girl," the impatient voice cut in.
"Let's have the letter, and be on your way before the Yanks
spot you here."

Laurel hastily removed the letter from her cloak pocket, a
man's hand reached out from the darkness and snatched it
up, then the door closed coldly.

She sighed and hurried back down the stairs. She couldn't
blame the man for being suspicious. Everyone in the city of
Galveston was on edge now, whether Southerner or Yankee.
The very air seemed charged with tension.

She hurried on, lost in thought. But then, rounding the
corner of Tremont and McKinney, she suddenly paused,
realizing that she was heading south rather than north. She
stared perplexed at the shadowy residential area in which
she stood. Where did she think she was going?

Toward Ursuline Academy, of course! she suddenly realized. She was already almost halfway there! But why? Why,
after all these months away, did she want to revisit the
boarding school where she had spent so many unhappy
hours?

As her feet continued, unbidden, toward her destination,
the answer hit her with the sureness of a thunderbolt—
home. Sameness, stability, security . . . for the time being,
the academy was the only remnant she had of a simpler,
more carefree time. Back at the Virginia House, the perils
and responsibilities of womanhood awaited her. But at the
school perhaps she could recapture a former peace and
safety, if only fleetingly. And perhaps—was it too much to

hope for?—the sisters might even take her back and she could escape her dilemma with Jacob entirely. Besides, it was high time that she let the sisters know she was all right; it had been cruel of her not to get in touch with them before now.

Hurrying past the intersection of Tremont and Broadway, Laurel froze as she heard the distant thudding of boots. For a moment she stood immobilized by fear; then she recovered, diving for the cover of a tree in a nearby yard. As two Yankees marched past her on the street, Laurel stood pressed against the tree trunk in the shadows, not daring to breathe, silently praying that she had not been spotted. Fortunately, the sailors filed past her in silence, and she noted with relief that Jacob wasn't one of them.

Watching the patrol meld into the blackness beyond her, Laurel dashed for the walkway and continued down Tremont, now running. After what seemed an eternity, her heart lurching at each suspicious shadow, she reached the intersection of Tremont and Avenue N. She turned west, racing down the sandy street by the light of the moon, now freed from the obscuring tendrils of foliage. The walkway was gone now, the buildings few and far between, making Laurel realize, with a shiver, that she could more easily be observed. But, she consoled herself, with the terrain open, she could also more easily spot the Yankees, perhaps giving her more time to hide should they approach. Besides, she thought, the Yanks would not likely patrol this deserted section of town, where the openness of the landscape made spying activities unlikely.

On she hurried through the cold moonlight until the huge, rambling hulk of St. Ursuline's loomed before her. Yet it was so very dark! Oh God, she thought desolately, what if the sisters had left for the mainland?

The white picket gate squeaked on its hinges as Laurel rushed into the tree-lined yard. She raced for the front door, half stumbling on a rock on the flagstone path. By the time she had climbed the board steps to the door, she was gasping for her breath, the frigid air stabbing her lungs like splinters of ice as she alternately pounded the brass door knocker and rang the small cast-iron bell hanging on its scrollwork stand next to the door.

She waited for a reply, but her only answer was the wind sending a ghostly, rustling shiver through the trees even as the moon showered the porch with a quicksilver light play.

Laurel now pounded the door with her fists, heedless of the pain shooting through her hands. "Please—please come," she begged hoarsely, tears filling her eyes.

As if in reply to her desperate entreaty, the door suddenly swung open. "*Mon Dieu*! Laurel!" came a choked, hoarse voice.

"Sister!" Laurel cried, falling into the motherly, plump arms of Sister Mary Joseph.

"Easy, *mon enfant*. Mind the candle. And come inside before the light is spotted."

Sister Mary Joseph drew back, taking Laurel's hand and tugging her into the foyer. Closing the door, the older woman turned to give Laurel a pallid, bewildered stare as she moved the candle about to study the girl carefully. "*Mon enfant*, we thought you were dead—drowned in the Gulf, we thought."

Blinking as her eyes adjusted to the candle so close to her, Laurel stared at the sister with frank curiosity. Viewing the nun in her long woolen nightshift, fringed shawl, and white drawstring nightcap, Laurel stifled a half-hysterical giggle. Never had she seen one of her teachers thus— without the inevitable habit. But seeing Sister Mary Joseph's blunt-featured, round face twisted in a combination of confusion and sorrow, Laurel felt a hard stab of guilt.

"Where have you been all these long months, Laurel?" The nun's voice was filled with anguish, and Laurel's heart wrenched. Sister Mary Joseph had always. been Laurel's favorite, as she was far more motherly than her tight-lipped, stern-faced companions.

Miserably, Laurel opened her mouth to reply, but the sister seemed to remember something and waved her off, then spoke with a sense of urgency. "Later, perhaps, we can talk. For now, I must immediately deposit you in Mother's office and go bid her rise."

Laurel's eyes grew huge. "Must you?"

"Certainment, mon enfant," Sister Mary Joseph said firmly as she started down the dark hallway, motioning for Laurel to follow her. "Mother took to her bed within a week of your disappearance, when we realized the situation was *despere*. She simply has not been the same since." Shooting a shaming glance at Laurel over her shoulder, she added, "I fear, *mon enfant*, that you have been the death of her, *peut-être*."

Laurel was silent, mentally bludgeoning herself for her thoughtlessness, as the two women moved down the long corridor in a pool of light. They entered Mother St. Pierre's office and Sister Mary Joseph lit a taper on the desk, checking the heavy drapes at the window to be sure no light could escape. She took Laurel's outer clothing and hung it on a peg, then turned to leave.

"Sister?" Laurel asked.

The woman turned.

"I—I forgot to tell you. Merry Christmas, Sister."

The nun smiled sadly, hugging Laurel. "Merry Christmas, *mon enfant*," she whispered, wiping a tear.

Sister Mary Joseph left, and Laurel sat down in the familiar chair across from Mother St. Pierre's desk. How many times had she been in this tiny room, she wondered, listening to the ominous ticking of the mantel clock as she waited for Mother to enter, pronouncing judgment for another infraction Laurel had committed? Yet tonight the circumstances were entirely different—oh, how her life had changed in two short months!

Shortly, the door swung open with a labored creak, and a gaunt Mother St. Pierre entered the room. Laurel reflected dismally that Sister Mary Joseph had not exaggerated—the sister seemed to have aged ten years since Laurel left.

"So you've returned, Laurel Ashland," Mother St. Pierre murmured woodenly, walking with a slow, tired gait toward her desk chair. Wearily, she seated herself, lacing long, thin fingers on the desk top as she stared at Laurel sternly.

Unlike Sister Mary Joseph, Mother St. Pierre had taken the time to don her habit and steel-rimmed spectacles. Adjusting her eyeglasses in a familiar gesture, she inquired, "Well, Laurel, do you intend to explain your disappearance? Or did you, like Lazarus, simply rise up from your grave?"

The gray eyes flickering at Laurel from behind the spectacles were cold, devoid of emotion, and Laurel cleared her throat nervously. "Mother, I must apologize," she whispered, staring at her lap.

"Indeed?" Mother St. Pierre murmured. Then, more severely, she asked, "Laurel, have you any idea of the torment your disappearance has caused me and the other sisters?"

Mutely, Laurel nodded. "I—I left for good cause, Mother," she offered lamely.

"Kindly explain," came the terse reply.

Haltingly, Laurel related the story of her disappearance— her escapades with Fancy, her subsequent decision to remain at the Virginia House and spy on the Yankees. When she told of her marriage to Jacob Lafflin, she received no response from Mother St. Pierre other than a raised eyebrow.

Finishing her tale and wrenching her hands, Laurel inquired worriedly, "Mother, I must know—my family, do they know of this?"

Mother St. Pierre shook her head. "Perhaps it was irresponsible of me, but I saw no need to cause them anguish, especially since we had no definite answer regarding your disappearance. Also, mail service has been at a virtual standstill in the past few months, and thus I considered it futile to send a message."

Laurel nodded, sighing her relief. "Again, Mother, I must apologize for the unhappiness I caused you."

"Unhappiness?" Mother St. Pierre repeated with a trace of bitterness. "An inadequate word, Laurel." Her tone growing abrasive, she continued, "Do you realize the other sisters and I spent days searching for you, that I even journeyed to Commodore Renshaw's flagship to ask his aid in locating you?"

"You did?" Laurel gasped incredulously.

"*Oui*, Laurel. The commodore promised his cooperation, but our search was fruitless nonetheless."

"Renshaw has seen me frequently at the Virginia House," Laurel muttered, scowling. "Though I suppose he assumed I was a quadroon, one of the serving girls . . ."

"*Oui*, you have covered your tracks well," Mother St. Pierre continued dryly. "So well, in fact, that after a time we assumed you and Fancy had gone swimming in the Gulf and subsequently drowned."

Laurel struggled to her feet, her face crestfallen, her mind splintering with remorse. "Mother, I'm so—"

"No matter," Mother St. Pierre commented resignedly, waving Laurel back to her seat. "It is done. Now you must tell me why you have come back here this night."

Seating herself, Laurel gazed at the impassive sister in confusion. "I—I suppose because I want to come back—to live here with you again."

But Mother shook her head vehemently. "It cannot be, Laurel. You are a married woman now."

Laurel's eyebrows flew up. "Mother, there is a war going on! Surely you cannot be enforcing schoolgirl rules!"

"Laurel, your place is with your husband," Sister St. Pierre maintained doggedly.

"But he's a Yankee!" she cried.

"That, you should have considered before you married him," Mother replied coldly.

"But Fancy was to be shot—"

"I thought you just informed me that the girl was never in any real peril—"

"Jacob never told me—"

"I'm sure had you thought, you would have figured out his ploy, Laurel. You have always been entirely too head-strong and willful for your own good, rushing into every situation without thought. If you're honest with yourself, I'm sure you must admit that your troubles are largely of your own making."

Laurel's hopes were sinking rapidly. "Mother, it's Christmas," she said miserably.

"Time to take in the needy, is it?" the mother superior replied with rueful humor. She shook her head. "No, Laurel, I'm afraid what you need we can no longer supply. This is not an institution for matrons."

Laurel was devastated. "You expect me to go back and live with Jacob Lafflin?"

Mother St. Pierre's expression was pitiless. "Forgive my bluntness, Laurel, but you have made your bed. Now you must lie in it, *n'est-ce pas?*"

"But he's a Yankee!" Laurel repeated weakly, close to tears.

Mother St. Pierre stood. "I'm sure God does not take sides in this war—and neither shall I. You are a wife, Laurel, and you can't run from your responsibilities. Go back to your Jacob."

Feeling utterly wretched, Laurel also stood up, tears now

brimming in her eyes. "Mother, if I go back to him, I shall betray my family—and all I believe in."

Laurel felt a gentle hand on her shoulder and peered up into Mother St. Pierre's gray eyes, which now appeared strangely sympathetic. "I've been rather hard on you tonight, haven't I, Laurel?" she asked.

"I deserved it, Mother."

"Perhaps. But don't take it too much to heart, my dear. I promise you, God will not judge you for performing your duties as a wife. And the rest will be resolved in time."

Laurel shook her head in disappointment and disbelief as the older woman took the taper from the desk. "Don your cloak, Laurel—you must be on your way home."

Swallowing her tears, Laurel put on her cloak, bonnet, and gloves, then followed Mother out of the small office. As they headed for the front door, Laurel suddenly asked in a strangled whisper, "Mother, may I see my old room?"

Mother paused, turning to eye Laurel curiously. But then her features softened and she replied, "Of course, Laurel."

Laurel followed Mother St. Pierre down the hallway, through a door into the long, narrow dining hall, now converted into a hospital ward. "No wounded soldiers as yet I see," Laurel couldn't resist commenting as she stared at the neat rows of cots, the light from the window dancing phantom images on the neat ironed sheets.

"Unfortunately, I fear the time will come, Laurel," Mother replied gravely.

Laurel nodded soberly, her mind unwittingly focusing upon Jacob, now out upon the dark, dangerous streets somewhere.

Leaving the hall, the two started up the stairs to the second floor. As they moved soundlessly down the upper hallway on the Persian rug runner, Laurel glanced sadly at the yawning doorways to the now deserted dormitory rooms. For a moment she could almost hear the ghostly echo of laughter, the prattle of schoolgirls during a happier time, before all her friends left.

Soon they entered the familiar confines of Laurel's room; Mother St. Pierre lit the lantern on the desk with her taper, then turned to face her former charge. "Mind the light, Laurel—you'd best leave the drapes closed. Do you wish to be alone now?"

She nodded.

"*Bien*. I shall wait for you by the stairwell."

Quietly, Mother St. Pierre left, and Laurel glanced about at the beloved room, now blurred by her tears. Everything was the same as she had left it—the massive mahogany bed with its quilted blue coverlet and gauzy mosquito netting, the Chippendale dresser with its matching armoire, the silk brocade daybed by the window.

The shrouded window beckoned her now. Heedless of Mother St. Pierre's warning, she walked over to it, pulling back the drapes and gazing out at the shadowy landscape below—at rows of starlight-strewn prairie grass, leading to the moonlight-swept beach, to the quicksilver waves billowing beyond. How many times had she and her friends romped upon that beach? Now their footprints were forever erased.

Choking back a sob, Laurel left the window and moved to the dresser. She fingered the familiar porcelain hair jar, with its bright spattering of hand-painted flowers. Then her eyes moved upward to the mirror, to lock with the eyes of her reflection.

She had left the academy a child. Now, the sad, troubled eyes of a woman stared back at her. Mother St. Pierre was right, she realized. There was no coming home now.

Grimly, she moved to the desk, blowing out the lamp. For one last time, she stared about the dark room, now faded into the memories of the past.

She left the room and quietly closed the door on her girlhood.

*   *   *

The instant Laurel entered the Virginia House, she knew
something was wrong. Though no one was about, there
were lights everywhere—bizarre, considering the Federal
dictate.

She thought for a moment of running away again. Then
she laughed to herself ruefully. There was simply no place
to go.

With greatest trepidation, she climbed the stairs. The
upstairs hallway was also lit, but deserted. Her heart lurched
into a frantic tempo as she approached the door to the room
she and Jacob shared, and her glove-clad fingers shook
visibly as she reached for the knob.

She swung open the door, then stopped in her tracks, her
features frozen.

He was there, as she knew he would be, sitting on his
favorite chair with his boots crossed upon a footstool, his
arms akimbo. "Where the hell have you been, my dear?"

Never had his voice been more restrained; never had it
held such a tense, dangerous undercurrent. But summoning
her bravado, Laurel arched a delicate black brow at her
husband and ignored his question, going to the dresser to
remove her bonnet, cloak, and gloves.

Hard hands grabbed her shoulders, turning her to face the
murderous countenance of her husband. "Do you know that
at this moment I've a dozen men out searching for you?
Now tell me. Where the hell have you been?"

Laurel's eyes were bright with bitterness as she replied,
"Where do you think, Jacob?"

"Damn you!" he cursed. "Tell me—tell me now!"

She glared at him in fierce silence.

He cursed again, then pivoted hard and started for the
door. But he paused, his hand on the knob, his features
gripped in conflict. "Laurel . . . God, Laurel, if only—"

"If only you hadn't deceived me, Jacob," she cut in savagely. "If only you hadn't used me, betrayed me—"

"The devil with you!" he growled, leaving the room, the door banging behind him.

It wasn't until he was gone that she thought of how tired and anguished his face had been. It wasn't until he was gone that she noticed the brightly wrapped present on the bedside table.

"Oh no, no," she found herself whispering in a tortured tone. "Oh, Jacob. And I didn't think of you at all."

She tossed aside her cloak and gloves. Then, brokenly, she sat down upon the edge of the bed and started opening the package, reading the card, which said, "Merry Christmas, dear wife—to keep you warm when I'm not there . . ." Sniffing, she removed the lid from the box, then pulled out a luxurious blue velvet robe, which was the exact brilliant color of her eyes. She donned the robe numbly, tying the lace-trimmed sash and digging her hands into the deep pockets. But one hand encountered something cold, and she pulled out a magnificent, luminescent strand of pearls.

"Oh, Jacob," she choked. "Jacob . . . God, I don't want to love you. I don't want . . ."

She collapsed upon the bed, the precious pearls clutched in her fingers as she wept her very heart out.

Chapter
Thirty-one

JANUARY 1, 1863

Laurel awakened to a loud banging at her door. Then, surprisingly, she felt the mattress shift as Jacob growled in the darkness, "Who the hell goes there?"

"Barnaby, sir."

Laurel heard Jacob mutter an obscenity under his breath, then felt him lumbering to his feet. He stumbled and cursed in the darkness, and Laurel heard the hiss of a match.

Sitting up, Laurel clutched the coverlet about her and shivered with the cold as she watched her husband, clad only in his trousers, move toward the door in a pool of lamplight.

"Well?" he demanded hoarsely as he threw open the door.

"It's the Rebs, sir," Laurel heard a shrill, boyish voice reply. "We just received a message from the docks. Reb boats have been spotted off Pelican Island, and our vessels flashed white, blue, then red."

Laurel strained to catch a glimpse of Barnaby, but the

317

broad bronze of her husband's back blotted out the boy's image as she heard Jacob order tensely, "Wait for me in the hall."

Jacob slammed the door and hurried to the chair where his clothes were laid. Laurel watched her husband hurriedly don his uniform. "Jacob, what is it?"

He looked up grimly. "It seems the city will shortly be under siege by your beloved boys in gray. Are you pleased, my dear?"

His words would have been cruel, yet they were tinged with anguish and despair, and sounded tragic and final instead. Laurel stared at him speechlessly. His sudden, frightening revelations were almost too much for her to absorb; indeed, she hadn't even known he was in bed with her until they awakened seconds earlier. The previous evening, Jacob and the other officers were granted the evening off from their duties so that they might celebrate the coming of the new year with Commodore Renshaw. Laurel had struggled to get to sleep, despite the din of drunken voices coming from the downstairs dining hall. Finally, exhaustion overcame her, and she hadn't even heard Jacob come to their bed.

Why had he come? Had he been drunk? For Jacob had slept elsewhere in the hotel ever since the day they went to the cemetery. She almost never saw him, and now he was leaving her again, to fight a dangerous battle. As she watched him finish donning his clothing, she tried to envision her life without him. Strangely, the thought of his not returning from the battle was unbearable. If she had ever doubted that she was in love with him, she would no more. She felt tears burning her eyes at the thought of his leaving with things so cold, so unresolved between them. They had so little time and such enormous barriers to surmount.

Shivering, she got to her feet and approached him. Her pride cast aside for once, she said haltingly, "Jacob, you will take care, won't you?'' She realized with an intense chill that he would be doing battle with men from her homeland, that he might be fighting against boys she actually knew. And if Fancy's premonition was true, Reba's curse might even follow him into the battle!

He finished hanging his sword from his waist and looked up at her, frowning; but then his dark features softened as he viewed the stark emotion on her face. ''Laurel, you shouldn't be out of bed. You're shivering.''

He took the robe he had given her for Christmas from the chair and wrapped it about her shoulders. ''There,'' he said gently, his dark eyes tender. ''Keep the bed warm for me until I return.''

''Oh, Jacob!'' she choked, clutching the blue velvet of the robe as she gazed up at him through the blur of her tears. ''Tell me—why did you come to my bed tonight?''

Abruptly, she was pulled against him, her head tucked beneath his chin. ''Don't you know?'' he asked.

Stroking her hair, he continued almost hoarsely, ''Laurel, when the battle is over, we must talk. You haven't always made things easy for me, but then I haven't exactly been a saint, either. For now, please remember that I married you because I cared for you and wanted to protect you. The rest will have to wait until later.''

She nodded, her face pressed against his neck, her senses absorbing the masculine smell of his skin. Savoring their physical closeness, Laurel poignantly wished the emotional distance between them could be overcome as quickly as with an embrace. Fearfully, she asked, ''Jacob, what do the lights on the ships mean? White, blue, then red?''

He said methodically, '' 'White light, enemy in sight, blue light, pray for might, red light, make ready to fight.' ''

''How awful!'' Laurel shuddered. ''That means the battle could begin any—''

Laurel's prophetic statement was drowned out as she and

Jacob heard a sudden explosive blast boom forth from the harbor area to the north of them. Jacob abruptly released her. "Damn, the shelling has begun. The Rebs may have already landed!"

Just then Fancy dashed frantically out of the anteroom, where she had slept in recent weeks. "What happening, Miss Laurel?" she asked hysterically, her eyes like saucers.

Laurel watched Jacob rush for the window, rip back the drapes, and gaze at the streets. As another volley split the air, Fancy shrieked and Laurel screamed, "No, Jacob! Come away from the window!"

"Damn, I can't see anything from here," he muttered. He hurried back to Laurel's side, gripping her shoulders with strong fingers, his face tense as he ordered, "Listen to me, Laurel. You and Fancy grab your clothes and wait in the hallway—I repeat, in the hallway. Do you understand? I'm going to the *Owasco* now, but I'll send Barnaby back to fetch you two to safety as soon as I assess the situation."

Just then Laurel heard a whirring sound above them— then she cried out and Fancy collapsed on the floor as a shell landed nearby. "No, Jacob!" Laurel yelled. "You can't go out in this—"

Jacob shook his head. "I must, Laurel. A captain cannot desert his ship during a battle."

"You'll be killed!" she shrieked at him, desperately clutching his arms with her hands. "Oh God, you'll be killed!"

She fell into weeping, and for a moment, Jacob held her, evidently quite touched by her words, her tears. There was an undercurrent of futility, of impending doom, between them. "Darling," he whispered against her hair, his voice near breaking. Then, as another shell whizzed overhead, he took charge of himself and pulled back to stare down at Laurel soberly. "Laurel, you must get your clothes."

At last Laurel obeyed him, grabbing her clothing and

Fancy's things as well. She pulled the sobbing servant to her feet, and without taking time for the girls to dress, the threesome dashed for the hallway. Then Jacob and Barnaby returned to the room, bringing all the pillows and mattresses to the hallway and positioning the two girls on the floor between layers of bedding. "Keep the mattresses about you and shield your ears with the pillows," Jacob directed the frightened girls. Turning to Barnaby, he said, "Let's be about it."

But Laurel bolted up from the mattresses, clutching her husband's arm. "Jacob, before you go, I must tell you—".

"Yes?" He turned to her expectantly while Barnaby waited by the stairwell, his gaze politely averted.

"Jacob, I—I—" She paused, biting her lip. "God be with you, Jacob," she said at last.

Jacob's creased face relaxed somewhat as he leaned over to quickly brush his mouth against hers. "And with you, my love."

Chapter
Thirty-two

The din of the battle could be heard long before the Confederate steamboat *Bayou City* slipped from the bay into the channel, her mission to give naval support to the Confederate ground forces that had earlier that night landed on Galveston Island. Captain Trey Garrison stood at the wheel next to the pilot, Captain McCormick. In the gray, miserably cold predawn, they watched bright flashes of shot and shell spew forth from the hastily placed Confederate artillery along the Strand and heard the answering boom of cannon from the Yankee gunboats in the harbor across from the Rebel forces. The air was thick with smoke and fog, making eyes and throat burn.

As the *Bayou City* made for the battle scene, the tall, blond Garrison thought of his purpose here in Galveston. He had specifically requested this assignment with Magruder's invasion forces, hoping to locate Laurel Ashland. Laurel's mother and sister back at Washington-on-the-Brazos had been worried sick about her ever since they'd heard the news about Federal troops being on the island. Trey was quite concerned about Laurel too; he had always considered the Ashlands a second family, and now they were truly his family, since he had just married Camille Ashland while home on leave. He had promised both Cammie and her mother that he would find Laurel and see her to safety, and he was determined to follow through. Yet the thought of eventually locating the young girl also wrenched his heart, for the news he would bring her was not good.

"There she is, the *Harriet Lane*!" Captain McCormick called, jarring Trey from his thoughts.

Trey turned just as McCormick lowered the spyglass and offered it to him. He took up the glass and squinted at the heavily armed Yankee gunboat. Whistling, he passed the glass back to McCormick, looking about ruefully at their own vessel, the *Bayou City*. She was no more than a steamboat packed with bales of cotton to protect her boilers and armed with one thirty-two-pound gun. The *Neptune*, the steamboat accompanying them, was similarly haphazardly rigged. Of course, each vessel was manned by well over one hundred of Tom Green's sharpshooters, cavalry they now called horse marines; yet all knew that the intrepid plan to capture the Federal fleet at Galveston with such a ragtag navy was the height of bravado.

From the bow, Major Smith, commander of the collective Confederate naval forces, gave the order to open fire upon the *Lane*. The first shot rang out from the rifled gun at the bow of the *City* and landed near an old schooner in the harbor. "No, you fools, fire at the *Lane*!" a voice called out.

The second shot came closer to its mark, but missed, splashing into the bay, as did the third. By now the *Lane* was answering fire, also ineffectually. The gun on the *Bayou City* was primed and aimed for the fourth shot when, suddenly and disastrously, the gun exploded, rocking the entire boat with the deafening blast. "Damnation!" McCormick cursed from Trey's side, wincing as he was struck in the arm by a metal fragment.

After the smoke of the ear-splitting explosion cleared, Trey looked at the grisly scene before him. Captain Wier, who had been in charge of the gun, was dead, his face unrecognizable, and a number of other men were badly wounded from shrapnel. Several soldiers moved and tended the dead and wounded as Major Smith called out the order to ram the *Lane*. McCormick, not badly hurt, simply pulled the splinter from his arm and continued with his duties, while Trey wrapped the sailor's oozing wound with a neck scarf one of the men had tossed him.

Trey watched the capable pilot maneuver the vessel, aiming to ram the *Lane* just forward of the wheelhouse. By now the *Lane* was firing at both the *Bayou City* and the *Neptune,* and while the *Neptune* returned fire with her howitzers, only rifle shot came forth from the horse marines on the decks of the *Bayou City*.

The first attempt to ram the *Lane* missed, just glancing her at the bow, due to a strong tide. The *Neptune* was more successful, striking the *Lane* on the starboard side. As the *Neptune* passed by the *Lane,* she took a number of shots broadside. "Hell's bells," growled McCormick, watching the *Neptune* retreat, making for the flat. "She's taking on water fast. Looks like it's up to us now, boys."

Soon the *Bayou City* had rounded to and built up a full head of steam. Trey braced himself against a railing as they made for the *Lane* at a breakneck speed, guns and rifles of the two vessels blasting out a ferocious, ear-splitting cadence. Then came the terrific crash as the *Bayou City* at last rammed the *Lane,* and Trey was thrown violently across the deck on impact, the breath knocked from him. When he arose, gasping, it was to watch horse marines throw grappling hooks onto the *Lane,* then climb ropes over the *Lane*'s railing and onto her deck, all the while yelling a wicked battle cry.

Gaining his bearings even as rifle fire shattered the air above him, Trey noted that the two vessels were now locked hard together. He followed the others, climbing a rope to board the *Lane,* carrying along his rifle with bayonet affixed.

When Trey got to the deck of the *Lane,* he found it splotched with blood and strewn with shrapnel. From somewhere near the foremast, he heard a call for surrender, then, at the bridge, he witnessed a Union officer, his coat already blood-soaked, crying out, "We'll die first!" just as, ironically, a bullet hit him in the head. By now, much of the Union crew had taken shelter in the hold to escape the deadly aim of the Confederate sharpshooters. All at once there was a deathly silence upon the deck, and Trey noted that many of the Confederates were gathered in a circle near mid-ship, along with the remaining Federals.

Breaking through to the center of the gathering, Trey witnessed a strange sight indeed upon the deck—a blood-spattered young Union soldier cradled in the arms of an older Confederate major.

"It's Major Lea's son—a Yank," McCormick whispered from Trey's side. "A father fighting his own son, wouldn't you know? Jesus—what is this cursed war about, anyway?"

Trey moved closer, desperately wishing there was something he could do. The boy, deathly pale and breathing in a death rattle, whispered, "My father is here," and the major answered, "Oh, Edward!"

While the anguished father wept, the boy died, men from both sides looking on with tear-streaked faces.

Suddenly, there was a terrific blast to the rear of the *Lane.* Trey whirled to see the *Owasco* bearing down hard upon them from the west, her guns blazing. Their position could not be more vulnerable. Oh God, he thought. He had

promised Mrs. Ashland he would see Laurel safely home.
And he had promised Camille he would live . . .

It had been a long night for Jacob Lafflin, who stood at
the rail of the *Owasco,* staring out at Kuhn's wharf in the
foggy dawn, his eyes burning from the smoke as he shivered
involuntarily in the cold. The *Owasco*'s guns had been
blazing for over three hours, but now there seemed a brief
lull in the battle. On the *Owasco*'s deck, two sailors
continued to man the eight-inch guns, bombarding the
Confederate batteries along the shoreline, while other seamen
tended the wounded and cleaned the other firing pieces.

Jacob thought back to the previous night. While he and
Laurel slept, Confederate soldiers and artillery had evidently
come down to Galveston on railway cars from Virginia
Point. Before any of the Federals knew what was happening, more than twenty Confederate artillery pieces had been
placed along the Strand and in front of the warehouses at
water's edge. Then, three hundred rebel soldiers had stormed
Kuhn's wharf. Colonel Bunell, the Union commander of
the three hundred and fifty men barricaded out on the wharf,
had foreseen this eventuality and had days earlier torn up the
entrance to the pier. Thus, the Confederate soldiers had
been forced to brave the cold waters of the channel as well
as fierce crossfire from the gunboats *Sachem* and *Owasco* as
they waded out. When the Rebel soldiers at last reached the
wharf, they found their scaling ladders too short to climb to
the Yankee stronghold and had been forced to abandon their
first attempt, retreating to a cotton press along the shoreline.

For now, the Union forces seemed to have the upper
hand. The Confederates seemed, gradually, to be abandoning
the attack—sharpshooters on top of buildings along the
Strand had either fallen or were forced to flee the merciless
Yankee fire, and a number of guns along the Strand had now
been either abandoned or hauled off.

The "expected" Confederate attack had caught the Union forces sorely ill-prepared, Jacob thought to himself ruefully. Yet it seemed the blue might win the day nonetheless, he reflected. Perhaps soon he might even be able to break away and go check on Laurel. He was grievously worried about her and had just sent Barnaby to fetch her and Fancy to a place of greater safety. Though he had made sure no shot from the *Owasco* was aimed in the vicinity of the Virginia House, he couldn't be sure the other two Federal gunboats shelling the city from the harbor were practicing such precaution.

"Sir!"

An alarmed voice jarred Jacob from his thoughts. He turned to watch Wilson approach, his distressed face streaked with soot from priming the cannon. "Sir, Reb boats are making for the *Harriet Lane*," the seaman said, pointing to the east.

Jacob cursed and took up the spyglass, turning eastward. "What the hell?"

The Confederate navy was almost laughable, he noted—two steamboats swaddled with cotton bales. Yet sharpshooters with rifles blazing crowded the decks of both vessels, and howitzers and a rifled gun volleyed shot and shell.

Luckily, though the *Owasco* was at anchor, she was already under steam, so they could swiftly make for the battle scene. Jacob shouted out the order to weigh anchor, at which four seamen ran for the capstan, bringing up the anchor. The *Owasco* backed out of the harbor, then started down the channel, building up a greater head of steam. The channel was narrow and the steamer grounded twice. The second time, as they struggled to break off a bar, Jacob observed one of the steamboats ramming the *Lane* broadside. He shook his head in disbelief as he watched Confederates throw grappling hooks onto the Federal gunboat. It seemed incredible to him that two ill-equipped steamboats could tackle such a heavily armed cutter.

With engines reversed, the *Owasco* at last got off the bar, steaming forward down toward the battle, passing the Confederate vessel *Neptune*, which was now sinking at the channel's edge. Jacob gave the order to fire at the Confederate forces now crowding the deck of the *Lane*, and the cannon of the *Owasco* boomed forth.

Yet when they got within a few hundred yards of the *Lane*, Jacob suddenly ordered a ceasefire. He took up the spyglass and more closely examined the *Lane*. A white flag now flew at her mast, and on deck, Union prisoners had been brought up from the hold to shield the Confederates from the brunt of the *Owasco*'s guns.

Jacob surveyed the channel to the east of the battle scene, hoping for some help or a signal from Commodore Renshaw's flagship. But he noted with dismay that the *Westfield*, also evidently trying to come to the aid of the *Lane*, was now hard aground in Bolivar Channel, listing to port.

"Damn," Jacob cursed in a moment of painful indecision. Then he shook his head. "I'll not order the butchering of our own men." He called out the order to come about and steam back up the channel.

As the *Owasco* retreated, Jacob again cursed under his breath. The tide of the battle had turned, suddenly and disastrously. "I'd best go fetch Laurel," he said grimly to himself.

Chapter
Thirty-three

JANUARY 1, 1863

While the battle raged in the harbor, Laurel and Fancy lay huddled in the upstairs hallway of the Virginia House, clinging to each other for dear life. The light from their lantern had long since expired, but with the approach of dawn, gauzy, grayish light filtered in through the window at the end of the hallway. Moments earlier, there had seemed to be a brief lull in the battle, but now the blasts echoing from the harbor area sounded fiercer than ever.

In the cold, dim corridor, Fancy screamed and quivered with each shrill shower of grape and shriek of shell, and Laurel was so busy comforting her, she hardly considered the peril to her own person. From time to time, the girls could hear pathetic human screaming coming from the streets of Galveston as citizens fled the destructive fire of the Yankee gunboats. The sound of the dogs was even more piteous, however, for it seemed every canine in the city joined in the awful howl as each shell burst.

"Oh, Miss Laurel, we is going to die!" Fancy screamed as a horrible explosion sounded nearby.

"God in heaven—that was close!" Laurel gasped, wrapping a pillow about Fancy's ears.

"Miss Laurel, we is got to run or we be blown most way to Washington!"

"No, Fancy," Laurel scolded. "Jacob said to wait here for Barnaby, and that we shall do!"

"But all the other servants is fled!" Fancy cried, her brown eyes wild with fear. "I hear them run out the front door ascreamin'!"

"You mean they panicked—and have probably been killed for their troubles!" Laurel retorted grimly.

The two fell silent, clutching the mattress about them as another volley burst to the east of them. Suddenly, a piece of shrapnel tore through the window at the end of the hallway, sending splinters of glass flying in every direction.

Fancy screamed, and Laurel was speechless with fright. Though the mattress covering them was splattered with glass particles, miraculously, neither girl was injured.

The instant the rain of shards ceased, the terrified Fancy sprang to her feet. "Sweet Jesus, save me!" she shrieked, racing for the stairs.

Kicking aside the bedding, Laurel struggled to her feet, intent upon catching the hysterical girl and dragging her back to safety. But just as Fancy got to the stairwell, she suddenly fell backward as she ran headlong into Barnaby, rounding the top step.

"Barnaby!" Laurel cried, tears of gratitude springing to her eyes as she watched the red-haired boy bend solicitously over Fancy.

"The wench just got the breath knocked out of her," Barnaby informed Laurel, who had now reached his side. While Laurel knelt down beside Fancy, Barnaby pulled the girl to a sitting position, whereupon the slave coughed and sputtered for air.

Barnaby's fawn-colored eyes met Laurel's seriously. "Ma'am, we must leave now. The Captain wants me to take you to the sand hills on the Gulf beach, since this whole area is in danger of being hit by Federal fire."

Fancy began wailing convulsively at Barnaby's words, while Laurel commented ruefully, "Believe me, we're aware of the fact. Let's go, then!"

"M-ma'am," Barnaby stammered, flushing miserably. "You can't go like that."

Scowling, Laurel looked downward, then blushed as she realized that she still wore her nightgown. The batiste gown did little to hide the curves of her figure, and her nipples were now tautened with fear. Covering her breasts with an arm, Laurel tugged Fancy to her feet and pulled her down the hallway toward the pile of clothing near the mattresses. Thankfully, Barnaby waited around the corner on the stairs while Laurel threw on her clothing and cloak, then hastily helped her sobbing maid dress.

The two girls were rushing toward the stairwell when Barnaby, evidently hearing them, hurried back up to meet them. "Ready, ma'am?"

As Laurel nodded, Barnaby said, "We'll have to go out the back, ma'am. On my way over here, I spotted a Reb platoon heading this way on Post Office."

Then, suddenly, it happened—a sickening, whirring noise directly overhead. Just before they heard the horrid sound of timber splitting, Barnaby uttered an incoherent cry, violently pushing Laurel and Fancy down the stairs. Tumbling to safety, the two girls heard Barnaby's blood-curdling scream above them. Then there was silence. A deathly silence.

Brushing splinters of wood from her clothing, Laurel sat up dizzily, her head throbbing. At first, her attention was drawn to Fancy, who whimpered near her. But as soon as she determined the girl was mostly just shaken up, she directed her gaze to the stairs.

Laurel screamed her horror, her cry so loud and awful that she didn't hear the door opening behind her. For Barnaby lay unnaturally sprawled across the top of the stairs, his frail body splattered with blood, while ghostly light filtered in through the hole in the ceiling above him.

Unsteadily, Laurel got to her feet, her voice a strangled whisper as she moaned, "Oh, Barnaby."

But then, abruptly, she was grabbed from behind, turned against a hard, familiar body. "He's dead, Laurel."

"Jacob!" Laurel cried, throwing her arms about her husband's neck, burying her face against his throat, tasting the sweat and the gunpowder on his skin.

But Lafflin's body was rigid as he disengaged Laurel's arms and stood holding her tightly by the shoulders. "You must come with me now, Laurel, you and Fancy," he directed, his features grim and intense, his face stained with powder. "The *Harriet Lane* has been captured by the Confederates, and the *Westfield* is hopelessly aground. If we go at once to my cutter, perhaps we can break out of the harbor."

Laurel's eyes grew enormous. "You—you want me to go with you to the *Owasco*?"

"Laurel, please, for once cease your parroting!" Jacob retorted impatiently. "Don't you understand that the whole island will shortly be crawling with Confederates? In case you haven't figured it out, we've lost, my dear."

"Lost," Laurel murmured, her face thunderstruck as she tried to digest this revelation. Strangely, the news of the Confederate victory brought her no feeling of elation.

Meanwhile, her husband cursed under his breath and strode off to the window, saying to Laurel, "Do something about the girl."

Laurel went to Fancy, who sat at the foot of the stairs

weeping incoherently. As she knelt by Fancy and patted her quivering back, Jacob muttered, "God's teeth. Here they come."

Her head jerking upward, Laurel watched him bolt the front door. "You mean the Confederates are coming?"

"Who else?" came the terse reply.

Laurel gulped, then suddenly uttered a gasp of dismay, her eyes fixing upon her husband's calf. "Jacob, you're wounded!"

He laughed mirthlessly. "Aye. A Confederate platoon spotted me coming, and unless I'm mistaken, they shall shortly break down the door to this hotel."

"Oh no!" Laurel cried. "Barnaby said there were Confederate soldiers out in the streets . . ." At the mention of the unfortunate boy's name, Laurel turned to look back up the stairs at the mangled, bloody corpse. "Oh, poor Barnaby! Jacob, he saved our lives!"

Laurel at last succumbed to hysterics and was immediately, roughly, pulled to her feet to face the stern visage of her husband. "Laurel, stop it. Don't look at him again," Jacob ordered. "I know he saved your lives, and peace be to him for it. But the boy is stone cold dead now, and unless we run for it this very instant, we'll be joining him!"

Sobering at her husband's words, Laurel argued, "But, Jacob, you can't run with your leg like that. You'll bleed to death!"

Suddenly, from out in the street, Laurel heard a guttural voice command, "Halt!" She gaped at Jacob, her features frozen, as the same voice ordered, "Search the premises!"

The door was tried unsuccessfully. Laurel's hand flew to her heart as a soldier shouted, "It's locked, Captain Garrison."

"Garrison!" Laurel whispered to herself, her face turning ghostly pale. Could it be? Was it Trey Garrison, her sister's beau?

"Break it down, then!" came the retort from outside. Oh, God, Laurel thought, that was unmistakably Trey's voice!

Laurel stared at her husband in panic, her heart racing, her mind splintering. She had been on the verge of trying to hide Jacob, yet Trey Garrison's voice outside had jarred her violently back to reality, making her realize that in siding with her husband, she would dishonor and betray her family and her country. She also realized, ironically, that this was, at last, the opportunity she had waited for, prayed for, ever since she first met Jacob Lafflin. She could now betray him, gaining her revenge for all the wrongs he had dealt her. Yet what sweetness could this victory hold when to obtain it, she must destroy the man she loved and perhaps shatter her very soul in the process?

While the soldiers outside rammed their rifle butts against the oak door, Laurel said to her husband in a small voice, "Jacob, I don't know what to do."

Evidently, Jacob sensed the conflict in her mind and heart, for he replied sadly, "Do you wish to turn me over to your brothers in gray, my love?"

Suddenly, the wood of the door began to splinter from the onslaught, but it was nothing compared to the wrenching of Laurel's heart as she faced her husband, seeing the hurt and disappointment in the depths of his brown eyes.

Then a voice called out, "Laurel—are you in there?"

Laurel died inside. In a hoarse whisper, she informed Jacob, "He—he's from Washington-on-the-Brazos—my sister's beau!"

Ironically, Jacob laughed. "You have a sister?" While Trey again called out Laurel's name, Jacob nodded toward the door and added, "Well, this makes the denouement rather tidy, doesn't it, my dear?" His hand moved to his belt. "Shall I give you my sword?"

Laurel's heart seemed to break in her breast at Jacob's words. Lost to her ears now was the sound of Trey Garrison's voice bidding her open the door as she faced the man she loved and saw the raw, naked pain etched upon his features.

For a moment, time froze as Laurel's teeming mind questioned, Who is the enemy? Is it the man I love—the man whom I betrayed, the man who risked his life and cut off his path to escape in order to come back for me? Or is the enemy pounding at the door—the South, my very own family?

"Laurel, open the door—now!" Garrison insisted, his voice at last crashing through Laurel's thoughts.

In a fraction of an instant, Laurel made her decision. A new maturity tightened her face, as if she had grown up in that very moment. Quickly, she pulled Fancy to her feet, hoarsely ordering, "Fancy, take Captain Lafflin to the cloak room, and both of you hide behind the coats. Do you understand?"

"Yes 'um!" Fancy half sobbed even as Jacob raised an eyebrow at Laurel, eyeing her with puzzlement mingled with new respect.

"Jacob, go with Fancy—and keep her quiet, or she may give us all away!" Laurel urged. Inclining her head toward the din outside, she added meaningfully, "I'll get rid of them."

Suddenly, Jacob smiled, a smile that seemed to come straight from his heart, and Laurel felt all aglow inside as he said softly, "Later, love."

Watching Jacob hobble off with Fancy, leaving a small, trickling trail of blood, Laurel bit her lip. Would the Confederates follow the path of blood to her husband's hiding place?

Laurel had no further time for the worrisome thought, for no sooner had Jacob and Fancy disappeared down the hallway than the door crashed open and a half-dozen soldiers barreled in, led by Captain Trey Garrison.

"Trey!" Laurel cried, rushing to the tall, blond Texan, giving him a quick, affectionate hug.

Like Jacob, Garrison looked exhausted and dirty as he glanced about the hallway warily. "Laurel, why didn't you open the door?" he demanded. "And who were you talking to in here?"

Laurel showed no fear as she turned toward the stairs. "The boy was dying from a shell wound," she said sadly, gesturing toward Barnaby's pathetic form. "I couldn't just leave him—"

"But he's a Yank, ma'am!" a tall, wiry soldier interjected in a heavy Southern drawl.

"He was a human being!" Laurel replied brittlely. Turning to Garrison, she said more calmly, "It's good to see you, Trey. You always said you'd come rescue me if necessary, didn't you? But—how did you know I was here?"

"I went to Ursuline Academy as soon as I could break away from the battle," Garrison replied, glancing about distractedly as if searching for someone.

Laurel felt her spine crawling. Had Mother St. Pierre told Garrison about Jacob?

"Laurel, I hate to ask this, but are there other Yankees about?" Garrison continued, his bright blue eyes scrutinizing her sharply.

Laurel met his gaze steadily, feeling the hard stare of the other six soldiers in the room. "Yes," she answered sincerely. "One of them came in and went out of here like a bullet." She pointed toward the dining hall. "He left through the back door."

"I see," Garrison muttered, frowning. "You don't mind if we look around, do you? After all, he might still be lurking about."

"I saw him leave, Trey," Laurel insisted. "That's when I bolted the door—to—to keep out the others."

Garrison smiled. "We'll just have a look to be sure you're safe, Laurel."

Laurel stood tensely silent as Garrison directed his men about the hotel, sending three of them upstairs, while the others began searching the rooms on the first floor. After what seemed an eternity of doors opening and closing and the sound of boots on the stairs, the men regrouped in the front hallway.

"You were right, Laurel," Garrison said sheepishly. "Now, would you mind telling me what you are doing here?"

Laurel's eyebrows flew up. "Didn't Mother St. Pierre tell you?"

He shook his head.

Laurel drew herself up proudly. "I've been spying for the South, of course."

Garrison threw back his head and laughed. "I should have known. Camille warned me that you'd likely be in the thick of it."

"Cammie!" Laurel cried anxiously, bolting forward to clutch the gray sleeve of Garrison's uniform. "Oh, Trey, have you seen my family?"

"Yes, quite recently, and they are just fi—"

"Is there news of Daddy or of my brother?" Laurel demanded breathlessly.

"We'll catch up on the news later, Laurel," Garrison replied gruffly. "For now, young lady, I want you to get back to Ursuline Academy." Turning to one of his men, he directed, "Wallace, escort Miss Ashland—"

"But, Trey, the shelling seems to have stopped. Surely I'm safe here."

Trey shook his head grimly. "A brief cease-fire has been established while the Union commander considers our call to surrender. But there's no guarantee the Yanks will comply. You'll be much safer on the south side of the island,

Laurel. The academy is being used as a hospital and will not be bombarded by either side.''

"I'm sure Mother is in her glory," Laurel muttered automatically.

"I beg your pardon?" Trey asked.

"Never mind, Trey," Laurel replied, biting her lip. "Look, I can't go yet, but I thank you for your concern—"

Garrison shook his head firmly. "Laurel, you're returning to the academy now. I insist."

Laurel felt near desperation as she heard Garrison's immutable order. Fishing through her mind for a counter strategy, she blurted, "Trey, I can't go! Not until Fancy returns with my cat!"

"Your cat?" Garrison echoed in astonishment.

"Yes," Laurel replied dramatically. "The poor darling spooked when the shelling began, and I sent Fancy out to fetch her."

"Good Lord—you didn't send your maid out during the siege?" Trey asked incredulously.

Laurel sighed. "Oh, Trey, I'm sure it was inexcusable of me, but you know I've a soft heart where animals are concerned."

Chuckling, Trey shook his head. "You did spend an uncommon amount of time in the barnyard as a child, didn't you?" he mused. "Well, no matter. Don't fret—just go with Wallace to the academy and wait for Fancy and the cat there."

"Oh no, Trey, she's so simple-minded, she'll never know I'm there."

"You mean Fancy?" Trey asked with a frown.

"No, the cat," Laurel replied, her blue eyes sparkling with mischief.

The other soldiers began laughing uproariously as Laurel pleaded prettily, "*Please*, Trey, I promise I'll come along just as soon as Fancy returns. Besides, the Yankees won't hurt us. They've been roaming the streets for months now, and they've brought us no harm.''

"Very well, you can stay for a while,'' Trey conceded grudgingly. "But I'm stationing a guard outside to take you to the academy the instant Fancy returns. And I'll be by Ursuline personally later today to make sure you've arrived.''

"Fine, Trey, we'll be there,'' Laurel promised smoothly. "After all, how can I miss hearing about things at home?'' She flashed him a bright smile, inwardly frustrated about the guard, but knowing it was futile to try to gain further concessions from Garrison.

Laurel and Trey exchanged farewells, and Laurel heaved a deep sigh as she stood at the window in the hallway and watched the soldiers outside meld into the early morning fog. She waved casually at the guard and drew the curtains.

At last, Laurel dashed down the hallway toward the cloakroom.

"Jacob?'' she quavered, throwing open the door and hurrying into the tiny room.

The rack of coats along the wall parted, and Laurel winced in horror as Jacob stepped out from a pool of blood, supported by Fancy. Thank God that at least the Confederates had not spotted the blood in the shadows!

Fancy's eyes were half wild with distress. "Miss Laurel, Captain Lafflin, he bleed something terrible!'' the servant cried to her mistress. "I know it Reba—it the curse—''

"Stop it, Fancy!'' Laurel scolded even as the thought chilled her to the bone. "Oh, Jacob!'' she continued wretchedly, watching him limp into the somber light cast by the room's tiny window. "We must get you to the academy at once so Mother St. Pierre may attend you.''

"The academy? Mother St. Pierre? What nonsense are you talking, Laurel?'' Jacob asked in bewilderment.

"Ursuline Academy,'' Laurel replied with worried impatience. "It's where I came from. Oh, I'll tell you all about it later. Now quit staring at me so queerly, and let's get you there!"

Jacob recovered his composure. "No, Laurel, I must return to the *Owasco*," he contradicted weakly.

"Fiddlesticks!" Laurel shot back, bending over to rip a strip of linen from her petticoat. "You're pale as a ghost, and if you try to return to the battle now, it'll be the death of you."

"And if I stay on the island, it's as good as turning myself over to the Rebs," Jacob countered.

Laurel uttered a cry of alarm as she touched the evil-looking wound on Jacob's calf, pulling back the torn leather of his boot to have a better look at the oozing, gaping hole. "Oh God, Jacob, you must come with me!" she pleaded. "This wound is bleeding horribly, and there's no doubt a bullet embedded in your flesh." Feeling sick with fear, she again thought of Fancy's dire warning. "Oh Lord, Jacob. Only Mother Celeste will know what to do with this."

"There's a surgeon on the *Westfield*," Jacob argued.

"Which is aground in the channel, didn't you say? And who knows when the battle may resume out in the harbor," Laurel retorted, wrapping the linen about Jacob's calf. "You're coming with me to the academy, where you'll be safe."

"I refuse to abandon my ship to the Rebs—Jesus, Laurel, you're killing me!"

"Sorry, Jacob," Laurel replied, grimacing as she finished tightly tying the bandage. "But it's the only way to stop the bleeding until we get to Mother St. Pierre." Quickly, she stood. "Come on, Jacob. I'm sure Mother will hide you if I ask her to."

She faced Jacob now, and he stared back at her, his features intense, brooding. "Very well, Laurel," he said at last. "But, mind you, I'm going to the academy mainly to see you and Fancy to safety. Then I'm returning to my ship. When we retake the island—well, I'll come get you then.''

Laurel sighed. ''I'll not argue with you now, Jacob,'' she said resignedly. ''Come. Let's be about it.''

The three left through the back door of the Virginia House, cutting across neighboring properties until they reached Twenty-third Street. Their progress in traveling toward the academy was agonizingly slow, for they knew not friend from foe in the dense fog. Again and again, they ducked into doorways at the sound of voices approaching, then they waited tensely in the shadows as a platoon of soldiers or a group of civilians passed by. Finally, they reached Avenue N and turned west, grateful now for the covering of fog that shielded them as they moved across the vast expanse of open terrain.

After what seemed an eternity, Laurel spotted the lights of the academy. Nearing the picket fence, the three paused, listening for sounds of movement nearby. But they heard only scattered distant gunfire. Cautiously, they entered the school yard and approached the building.

Starting up the cobbled walk, the threesome suddenly froze as they heard the front door to the academy swing open. While the sound of conversation drifted toward them from the porch, Jacob grabbed the hand of each girl and they dashed to hide behind the trunk of a large tree.

Laurel held her breath, hearing Mother St. Pierre say, ''We will be most happy to assist you in any way we can, Colonel Cook.''

''Thank you, Sister,'' came the masculine reply. ''We'll send you all the medical supplies we can collect—to treat the wounded of both sides.''

The two now moved through the schoolyard, two dark figures shrouded by fog, and Laurel heard Mother St. Pierre say, ''I am pleased, Colonel, that we understand each other.''

"Good day, Sister," Laurel heard the Confederate officer murmur, the gate hinges squeaking.

Now a solitary figure moved back down the cobbled path, and Laurel sprang out from the shadows to clutch the habit of Mother St. Pierre.

"*Mon dieu!* Laurel!" the mother superior gasped.

"Mother, you must help us!" Laurel said in an urgent whisper. "I'm here with my husband—you must hide him and treat his wound!"

"Your husband? But where?" Mother St. Pierre asked confusedly. Then she caught her breath sharply as two additional figures stepped out from behind the tree.

"I'm Captain Jacob Lafflin, Sister," Jacob explained in a brittle voice. "I'd be greatly in your debt if you would help us."

"You understand, Captain Lafflin, that this hospital is under Confederate control?" Mother St. Pierre inquired.

"Yes, I know," Jacob replied. "I'm here to ensure my wife's safety and have my wound treated so I may return to my command and see my vessel safely out of the harbor. If you tell the Confederates I'm here, well—"

"I see," Mother said carefully. She paused for a moment, her face lined with perplexity. At last, she turned to Laurel. "Bring your young man to the east entrance, Laurel. I'll meet you there and lead you up the back stairs to your old room. Then we'll tend Captain Lafflin's wound."

"Oh, Mother, thank you!" Laurel replied joyously, impulsively hugging the older woman. Though Mother St. Pierre returned the embrace, Laurel couldn't read her expression as the nun quickly disengaged herself from Laurel and headed off toward the steps, calling over her shoulder, "Hurry—before more soldiers arrive bearing the wounded."

Quickly, Laurel, Jacob and Fancy moved to the side entrance. Momentarily, the door creaked open, and Mother St. Pierre motioned them inside. As they entered the dark tomb of the first-floor hallway, Laurel heard the faint sound of feminine voices coming from the direction of the hospital ward, along with the moaning of the injured, the clatter of bottles and trays.

With Mother St. Pierre leading the entourage, the group climbed narrow stairs to the second floor, then moved silently down the hallway to Laurel's room. Inside, Mother St. Pierre lit the lantern on the desk, and as the light filled the dimness, Laurel's gaze moved protectively toward her husband, who stood in the center of the room, his back to her.

"So you hailed from a nunnery, did you, my dear?" Jacob inquired, turning unsteadily to face her.

His face was ashen. Laurel screamed as he collapsed upon the rug.

Chapter
Thirty-four

JANUARY 4, 1863

Laurel sat by Jacob's bed clutching her rosary beads as early morning light filtered in through the cold pane of the window. Funny, she reflected, she hadn't even thought of prayer over the past few months, but during the previous three days, with her husband deathly ill, she had spent hours on her knees. Having Jacob wounded was frightful enough, but the constant awareness of Fancy's warning—that the vile legacy of Reba's voodoo might somehow be responsible for his proximity to death—was simply unendurable. Thus Laurel tried to keep her mind and heart on the endless "Hail Marys" and "Our Fathers" she recited in an attempt to ward off all evil.

Jacob moaned now, and Laurel hurt for him. Laying aside the beads, she reached for the basin on the stand near the bed, taking a cloth from the cold water and wringing it out. As she placed the cloth on Jacob's forehead, he seemed somewhat soothed, for he relaxed in his sleep. But his eyes remained closed, his face hot and flushed.

Laurel had not left the room since they came to St. Ursuline's from the Virginia House. After Jacob fainted upon their arrival, he had fortunately remained unconscious while Mother St. Pierre removed the bullet from his calf and treated his wound. Since that time, though, he had been in and out of delirium. While his wound did not appear badly infected, Mother had explained that Jacob was weak from loss of blood, and also that some of the poison from his wound had probably escaped into his bloodstream. Nonetheless, the fact that Jacob had become so very ill so quickly made both Laurel and Fancy fear something worse.

Every effort had been made to see to Laurel and Jacob's comfort. Even though the downstairs hospital ward was jammed with the wounded of both sides, cloth-covered trays were sent up to Laurel's room regularly, double portions of food and fresh bandages hidden beneath the linen napkin. However, Jacob had not eaten—it was all Laurel could do to force a few spoonfuls of broth down him in his more lucid moments.

The hours were long for Laurel. Mother St. Pierre checked on Jacob only during rare moments when she could break away from the ward. And Fancy was largely absent, too, having been conscripted to help with the enormous kitchen chores involved in feeding the wounded. Thus, Laurel's companions became silence, fear, and worry.

A knock at the door now caused Laurel to stiffen. Quietly, she got to her feet, clutching her white wool shawl about her as she tiptoed to the door. "Who is it?" she whispered.

"Mother Celeste," came the barely audible reply.

Laurel opened the door to face the weary countenance of Mother St. Pierre. "Come out into the hall, Laurel," the nun directed gravely.

Laurel moved silently into the hallway, closing the door and facing the sister. "Yes? What is it?"

Mother St. Pierre sighed. "It's Captain Garrison, Laurel. I can't put him off any longer. He insists he must see you."

Laurel bit her lip. Trey Garrison had been asking to see her every day since they arrived at the academy, and she had sent down one excuse after another as to why she couldn't come.

"I can't tell him you have another headache, Laurel," Mother St. Pierre continued. "He simply won't believe me."

Laurel sighed resignedly. "But what of Jacob?"

"I'll sit with him while you go downstairs."

"Very well. Where is he?"

"In my office."

Laurel reached out and touched the black sleeve of Mother's habit. "Thank you, Mother. You've been an angel to us."

The tall nun smiled fleetingly as she turned and opened the door to Laurel's room. Laurel moved toward the stairs, her gait slow and hesitant. She should have met with Trey before now, she knew, since he undoubtedly had news of home. Yet she had felt obsessed to remain with her husband. Worst of all, she had a horrible intuition that Trey would be bringing her bad news.

Laurel trudged down the back stairs, distractedly brushing a wisp of black hair from her eyes. In the downstairs hallway, she heard sounds of conversation mixed with moans of pain drifting toward her from the hospital ward. She shivered, drawing her shawl more tightly about her. No longer did she feel insulated from this tragic war—as if the threat to her husband's life were not bad enough, she had also had to cope with the periodic wrenching screams of the men in the hospital ward, horrible shrieks that awakened her many times at night. And often during the day, while she stood at the window, she saw soldiers bearing cloth-wrapped corpses toward the cemetery—for there was not enough wood to be found on the island for coffins. The Confederates had won the battle, but men from both sides had paid the price.

Slowly, Laurel opened the door to Mother St. Pierre's office. As she stepped inside, Trey Garrison got to his feet. "Good morning, Laurel."

Laurel nodded to Trey. He looked quite handsome this morning in his gray brass-buttoned uniform, and the sun, shimmering in from the window behind him, danced golden highlights in his hair. Laurel moved around the desk to seat herself in the familiar chair where she had spent so many unhappy hours previously.

"Have you recovered from your malaise?" Trey asked, folding himself into the mother superior's chair.

"Yes, Trey," she replied uneasily. Seeing Trey in Mother St. Pierre's chair made her feel at a distinct disadvantage.

"That was quite an extraordinary headache you had," Trey continued casually. "Complete with vomiting, I understand."

"It was the shelling, Trey," Laurel said sincerely while her spine crawled at the trace of suspicion in Trey's smooth tone. She was also unnerved by his bluntness—he must be suspicious to refer in such an ungentlemanly manner to her supposed physical illness. "The—the shelling truly prostrated me," she continued earnestly, praying he would believe her.

"I see. I'm pleased you're better." Trey paused, his fingers toying with the pen in the inkwell on the desk, his brow creased in a thoughtful frown. "Laurel, aren't you at all curious about your family?"

She stared at her lap. "Frankly, Trey, I fear what you have to say."

"Laurel, look at me."

Her heart racing in trepidation, Laurel looked up at Trey

and saw the pain in his bright green eyes. "Oh God—I knew it! It is bad news, isn't it?"

He nodded gravely.

"Daddy . . ."

"Yes. And your brother, Charles, too. I'm sorry, Laurel."

"Oh God, no!" Laurel cried, her head in her hands, her mind and heart torn by excruciating pain.

As Laurel sobbed, Trey got up and moved around the desk, pulling her up into his arms. "What can I say?" he said hoarsely, lamely patting her on the back and handing her his handkerchief.

For long moments they stood thus, Laurel weeping her heart out, while Trey awkwardly tried to comfort her. Finally, the initial shock subsided somewhat and Laurel returned to her chair. Bravely, she met Trey's gaze as he again sat down across from her. "I want to know what happened to them. When—and—and where."

"Laurel, what purpose can it serve—"

"Tell me, Trey," she insisted adamantly, wiping her tears.

Trey sighed, then explained to Laurel the circumstances of her father's and brother's deaths, during the second battle of Bull Run. He told of how he had gotten special leave to come home and break the news to her family. Afterward, he answered her questions regarding her mother and sister, assuring her that both were in good health and adjusting to the tragedy. "By the way, Cammie and I did get married while I was home on leave," he concluded almost shyly.

Laurel was too numb to feel much elation at the news. Yet she did manage to say sincerely, "I'm happy for you, Trey. But, mind you, don't go getting yourself killed and break my sister's heart."

"I'll do my best not to, Laurel."

Laurel glanced at her lap, at her fingers now twisting the

handkerchief. "Are Mother and Cammie distraught with worry about me?"

"I'm afraid so," came the reply. "In fact, I secured this special assignment with Magruder just so I could locate you. But don't fret. We'll arrange to get you home just as soon as possible."

Laurel glanced up, undisguised fear on her face. "Oh no, Trey, I couldn't!"

"Why not?" Trey countered, raising an eyebrow at her.

Laurel brought her hands up to her face, her mind splintering. All at once, she was overwhelmed by it all—her fear, her confusion, her grief, Trey's questioning. "Trey, I must go back upstairs," she whispered desperately. "My head is again beginning to throb . . ."

Her voice trailing off, she got to her feet and numbly moved toward the door. But in an instant Trey was beside her, his broad back against the door, barring her exit. "Not yet, Laurel. First you must tell me who you were hiding at the Virginia House."

Laurel glanced up at him thunderstruck, her eyes wild. "W-what do you mean?"

"Surely you don't think I believed that absurd story about your cat," he replied, scowling down at her. "I saw the trail of blood leading to the cloakroom and the pool of blood on the floor beneath the coats. You were hiding the Yank one of my men wounded, weren't you, Laurel? Why? Is he upstairs now? Is that why you wouldn't see me?"

There was hurt and suspicion in Trey Garrison's green eyes. Laurel gaped at him wordlessly, too taken off guard to respond.

"Are you hiding a bluecoat, Laurel? Tell me!" Trey demanded.

Laurel shuddered, feeling utterly defeated. "Yes, Trey," she said tonelessly.

Trey's eyes darkened with disappointment and dismay as

he took Laurel's arm and firmly led her back to her chair. "My dear, this is quite serious. You've some explaining to do."

Laurel realized that further resistance was futile. Sitting across from Trey, she spilled out her entire story—of coming to the Virginia House, of spying on Jacob, of her subsequent marriage to him. After Laurel finished, Trey was silent for a long moment, his chair creaking as he rocked back and forth on the legs. Finally, he asked, "And how do you feel about this Captain Lafflin, Laurel?"

Laurel's heart was in her eyes as she breathed, "I love him, Trey."

"I gathered as much," Garrison replied, his jaw tight. Looking at her steadily, he inquired, "So he's upstairs now, is he?"

"Oh, Trey, please don't turn him in!" Laurel pleaded.

Abruptly, Garrison got to his feet, and moved to the window, his shoulders slumped. "You're asking a great deal, Laurel."

"But, Trey, surely if you were going to turn him in, you would have done it at the Virginia House—"

Garrison turned to face her and said with anguish, "I had no desire to watch my men kill you, Laurel—or worse."

"You can't mean—surely you could have stopped them—"

He silenced her by raising his hand and shaking his head. "Bitterness runs deep in this war. Soldiers crazed with blood-lust have been known to turn on their own officers when thwarted."

Laurel shuddered silently.

"You've put me in a very awkward position, Laurel," Garrison continued, folding his arms across his chest.

Confused and frightened, Laurel blurted back, "Well, perhaps Jacob will die and assuage your conscience, Trey. He's had a raging fever for days, and God only knows if he'll make it through the night!"

And she burst into tears.

She heard Trey move to her side and felt his strong hands on her shoulders. There was a long, awkward silence, then Trey said miserably, "Jesus, Laurel, I didn't mean to make you cry again. God, I've been hard on you today, haven't I?"

Her only reply was a sob. He sighed, patting her shoulder, trying to comfort her as best he could. Finally, he gently pulled her to her feet. "Go tend your husband, honey."

She stared at him, her tears frozen on her face. "You're not going to—"

He shook his head. "I'll not take from you the only man you have left, Laurel," he said sadly. Pulling her toward the door, he urged, "Now get back upstairs before I change my mind."

Laurel dabbed at her eyes. "Thank you, Trey."

At the door, he paused, frowning thoughtfully. "I can't promise anything, Laurel, but I'll see if I can arrange to get you and Jacob away from the island once he recovers."

Trey's words were sobering to Laurel, but they made sense. Neither she nor Jacob would be safe staying on the island indefinitely. "Oh, Trey, that would be good of you," she said, but added worriedly, "*if* Jacob recovers."

"He will." Trey grinned. "He'd have to be a fool to leave a pretty thing like you a widow."

Laurel smiled bravely. "He's so like you, Trey. At another time you might have been friends—brothers, even."

He nodded sadly, opening the door for her. "That's what makes this damn war so obscene."

The two exchanged goodbyes and Laurel hurried for her room. In the upstairs hallway, she spotted Mother St. Pierre coming toward her, tears streaming down her cheeks. "Oh my God—Jacob!" Laurel choked, racing past the nun and into her room.

She immediately spotted Jacob on the bed—he was very still, his face pale, his eyes closed. "No no," Laurel moaned, wringing her hands.

"Laurel, our prayers have been answered," Mother St. Pierre said from behind her.

Laurel whirled to face the nun. "The fever has broken—I was just coming to fetch you, Laurel," Mother said, and Laurel at last realized that Mother's tears were of joy, her eyes glowing.

With a cry of ecstasy, Laurel turned to her husband. He looked, indeed, quite wan, but the fever flush was gone, a good sign. She moved closer and with trembling fingers reached out, touching his forehead to make certain the fever had abated. His flesh was warm to the touch, but not hot.

He would live . . . he would live. . . . Indeed, their prayers had been answered! They had survived all—the war, even Reba's curse. She began to sob, her tears trickling down upon her husband's face.

Jacob's eyes slowly opened, and he stared up at Laurel gravely. His hand, unsteady but warm, took hers, and he pressed his lips against her palm as he whispered, "Don't cry, darling. I'm here."

Chapter
Thirty-five

While the setting sun cast an amber glow in the room, Laurel sat by Jacob's bed, watching him sleep. It had been an emotional day for her—Jacob had been awake and lucid all morning. Laurel had explained to him what news she had gleaned from the sisters regarding the battle days earlier— that the Confederates had indeed won, that most of the Yankee gunboats, including the *Owasco,* had fled the harbor during the cease-fire period. When Jacob expressed his concern about returning to his command, Laurel had scolded back that there was absolutely nothing they could do until he recovered his strength. Then, after consuming a large bowlful of soup, Jacob had fallen asleep, resting peacefully all afternoon. While he slept, Laurel had sat in a straight chair near the bed watching him, occasionally wiping a tear of joy from her eye or getting up and moving to his side to press her lips against his forehead, reassuring herself over and over again that he was alive and free of fever. Occasionally, she fell into weeping as she thought of her dead father and brother. The initial shock had faded somewhat, but there was a deep wound in her heart that would take a long, long time to heal.

Now, Jacob stirred slightly in his sleep, tossing aside the covers. Distressed, Laurel watched gooseflesh spread across the bronze of his chest due to the chill in the room. She tiptoed to his side and reached for the covers. Suddenly, she was pulled downward, atop a hard chest, and her husband's warm lips covered her mouth.

"Good evening, sweetheart," Jacob said sleepily as they came up for air.

Laurel drew back, resting her elbows on either side of her husband as she gazed down at him in astonishment. How handsome he looked—his black hair sensuously tousled, his brown eyes glowing. Even the heavy growth of whiskers on his face added to his masculine appeal.

"Jacob, mind your leg—I don't wish to injure you," Laurel admonished, trying to sound severe despite the quiver of excitement in her voice.

His hands slid down her body to grasp her bottom. "Good—then you'll not put up a fight." And giving her a wicked wink, he again fastened his mouth upon hers.

For a moment Laurel lost track of all else. It felt so good to be in her husband's arms again—to feel his warm, firm mouth on her lips and throat. But as his hands reached for the buttons on her blue wool dress, she suddenly, illogically, burst into tears.

"Laurel?"

Sounding baffled and alarmed, Jacob pulled them both to a sitting position. For long moments, she wept desperately, while he held her.

"What is it, sweetheart?" he asked at last, when she had quieted somewhat.

Laurel looked up at him through her tears. "I—I've been

so worried about you, Jacob. You've been so very ill. Fancy was even afraid that Reba's curse might still—''

"No, no, darling. It's over. You must never think of that again," Jacob interrupted hoarsely, pulling her close. But when her slender figure continued to tremble with the threat of new sobs, he added worriedly, "There's more, isn't there?"

She nodded as she looked up at him in sorrow. "I—I couldn't tell you this morning when you seemed so weak, Jacob. But Trey Garrison came to see me today. My brother and my f-father are both dead."

"Oh, darling—I'm so sorry," he said, holding her tightly and tucking her head beneath his chin as she continued to cry brokenly. "But you know, Laurel, you told me your father and brother were already dead and lying in Episcopal Cemetery."

"Oh, good grief," Laurel choked, with a laugh that was half a sob. "I suppose it's time I told you the truth, isn't it?"

Jacob nodded gravely. Haltingly, Laurel explained to him about her background, telling him of her childhood at Washington-on-the-Brazos and of coming to St. Ursuline's three years previous. Jacob listened patiently, comforting her several times when her speech disintegrated into weeping at the mention of her father's or her brother's name. "I'm so relieved, darling, to have the mystery cleared up between us," he said when she finished, kissing her wet cheek. "And I'm deeply sorry that the circumstances of your telling me are so tragic. But I wish you had told me before. I wish you had trusted me."

She nodded sadly. "I guess trust was always our biggest problem, wasn't it, Jacob?" Stifling a sob, she continued, "It's all so unreal. Daddy and Charles are lying in a grave somewhere in Virginia, and I'm here in the arms of their enemy."

Jacob stiffened. "So I'm your enemy, Laurel?"

"No, no," she choked wretchedly, twisting her hands. "You're not my enemy, but you're their enemy. You're my husband, Jacob. When I married you, I betrayed everything I hold dear—my family, my home. Now, I can never go back because—because you're my husband and I love you!"

This revelation bursting from her, Laurel fell into renewed spasms of heartbroken weeping.

"Oh, Laurel!" she heard Jacob breathe as his hand gently stroked her hair. "How I have longed to hear those words from you!" His arms tightened about her, and he pressed his lips against her forehead.

She drew back, awed by the reverence in his tone. "You have? Why?"

Jacob looked down at her, his eyes glittering with amusement mixed with tenderness. "Why? Because I love you too, silly goose." He leaned over and kissed the tip of her nose.

"You do?" she quavered.

Jacob shook his head and laughed. "You should see your face—full of innocent amazement. Of course I love you, Laurel. I think I fell in love with you the very first instant I saw you. You were so full of life and bravado—telling all those outrageous lies and insisting we all believe you." Thoughtfully, he reached out and stroked her flushed cheek. "I could tell immediately that you would need some looking after. When Carter tried to attack you, I literally wanted to disembowel the bastard. I soon realized that if I didn't claim you for my own, one of the others would ruin you. And the thought of your innocence being used by the likes of—" he paused, gritting his teeth.

"But you played a wicked trick on me, marrying me, letting me think Fancy's life was hanging in the balance!" she accused indignantly.

Jacob smiled devilishly. "You did play right into my hand. And may I point out that you deserved it?"

"I did not!" Laurel maintained stoutly, setting her arms akimbo.

Jacob chuckled and quickly kissed her pouting mouth. "Oh, what a devious little chit you were. I didn't believe a word you said regarding your background, of course. Do you know I actually thought you were a quadroon or an octoroon and a serving girl at the Virginia House?"

"You did?" Laurel stared at her husband with her mouth agape. "You thought I was part black and you married me anyway?"

Jacob frowned. "Would your being part black have made you less than human, Laurel?"

Laurel blustered, "But blacks are slaves—"

"And slavery is wrong, Laurel," Jacob said gravely. He stared off toward the window. "Oh, I didn't used to think so—like many Southerners, I once believed slavery was the mainstay of a chivalrous way of life. At least so my father used to tell me."

"Your father?" Laurel prodded gently, her caution spurred by the trace of bitterness in her husband's voice. "You mean Jean Lafitte?"

"Yes. He took me on a voyage once," Jacob continued, his eyes holding a faraway look, almost as if Laurel were not there. "I was a lad of ten at the time; my father was past sixty. We toured most of the Gulf coast—New Orleans, Galveston, Indianola. He told me tales of his adventures on the high seas and showed me the locations where his booty is buried."

"You mean you know the hiding places of Lafitte's fortune?" Laurel asked excitedly.

Jacob nodded grimly. "We retrieved some of the gold during that very voyage—"

"So that's why you sent me the gold dubloons!" Laurel interrupted, snapping her fingers.

"Aye. My father also left enough gold buried in these parts to gild the *Owasco*."

Laurel was amazed. "What are you going to do about it, Jacob?"

He sighed heavily. "That's a difficult question. It's blood money. Many good men were killed for it and even now lie in a watery grave. And what my father didn't gain through privateering booty, he obtained through selling human beings."

"You mean when he smuggled slaves?"

"Yes. As a child, I accepted his romanticized version of his exploits. But soon after I graduated from Annapolis, the cutter I was assigned to stopped a slaver off the coast of Florida." Jacob's hand gripped the counterpane and his eyes darkened with anguish as he said, "When I saw the suffering those poor, tormented souls endured in the filthy, stinking hole of that ship—well I was actually physically ill, Laurel."

Laurel found her husband's words quite sobering. "I just never thought—"

"That blacks are people, too?" Jacob put in, staring at her earnestly. "That it's wrong to keep them in bondage?"

Laurel nodded slowly. "I suppose I realized that recently, with Fancy. She risked her life to save me, yet never before had I thought of her as anything but an object—that is, not until I nearly lost her." She sniffed, staring at her tightly clenched fingers in her lap. "I guess you taught me an important lesson, Jacob. But if what you say is true, then my family—all our friends—are wrong, bad."

"Not bad, Laurel—just misguided," Jacob said gently.

Despite her husband's reassurance, Laurel felt a lump building in her throat, and new tears stung her eyes. "It's just so tragic, so senseless, this war. To think my father and my brother died for naught."

"Laurel, they did what they thought was right, just like you did, even though you scared me halfway to the next life."

"Oh, Jacob." Again she began weeping, her feelings of turmoil and grief tearing her apart.

Jacob held her and stroked her trembling back, whispering again and again, "I love you, Laurel." But she continued to cry brokenly, pathetically.

After a moment, he pulled her body on top of his. She lay with her wet cheek pressed against his bare shoulder and felt his warmth spreading through her body.

"You've been through so much, my darling," she heard him say huskily. "And you've been so brave. Don't give up now. Where's that courage I'm so proud of?"

She gazed up at him, momentarily distracted from her weeping.

"That's better," he whispered, smiling tenderly. "No more crying. It's time to forget all this sadness, at least for a while. Time to love your husband."

She felt a blush spread rapidly across her face. "But—we can't—I mean, your leg—"

He chuckled. "It's time you learned to properly pleasure your man."

"Haven't I?" she demanded indignantly, her embarrassment for the moemnt forgotten.

"Oh yes, thoroughly," he laughed. He reached out and stroked her cheek, giving her a passionate look that made her senses flutter in anticipation. "But I've an even more delicious torment in mind for you tonight, love."

He propped pillows behind them, then boldly pulled her astride him. Realizing his intent, Laurel felt herself begin to ache and throb for his touch, albeit his design seemed wantonly wicked.

"Doesn't—doesn't your wound hurt?" she managed, her face burning.

He pulled her harder against him. "I'll tell you what hurts."

Her eyes grew enormous. "I think I already know."

He laughed and kissed her. "Besides," he continued, after a moment. "I must know if you've forgiven me for the last time, on board the *Owasco*."

She stiffened slightly, but he drew her closer and said, "You must understand, Laurel, that I was wild with love for you, yet I was sure you would never trust me, never share your life with me, never tell me the truth. When I took you—well, I think I wanted to brand you mine, to make your body yield completely as your heart and mind never would." He sighed, stroking her hair. "So many times when I was hard on you, darling, it was just my frustration and my damned pride. Can you forgive me?"

Reaching upward to stroke his face with her hand, she said quietly, "Of course I forgive you, Jacob. And I understand. It was wrong of me to lie to you all those times. I should have been more willing to meet you halfway. I—I guess I'm quite proud, too."

While she spoke, he began unbuttoning her dress. "Not a shred of pride between us now, fair lady," he whispered, his hand undoing the ties on her chemise, then reaching for her bare breast. "Not a shred."

She trembled with expectation as his deft hands undressed her. Moments later, when she was perched, gloriously naked, above him, he whispered reverently, "God, how beautiful you are. Your skin is pink and white and smooth as silk, your hair is like the sea at midnight, your eyes are glowing—"

"With love," she supplied, her voice breaking. "With love . . ."

They kissed and caressed, their passion building to a voracious hunger. At last, no longer able to wait an instant, Laurel began to take him into herself, and when he responded by pulling her violently downward, she cried out in intense, indescribable pleasure. She was totally undone by him yet totally at one with him. Their eyes locked for an electric moment, then their lips melded in a ravenous kiss. Tears filled her eyes as the pain and grief faded from her mind and her entire being became the love she felt for her husband.

She rode with him to rapture, to the deepest fulfillment of their love.

Chapter Thirty-six

On a chilly January morning four days later, Trey Garrison sent a message to Laurel's room that he wished to meet with both Laurel and Jacob. Jacob was now recovering nicely and hobbling about the room without benefit of crutches. For the sake of secrecy, he and Laurel agreed to meet with Trey in the upstairs sitting room.

The upstairs parlor was more of a sun room, and when Jacob and Laurel first entered, they did not see Trey as they glanced at a sea of palms and other lush plants facing the long row of tall windows flanking the room on the south.

They heard a shuffle of boots, and Trey Garrison unfolded himself from a large rocker near the windows. "Good morning, Laurel. Captain Lafflin."

Trey approached the couple, his green eyes solemn as he shook hands with Jacob. The two men, in uniforms of contrasting blue and gray, eyed each other guardedly.

Laurel and Jacob seated themselves in Windsor chairs strewn with colorful pillows and Trey returned to his rocker.

Laurel was now between the two men, and she eyed each of them covertly as she smoothed her green velvet skirts about her.

At last, Jacob broke the silence. "Captain Garrison, I wish to express to you my gratitude for your not turning me in to your superiors, both here and at the Virginia House."

Trey shrugged, inclining his head toward Laurel. "I kept silent only for Laurel's sake."

Jacob nodded gravely. "I understand. But I am in your debt, sir—an obligation I do not take lightly."

Trey Garrison studied his enemy appraisingly, a new respect shining in his green eyes. "I see that you are a man of honor, Lafflin, Yank though you be. And from what Laurel says, you have acted in her best interests."

"I've tried to," Jacob replied, shooting Laurel a smile.

The tension between Trey and Jacob seemed to lessen somewhat as they spoke. The two briefly discussed the battle days earlier, with Trey filling Jacob in regarding details of the conflict. "I understand you were captaining the *Owasco*, Lafflin," he commented. "Since I was on board the *Bayou City*, it's a wonder we didn't kill each other."

"Aye," Jacob concurred. "It truly is. Tell me, Garrison, what happened after I left the harbor and went to the Virginia House? How did Renshaw respond to your commander's call to surrender?"

Trey shook his head, his expression grim as he stared out at the cold expanse of sky, gray surf and pristine sand before them. "I'm afraid that during the truce period, your commodore ordered the entire Federal fleet to flee the harbor under flag of truce. Since the *Westfield* was aground, Renshaw ordered it blown up rather than abandon it to our forces. Unfortunately for your commander, the charge left on the *Westfield* did not detonate, and when Renshaw and his officers rowed back to check on it, they were blown to the four winds for their troubles.''

"My God!" Jacob exclaimed, his features incredulous. "You mean Renshaw ordered our forces to flee during the cease-fire, then he blew himself up with his own ship? The commodore must have lost his head.''

Trey nodded. "So it appears. Anyway, the balance of your fleet managed to steam out of the harbor.'' He turned to Jacob. "They left us with a ticklish problem, however— getting you and Laurel out of Galveston.''

Jacob nodded, studying Garrison cautiously. "Laurel said you might be willing to assist us. What do you have in mind, Garrison?''

Trey gestured toward the Gulf. "Though your fleet is now long gone, yesterday your frigate *Brooklyn* anchored off the bar, reestablishing the blockade.''

Jacob nodded, half smiling. "I didn't think our navy would leave Galveston open for long.''

Trey crossed his legs and continued, "Last night, I signaled the *Brooklyn,* then rowed out, under white flag, to speak with Commander Bell.'' He sighed. "It's all arranged. Bell expects the two of you to board tonight.''

Laurel and Jacob exchanged looks of amazement as Garrison continued, "I've tied up a rowboat for you near the ruins of Lafitte's Maison Rouge. Tonight I'll take the two of you there—I've arranged a signal with the captain to let them know of your approach.''

"Are you sure Bell believed you—that they'll be waiting for us tonight?" Jacob inquired with a trace of suspicion.

Trey nodded. "I explained to him the situation—about Laurel.'' With a meaningful glance at Jacob, he added, "It's best that you get her off the island immediately. If my compatriots should discover that she wed a Yankee—for whatever reason—I should truly fear for her life.''

"And should your fellow soldiers discover what you've

done for us," Laurel put in meaningfully, a tear burning her eye, "then they'd kill you, Trey. Wouldn't they?"

"They would," he agreed gravely. Glancing over Laurel's head, Trey stared at Jacob. "But they won't find out."

"Certainly not from my lips," Jacob replied, meeting Trey's gaze levelly. "Or from Laurel's."

Trey stood up, helping Laurel to her feet. "Good. Then I'll come for the two of you at midnight."

"And Fancy," Laurel put in.

"Of course," Garrison agreed, smiling.

"You're coming tonight won't be necessary, Garrison," Jacob remarked, now standing beside them. "You've endangered your life enough for us already. Laurel and I can get to Maison Rouge on our own."

But Trey shook his head as he approached the door. "No. I promised Laurel's mother and sister that I'd see her to safety." He turned to smile at them sadly. "While I doubt this is what the Ashlands had in mind, I must see the drama through to its conclusion."

The couple thanked Trey profusely, but as the Confederate soldier left, Laurel fell, trembling, into Jacob's arms, clutching him tightly.

"What is it, sweetheart? You're not crying again, are you?" Jacob asked gently.

She shook her head in denial even as her body shook with silent sobs.

"Don't you want to come with me, Laurel?"

"Yes," she choked, her face pressed against his shoulder. "But I'll be leaving my home—maybe forever."

"Your home is with me, Laurel," he admonished, his arms tightening about her. "And don't grieve. When the war is over, I'll bring you back to visit your family."

"You promise?" she asked tremulously.

"I vow it, sweetheart."

*   *   *

"Fancy, are you sure?" Laurel asked. The two girls and Jacob stood braving the cold night breeze cutting across the crumbling foundation of Maison Rouge as they stared out at the Gulf just beyond them.

"Yes 'um," Fancy replied. "I want to go home to Brazos Bend."

"But, Fancy. Won't you miss me?"

"Yes 'um," Fancy croaked in the darkness. "But I don't know nothing about no Pennsylvania, Miss Laurel. And I ain't goin' there."

As she felt Jacob slip a comforting arm about her waist, Laurel wiped a tear from her eye with the sleeve of her wool cloak. She felt cold to the bone, for they had been standing on the deserted foundation of Maison Rouge for nearly an hour, waiting for the approach of the *Brooklyn*. Even now, Trey Garrison stood beyond them down by the water, his cape whipping about him as he strained to see a sign of an approaching ship.

It had been a difficult day for Laurel. She had packed for herself and Jacob, squeezing the bare necessities for them into her portmanteau. Then, almost offhandedly, she had informed Fancy to be ready to depart with them that night, only to be utterly appalled when the servant steadfastly refused to go with them.

"I ain't goin' north wid you, Miss Laurel," Fancy had maintained vehemently. "Galveston done give me my fill of goin' places. I is tired and I is goin' home. 'Sides, one of them wounded Yankees, he tell me I is free now, since the first day of this year. I is goin' home."

Laurel had argued with the servant to no avail, then had hurried to Jacob, begging his help with the wayward servant. But her husband had shaken his head. "Fancy's right, Laurel. It is her choice, and she is free. The Emancipation Proclamation became effective January first."

"But I'll miss her," Laurel had wailed.

"You don't own her, Laurel," Jacob had admonished.

Now Laurel tried to imagine her life without Fancy and found the idea unthinkable. Though she was three years older than the girl, she simply could not remember a time when Fancy was not a part of her life. She had taken the girl for granted, and now there was no time left.

Yes, Laurel thought sadly, the coming years would be difficult without her friend and companion. Jacob would be leaving her alone in an alien place with a stranger, his mother. He would then spend the balance of the war at the helm of the *Owasco,* and God only knew if she would ever see him again—

"She's approaching!" a voice called out.

Distracted from her thoughts by Trey Garrison's voice, Laurel turned and spotted a shadowy hulk in the distance out in the channel. She watched Trey light a lantern and begin signaling the *Brooklyn.* Leaving Laurel to wait with Fancy, Jacob hobbled down to the beach to place the portmanteau in the rowboat and to ready the small skiff.

Laurel realized that when she stepped into the rowboat, all her ties with the past would be cut. Whatever the future held, she could depend on no one but herself—her own will—until the war ended. Would it be enough to see her through?

Suddenly, Laurel smiled, a mixture of sad awareness mixed with exultation. She had made it this far, hadn't she? She had gotten through a war, through losing her father and her brother, through marriage to a man she thought she hated, only to come out on the other side, to the full awareness of what true love between a man and a woman could mean. Yes—somehow she had prevailed, and would always prevail.

Filled with a new strength, Laurel turned to bid Fancy farewell. "I'll come back," she whispered, clutching her friend tightly to her. "Goodbye, Fancy. I—I love you."

For a moment the two girls stood quietly embraced, communicating their feelings in the cold silence. Then, as Trey Garrison called Laurel's name, the black girl whispered back, "Goodbye, Miss Laurel."

Laurel released Fancy and walked down to the beach to meet the two men. As Jacob held the rowboat in readiness at the water's edge, Laurel said to Trey, "You'll see that Fancy gets home?"

Trey smiled. "Of course. I'll make arrangements for her as soon as possible."

Laurel stood on tiptoe and kissed Trey on the cheek. "God bless you, Trey. And goodbye."

Laurel moved forward and took her husband's hand, the smile on her face showing the full commitment of her love and no trace of regret. Together, they rowed out toward the *Brooklyn*, beginning the long journey that led to their future.

Author's Historical Notes

The following historical facts may be of interest to readers:

Ursuline Academy actually existed at the time of the story, and the female students were rarely, if ever, allowed to leave. The names of the Ursuline sisters are authentic.

The Virginia House Hotel did exist at the time, and there was actually a sign on the hotel that read: "Not a rat or a mouse/Dare enter the Virginia House."

William Hendley and John Sleight did run a shipping agency on the Strand during this period; it was known as a headquarters for Confederate spying activities during the Civil War. The William Hendley Building still stands on the Strand in Galveston today.

The names of Commodore Renshaw and Captain Law are authentic, as are the names of all naval vessels in the book.

A battle between the Federals and the Confederates did occur at Indianola on October 25, 1862.

Jean Lafitte headquartered himself in Galveston around 1817; he did burn Maison Rouge before he left in 1821, and it's rumored that he left a fortune buried in the Galveston vicinity. One theory regarding the rest of his life asserts that he took the assumed name of John Lafflin, married, and lived quietly for the remainder of his days.

A citizen by the name of Rohledder was actually killed by Confederates trying to retake Galveston Island from the Federals during this period.

Reverend Benjamin Eaton was actually pastor of Trinity Episcopal during this period.

The Federal fleet at Galveston opened its guns upon the city on the night of December 1, 1862, after gunfire was exchanged between Confederate Thomas Barnett and a Yankee sentinel who ordered him to halt.

The Confederates defeated the Federal fleet at Galveston on January 1, 1863, using two steamboats swaddled in cotton bales. Captain McCormick, Major Smith, and Captain Wier were actually aboard the Confederate steamboat *Bayou City*.

Confederate Lieutenant Edward Lea did actually die in the arms of his father, a Union major, aboard the *Harriet Lane* during the battle of Galveston. Lea's grave can be found in Episcopal Cemetery in Galveston today; his tombstone bears the words, "My father is here."

The U.S. frigate *Brooklyn* anchored off the bar near Galveston Island on January 7, 1863, reestablishing the blockade.

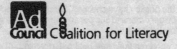